JOHN GARDNER

THE SECRET HOUSES

J

JOVE BOOKS, NEW YORK

This Jove book contains the complete
text of the original hardcover edition.
It has been completely reset in a typeface
designed for easy reading, and was printed
from new film.

THE SECRET HOUSES

A Jove Book/published by arrangement with
the author.

PRINTING HISTORY
G. P. Putnam's edition published November 1987
Published simultaneously in Canada by General Publishing Co.
Limited, Toronto
Jove edition/February 1990

ISBN: 0-515-10237-7

Jove Books are published by The Berkley Publishing Group,
200 Madison Avenue, New York, New York 10016.
The name "JOVE" and the "J" logo
are trademarks belonging to Jove Publications, Inc.

PRINTED IN THE UNITED STATES OF AMERICA

10 9 8 7 6 5 4 3 2 1

The secret houses
Which are our souls
Remain uncharted
Except by God,
Who Made the map...

Anon.

The secret fear of being denounced,
The secret terror of a knock on the door.

Yevtushenko: *Fears*

THE RAILTON

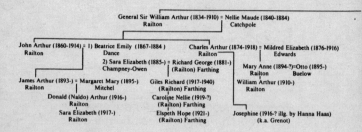

General Sir William Arthur (1834-1910) = Nellie Maude (1840-1884)
Railton   Catchpole

John Arthur (1860-1914) = 1) Beatrice Emily (1867-1884)   Charles Arthur (1874-1918) = Mildred Elizabeth (1876-1916)
Railton   Dance   Railton   Edwards

                         2) Sara Elizabeth (1885-) = Richard George (1881-)   Mary Anne (1894-?)=Otto (1895-)
                            Champney-Owen   (Railton) Farthing   Railton   Buelow

James Arthur (1893-) = Margaret Mary (1895-)   Giles Richard (1917-1940)   William Arthur (1910-)
Railton   Mitchel   (Railton) Farthing   Railton

      Donald (Naldo) Arthur (1916-)   Caroline Nellie (1919-?)
      Railton   (Railton) Farthing

      Sara Elizabeth (1917-)   Elspeth Hope (1921-)   Josephine (1916-? illg. by Hanna Haas)
      Railton   (Railton) Farthing   (k.a. Grenot)

THE FARTHING

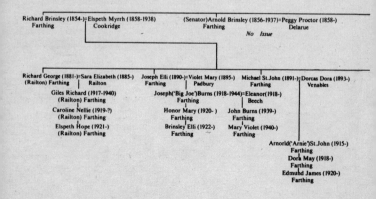

Richard Brinsley (1854-)=Elspeth Myrrh (1858-1938)   (Senator)Arnold Brinsley (1856-1937)=Peggy Proctor (1858-)
Farthing   Cookridge   Farthing   Delarue
                                                                         No   Issue

Richard George (1881-)=Sara Elizabeth (1885-)   Joseph Elli (1890-)=Violet Mary (1895-)   Michael St.John (1891-)=Dorcas Dora (1893-)
(Railton) Farthing   Railton   Farthing   Padbury   Farthing   Venables

      Giles Richard (1917-1940)   Joseph('Big Joe')Burns (1918-1944)=Eleanor(1918-)
      (Railton) Farthing   Farthing   Beech

      Caroline Nellie (1919-?)   Honor Mary (1920-)   John Burns (1939-)
      (Railton) Farthing   Farthing   Farthing

      Elspeth Hope (1921-)   Brinsley Elli (1922-)   Mary Violet (1940-)
      (Railton) Farthing   Farthing   Farthing

                                                                     Arnorld('Arnie')St.John (1915-)
                                                                     Farthing
                                                                     Dora May (1918-)
                                                                     Farthing
                                                                     Edmund James (1920-)
                                                                     Farthing

FAMILY IN 1946

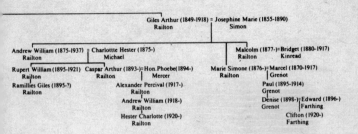

Giles Arthur (1849-1918) = Josephine Marie (1855-1890)
Railton   Simon

Andrew William (1875-1937) = Charlottte Hester (1875-)
Railton   Michael

Malcolm (1877-)= Bridget (1880-1917)
Railton   Kinread

Rupert William (1895-1921)   Caspar Arthur (1893-)=Hon. Phoebe(1894-)
Railton   Railton   Mercer

Marie Simone (1876-)= Marcel (1870-1917)
Railton   Grenot

Ramillies Giles (1895-?)
Railton

Alexander Percival (1917-)
Railton
Andrew William (1918-)
Railton
Hester Charlotte (1920-)
Railton

Paul (1895-1914)
Grenot
Denise (1898-)= Edward (1896-)
Grenot   Farthing
Clifton (1920-)
Farthing

FAMILY IN 1946

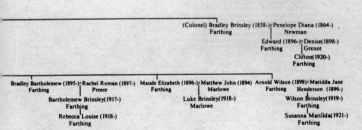

(Colonel) Bradley Brinsley (1858-)= Penelope Diana (1864-)
Farthing   Newman

Edward (1896-)= Denise(1898-)
Farthing   Grenot
Clifton(1920-)
Farthing

Bradley Bartholemew (1895-)= Rachel Roman (1897-)
Farthing   Preece

Maude Elizabeth (1896-)= Matthew John (1894)
Farthing   Marlowe

Arnold Wilson (1898-)= Mattilda Jane
Farthing   Henderson (1899-)

Bartholemew Brinsley(1917-)
Farthing
Rebecca Louise (1918-)
Farthing

Luke Brinsley(1918-)
Marlowe

Wilson Brinsley(1919-)
Farthing
Susanna Mattilda(1921-)
Farthing

Prologue

▼

NOTHING MUCH EVER happened in St. Benoît-sur-Loire. The Abbey still stood where it always had, and the town went about its business with almost painful normality, philosophically shrugging off the fact that it had spent four years under the Nazi tyranny. German soldiers were regular customers in the bars. Occasionally the military police came asking questions; sometimes a girl would get pregnant by a German. They would take her away, and people presumed she was cared for.

They had all heard of the Gestapo man in Orléans—Klaubert. Who had not heard of him? The man was a beast. *Le Diable d'Orléans* he was called, and not without reason.

You heard things. If you went into the city you might see things also—as well as the damage.

They knew of course that there had been acts of sabotage right across France. Certainly there had been mishaps and explosions near St. Benoît-sur-Loire, as well as the damage already done to Orléans during the fighting, and in the bombing. But, like everybody, the good citizens of St. Benoît-sur-Loire now held on to hope. Five weeks ago the Americans, British, and their own Free Forces had landed in Normandy at long last. France would soon be at liberty again, so there was no need to fear the Nazis. During the previous week there had been talk of American parachutists near this very place. Some claimed to have heard shots fired.

Then, suddenly, in the small hours of dawn, it happened.

Some heard it from their beds, others as they rose before sunup: cars and trucks driving into the town at full speed, the knocking on doors, and the sound of heavy boots on the pavement.

The men who came were mainly Gestapo, with some regular troops for weight. They went to three houses and shots were fired in one of them. Later some people saw two bodies being carried

1

out. Nobody viewed the other people—men and women—being jabbed, punched, and hustled into trucks, just as nobody saw the radio set being taken from the house where there had been shooting.

A Wehrmacht sergeant, fat, friendly, and without malice, told one of the local barmen that criminals had been arrested and were being held by the Gestapo in Orléans. Nobody believed that. They knew it was a Resistance *réseau*—a network or circuit—that had been crushed. Nobody fancied the chances of the people who had been taken to the Gestapo headquarters in the Rue de Bourgogne, Orléans.

They did not know the *réseau* was called *Tarot*. Nor had they ever heard of the English family called Railton, or the American family named Farthing. How, then, could they know the deep effect the breaking of *Tarot* had on these two families—bound together by marriages and an affinity for their work?

For the Railtons and Farthings it had started even before the war. It did not end until long after the conflict was over. For two in particular it began in the summer of 1940.

PART ONE

▼

THE
FRENCH
HOUSES

1

▼

"WELL?" CAROLINE STOOD at the turn of the stairs, outside the cracked and scarred door to their flat. Through the opening Jo-Jo could glimpse the familiar simple furnishings of the place they had called home for the past two years. She now knew it would be home for only a few more hours.

"It's come." She lifted her hand to wave the postcard pulled from her purse. "The boy said he should have brought it yesterday, but they needed him for other things. I didn't believe him."

Caroline turned, walking back into the five-room dingy apartment. Each room was no larger than a small cell. Jo-Jo, four years Caroline's senior, and the taller of the pair, saw that her cousin was frightened. Caroline stopped, looking down from the square window into the Rue de la Huchette. The whores, and the men who protected them, were there arguing.

The street was notable for two things—the dowdy, run-down third-rate hotel which had been Oscar Wilde's home, and the brothel, with its ornate doorway flanked by statues of two black pageboys, that made the area safe for *les petites Anglaises* as the locals inaccurately called them. The whores were friendly, and men employed to watch the place always made certain the two girls were never bothered by passing trade. Further, the apartment was cheap.

Not that there was any shortage of money, but Jo-Jo and Caroline were, like so many of their tangled family, stubborn and determined young women. Girls of a new breed, they lived almost ahead of their time with a shining idealism that put rank and power to one side, choosing instead to work and exist among ordinary people and so share lives vastly different from the glittering, privileged ways of their sisters and cousins back in England.

Barely a month previously, the war, which had seemed until

then unreal, had exploded into the horror of battle and rout. Hitler's legions were unleashed, first on Holland, Belgium, and Luxembourg, with bombs from the air and storm troopers landed by glider and parachute. The great force massed itself, and within hours General Guderian's Panzer divisions clattered, rolling into France, the ground ahead blasted by Stuka dive bombers; the Panzers, followed by half-tracks towing guns; and the leapfrogging infantry of the Wehrmacht, with the gallant, brutal, expert soldiers of the Waffen SS. The lightning war—Blitzkrieg—had struck, moving across Europe like a giant warm knife through a mound of butter, beating back the defenders, pushing the British toward the sea, and the French into their graves and panic.

Paris had been chaos for the last two weeks—noisy, the streets clogged with those who wished to flee, the air rife with rumor, the eyes of its people wary with fear. Slowly they heard the approaching thunder of war, until the Panzers were poised only a few miles east of the city, with others working to the north and south. Then, today—Thursday, the 13th of June—Paris sighed and lay back silently like a woman bracing herself for rape. The streets emptied; houses closed their shutters; traffic disappeared; there were stories of looting; others said the Métro had come to a halt. Only occasional, and sometimes desperate, people were seen on the great thoroughfares. Jo-Jo had been one of them.

Now she could see the nerves and muscles of Caroline's small body go taut with tension. Jo-Jo knew the girl's feelings and emotions by the look in her eyes or the way she moved. When Caroline was born, Jo-Jo had only recently arrived at the great house which was their true home in England. The other children seemed alien to the little girl, and she fussed around the new baby like a tiny second mother. When Caroline had started to toddle, Jo-Jo was always at hand, and, as they grew, the pair became inseparable.

Caroline glanced into the street again. "What does the post-card say?" Her long fingers grasped at the pasteboard—a familiar black and white view of a marketplace with the statue standing proud in its center, and Caspar's neat hand on the back, in green ink—*Things much the same here. We think of you. Remember the tempest will not last forever.* Her eyes seemed calmer now as she looked at her cousin.

"It means we have to get out now. Come home, or do as we agreed," Caroline said in almost a whisper. Her nostrils flared briefly. Since childhood this had been a habit, a sign of anger about to burst. But this time she held back the fury. "He didn't mean us to get out, back to England, did he?"

Jo-Jo shook her head, a hand tight on the other girl's shoulder. "I shouldn't think so. Would you, if you had been Caspar?"

There was a pause, the sounds of the squabbling whores sucked in through the half-open window. "Come on, Caro. We've known for a week there was no way out." She gave a little laugh, like the twitter of some bird. "We *did* agree to do it."

Caroline dropped her head, the tousled dark hair falling almost to hide her face, then she swept it back with one hand. "We agreed, but nobody thought it would happen."

"Caspar did. Two months ago Uncle Caspar did."

Was it really two months? Caroline thought. More than sixty days since Caspar had sat in this room with bread, ham, and a cheap red wine, laughing and eating with them. Jo-Jo also thought of him: how he had sat opposite her across the table and taken her long hands in his, and how she felt the metal of his false left hand through the glove he always wore.

When Caspar had lost his arm and leg in 1914, he had worn the makeshift artificial limbs of the time, but now things were more sophisticated and, unless you knew he was a cripple, it was difficult to detect his disablement at all, except for the gloved hand.

"I have no right to ask this," he had said, smiling as though preparing them for some household chore.

"But you're going to ask it just the same, Uncle Caspar." Jo-Jo laughed. He was one of the first men of the family she could remember from childhood. Now Caspar Railton was in his late forties, but Jo-Jo recalled the jolly limping figure who had met them after the strange journey which now seemed like a dream, sometimes returning to haunt her—especially after she had been told the truth, on her sixteenth birthday.

Jo-Jo Grenot had been brought, at the age of four, to the big, exciting, and beautiful Berkshire house called Redhill Manor. The manor seemed to belong to Uncle Richard and Aunt Sara. It was always full of people, and there were a lot of children. Quickly, as she grew, Jo-Jo became aware of the complexities of her family—how Uncle Richard Farthing was an American who had married Sara Railton, a member of the powerful Railtons only through her previous marriage, yet accepted by the family as truly one of them.

Maman was a Railton who had married a Frenchman. That was why she was called Grenot. The Railtons, and the large

American family of Farthings, had become inextricably entwined because of Sara and Richard. Later *Maman*'s other daughter, Denise, had married a Farthing. The two families were like great trees, planted close to one another, so that underground their roots had entwined, just as their trunks had become covered in ivy which prevented one from seeing the true texture of the bark.

On the evening of Jo-Jo's sixteenth birthday *Maman* had taken her to the rose garden and told her the truth: how she was really a Railton; how her father, who had died in the 1918 influenza epidemic, had been a member of part of the Secret Service during the Great War (as they then called it); how he had helped catch a woman German agent and made her work for the British. They had become lovers, and the woman had been murdered by the Germans, but not before she gave birth to Jo-Jo. *Maman* was not really her mother, but Jo-Jo was still a true Railton and could, if she wanted, take her proper name when she was twenty-one. She refused immediately, telling Marie Grenot that she would always regard her as mother, and wanted no new name.

Soon after this, Jo-Jo was sent to the Sorbonne, in Paris. Her grades were exceptional, so she was asked to stay on as a junior lecturer in English. In due time Caroline came to Paris as a student.

It was through Jo-Jo's influence that Caroline pleaded with her parents and was allowed to stay in Paris, taking a junior post, with Jo-Jo, at the Sorbonne. Richard and Sara Farthing did not really want Caroline living away from home, or in this manner. They had made her promise to return if things got too difficult. When war was declared in September 1939, Richard had even come over to see his daughter, but left feeling proud of her, and certain she would return to England if Hitler's armies started a shooting war.

Now, like Jo-Jo, she thought of Caspar, and the conversation a month previously. "I work for a government department," he had said, and the girls knew immediately what he meant. It was not talked about among the family, but they all knew some of their kinfolk were involved in secret matters. Caspar had been Chief-of-Staff to the first head of the modern Secret Intelligence Service, Sir Mansfield Cumming: "C" as he—and all his successors—was known.

"People said you'd retired," Jo-Jo said.

Caspar had laughed. "I did. The business became very boring, and a bit unprofessional. They persuaded me back in '38, though. Gearing things up for this show." He spoke of the present war, which everyone had expected in 1938. "Now, I feel damned awkward about asking this—and you can refuse." He talked to them for almost two hours, and they agreed to examine the situation if it should ever arise. He gave them simple codes: the sending of postcards which would warn them to make up their minds—*Come home, or do as we agreed.* The alternative was simply *Come home.* When he left, Caspar looked shamefaced, saying they should not discuss this with their respective parents. There was little likelihood of Caroline doing this, as Richard and Sara were in America. But Marie Grenot still lived in Berkshire.

Now, standing beside the window, Jo-Jo said it all seemed inevitable once Hitler had made his unstoppable move.

"Damn! Everything's been for nothing." There were brightred spots of frustration high on Caroline's cheeks.

"What has?"

"Living like peasants. Sharing our beds with fleas and our bread with beggars."

"How can we tell? *We* chose to do that, Caro." Jo-Jo had a way of suggesting a truth, then leaving it to hang in the air, waiting for the other person to speak.

At last Caroline said, "I suppose we go, then."

Jo-Jo gave a sigh. "Right, then. We burn the passports and papers. Use the ones he gave us and head west. It's less than one hundred fifty kilometers."

"Jules Fenice." Caroline said the name as though she had known the man since birth, and wondered what he would be like—this man trained by Uncle Caspar and waiting for them in a village on the Loire, near Orléans.

First they had the job with the weapons and ammunition. Then they were to link up with Jules Fenice, whose code name would be *Felix* in the years to come.

They stayed in the little apartment until it was dark, burning the papers and anything that linked them to England. Then, with a few belongings packed in their cheap cardboard suitcases, they set out from the Rue de la Huchette, Paris, to the village of St. Benoît-sur-Loire, within spitting distance of Orléans.

They dodged German soldiers who entered Paris in the morning, and then the French police—for France gave itself over to Hitler's Reich during their journey, with Marshal Pétain setting up his puppet government in Vichy. They used their French papers, which turned them at a stroke from Caroline Railton Farthing and Josephine Grenot into Catherine and Anne Routon. Sisters.

They were to be known, later and to others, as *Maxine* and *Dédé*—part of a network called *Tarot*, which became famous, and infamous.

For the two girls the journey from Paris was a trip into fame which ended in oblivion, mystery, and intrigue.

2

▼

FOUR YEARS LATER, when the secret underground network known as *Tarot* broke down—five weeks after the Allied armies landed in Normandy on D-Day, June 6, 1944—Caspar Railton did not know how to break the news to Richard and Sara, nor to Jo-Jo's "foster mother," his own Aunt Marie.

He was due to spend the weekend of July 15 at Redhill Manor, set above the small market town of Haversage. There would be no chance to avoid questions about Caroline from Richard and Sara.

Sara had continued to live in the splendid house—which dated back to the reign of Henry VIII—managing the large estate and farm since the death of her first husband in 1914.

When Richard Farthing married her, later in the First War, the family had been all too pleased to allow the couple to remain in what was strictly Railton property. During the passing years, this one act had drawn the families closer, and between the wars almost all the senior Railtons visited the Farthings' magnificent homes in Washington and New England; while the Farthings, in turn, crossed the Atlantic to spend time at Redhill.

Now, in his concern, Caspar sought out his cousin James, who knew almost as much about the network called *Tarot* as Caspar did. Possibly more, in the light of certain events which had taken place a week earlier.

James and Caspar were not only cousins, but also close friends, for their careers had run along similar tracks. Their birthdays were within a couple of months of each other; together they had entered the Army, passing out on the same course at Sandhurst—Caspar going to his regiment, and so to France, where he had been so shockingly wounded in 1914; James moving with dangerous stealth into the field of Intelligence, finally becoming an agent in Berlin where he was arrested, escaping

11

execution by devious plots about which the family rarely spoke.

The cousins arranged to travel to Redhill together by car—
their respective wives would go earlier, by train. Caspar needed
to talk, and the journey by road would allow that.

So far his war had been exhausting, and—now that everybody
thought the end was in sight—Caspar felt the fatigue. People
who knew him well said he had aged incredibly in the past years,
looking more like a man of sixty than one in his early fifties.

When he was enticed back into the Secret Intelligence Service
—known to most as MI6 by this time—Caspar was appalled by
the disorganization. His first posting, in 1938, had been to Section D, dealing with what was euphemistically called "irregular
warfare."

Caspar stood two days of sitting around discussing farcical
ideas, then went quietly to "C"—the Chief of SIS—bluntly asking for a special brief to, as he put it, "Follow a version of
Christ's instructions to go out into the highways and hedgerows
and compel them to come in." By which he meant that he wanted
to collect some really useful covert talent against a possible sea of
trouble. All he saw around him was, as someone else put it, "An
establishment of very limited intelligence, with professionals who
were by and large pretty stupid—some of them very stupid."

His wish was granted, and, an old hand at the business he had
learned from the eccentric Mansfield Cumming, he began snooping around Europe and the quieter corners of the major universities, revealing nothing to his Service colleagues.

Caspar's recruiting campaign was so successful that following
Dunkirk and the collapse of France, *Tarot* became operational
very quickly. The first signals from this network were in fact
received long before any of the trained Special Operations Executive officers could be sent into occupied Europe. SOE was
formed, late in 1940, to support resistance movements in the
Nazi-occupied countries and, as Winston Churchill proclaimed,
to "Set Europe ablaze."

Soon, Section D was swallowed by SOE, and Caspar found
this an excellent vantage point. He could also salve his conscience regarding the recruitment of his nieces by reporting to the
girls' parents that they were safe.

He continued to do this until *Tarot* went dead. But the death of
Tarot posed him a plethora of problems.

The major difficulty was even better known to James, who
was similarly concerned when lured back to clandestine pastures
in 1939, a week after the outbreak of war. James had been part of

that idealistic band who saw, in spite of its eccentricities, the necessity for a good, sound, professional Intelligence Service. He had left the work after being ordered to spy on the Labour movement on behalf of the Conservatives. While being a Tory at heart, James was shocked at the idea of such an undemocratic order. "The Security and Intelligence Services," he snapped at his superior, "are here to serve country and democracy, not political whims!"

When he returned to work, there was still little to be happy about, particularly after the Service lost the bulk of its agents abroad, following the kidnapping of Stevens and Payne Best—Chief and Deputy Chief of the SIS Continental office—in a crafty operation on the Dutch-German border at Venlo: a plot skillfully handled by the Germans and known to all by the understated title of the Venlo Incident. Later, after the invasion of Holland, one of the remaining agents, in a moment of exceptional dereliction, mislaid a suitcase containing every contact address. The entire SIS operation in Western Europe was blown, and James played a large part in attempting to rebuild a realistic and ordered Intelligence apparatus, until the United States came into the war and the Office of Strategic Services was set up as the American counterpart to SOE. James Railton was given the uneasy job of liaison between the American OSS and MI6.

The cousins left London at around four in the afternoon, James picking up Caspar from Wimpole Street where he had his offices—discreetly removed from the main Baker Street complex that was SOE headquarters.

Caspar said little until the red MG was on the Oxford road. Sitting in brooding silence next to James, his mind strayed to times past when the prospect of a weekend at Redhill was exciting. There was nothing remotely happy about having to break the news that for the first time since 1940 he did not know whether Jo-Jo and Caroline were safe.

"Ever worked out how many of the family are in the lunatic trade?" he finally asked James.

"Counting Jo-Jo and Caroline?"

Caspar winced as his cousin went straight to the heart of the matter. "And 'Big Joe' Farthing, who's missing, presumed killed, after last week's cock-up." James spoke of an OSS operation called *Romarin* which had been closely linked with *Tarot*.

"Touché," Caspar murmured. "I didn't know Joe was with the 'Outfit.'"

"Well, he was—and Bradley junior; *and* Arnold junior. Count them in, and add Naldo for luck. If you count ourselves, together with Richard's work in the States—and he's still active here of course—there *were* nine of us. What of the girls, Cas? Chances?"

"They've had a good long run. Their chances're very low."

James nodded. It was a bright summer's day with the countryside at its best, everything at odds with their thoughts, for neither man shirked the feeling that he had contributed to the deaths of agents who were related to them by blood or marriage. Both men had the girls uppermost in their minds. Caspar and James had loved them as their own, which in a way they were, for the Railtons tended to close ranks quickly in moments of crisis. Once at Redhill Manor, Caspar would not be able to avoid saying something about the girls, any more than James could dodge talking to Richard about his nephew, Joe.

They watched the road and the passing landscape: the trees in their dusty full foliage; the farmland golden with corn and wheat, almost ready for the harvest; and they knew that all was *not* safely gathered in, yet the winter storm for them might be almost here.

"I'm worried about *Tarot*," James said. "Concerned since last week. Since *Romarin*. They knew, Cas. They knew just where the boys were going in."

Caspar did not reply until they had covered a good mile. "Me too. I'm worried stiff." He said it in such a strange quiet way that James took his eyes off the road to glance at his cousin's drawn face. "You in pain, Cas?" He knew that Caspar's old wounds— the stumps of missing arm and leg—still caused him pain, even after so long a time, and that he was starting to feel the onset of circulatory problems which had been expected for years.

"A little gyp." Caspar was curt. "Get it sometimes. Funny. Stress brings it on." Then suddenly he slewed the conversation back to *Tarot*. "I've been concerned for a while, old son. You seen the file? *Tarot*, I mean?"

"Bits of it."

"After *Romarin* I did some adding up. At the start, the sabotage and all that wasn't bad, but it takes an alarming dive when you look at the figures for 'Action Demanded'—when we gave them specific targets. They've only given us two percent accuracy since 1941. It's been more a case of setting Europe afizzle than ablaze."

James whistled.

"Other things," Caspar continued. "Over the past four years

we've sent them fifteen officers. Only three made it to the network, and all but one of those got bagged within two months." He paused as they overtook three American ambulances en route to one of the nearby airfields into which the medical Dakotas brought wounded from the brutal fighting which continued in France. There was the irony, he thought. They were going armed to Redhill which, even in bleak moments, echoed with laughter and happiness—a place of safety. And arms were being used just across the channel, where young men faced the horrors of battle. For a second he wondered if there was still any life, or laughter, in the house at St. Benoît-sur-Loire—Fenice's house from which *Tarot* had operated for so long. *Where be your gibes now? Your flashes of merriment . . . ?* He could hear Jo-Jo and Caroline as very young girls doing a party piece at a long-gone Redhill Christmas.

Caspar pulled himself back from the pictures in his head, turning to James. "I've been on to 'Nine' as well." He meant MI9, the department which dealt with escape and evasion by aircrew shot down over Europe. "*Tarot*'s managed to get almost five hundred aircrew out—or at least on to the next stage and then out. But they're blackmarked by 'Nine,' and as usual I'm the last to be told. *Tarot*'s had over a thousand through their hands. Which means half of their product went missing and didn't make it home." He gave a quick, deep sigh. "They weren't so hot on the intelligence stakes either. Not at all dependable to say the least. We didn't ask much from them, but we got a good deal less than they should have given. And to think *Tarot* was the apple of my eye. I was blind to its excess of faults. In other words I should never have sanctioned *Romarin* for you, James. There's something very rotten about *Tarot*."

You always see it too late, he thought. Even when it is under your nose. Because he had been instrumental in setting up the network—trained Jules Fenice; pushed Jo-Jo and Caroline toward it; watched the *réseau* become active and grow very quickly. Taking such a pride in it, Caspar had failed to see that something was very wrong.

James also had thoughts. *He* should have examined the logistics of *Romarin,* and asked far more questions—for *Romarin* was a daring OSS operation aimed at kidnapping the Orléans area Gestapo Chief—*Standartenführer* Hans-Dieter Klaubert, together with his mistress, Hannalore Bauer. The unit had been dropped directly on the DZ after receiving the code signal, flashed from a field. The aircrew said they saw flickers of machine-gun fire from the ground, and, two days after, word had come from *Tarot* itself. The operation had gone very wrong. The OSS team were all presumed dead.

The time for *Romarin* had been chosen in order to spread confusion among the SS in Orléans and encourage them not to continue with the vicious acts of their leader. During his years at Orléans, Klaubert had been responsible for the torture and executions of more than five thousand French men, women, and children; a further seven thousand had been deported—on his personal order—to the death and slave camps. Little wonder that he was known as the Devil of Orléans. With an officer as efficient as Klaubert, it seemed strange to James that *Tarot* had been able to continue operating in the area at all, for it had been the man's avowed intention to crush the Resistance in his personal satrapy. Nothing matched up, James considered. Then he said it aloud.

"I know." Caspar's usual bonhomie was quite gone. "By Christ, I know, James! Something smells, and heaven knows if we'll get to the bottom of it." He sounded a sad and beaten man.

"Oh, we'll get there, Cas. Don't worry. Once France is free of the Nazis, we'll backtrack through hell if we have to. *Tarot* stinks, old chum. All we have to do is follow our noses."

Neither of them could know, as they passed through the market square of Haversage to begin the long climb up Red Hill, toward the Manor, what horrors would be disturbed once the stones of *Tarot* were turned over and the true stench reached their nostrils.

3

▼

TWENTY, THIRTY, EVEN forty years later, public disclosures were being made about the networks of agents in occupied Europe during World War II. It was two decades before the first history of Special Operations Executive was released, and about the same amount of time elapsed before the United States opened its filleted OSS files to the historians. Yet even now arguments continue; and secrets remain hidden. One of these concerns the *Tarot* network.

In occupied Europe there had been betrayals, great courage, treachery, vengeance, and splendid guile, from both the *Mouvement*—as the Resistance was first called in France—and the German Military Intelligence, the Abwehr.

The truth about *Tarot* did not immediately come to light—even to the guardians of secrets—once France was liberated, as James had prophesied. Much that had gone on in other networks needed no investigation—or very little—yet an inquiry into *Tarot* was obviously necessary, and quickly scheduled for the spring of 1946.

Before that, an event which was to have much bearing on the truth took place among the strewn ruins of the now segmented and quartered German capital of Berlin. By pure coincidence the event concerned one Railton and one Farthing.

The Railton was James' son, Donald. As a small boy he could not pronounce his name. Instead he called himself Naldo, and so became Naldo, or Nald, to everyone, inside the family or out. He even thought of himself as Naldo.

Naldo Railton had come to the SIS via his father. At Cambridge there had been a short, if furtive, dalliance with the Communist Party. Later, putting the half-baked, emotional ideals to one side, the young man embraced the cause of pacifism, swearing that, should war be declared, he would rather be imprisoned

17

than go forth to kill. When the shooting war overtook the phony war in May 1940, Naldo Railton quickly changed his mind. As he said to his Great Aunt Sara, "If you happened to be in Harrod's with your wife and children and an armed gang began shooting, you'd do everything in your power to defend them. You'd even shoot back." Naldo did that very thing from the cockpit of a Spitfire toward the end of the Battle of Britain, becoming one of those hastily trained young men who went to war with a minimum number of flying hours to their credit. A midair collision nearly cost him his life and certainly finished him for any further operational flying. By then he had seven confirmed kills and a DFC.

Somewhere along the line James pulled strings and Naldo was quietly seconded to SIS, where he acquitted himself well in training and then went into the field—mainly controlling agents through Lisbon and Gibraltar for the Iberian subsection headed by one H.A.R.—"Kim"—Philby.

Early in 1946 Naldo found himself in Berlin, one of the sadly depleted number of SIS officers running Berlin Station. The times were badly out of joint. Berlin, neatly divided into four zones, policed by American, British, French, and Russian forces, had already become an island in the huge section of blasted Germany claimed by Russia. The winter had been almost unbearable —the black market flourished and was unstoppable, the city remained in ruins, peopled by a pitifully proud, yet defeated civilian army. Women were to be had for a few cigarettes; murder could be done for an hour of warmth. Many who had survived the bombings and the last weeks of the battle of Berlin died from cold or hunger. Most significant, by this time the enemy had ceased to be the Germans.

Eyes turned Eastward, and Russia had become the bogeyman. Many politicians and large numbers of senior military officers thought that a war between the former allies was inevitable. Some thought it to be expedient. There was a feeling that it might happen at any minute, while America still held close to the atomic secrets that had brought about the final capitulation of Japan. After a lull of wartime alliance, Communism again became the dark red cloud on the horizon.

In the meantime, the hollow-eyed, dazed German population was starting to reorganize itself, and the abiding picture Naldo carried from that time was of old men, boys, and women forming human chains to sift through the rubble, certain that Berlin would rise from its own ashes to become a prosperous city once more.

One evening, in his relatively comfortable billet within the British Zone, Naldo's telephone rang. The caller was Arnold Farthing, one of Richard's nephews who had been with the OSS almost from the beginning. Naldo knew him well, not only as a relative, but also as a shrewd and ruthless Intelligence officer. Arnold sounded distinctly rattled.

"Nald—" He spoke briskly but in almost a whisper, as though certain that he was being overheard. "Nald, I need to see you. It's urgent. Can you meet me?" The night was bitter and Naldo had no desire to go through the business of getting transport and carting himself over to the American Sector. "Can you come here, Arnie?" he found himself whispering, as though imitating his cousin.

"Fifteen minutes. You alone?"

"And palely loitering." Naldo smiled.

Fifteen minutes to the second and Arnold Farthing was at his door.

Naldo lived on the third floor of a broken-down building which had miraculously escaped the bombs and shells near Hitler's proud Olympic Stadium. It had once been a small hotel, and one wall was propped up with heavy wooden braces. Using the stairs always seemed perilous, for they leaned drunkenly to one side at the rise from second to third floors. The whole place was inhabited by British officers and diplomatic staff who knew one another only from passing on those stairs. Each kept his own peace in this place. It was not wise to ask questions or show too much interest in one's neighbor.

Before the tap on the door, Naldo became slightly alarmed. From his window he had clearly seen the American's car draw up in front of the house. He thought there was a passenger.

"Jesus, it's cold. You got a drink?" Arnold wore a heavy overcoat, muffler, trilby hat, and thick gloves. If his mission had been dangerous, Naldo reflected, there would have been no gloves. You could not use a peashooter with the gauntleted, fur-lined specimens which warmed Arnold's hands.

"Sure, come on in. Get warm." He motioned toward the pot-bellied, wood-burning stove. "Don't touch it, you'll get third-degree burns." Naldo opened a cupboard, brought out a bottle of Johnnie Walker and two glasses, poured a liberal shot into each, and handed one to Arnold, who had taken off the gloves and hat and was now unbuttoning his coat. He wrapped a large hand around the glass, raised it, then smiled and muttered, "Hail and farewell."

Arnold was a tall man, broad as a football player, and with a face that was more battered than attractive. The slightly bulbous nose tilted to one side where it had been broken a dozen times, and his smile was lopsided. The eyes were his best feature—sea-gray and relaxed. They said of Arnold Farthing that nobody could ever tell the truth, or his next move, by looking at his eyes, which had in them a permanent twinkle, as though life was a constant series of amusing episodes.

The eyes smiled down at Naldo now as he spoke.

"Hail and farewell?" Railton queried.

"We're moving out, old friend. Going. Washington's rolled us up."

"What?" He genuinely could not believe it.

"It's true. OSS is disbanded. They've given Wild Bill the old heave-ho, and most of his buddies with him." Wild Bill was General William Donovan, head of the OSS and would-be architect of a major U.S. Intelligence community.

"But why? It's crazy. Your people're needed here. Needed all over Europe—"

"*You* know that, Naldo, and *I* know it. But nobody appears to have shared the knowledge with President Truman. The scuttlebutt says we're too expensive, and Wild Bill's been trying to build an empire. Things'll go on much as before, and will be the foundation of something called CIG—Central Intelligence Group. But around a quarter of us are being sent home. The shit hits the fan as from 23:59 hours tonight; and I'm one of the guys being shunted back to a desk in Washington."

Naldo dropped into a chair—a relic from the thirties, black leather, split and cracked, with horsehair pushing its way out of several slits. Somehow he had thought of the OSS as a permanent fact of his life. He had spent a fair part of his career in SIS working and liaising with the Americans—swapping favors and information. In the few months spent in Berlin, the communications were even closer. Change he had foreseen, but not this sudden eclipse, for the United States had never boasted an active Intelligence organization until "The Outfit" arrived on the scene. To Naldo it was madness to throw away people like Wild Bill Donovan and the many others who had built such an efficient, cohesive team. Within his own Service, Naldo was in a minority of officers who thought the OSS was worthwhile. "What do you want with me, Arnie?" he asked at length.

"Thought you might like my one and only asset."

"You're down to asset stripping? Doesn't this other crowd—the, what d'you call them? CIG—"

Arnold shook his head. "They want no part of my asset. I've tried to explain his usefulness, but Dick—Head of Station—figures this one's too young to handle. Too hot as well. So I come bearing a gift. Dick's clinging on to assets like a leech, but for some reason he wants no part of this one. Difficult to understand, because he's hot to go. I guess it's possibly his age."

It had started to sleet outside, the cold frozen spikes hitting the window like shrapnel.

"Tell me?"

"He's fifteen years old and has the instincts of a trained snoop and the makings of a natural Intelligence operative. He's German and speaks English none too well, but he's already put up seven Nazis for me. Hates 'em. Blames 'em for his daddy's death. Daddy was a Luftwaffe pilot. Bought it in the Battle of Britain, but this guy blames the Nazi Party in general and Hitler in particular."

"You sure he's not working his ticket?"

"Pardon me?"

"Swinging the lead. Nazi-hunting because it's the fashionable thing for him to do and earns him a dishonest crust?"

Arnold slowly shook his head. "Any fifteen-year-old who looks almost thirty, and could easily kill with his bare hands would not be doing the job this guy's been doing for me if he wasn't for real. Hell, Naldo, he's been living in the POW and DP camps, sniffing out SS guys and Party members like a gundog." He gave a brilliant smile. "I've been moving him around. If I thought they were likely to get wind of him, I pulled him out, fed him for a few days, then socked him back into another camp. This guy's a *Wunderkind*. I promise you."

All over Europe there were still camps, not as sinister as the Nazi concentration camps, but some unpleasant people hid in them. There were camps for DPs—displaced persons—for prisoners of war; even for displaced prisoners of war. Many wanted Nazis hid among the inmates of these camps.

"At fifteen?" Naldo was far from convinced. "How the hell does he do it?"

"Don't ask me, but he *does*. He's like a ferret. This guy can smell SS or real baddies a mile off. You put him into a camp; he cozies up to one or two people, and the next thing you know, he's got names and faces. I tell you, Nald, he's a natural. Put him in and you get results."

"When do I get to meet him?" Naldo was impressed by Arnold's passion. The man would not talk like this unless the German boy really did have an inexplicable gift.

"He's outside. In the car. Lying crunched up like a dinosaur's fetus in the back. This guy is really big."

"Get him up here then."

Arnold held up a hand, palm facing Naldo Railton, to stop him. "In a minute. He's turned up someone who might be very important to you. *You* in person."

"Why me?"

"Look, like all of us, I read the circular about Klaubert and anyone with connections to SOE's *Tarot* network. The Enquiry's in a few weeks, yes?"

Naldo nodded, the smile wiped from his face.

"Who have you got so far? Apart from the people involved in London."

"One of the 'pianists' has been found." A pianist was a radio operator. "One who was with *Tarot* for six weeks. He got out and went to work elsewhere. And there's one of the *Romarin* team, one of yours. Injured but talking."

"Yeah? Well, my guy's got Klaubert's second-in-command. How would you like him?"

"Very much."

"He might also be onto a Frenchman, posing as a German. This guy claims to have been around the Orléans area and knew people."

"What kind of people?"

"You know what kind of people, Nald. *People-people*."

"Bring him up. I'd like to talk to—what's his name?"

"Kruger." Arnold was already at the door, pulling on his gloves. "Eberhardt Lucas Kruger. I call him Herbie for short. He answers to it, anyhow."

The youth who returned with Arnie was tall. Very tall. The Farthings had always bred men with long bones, as indeed had the Railtons, but neither family had anything on those who produced Kruger. Not only was he tall and emaciated, but also, through the gangling undernourished frame, Naldo could detect the boy was broad-boned. He would be very large when properly fed and fit.

He gestured to a chair near the stove, and Kruger sat eagerly. Arnie had been right, he looked more like a man in his late twenties than a lad of fifteen. He also had that attribute Naldo was aware of in many good Intelligence officers. He was quiet, the big body used in sparse movements, the eyes calm, giving nothing away. For a second he wondered if this art had been learned from Arnold.

"You want a drink?" Naldo spoke carefully to him, spacing the words as he would to a very small child.

"Coffee, maybe?" The voice was that of a man, and the two words in English came out haltingly.

"Not whiskey? Gin? Brandy—Schnapps?"

A broad smile crossed Kruger's face. "If I am drinking the Schnapps I become drink, yes?"

"Drunk, Herb. The word's *drunk*," Arnold prompted.

"Say again." Kruger looked up at the man as though he was an object of love. Case officers and agents, Naldo thought. Tied together like man and wife. Sometimes like man and wife who wanted a divorce: but not these two. Arnold Farthing was going to be a very hard act to follow.

"Drunk," Arnold repeated slowly. "You get too much liquor in you, then you get drunk. Okay?"

"Okay. Drunk." Kruger smiled as though proud of learning his lesson.

"So, do you want a drink?" Naldo asked.

"Coffee please. Only coffee. Else I am getting . . . drunk."

"Otherwise I will get drunk," Arnold said automatically. "Look, Herbie," he paused as Naldo went into the tiny cubicle that doubled as a kitchen. "Herbie, this is Mr. Railton."

"Railton?" Kruger repeated like a parrot mimicking its owner.

"He's a very good man, Herbie. I want you to tell him all you've told me."

"Why?" As though he sensed already that he was going to lose Arnold.

There was a long pause—Arnold wrestled with his conscience. Should he tell the boy now or later? Naldo settled the matter, "I need to know about the officer you say was second man in the Orléans-area SS. I need to know about the Frenchman pretending to be a German."

Kruger looked at Arnold, as though waiting for a sign that it was correct for him to repeat the information.

"Mr. Railton's a good man, Herb. He's the best. Better than me. You must tell him everything." Arnold smiled.

Kruger nodded very slowly. "Okay," he said, though not

sounding pleased. "Okay, you tell me. I work for this Mr. Railton now, eh? I get the kick from your people."

There was another pause, with the hail clattering at the window. The wind gusted outside and the lumps of ice splattered ever harder. The three men looked at each other—a strange dueling of eyes, each of the three pairs flicking from one to another.

Naldo broke the silence. "Herbie, you are *not* getting the kick, as you call it. It's the other way around. Mr. Farthing's getting the kick. You must know this now, before you tell me anything. Mr. Farthing's organization, the people you've been working for are going—or at least Mr. Farthing's people're going. I am staying. I do the same job as Mr. Farthing. He's asked me to look after you. He cannot protect you anymore. No money. No food. Work for me and you'll still get paid and fed." He wanted to add clothed, for Kruger wore a varied form of dress—German army boots, a pair of GI trousers, a mongrel shirt, and a couple of pullovers that needed darning. Over these last items he had a jacket that was much too small for him. His arms sprang from the grimed sleeves like thin extensions of a telescope. He looked, in fact, what he was supposed to be—a DP, a displaced person from one of the camps. It was very good cover.

"This is true?" Kruger looked, almost spaniel-eyed, at Arnie, who nodded, reaching out, and patting the boy's shoulder. "It's true. I'm only trying to help you, Herb."

Kruger nodded again, very slowly, then began to talk. What he had to tell Naldo Railton could be dynamite as far as *Tarot* was concerned. It was the first information Herbie Kruger ever passed to the British, and certainly it would not be the last.

There would be much to do from a point of logistics. Naldo knew he was going to have to sell Kruger to his Head of Station, for Arnold had a whole system of covert action working for him—officially and unofficially. He had been flying Kruger in and out of Berlin for over six months, taking him into West Germany and going through a whole magic circle of tricks to place the boy into one or another of the camps. It required a lot of cooperation and some fancy footwork that neither Victor Sylvester nor Arthur Murray could teach in the time he had to spare.

In the end, Naldo did what so many intelligent men caught up in arcane rituals had done before him. He called in sick, dressed Kruger in a decent suit, got papers for him, and flew with him out of Berlin. Then he took the boy to the camp about which he had spoken, explained the situation to the British Commanding Officer—omitting that he had no official sanction for what he required—and arranged for Kruger to view men in the camp without being seen.

Herbie identified both of them. Naldo interrogated the pair for two days, with either the Commanding Officer or his adjutant present. In the end both men broke down. The Frenchman's true name turned out to be Fenice—Jules Fenice, known to SOE as *Felix*. He sobbed out a story of fear, saying that he had never collaborated, but knew things had gone very wrong with *Tarot*. "I was afraid of reprisals—in the end I was the only one left. Who'd believe me? I spent almost four years trying to find out what was wrong; who was meddling with *Tarot*. I knew vengeance could fall only on me."

The German was not Klaubert's second-in-command, but an SS-*Sturmbannführer*—a man in middle age, who had been posted to Orléans only a few months before the invasion of Normandy. His name was Otto Buelow, and when he heard Naldo's real name he talked for the best part of twenty-four hours.

Naldo then did the only thing possible. He telephoned his father, and when James heard the name Buelow he jumped like a scalded cat. "Don't leave the place! Don't leave those two unguarded for a second," he snapped. "I'll fix your Head of Station, Naldo. Oh, and keep this fellow Kruger around. Don't lose him, he could be useful." He put down the phone and rang Caspar. "Cas, old dear," he said very quietly. "Your man *Felix* has turned up."

"Good God!"

"And another member of the family with him. The Otter's surfaced."

4

▼

"THE OTTER" WAS old Railton family history, and known well enough to the Farthings also, for the Otter was, in his way, a small scandal.

Mary Anne Railton—in truth Jo-Jo's half sister—had been a nurse during the Great War. While working in a field hospital close to the Front, near Ypres, she had tended a man who wandered in one evening, almost naked, his clothes blown from him by the blast of shells. For weeks he could only say one word—"Ott." They called him "the Otter," and, not knowing who he was, nor even his nationality, they kept him safe. He was suffering from shell shock but his brain had not been damaged, so he was able to assist with light duties. Later he had saved Mary Anne when she was attacked and raped by a disturbed patient. In that moment of trauma the block cleared and he was revealed as a German artillery captain—Otto Buelow.

Buelow was brought to England and used, by the Secret Service, who put him in POW camps to spy on his fellow countrymen—rather as Arnold Farthing used young Kruger. Otto and Mary Anne kept in touch and after the war, when he was free to go home or stay, Otto Buelow opted to return to Germany, for he had a driving belief that he should try to help rebuild his shattered country. Against the wishes of her family, Mary Anne Railton followed him and they were married soon after her arrival in Berlin.

The couple was all but ostracized—though, secretly, Sara wrote to Mary Anne often from Redhill, for Sara thought that one day the girl might need her help. But gradually Mary Anne's replies became shorter and less frequent, finally petering out altogether in the late 1930s. Nobody knew what had become of her or the former artillery captain, until now.

When he heard the news that Fenice and the SS officer Bue-

26

low had been discovered, Caspar went straight to C—the Chief of the Secret Intelligence Service—who arranged for the men to be brought back and interrogated by one of his special teams. Caspar was not allowed to see either of them, for his position within the Service would be under consideration until after the inquiry. It was always possible that he might be held responsible for the whole *Tarot* debacle—for the extent of the treachery within that network was now thought to have provoked a major failure in the British resistance setup.

The weekend before the inquiry was due to start, Caspar and his wife, Phoebe, went to Redhill Manor.

As they turned off the main road, through the gates and into the drive, Caspar thought that surely this was the most beautiful house in England—not the greatest, largest, nor the most splendid, but magnificently proportioned, its glowing Tudor stone well matched with that used in later additions to its buildings.

They stopped on the gravel within the squared U-shape of the building, before the large weathered front door. Sara stood in the doorway, smiling at them. To Caspar she looked now exactly as she did when he had first seen her. Then he was at the turn of adolescence, and he thought she was the most gorgeous creature upon whom he'd ever set eyes. "Lucky devil," he had said to James, "to gain a stepmother like that." James had been the envy of the Sixth Form at Wellington College.

Now, at almost sixty-one, Sara Railton Farthing had suffered no horrific signs of aging. Naturally, there were some lines in her face, mainly at the corners of the eyes—tiny grooves, gouged out by the pain of the last years. She and Richard had suffered like so many in the land. Their only son, Giles, had died at Dunkirk, and there was the more recent unexplained disappearance of Caroline. Only Elspeth—named for a Farthing—remained.

Sara greeted them with warmth and smiles, kissing Phoebe and holding on to Caspar for a shade longer than usual, as if trying to tell him that he must not hold himself responsible for Caroline. But he felt the cloud of guilt hanging around him whenever he came to the Manor now, and it did not help to know that his own children had all survived the war—the eldest, Alexander, had been at the Government Code and Cipher School, later GCHQ, at the famous Bletchley Park Headquarters. Their second son, Andrew, was a lawyer, and, as such spent the war with the Judge Advocate General's staff at the War Office. Their only daughter, Hester, had been in the WRNS—the Women's Royal

Naval Service, usually referred to as the Wrens. There was a
sailors' joke about being up with the lark and to bed with a Wren.

It was not until just before dinner that Caspar realized James
was also in the house, with Margaret Mary. Dick was in a hearty
mood at table, and there was no talk of the impending inquiry—
except for a *faux pas* by Elspeth, who had clamped her hands in
front of her mouth when Caspar arrived in the drawing room and
blurted, "Oh Lord, Uncle Cas, I didn't know you were coming.
Ma never tells me a thing, and I shouldn't really be here because
I'm giving evidence at the Enquiry."

Dick had sharply told her to shut up and not be stupid.

"But he's—" She stopped abruptly, seeing the look in her
father's eye. Elspeth had been with the First Aid Nursing Yeo-
manry—the FANYs—who provided not only field agents for
SOE, but also signals staff. At Bicester, not far from her home,
she had been at No. 53A Signal Station and personally monitored
many of the *Tarot* messages.

When the ladies retired after dinner, leaving the three men
alone, Richard apologized for his daughter.

"What was she going to say when you stopped her?" Caspar
asked, recalling the look Dick had given his daughter when she
began, "But he's—"

Dick gave a small sigh. "'But he's going to be charged with
incompetence.' That was probably what she had in mind. You
must know, Cas, there's a witch-hunt in the making."

"They're really after my blood?" Caspar was surprised.

"Scapegoats're being found for everything, Caspar." James
did not meet his cousin's eyes.

"They can have my wretched job any old time," Caspar
laughed. "Press-ganged back and now—"

"Shat upon," Dick supplied with a laugh. "I'd have a word
with C, but—"

"He won't have anything to do with it." Caspar sipped his
port. "I should've known when he told me the Enquiry was only
for the record—'Setting matters straight.' C wants no involvement."

"No. No, he wants no involvement." Dick spoke as though he
knew something else. "Who's on the Board of Enquiry, then?"

Caspar gave the names of a former senior SOE man and two
departmental heads from MI6. "The usual legal inquisitors, as
well, I should imagine. There'll also be three of Torquemada's
Terrors borrowed from 'Five.'" He grimaced.

There was a long pause before Dick spoke again. "Cas, Caro

did know what she was getting into, didn't she?" It was not said to twist the knife in the wound. His tone was professional, not fatherly.

"Jo-Jo and Caro, both." Caspar looked at him with sad eyes. "I spelt it out to them. They knew when I talked with them in Paris. The only thing I reproach myself for is that, finally—in 1940—I did not give them time to back out even if they had wanted to. But that wasn't altogether my fault. Guderian and the Luftwaffe moved much faster than anyone expected. The French collapse came quickly as well."

"And this fellow *Felix*. Fenice. You spoke to him a lot. Any hints that he was a Red—a Communist?"

"He was a Frenchman, first and foremost. Didn't like the thought of the Nazis running all over his country. I spent a lot of time with him, but we didn't go into the finer points of his politics. Why?"

"Oh, come on, Cas!" Dick thumped the table. "You *know* what problems everyone had with the Allied forces. Different shades of politics were the booby traps we all dealt with after the Fall of France. The inquisition's going to ask a lot about *Felix*'s politics."

When refugees and fighting men, fleeing from the Nazis, had managed to reach England, and the country seemed to stand alone after Dunkirk, there had been many political difficulties. Not just with the Free French, but with Poles, Czechs, Belgians, Dutch, and others also.

At that time Germany and Soviet Russia had stood shoulder to shoulder because of the nonaggression pact between their two countries, signed barely days before the war began in 1939. The Nazis and Communists were strange bedfellows and before Hitler reneged on the pact, by invading Russia in the early summer of 1941, any refugee with Communist leanings was suspect—particularly as Germany and the Soviets had, together, carved up Poland at the outbreak of war.

When Hitler invaded Russia he also pushed her into the arms of Britain—another strange alliance. At the time, Richard Farthing had remarked, "We're getting into bed with Hitler's unsuitable mistress. We should sleep with one eye open and make sure she's not going to cut our throats." Now he said, "Saving money —austerity—and the revolutionaries among us are this government's obsession.

"You mean if *Felix* comes right out with it, they'll brand me as a Red as well?" Caspar asked, as though the idea was ludicrous.

"We all know that our Russian comrades are no longer allies." Richard Farthing laid his palm on the table. "You know what went on and what's going on now. On both sides of the Atlantic they see Communist plots everywhere. God knows, I've talked to generals who say we should use the atomic weapons on them tomorrow and have done with it. You Brits have always been a secretive and suspicious race." He laughed, knowing his own habit of thinking himself British and not American—or vice versa—when it suited his purpose. "Anyone who had close dealings with the Reds is suspect."

Caspar bridled. "*Tarot* was the *first* operational network. It was part of the *Mouvement*. Jules Fenice only called it a *réseau* after Hitler turned on Russia—and that was when all the pro-Communist Frenchmen joined in arms against the Nazis. Until Hitler invaded the Soviet Union, one hell of a lot of French Communists stayed out of the fight—simply because there was a Russo-German treaty. If Fenice was bright crimson politically, I hardly think he would have had a go against the Occupation forces while Hitler was still Stalin's buddy."

"Don't be too certain." Dick looked at him gravely. "Beware questions that're loaded, Cas. They'll weigh down the questions with Communist traps. Be sure of it. I tell you, Cas, the Soviets are not this year's favorite people."

Caspar nodded, but Dick continued, overlapping what the younger man started to say. "The thing you have to remember is that the real interrogation is over. They've had your man —*Felix,* and the 'pianist,' *and* the guy from operation *Romarin,* and the Otter under a microscope—and they've extracted the dawn chorus from them. What they have said—true or untrue—is already on secret record. From those sources they *know* what they think is the truth about *Tarot.* Nothing you say in defense is going to surprise them. Their minds are already made up—unless C has the secrets locked away where nobody can touch them, which I doubt. They *do* have something up their sleeves, Cas. *I* know. I've tried to get hold of the transcripts."

"Me too," James murmured.

"Nobody's selling. So they'll let you say your piece, then they'll bring out the treasures from the dig. They've been on an interesting expedition wherever they do their work these days. Archeology of the mind, Cas. And they'll bring up the artifacts and the jewels from the tombs and parade them especially for you. Mark me, my dear Caspar; and mark me well."

THE BOARD OF Enquiry assembled on the second floor of a house off St. James's, far enough away from the SIS headquarters in Broadway Buildings to make it comfortable.

The chairman, a much-liked Cambridge don who had made his name in the Service, reminded everybody that it was not a trial. "We're not here to accuse anyone, nor apportion blame, nor even to recommend disciplinary action," he said in his thin, reedy voice. "We're here simply to sift the facts and try to reach some conclusions for the record."

The lawyers all looked as though they did not believe a word of it.

There followed a reading of the guidelines on which the Board would act. Caspar Railton, as the SIS officer who had been on loan to SOE and had much to do with *Tarot,* could be questioned about the part he had played and the decisions taken. There was a list of witnesses, and Caspar could be present at the giving of their evidence. Each one could be questioned, and crossques- tioned, by the Board, and by Caspar. It was his right, but it made him feel uneasy.

The chairman smiled at him. "I think we should begin with your own view, Mr. Railton." His body matched his voice, thin, as though bundles of twigs had been fashioned into human form.

"Where would you like me to begin?" Caspar heard the un- dertow of hostility in his own voice.

One of the lawyers shuffled his papers, glancing at them. "Why not do as the eminent Lewis Carroll suggested, Mr. Rail- ton. Begin at the beginning and go on till you come to the end: then stop." His manner and tone contained all the signals of pomposity which Caspar loathed.

"You will, I presume, already know that I was invited to re- join the Service in 1938," he began. Noting the lawyer was about to interrupt him, Caspar raised his voice to override any attempt to stop him now. "I was appointed to Section D and later received a brief from the CSS himself to carry out a recruiting drive for likely informers, agents, provocateurs, and saboteurs throughout Northern Europe. We were most interested in possible target countries . . ." So he started, not mentioning names until he got to those directly connected with *Tarot*, and taking care to be as precise as possible.

Caspar talked solidly throughout six sittings of the Board— for three days. And, as he spoke, he found himself being transported to the time, nearly seven years before, when he followed the trail which led him to the man they called *Felix*—Jules Fenice. He saw places, recalled weather and smells, remembered the stains on tables of estaminets, or marks on old furniture, the rise and fall of particular voices, looks, gestures and off-stage noises. "I have a distinct picture of all the 'alarums and excursions'—as Shakespeare would say," he told them.

To give the Board credit, the members listened attentively to his narrative.

It started in a bar—

5

▼

THE BAR WAS near the abbey ruins in Loudun. Later Caspar was to reflect on the irony of being in this ancient little town, with its narrow streets and flamboyant square-towered church, when he first heard of Jules Fenice.

It was almost autumn, 1939, but the leaves had yet to turn into gold and brown. The smell of war was in the air, as it had been last year. But this time everyone seemed to know it would happen. Two workmen talked seriously, leaning against the zinc bar, gesturing with a violence that in other countries might have precursed an alarming personal feud.

Caspar sat alone, and waited. It was past six o'clock and twilight was nearly upon them. His contact—Claude Fremet—a name filched from the files as one who had operated behind the German lines during the last war, was late.

Caspar sucked at his cigarette, knowing the man might wish to dodge the meeting. He glanced at his watch and thought briefly of the scandals, sights, and horrors that this place had seen. There had been a short episode of terror here in the early 17th century when a fever of so-called demonic possession had broken out among Ursuline nuns, led by a hunchbacked prioress. They had denounced the local priest, Urbain Grandier, as the devil, and he had been put to the question, tried, tortured, and burned in this place.

He swilled back his brandy and was about to leave when the door opened and his contact appeared—a small old man, bearing his body on a crutch, the tiny ribbon of the Croix de Guerre just visible between buttonhole and lapel on his shabby dark jacket. He did not wear a false limb. Instead, one trouser leg was pinned up around the calfless knee.

The barman nodded at Claude Fremet. A wary nod, as though

he knew the man's reputation. The two workmen did not even look up. One was saying that this time it would be different, this time they had the Maginot Line.

"There will be war," Caspar said. His French was excellent, though he spoke it with a Parisian accent.

"When was there not war?"

It was the agreed exchange of words. Caspar had spoken to the man only on the telephone, though he knew Fremet was short of his right leg from the knee down, and that he had lost it, not in battle, but falling from a window when trying to burgle a house not far away in Châtellerault. Both men nodded. Caspar asked what he would drink, and went to the bar, carrying two glasses of *fine* back to the table.

Fremet had been in trouble with the police many times yet still managed to make a living. How, nobody was quite certain, but those who knew about these things maintained that his absences from Loudun denoted time spent planning robberies for some big gang in Paris. Fremet had always been a better planner than burglar.

"You want something arranged?" he asked Caspar, who saw immediately that the Frenchman spoke in that manner beloved of convicts the world over—a sort of ventriloquial speech, with the lips hardly moving, the sound directed low toward the ear of the listener.

"I would like your advice, Monsieur Fremet."

"So? Advice is not cheap."

Caspar nodded, slipping the envelope from his breast pocket and dropping it onto his knees. It was the act of a close-up magician who worked the tables of nightclubs, sitting with customers and amazing them with sleights and card tricks. Only Fremet was allowed a tiny glimpse of the envelope. Nobody else had time to see it.

"War *is* coming," Caspar repeated. "Any day now. This time we wish to be ready."

"I'm too old to fight, and my leg cannot help me. I shall sit this one out, as they say in the dance halls."

Fremet slid his hand under the table onto Caspar's false knee, to nip the envelope away and pocket it. "Okay." He smiled, the eyes searching behind Caspar, constantly moving. "What can I do?"

"I need to know of men who could be trusted if the Boche

ever got here." It was a variation of a phrase he had already used in Belgium and other parts of France.

"In this area?" Fremet opened his eyes wide, making a joke of it.

"Somewhere near at hand."

The Frenchman shook his head. "I cannot give you any introductions here. But I might have one man for you, elsewhere. A good man, and an even better Frenchman. Though the cops would not say it."

"Where?"

"West. Nearer Paris. A village outside Orléans. Not so far in your machine." Fremet had the acute observation of a criminal, for Caspar had parked the old Citroën three streets away. Caspar nodded, indicating admiration.

"Name?"

"He is named Jules Fenice. Lives alone since his wife left him—or died. Nobody really knows which. He went away for a time."

"Away? Away in prison?"

There was a ghost of a smile on Fremet's thin lips. "Away to the Foreign Legion. He did five years with them. They are the worst. The hardest. But not as hard as the guillotine, if you follow me." Then, almost as an afterthought: "But he's trustworthy, I promise you. Loves his country. Hates the Nazis. Doesn't care much for our own politicians."

"How does he live?"

"Small house. A portion of land. Breeds pigs. Not in a big way. He's not prosperous, but he's the kind of man you want. I give my word on it. I know. You wish to meet him?"

"Maybe."

"He has the telephone. I shall tell him you're coming."

Fremet gave him careful directions, and as Caspar left it began to rain. He drove to Poitiers, booked into the Armes d'Obernai and overslept the next morning. The weather was bad right across France, so he did not get to St. Benoît-sur-Loire until late at night.

Here, in the present, as he told the story of his first meeting with Jules Fenice, Caspar knew what it must feel like to be an actor holding an audience in the palm of his hand. Each member of the Board had his full attention. There was no shuffling, fiddling with papers, or exaggerated sighs of weariness. He relived it all for them—and for himself.

"It was a filthy night," Caspar continued. "The rain was all I could see in my headlights. The drive seemed to go on forever. The roads were bad, and I lost the way once, nearly finishing up in a ditch. But Jules Fenice was waiting for me. He had put an oil lamp in his front window. Fremet had said it would be the signal that Fenice was willing to talk with me."

6

▼

IN THE BLUSTERING downpour the house at St. Benoît-sur-Loire seemed only a dark mass, merging with the night. The rectangle of light, which was the first ground-floor window, appeared and disappeared as the wind sent squalls over it. Caspar approached the house by driving down a rutted muddy track on the outskirts of the village. His wheels spun on the sodden earth, finally bringing the car to a halt. In the headlights he saw two poplars, whipping in the wind, standing sentinel over a small latched gate.

On the following morning, when the storm had gone, the house was revealed as a long, narrow, ugly building of gray blocks, with a slate roof the color of a thunderhead. It looked more like a large farm outbuilding than a dwelling. But on that first night he heaved himself from the car, grabbing at his attaché case, turning up his collar, and squelching through mud, as he moved toward the house. The door opened as he reached it, as though the man inside had watched his progress.

At first sight Jules Fenice did not appear to be the kind of man Caspar required—thickset, in his mid-forties, with a square face and sparse light hair which lay flat to his scalp as though someone had painted it on. To start with, Caspar could not put his finger on what was wrong. Fenice moved with tight precision and the gray eyes never showed any sign of speculation: revealing instead an instant wariness, as though everything and everyone with whom he came into contact was potentially dangerous. He opened the door wider, motioning Caspar to come in.

"Claude said you were coming." Fenice closed the door, leaning against it, waiting as Caspar's eyes flicked quickly around the room, which seemed to take up the bulk of the ground floor— bare flagstones and an old, open range with sides of ham and cured bacon hanging from hooks set into the stone hearth, func-

37

tional furniture and the smell of animals which pervaded the atmosphere.

"Thank you." Caspar returned the man's guarded look.

Fenice helped him off with his coat, hanging it over a chair in
front of the range. Already a bottle of Cognac and two glasses
stood on the table, and Caspar's host poured a liberal dose into
one of the glasses. "Drink it. It will kill the damp. You wish to
talk or eat?"

"You're generous. Can we do both?"

"But certainly. You stay here the night. Claude said it was a
matter of being ready for war."

"A precaution." Caspar smiled. "In case the worst comes. In
case Hitler's army gets the better of us. Unlikely, but we're trying
to be ready." It was the line he had used in other parts of France,
Belgium, and, even once, in Poland. Fenice's reply might give
him a clue to the man's possible use.

"It is likely, not unlikely." The Frenchman was dropping lard
into a big frying pan set on the range. He took down a side of
bacon and deftly cut a dozen slices from it, dropping them care-
lessly into the pan where they hissed and sizzled as he shook the
handle with one hand and took plates from a rack with the other,
setting them on the back of the range.

They ate almost in silence, Fenice breaking hunks of bread
from a crusty *baguette*, handing them to Caspar.

The bacon was thick and full of flavor. Caspar commented on
how good it tasted.

"That was Gretchen." Fenice smiled. "I call them all by German names. The Boche killed my father and his brothers. I have
reason to dislike them."

Caspar nodded. It would take time to test the man's reactions,
but the geographical portents were good: the small house was
unlikely to be commandeered or pillaged by any advancing army
—except for the pigs. But a man like Fenice would be clever
enough to do deals with any military authorities. Lord, Caspar
thought, I hope it doesn't happen. Silently he prayed that none of
those he had already recruited would be needed.

It was during their first guarded conversation that Caspar detected what worried him about Fenice. The man held himself like
someone with military training, yet there was a disadvantage, for
it became increasingly obvious that he was more used to obeying
orders than giving them. If he was to be recruited it had to be as a
leader. The man would need further training. He had already

volunteered a hatred for the Germans. Caspar did not always respond well to people who gave that kind of information freely on a first meeting. Recruiting agents required patience, playing them like fish, even seducing them over a long period.

They talked late on the first night, though afterward Caspar realized that he had done most of the speaking, to establish beyond doubt that he was on the side of the angels, and not what Fenice called "a fox in lamb's wool."

In turn, the Frenchman told his own story, using few words but providing evidence by way of photographs and documents.

The house had been his father's home, and it was from here that Fenice senior had gone to war in 1914, never to return. Jules was brought up by women—"There are two aunts still living. One here, the other in Orléans." He had chosen his own bride from the village, but she was a flighty girl whom his mother did not like. "This house was a battlefield between Annette and my mother, until the old lady died. Then it was a battlefield for me."

The girl was a scold, and had a lover, the son of a prosperous builder who lived in Orléans. One day both Madame Fenice and the builder's son disappeared. The police searched, and had Jules in for days at a time, questioning him. Nobody ever heard of the lovers again, and soon the police grew tired, though the locals kept their distance. For Fenice, though, it became difficult. A friend accepted the offer of the house and pigsties for an unspecified time. "I left and went where so many criminals go—to the Foreign Legion." He grimaced. "There were times when I wished I had stayed here, I can tell you. The Legion is not for the faint-hearted. I gave it five years. It gave me my life and respect."

He talked occasionally of hardship and brutality, but never in any detail. Caspar observed that the man was intensely proud of having served with the Legion, which meant he was also proud of his country. Sitting, on that first night, drinking Cognac in the flagstoned room by the light of oil lamps, it soon became plain that Fenice should be wooed, possibly won, and, if so, given further training.

Before retiring, Caspar asked to see around the house—it was something he usually did as soon as possible when priming a possible recruit. He did not like to sit in a strange house without knowing if anyone else was there, but in this case he waited for the moment. Fenice was, by the very look of him, a hard man. To upset him before gaining confidence could be fatal to the final outcome.

There was no electricity, so they did the grand tour by oil lamp—the long passage upstairs was uncarpeted, as were the wooden stairs themselves. It was difficult for two men to pass one another along that passage, and all the rooms, except for the large one downstairs, were like boxes. He could sleep four at a pinch, and there was loft space in the roof which might prove useful. But there had to be electricity. That was Caspar's first and only concern about the house.

In all, he visited Fenice six times before the Fall of France. The first visit lasted for three days while the men fenced back and forth about the true reasons for the Englishman's visit. But when Caspar left, he knew there was a fair chance of opening up a cell here, just outside Orléans, should there be real disaster.

War came, and, during the bitter winter of 1939–1940, Fenice allowed himself to come under discipline, and put it about that he had to visit friends in Paris. In reality he went to London for ten days where, under Caspar's guidance, he refreshed his memory of weapons and skills. He also learned something about signals, together with simple tradecraft. Caspar also tried to expand the Frenchman's attitude toward leadership. Alone with Caspar, Fenice committed various passwords and code names to memory, so that they played games, tossing simple phrases or initials back and forth like jugglers as they sat in a quiet Hampstead basement.

"I last had physical contact with *Felix*," he told the Board of Enquiry, "in April 1940. We already knew of movements within the Wehrmacht and had a good picture that *Fall Gelb*—Case Yellow, the battle plan against the West—was being altered. But, as we all know to our cost, the Allied Supreme Command preferred to believe *Fall Gelb* had not been altered one iota. With the permission of the CSS and, I am told, a grudging nod from the military, I set out to do the rounds of five possible cells within Belgium and France. In the end, only one of those cells became switched on in its original form—*Tarot*, led by *Felix*. I arrived at St. Benoît-sur-Loire on April 3rd." Jesus! he thought as he said it, *Tarot* was the only network I managed to run from afar. My other recruits were swallowed up by different networks, many of which came unstuck, like *Prosper* and the penetrated *Interallié*. If *Tarot* really was an undiscovered disaster, he might even be linked in to the other blunders. Pushing the thought to one side, Caspar continued his narrative. He painted more word pictures, and his visits to St. Benoît-sur-Loire and Orléans during that first winter of the war came into the mind as those icy, snowdrift paintings by Bruegel.

THE HOUSE had been connected up to the electricity mains just before the long, hard winter set in—Caspar had pulled strings through the military, then covered his tracks so that anyone investigating the possibility of Fenice getting preferential treatment would put it down to a deal between the military authorities and large quantities of pork and bacon finding their way into army messes. He even suggested to Fenice that this ploy should be used with the Germans if they came.

On this, last, visit, Caspar sat opposite Jules and saw him clearly in the light from the one bulb which dangled above them. There, over one night, he told *Felix* of his final fears, and what would have to be done.

"The battle's coming, my friend, and I don't think the military, however courageous, realizes what kind of war is going to be unleashed."

Jules shrugged. "It was ever thus. *Merde*. We're in for it."

"Let's see." Caspar gave details of arms and explosives caches, already set up, and the possibility of the first couriers. Going through the passwords again, he said casually, "Oh, don't be surprised if your two nieces from Paris decide to come and stay here."

"Ah. But I have no nieces."

"You might have. If that turns out to be the case, their names will be Catherine and Anne Routon." Caspar's eyes almost mocked him.

"Homework well done." The twinkle appeared around Jules' lips. "They come from my late wife's side of the family. I hope they're pretty."

"Very pretty, but they don't know about you yet. To us, as you will be called *Felix*, they will be recognized as *Maxine* and *Dédé*." He made *Felix* repeat the names and thought of the passports and documents secreted in the false bottom of the glove compartment in the car outside.

After a while he asked *Felix* whether *he* had yet started to recruit any friends.

"No, but I have my eyes open."

"Your open eyes, Jules; whom have they rested upon?"

There was distinct hesitation before he spoke. Jules Fenice

could never put his trust lightly in any fellow man. It was the one thing that still concerned Caspar. Would he have the strength to take an active lead? Getting facts from him was like pulling teeth.

"Well," he said eventually, "there's the butcher, Henri Villar —he's loyal, fat, and fancies the widow Debron. I think he would be trustworthy, but I shall be careful. Not too fast with him. The Abbot and his monks should be left alone, but the Curé Sicre would be reliable; the doctor—Monsieur le docteur Clergue; and an *avocat* in Orléans who does work here once a week —Maury. Jean Maury."

"If it comes, good luck, my friend." Caspar held Jules Fenice's hand in a tight grip. He had come a long way toward knowing, even respecting, this secretive, introspective man over the past months in lengthy face-to-face sessions, both at St. Benoît-sur-Loire and in London. Yet, as he drove away from the strange rectangular house, he admitted to himself that he really knew little of the true man. Only the bare facts—that he may have murdered out of passion or jealousy; that he had served his country, could keep his mouth closed, was quick with a pistol and unconcerned when handling explosives; that he had a good memory. It was probably just enough to forge the bond between agent and handler.

Caspar was confident that his agent knew what was to be done if his area became occupied by Nazi troops. "Havoc! Chaos! That's what we want. Little things like trains being held up for hours; transports with sudden problems—their engines or tires." In London they had told Fenice, "Don't run amok. That'll just draw attention to your people. Better to injure a couple than kill a hundred. Injuries mean hospital treatment and paperwork. Injuries complicate matters and cause more work." Caspar had advised of yet another way. "If you discover a girl is infected—and the doctor could help you there—let her infect a few of them before she gets treatment." His grandfather, Giles Railton, whose ruthless ways were legend, came into his mind.

So Caspar drove to Paris in order to drop in on his nieces, Jo-Jo and Caroline, where he gave them money for ham, bread, and wine, then told them stories which made all three laugh in the Rue de la Huchette. After that, over the space of four hours, he seduced them to work, if need be, with *Felix*. It was easy, for they were both Railtons, and the world of secrets ran in the Railton blood like strong wine. There had even been a Railton who worked gathering intelligence concerning the Spanish Armada during the reign of Elizabeth I. To recruit Railtons was as simple as falling from a log.

He felt no guilty conscience; yet, once more, thoughts of his grandfather Giles hurled themselves into his head.

When Caspar returned to London he could not understand why, on the night of his homecoming, "old Phoebe"—as the family called his wife—had to shake him, sweating, from a nightmare, recalled clearly on waking. A man dressed in a bloodstained white robe, with gore running from his misshapen legs, together with a deformed woman in black, beckoned him down a narrow cobblestoned street. The stones were hot under his feet. He followed. They turned the corner. He still followed, and at the corner dropped, screaming, into a crevasse of fire.

Three weeks later, on May 10, the shooting war began. For Belgium and Holland it lasted a bare five days. For the rest it was over in only six weeks.

Caspar could hear the traffic from nearby St James's as he told the Board how his first courier—a Swiss called only by a street name, *Night Stock*—had made contact with *Felix* and reported that *Maxine* and *Dédé* had arrived. He also brought a message in cipher which said that *Tarot* now consisted of eight people and the weapons were secure.

"It was a start. A beginning," Caspar told them, and the six members of the Board looked back at him with hungry eyes. He could not divine whether they were now ravenous for more of his tale or for his blood.

7

▼

OUTSIDE, IN THE real world of the present, other things were happening. Naldo Railton, son of James and nephew of Caspar, had been removed from Berlin Station and given the task of handling his own agent—the lad Kruger.

The results Kruger had obtained regarding the *Tarot* affair had so pleased C that he had given the order himself, in spite of counsel against the action from the Deputy Chief and two Heads of Departments.

Naldo handled Herbie Kruger with skill, running him through two of the DP camps in West Germany before moving into Austria. This did not please the Resident—or Head of Station—in Vienna. Vienna was regarded as "most sensitive," and the handful of SIS people there took great umbrage at Naldo Railton's arrival with his lumbering, youthful, and clumsy-looking agent.

They were less happy when the agent produced results in the form of two senior SS men and a particularly brutal woman SD guard who had disappeared from the terrible female camp at Ravensbrück.

Things appeared to be going very well. Naldo and Kruger even had an operational name, *Weed Killer,* with Herbie Kruger known, in all signals, as *Digger*. The names were obvious, but, a handful apart, the nucleus of SIS in London was not known for brilliant mental agility.

Then the unthinkable happened. *Weed Killer* was closed down.

Naldo had the news from a young, haughty SIS type, straight from the head of Vienna Station's office, just after breakfast one drizzling Thursday morning. It came on heavy stationery emblazoned with the Foreign Office crest. Most insecure, Naldo thought.

Running his eyes over the document, Naldo made up his mind

to report the insecure method. It was flagged as "Confidential," though not "Classified," and contained every last detail—passport and papers collection, times of travel, mode of transport, right up to the fact that they would be met on arrival, for they were to return to London: Naldo and Herbie both. To cap it all, the orders had C's personal sanction.

Kruger, naturally, was overjoyed at the prospect of seeing London, while Naldo could not shake off a sense of foreboding.

They were flown into Northolt by the RAF and met by two teams: a pair of heavy men from "The School," as they called the Training Department; and three smooth, wary types whom Naldo identified as "Staff." The heavies took Kruger off in a plain white van, while Naldo was driven into London in an old Daimler, flanked, in the rear, by two of the smoothies.

The first held out his hand. "We have to take your passport, old boy."

"What's going on?" Naldo asked grittily.

"C's instructions. Ours not to reason why, and all that rot."

Naldo handed over the passport they had given him before leaving Vienna. "And the real one." The first smooth operator smiled, showing perfect teeth.

"I presume I can keep the rest of my ID." Naldo fished in his pockets.

"'Course. Only temporary."

"Indefinite leave, old chap. But you mustn't go out of London."

"So where can we drop you, old horse?"

"Corner of Exhibition Road, Kensington," Naldo snapped.

"C says he'll be in touch," they chorused as the car stopped near the entrance to Kensington Gardens. Naldo hefted his small case in his right hand and turned in the direction of the house he called home.

As well as Redhill Manor, the Railtons had a number of London properties, but home for Naldo was none of these—not the grand house in Cheyne Walk, nor the property in Eccleston Square, where his Uncle Caspar now lived, but the three-story house in which he had been brought up. The place belonged to his father, who had bought it during the First World War as a home for his wife and children.

He had not been back for weeks. The last time was shortly after Arnie Farthing had bequeathed Herbie Kruger to him, and then only for a weekend. It smelled musty and a little damp, but everything else appeared to be in order.

At thirty-one, Naldo was not married. There were plenty of girls, for he was a big, fine-looking man in the Railton mold: tall, muscular, and with a distinctive bone structure—strong jawline, high forehead, and the "Railton nose": straight, patrician, and flaring slightly at the nostrils.

There was a woman who came in to clean twice a week— more often when he was there—so the living room fire was laid. He set a match to it, rubbing his hands and thinking that if C had given him leave there was no point in worrying about the whys and wherefores. Sufficient unto the day.

He went to his small study where he unlocked a desk drawer and took out his "little black book." Might as well have some fun. Eat, drink, and be merry, for tomorrow...

But London was almost empty of his friends. It was Saturday and the girls he took out when on leave all seemed to be in the country or otherwise engaged.

At lunchtime he put on a coat, went out, hailed a taxi, and headed for the Ritz—the grillroom, which was still full of uniforms, male and female. He felt like a shirker and, indeed, was almost treated as a pariah. The staff in the grill had become used to ranking officers and their ladies, and, even though the war was over, they still kept up a kind of snobbery where civilian clothes were concerned.

He ate a mediocre meal and was about to order coffee when someone spoke from just behind him.

"Naldo? What the hell're you doing here?" It was the last person he wanted to see, "Buzz" Burville, sporting the crown and pip of a lieutenant colonel and the flashes and badges of the Airborne. They had been at Wellington together, then Cambridge for a while, and Buzz was not only a prize bore, but one of those career officers who knew of Naldo's occupation and was given to pumping him so that he could boast secrets in the Mess—secrets that usually emanated from his own brain.

"Hallo, Buzz," Naldo greeted him flatly. "You okay? I heard you got out at Arnhem. And a gong as well!" He stared at the white and purple ribbon above the breast pocket.

"Came with the milk train." It was the standard answer of "heroes," and as Buzz said it, Naldo's eyes flicked to a point behind the officer's right shoulder. A slim young woman with a cap of dark hair neatly shaped over her ears was approaching them. "So what's new in the world of cloak and dagger, Nald? Bagged any good spies lately? I hear your honored uncle's going through the mill. Inquisition and all that, about baddies in France . . ."

How the hell did he know that? Naldo thought as the young woman reached a point six inches or so behind Burville and coughed. She wore a smart and expensive gray suit which must have taken all her clothing coupons for the next six months.

"Yours, I think." Naldo nodded over Buzz's shoulder.

"Oh, lord. Yes. Don't think you've met my sister, Barb. Barbara, this is an old school chum—Wellington and John's, Cambridge—Naldo Railton, my young sis, Barb."

Naldo rose and stretched out a hand. How could a crashing bore like Burville have such an elegant, beautiful sister? "How d'you do?" he said lamely.

"I do very nicely." She smiled, eyes shining black as her hair.

"Careful of Nald, Barb. Cloak and dagger merchant," in a stage whisper. "Codes, secrets, spies, you know."

"No, Bertie, I don't know." She went on smiling at Naldo. Bertie, he thought. Lord love him, but after all the years at Wellington and Cambridge he had never known Buzz's Christian name. "Bertie"—my God, suits to a t.

Burville looked nervous. "Just going, actually." He moved his lips into a smile, an action he always seemed to find difficult. "Been getting a bit of stick from Barb. I was late. She's only had a main course and I have to dash."

"You care to have some pudding and coffee with me?" Naldo, still standing, did not take his eyes from Barbara.

"I'd love to. Thank you, Mr. Railton."

"Well . . ." Burville began to stammer out apologies to his sister for being late and messing up the lunch.

"Oh, off you go, Bertie, and don't hurt yourself jumping out of aeroplanes. It's dangerous."

Burville shrugged. "Decent of you, Naldo. Thank you. Must dash. Love to the aged parents, Barb, when you see them." For a terrible second Naldo wondered if he had been wise to invite her. Her looks could camouflage an empty head, with thoughts that stretched no further than the next cocktail party or whether she would get her photograph in *The Tatler*. He looked at her in silence for a full thirty seconds, which felt like an hour.

"Where does the name come from?" she asked.

"Name?"

"Naldo. Is it Italian or something?"

He explained. "My close friends call me Nald."

"Can I be a close friend, Nald?"

It took only minutes for Barbara Burville to allay his fears. They knew immediately that they spoke the same language. She was on demobilization leave from the WAAFs, and, within an hour, Naldo discovered that her elegance and beauty were not just skin deep. She had a sharp sense of humor, and an even sharper brain. She also liked music, theater, and poetry. These were the easy things to discover about Barbara Burville, the kind of surface qualities most men find out quickly, latching on to them as they idle toward an acquaintanceship which might just possibly lead to something else.

They went to see a film that afternoon and had dinner at the Hungaria in the Haymarket. She had a flat above the shops in Cecil Court and after he had dropped her off that night, Naldo went back to Kensington and telephoned her.

As they left the Hungaria, he had watched her back, straight as a soldier's, and saw her body move inside her clothes. Naldo desired her more than he had wanted any woman. He was not one for casual affairs, though healthy lust had always played a part in his life. On the telephone, they talked for half an hour, and she flirted with him, though it was not the usual emptyheaded banter. Barbara's quick wit went deeper. As they arranged the next day's events—for it became clear they would be meeting on a regular basis—she suddenly quoted Auden at him. "Woken by water/ Running away in the dark, he often had/Reproached night for a companion/Dreamed of already." Barbara spoke the lines in a soft whisper, as though playing at being a seductress. "Do you reproach night for a companion, Nald?" she teased.

"Constantly," he said, then, when he put down the telephone he looked up the poem. It was called "The Secret Agent," and he smiled at the complexity of her jest, and knew that if it was to happen between them, it would be very fast indeed. In so short a time, Barbara had climbed into his mind and taken possession.

On Monday night they became lovers, and it was sweet as apples and soft as down for them both. She wept after the act, and Naldo Railton held her close as the sobs ran through her like knife thrusts.

"I'm sorry, you're the first since . . ." she began, then stopped herself.

"It's okay," he whispered. "I'm not jealous of your past and never will be."

She looked up at him, the big dark eyes damp with great thunderstorm tears. "And now?"

"Now, I'll be jealous if you even look on another."

"I'm glad, for I can be the most jealous woman known to man. I'll be jealous of every moment you're not with me." He had a feeling she had never said that to anyone else. She spoke again. "For the first time in my life, Naldo, I'm truly sorry that you weren't the one to chop down my little cherry tree."

He took her again and she cried out at her climax—loudly as though trying to exorcise the traces of any other man who had ever touched her. She was twenty-six years old and had been engaged to a bomber pilot. Like many, he had not returned one night and part of her still grieved for him.

By the next morning Naldo knew this was not merely a passing thing. Naldo was not the type to be suddenly moonstruck, he had never "fallen in love with love." He had too much inbred caution for that, instilled into him not only by family background, but also by his chosen profession.

On Wednesday night they dined early, at Gennaro's in Dean Street, then went back to Kensington and sat by the fire for a time, Barbara with her legs tucked under her, on the floor, her head on Naldo's knees. They talked of marriage and their respective families.

"My life's far from normal," he said. "I could be away a lot—with no explanations. It can be difficult; I know from my own parents. My father was—is—in the same line of business. They close ranks around the wives when the men are away, though. Bloody good about that."

"I'm used to it. It's been most people's life for the last few years. But it runs in my family. Army, like yours, I imagine."

Presently she uncurled herself and began to undress. They had switched no lights on and the fire threw red flares around her body, giving new textures to her skin. He took her in his arms, and was about to place her on the rug before the fireplace when the front doorbell started to ring—quick bursts of single dots.

"Who the hell . . . ?" he began.

"Your bell's having a little orgasm," Barbara laughed, gathering up her clothes and running barefoot to the hall and up the stairs. He caught sight of her, nimble with no extra flesh moving on buttocks or breasts, as he turned on the hall light.

"I go, I go . . ." she quoted Puck at the first turning of the stairs, then, plaintively, lower lip pouting, "Look how I go . . ." disappearing from sight with a chuckle. The memory of her smooth black hair remained in the retina of his mind, and from somewhere in his past a name sprang into his head—*Ranuccio Farnese*. Though he spoke good French, German, Spanish, and

Italian, he had no idea where the name came from. It was certainly not any Italian contact he had ever known.

Naldo took the chain off the door and opened it, heart suddenly pounding as he did so, realizing he had not taken the simplest precaution his Service demanded.

In an uncoordinated windmilling of arms and legs, Kruger burst into the hall. "Naldo. Good. I find you. It is good. But please close door."

They had done him up a bit—given him new clothes, but with Herbie the clothes found their own level, fitting where they touched, the trousers bagged and the jacket hung like a sack. His tie, loud as a twelve-bore shotgun, was almost at right angles to his collar. The man was animated. You could read excitement in his eyes, yet apart from his lumbering entrance, his body was still and calm, like the air before a tropical storm. He had not broken from the basic technique learned, Naldo suspected, from Arnie Farthing. He stood still now as he said, "Good. I do well. I find you. It is my objection."

"Your what?"

"Object . . . something. They start English lessons, Naldo. Object—"

"—ive?"

"So. *Ja*, objective."

"I'm part of a training exercise?" Naldo sensed anger rising.

"*Ja, und nein*. Yes, but no. Is very important, Nald. *Very* important. Tonight is exercise, but this afternoon I am havink meeting, how you say it? Interview? *Ja*, interview with the Chief. He gives me envelope. For you. Very important. He says that tonight I do this, what do you call it? Invasion exercise where I must not be caught. Must not be followed."

"Evasion," Naldo supplied.

"Is what I say, evasion exercise. They have teached me—taught me—how not to be followed by the surveying teams . . ."

"Surveillance, Herb." He sounded like Arnie Farthing at that first meeting in Berlin.

"Only if I am certain that I've outrun the hounds am I to come here. Come to you. Give you letter."

Naldo said nothing but moved to switch off the hall light. The flames from the fire in his sitting room allowed him to lead Herbie inside, then take a peep outside, drawing back the far edge of one of the heavy curtains. Nobody lurked. Not even a parked car. "You're certain you weren't followed?"

"I give them slip. Four of them." He held up four fingers.

"They think I go on Bakerloo Line, but I switch trains, then walk. Make certain nobody follow."

"Well done, Herb . . ."

"*Ja*, they are good fellows. They teach me song about Piccadilly." And before Naldo could stop him, Herbie launched into a tuneless dirge—

> "*Oh my little sister Lillie is a whore in Piccadilly,*
> *And my mother is another in the Strand,*
> *Ja*, mein Father hawks his—"

"Shut up, Herb!" he shouted above the crudity, hoping that Barbara could not hear upstairs, though he knew the bawdiness would never bother her. She could swear like a trooper, he already knew. Herbie stopped, looking crestfallen. And Naldo gave him a friendly nod. "Now, just let me read this." He tore open the envelope, eyes racing down the page. It was in C's own hand and in green ink, an affectation which had caught on from the first C. Naldo's father said it had become superstition.

Your good man will have got to you safely with this. Please instruct him that he is not, repeat not, to divulge his visit to you, nor that this note has reached you. Burn after reading. I wish to see you under most secure conditions. In plain language, nobody else should know of our meeting. Tonight, and, if necessary, for the next three nights, I shall be alone— from 11pm to 1am—at the address in Northolt at the foot of this note. It is near The Target public house. I would be grateful if you would please observe field rules and abort if you are followed.

Naldo tore the paper into four pieces and dropped them on the fire, waiting until it was completely consumed. Then he turned to Herbie.

"You've done well, Herb. Now, did C tell you that you mustn't talk of this to anyone?"

"I tell nobody. Not now. Not never, Nald. I promise. They can beat me to pulp. I tell nobody."

It was enough. They talked for a few minutes, then Naldo let the big German boy out of the back entrance, where he was quickly lost in the shadows.

Upstairs, Barbara lay in bed, the sheets pulled up to her chin.

"I'm sorry," he said. "I have to go out. Business. Will you

wait? Stay here all night? Don't know when I'll be back. Maybe not till the morning."

She did not open her eyes, whispering, "I'll wait. If you're very late I'll go home and you can ring me there. I love you, Nald."

"Yes." He felt suddenly idiotic. "You too . . . Very much."

At the door, he paused.

"Naldo?" she called.

"Yes?"

In almost a whisper she quietly sang—

> *"Oh my little sister Lillie is a whore in Piccadilly,*
> *And my mother is another in the Strand."*

"I love you very much, Barb," he said, grinning back at her giggling face. "Will you marry me?"

"Yes, please, even if your father does hawk his—"

"'Enough, no more: 'Tis not so sweet now as it was before.'" The Railtons had a habit of quoting Shakespeare. Some said they even thought in the Bard's words, and treated the text as some religious people did with the Bible.

8

▼

THE PLACE WAS situated in a long, climbing row of semidetached houses—white stucco walls, the doors and windows of each painted in different shades, as though to express some form of individuality among the rising river of uniform buildings. Only one in four of the streetlights had been reactivated after five years of enforced blackout, so Naldo saw the changing colors, and the various front hedges and fences, only in spasmodic bursts.

The house C had designated stood in shadow, as did its partner. After negotiating his way through a small gate and up an erratically paved walk, Naldo could just make out the number, screwed to the door and painted over, as though the wartime occupants had felt it wrong to polish brass which might cause reflection and so twinkle to a passing Nazi bomber. He smiled, remembering the tale that went around Haversage after the bomb had killed the cow. It had been the cowman's fault, everyone claimed, because he had left the light on in his cottage. Opening the door had drawn the Heinkel's attention. The uninitiated held great store by chinks of light. It was the sense of vulnerability that did it.

Hardly had he pressed the bell than the door was opened without sound—lock and hinges newly oiled.

"Come in, young Railton. Good to see you." The door closed and the light came on. There, in the tiny hallway stood the somewhat avuncular, though quite unimpressive figure of C—heavily built, with small eyes embedded in a round pale face topped by gingery hair.

C took his coat and hat, hanging them neatly on an old-fashioned hallstand, then, with outstretched arm, shepherded Naldo into the main living room.

It was completely out of keeping with anything Naldo would ever connect with the Chief—a glowing cave of pink. Pink curtains through which he could glimpse old blackout frames still in place, pink walls, pink lampshades and chair covers. Even the beveled 1930s mirror was pink, huge above the tiny fireplace with its pink tiles and hissing gas fire.

"Ghastly, isn't it?" C chuckled. "Sit down, Railton. You came by car?"

"Yes, sir. Parked well clear."

"Good. No tails?"

"Nothing."

"Fellow Kruger got to you without any trouble?"

Naldo nodded.

"Odd boy, Kruger. But I care for him. He'll go far. Knows what he's about. Only a lad, but he already has the touch."

"I think he grew up very quickly in Berlin, sir. Most young people *had* to grow up fast."

"Dare say. Yes. Well, business. I own this house, by the way, and the one next door. Picked 'em up for a song and kept them to myself. Really belong to the 'shop' of course but they're not on anyone's books." He gave the suggestion of a conspiratorial smile. "So, rather you didn't mention them to anyone. Private safe house. In fact everything we talk about is strictly between us."

"Of course, sir."

"It starts with Kruger. What we winkled out from the couple of people he identified for us: Buelow and Fenice. Care for a drink?"

He could have done with coffee and said so. There was some—"Perking away in the kitchen," as C put it. In a few minutes they were again seated, armed with coffee, the percolator and accessories on the pink glass table between them.

C began once more. He had, naturally, seen the full reports that came from the interrogations of Buelow and Fenice, together with statements from the "pianist"; the OSS man who had escaped from *Romarin;* plus others who would be giving evidence at the *Tarot* investigation. "They've all seen them now, of course. The Board of Enquiry, and a couple of other people with need-to-know. But there are other bits and pieces on file. Interesting tidbits which almost go to make up a rather gaudy jigsaw. I've put in a lot of time digging into history, old cases, dusty files. In a way I've been resurrecting the dead."

Naldo suddenly recalled something his father had remarked, in private, about C. "He loves the games," James had laughed. It was a kind of aside. "Conjures operations from dreams some-times. Bit of a fantasy man is our Chief."

C paused, gave another smile, and then wrinkled his brow before asking, "What would you say were the prime subjects on the agenda of our Service, Railton? At this very moment, I mean."

This was all delivered in a matter-of-fact tone. Naldo did not think twice about his answer. It was elementary. Since the atomic bombs on Hiroshima and Nagasaki, plus the division of Germany and Berlin, their main concerns had been plain. "Defense of atomic secrets, and Russian intentions in the East—particularly Berlin."

C nodded. "Not far off the mark. They're both high on the list. In fact they're going to be high on *your* list. How much do you know about this enquiry into your uncle's network, *Tarot?*"

"Only the minimum. I thought it was an SOE network, though, not my uncle's."

C gave a small grunt, his head dropping to one side. "Your uncle recruited its leader and did a lot of long-distance handling."

Naldo shrugged. "I suppose so."

"Look." C's tone became more avuncular. "I don't think for a moment that Caspar's done anything to be ashamed of—nothing out of the ordinary, though there *are* people who'd like to make the enquiry into a kind of secret show-trial. Unhappily for them, there are weightier matters that've come to light. Sit back and let me fill in the picture with what we know—from Buelow, Fenice, and the sources that're in *no way* connected with the damned enquiry. Yet—and here's the paradox—they *are* connected with your Uncle Caspar's *Tarot* network, and with events in Orléans itself: or at least with Klaubert, the so-called Devil of Orléans."

Naldo had begun to feel tired in the hot, pink suburban room. Now, as C spoke, he came wide awake, his senses tingling, reacting to C's story. For his Chief began to reveal secrets, like a magician opening a nest of Chinese boxes—cross-referencing fragments of Buelow's, and the others', evidence with things buried deep in files within SIS Registry. He was clear and con-cise, and the story ranged across half of Europe, springing to the United States, then to Soviet Russia and back again.

It was a complex tale, but the way in which C laid out each equation, and then provided each answer, finally made up a sin-ister and labyrinthine thesis. Ploy followed ploy, movement be-came action, and, at the end—if C had really followed the logic correctly—there could be only one answer.

"You see what I'm getting at," he said in conclusion. "We have to put our own questions to the answer."

"Yes." Naldo could not completely take in the enormity of C's thesis. "You'd claim, sir, that things which happened within *Tarot,* and were connected to the Gestapo in Orléans, are directly linked to our own Service—and, from there, to Russian attempts to gain atomic intelligence?"

"Correct."

"And we have to test this theory?"

"Correct again."

"But you have diverse intelligence, from good sources, sir. How *can* we test its accuracy?"

"An operation by stealth. Your operation, Railton—well, yours and mine."

"Where do we start?"

"Here and there." C tilted his hand. "First, you'll have to go through the files I've gathered under one classified heading. I have the one copy. Nobody else has seen them as they are—rearranged under one roof as it were. And of course you'll have access to the *Tarot* Board of Enquiry transcripts as they become available." He gave yet another thin smile, as though passing a trust to Naldo. "After that? Well, we shall see. London. Berlin. Maybe Russia. Certainly the United States. You'll have to go deep. You'll need to run young Kruger into the Berlin Russian Zone for a start. I also think, bearing in mind what we know of the United States connection, you should have an American officer on detachment. I'd like to keep things in the family—your family, that is." He regarded Naldo with his solemn eyes. "I'm trying to get Arnold Farthing seconded to us. They've given him a desk job in Washington, but there are ways and means. I should know soon. Maybe in hours. Hang on until then."

He cautioned Naldo again. Nothing must be breathed, even to members of his own family, and certainly not to any of the SIS. "It's an enclosed operation. *My* operation." His voice rose slightly, and he went on to arrange a further meeting.

Thinking his Chief had finished, Naldo made to stand up, but C held out his hand, palm toward his agent's chest as though to push him back. "There is one more thing, and it might just be your first key into all this." He leaned to one side of his chair, extracting a file from a briefcase on the floor. "Photographs I want you to look at. Tell me, do you recognize this man?" He slapped an aging print onto the table and Naldo nodded. "Yes, of course. I've seen it many times. My late Uncle Ramillies, Caspar's brother."

"What about this young fella, eh?" C tapped the photograph with a forefinger.

"I think you know, sir. He was a member of this Service. Went on an operation into Russia in October 1918—"

"At the instigation of your great-grandfather, Giles—"

"He was never seen or heard of again."

"No. There's nothing on file. Of all the people we sent in during that time of revolution and civil war, we heard no more of Ramillies Railton." As he said it, C pushed another picture forward, and then another and another.

Each photograph was obviously of the same man—taken over a passage of years. They were all blown up from smaller prints: each one with a grainy texture. Slowly Naldo emptied his mind of emotion; as the fourth and fifth photographs were passed in front of him, he realized what was coming. It was the answer to something that had troubled him for over a decade now.

"How about him?" C was not gruff in manner. You could even have said that he showed pity as his finger pushed the photograph closer.

"Yes." Naldo heard the rasp in his own throat. "Yes, I recognize *him*. I also see now who he is."

During that fleeting flirtation with leftist politics while at Cambridge during the thirties, Naldo had gone one icy night to the rooms of a friend in Trinity College. There they had been given tips and invitations by ". . . a comrade . . . who has British origins, but has lived in the USSR for some time." On that evening, Naldo thought there was something familiar about the man, and the face of the man from Russia had stayed alive in his imagination ever since—like somebody he had met before that time but could not place. Now, he saw in the progress of photographs that it was his own uncle, his Uncle Caspar's brother, Ramillies Railton.

The SIS was also well advised about Naldo's political shuttling during his Cambridge days.

"Does my father know?"

C shook his head. "Time enough. He will be told, and Caspar also. Ramillies calls himself Rogov nowadays. Gennadi Aleksandrovich Rogov. NKVD of course. Quite high in their scheme of things. Spends a lot of time in the Russian Zone of Berlin. Wouldn't it be rather charming to arrange a meeting?"

Bearing in mind the whole thesis upon which C's conclusions

rested, it was a breathtaking, daring, and very dangerous idea. Naldo's heart leaped at it. He raised his eyebrows. "I wish I had thought of that, sir."

The Chief smiled back. "Maybe we'll tell certain people that you did," he said as though sealing the bargain on the operation upon which they were about to embark.

In the hall, he put a Yale key into Naldo's hand. "My house is your house," he said. Then he made Naldo repeat the telephone number three times. "It's unlisted and, as far as I can tell, the line's secure. We will probably use this place a great deal."

NALDO RETURNED TO the house near Kensington Gardens at five in the morning. Barbara stirred in her sleep as he slipped into the bed beside her, then she moaned and wrapped herself around him.

Even though his mind reeled under the information entrusted to him, and the dangers that he knew must follow, Railton fell into a deep sleep.

He was wakened only by Barbara's kisses.

"Oh, you didn't turn into a frog," she laughed as he came awake. She had made toast and coffee and she waited, close to him as he drank, ate, and began to come alive again.

"You got in very late," Barbara said.

"Yes, and the last hours have been a short course in death."

She asked no more questions, and he made up his mind to put her name to Security for clearance. It was routine, but in standing orders when it came to possible wives.

"When do I meet the mighty Railton clan?" she asked.

"When I've told my father about us."

As she leaned over him, he noticed that her hair, like her breasts, stayed in perfect order—the smooth, neatly cut black cap of hair which made her look vaguely like a page boy in some painting he had once admired. There was a boyish look about the way she walked also, though nothing boyish in the breasts, which remained the same whichever way she turned. They did not even seem to flatten when she was on her back, as some girls' did.

Suddenly the name—*Ranuccio Farnese*—returned to his mind, and he knew where it came from. When he was still very young, his mother had spent hours showing him colored reproductions of the works of great classic artists. She had even taken him to galleries as a boy, for two of her great interests were music and art. Ranuccio Farnese was the name of a 16th-century boy, painted by Titian. The name, and the painting, had stayed, locked in perfect memory through all the years. The black cap of hair in the painting was identical to Barbara's hair, re-created by God and a *coiffeur*.

Naldo told her of his childhood and how his mother and father had a strange, almost telepathic sympathy regarding music. "Father swears he heard my mother playing the piano when he was in prison—in Germany. She also claims to have felt him standing behind her when she played. Everyone else gave him up for dead, but Ma knew he was alive. Apparently they swapped times, dates, and pieces of music. They matched up. They still have experiences." Naldo said he could remember the day, as a small child, when his mother had played happy music and said, "Daddy's coming home."—"And, sure enough, he did. A few days later."

"I think *we* could be like that," she said. "I knew the moment I saw you that I would fall in love with you."

He reached out, holding her close. They stayed like that, in bed, for most of the day.

At five o'clock the telephone rang and Naldo went, naked, to answer it.

He recognized Arnold Farthing's voice immediately.

"I only had to wait an hour for the call to be put through. I had to speak with you. I've been posted back to Europe and I don't know why. They mentioned your name."

Naldo asked when he was coming.

"Hope to be there by the end of the week."

"Good. You can be my best man. I'm getting married. Nobody else knows yet."

"Does the bride know?"

"I think she's got the idea. I suspect we're having the honeymoon now."

9

▼

CASPAR SPOKE WITH controlled passion to the Board of Enquiry. "During the whole of the war I felt like one tiny piece of several living jigsaw puzzles that had been scattered across the floor of Europe. Some burned near me; some exploded; some I could see and touch; others I could not relate to at all."

Naldo read the latest transcript in the nauseating pink room at the little safe house at Northolt.

If Caspar had the power to evoke pictures in the mind to the Board, this particular feat was even more apparent when read from the transcribed pages. He told of the thousands of jobs he had done, and the hundreds of decisions he had been forced to make during the war, as he traveled between Secret Intelligence HQ in Broadway Buildings, the SOE HQ in Baker Street, and his own office set well apart from both.

The catalog ran from recruitment and training to meetings with agents—not always in Britain—interrogations, briefings and debriefings, planning conferences, deals, and straightforward nail-biting waiting at Tempsford or one of the other Moon Squadron stations from which agents were flown out to occupied Europe.

He also spoke of days in Cornwall, on the Helford River, dealing with seaborne agents, coming in or going out.

Worse were the individual decisions made like any military commander with the added knowledge that, upon his orders, someone was going to certain death.

"The rest of the war was there, somewhere," Caspar told them, "and I was conscious of it. But, like a soldier in battle who sees only the small arc of his field of action, everything else seemed insignificant compared to the job I was doing at any given time.

"*Tarot* was but one of my responsibilities, so you'll have to give me chapter and verse on any *Tarot*-connected operation; and, in turn, I'll have to be given time to consult the files before I answer. You *cannot* expect me to give you off-the-cuff replies to the kind of question I've just been asked." —The question concerned the sabotage of certain aircraft under test: the Messerschmitt 110s designated G-4 with special forests of radar antennae sprouting from their noses for the successful role they played as night-fighters.

Over three days, Caspar had regaled them with an almost Arabian Nights' tale concerning the setting up of *Tarot*. Now, the inquisitors of the Board had begun to question him concerning the network's individual operations. What they actually said was that they wished to "consult you regarding certain actions." But, when it came down to it, Caspar was being interrogated, and he fought back like some snappy old general.

Before they began this so-called consultation, another witness was called—a former FANY cipher clerk who had served at No. 53A Signals Station and, while there, was responsible for the major decrypts to and from *Tarot*. C had written in the margin, *C. Railton did not appear surprised that the FANY was a relation*. The transcript did not give her name, but Naldo knew it was Elspeth—only known living daughter of Richard and Sara from Redhill.

She recited a string of signals *en clair*, including operational instructions they called "Action Demanded"—mainly sabotage orders of some priority. These last concerned the derailment of specified trains, the sabotaging of military convoys, or electric pylons, and that oldest of tricks, the insertion of sugar into the gasoline tanks of various Panzer units which passed through the Orléans sector. The messages which had come in regarding ad lib actions ranged from the wounding of Wehrmacht soldiers to the detonation of explosives in key military installations.

Now they had asked Caspar if he knew or suspected, at any point before the Allied invasion of Normandy, that a large number of the Action Demanded orders had *not* in fact been carried out with any success—though *Tarot* claimed in its messages that every single such operation had been pressed home with vigor, producing exceptional results. All of these actions were supposed to have taken place between the winter of 1942 and the late autumn of 1943, when plans for *Overlord,* the Allied invasion of occupied Europe, were well advanced.

"Very well, Colonel Railton, could you tell us if you had any opportunity, between 1942 and the autumn of 1943, of getting *firsthand* evidence of the success, or opposite, of your people in Orléans and St. Benoît-sur-Loire?" one of the Board asked.

"I've already said that I need to consult records myself!" Caspar barked. "Do I have to spell it out to you, gentlemen? And do I have to remind you that the members of *Tarot* were not *my people* as you put it; they only came under my control from time to time."

"At least two were related to you by blood, Colonel Railton."

"That has absolutely nothing to do with it. I ask to be allowed to consult the records."

"Even about your own relations, Colonel? Very well, but we must defer to the chairman."

The chairman was quite willing to give Caspar time to examine the files, yet the whole passage of words troubled Naldo for two reasons. From what he had already read, in C's special file, he knew Caspar would not *need* to look at any records. There was an incident in the summer of 1943 that could never in a thousand years have left his mind. On the other hand, there *were* certain things which Caspar had yet to discover. Things already in the thumbed pages of C's special file.

The chairman of the Enquiry Board on *Tarot* adjourned the sittings for ten days so that Caspar could "Read and revise all necessary documents." He also indicated that in his judgment three more of the witnesses should be heard before any further questions or cross-questions should be put to Caspar Railton. They would be an officer from the Government Communications Headquarters, the "pianist" who had spent some weeks in St. Benoît-sur-Loire, and *Felix*—Jules Fenice himself.

The adjournment gave Naldo an opportunity to catch up on the mounting pile of paper, there in Northolt, for him to study.

For Naldo, life was taking a new shape. A precise pattern was now laid over his waking hours. The evenings and nights were often spent with Barbara, but early each morning he would travel out to the Northolt house where he spent hours reading—the previous day's transcripts from the Enquiry, and C's reassembled file. The documents were brought to him each morning in a little red General Post Office van. The driver wore a GPO uniform, and the same man never knocked twice.

At first, C's File, to which they gave the name *First Folio*, appeared incomprehensible. Some of the documents were from recent days and showed only slight signs of wear and tear. Others reached back to the early days of the war, some even to the late 1930s. Many of these had the ring file holes heavily reinforced with little gummed eyelets; pages were patched together with tape—some already beginning to take on yellow marks at the edges where sun had beaten on their shelves through a Registry window.

They also required a cross reference, yet there was none. Only on certain files had C marked in his neat green ink *See XC*105 or some such clue. Apart from that, Naldo found himself reading reports and dossiers which appeared to have no interconnection. It was a giant puzzle, and C relished it as an academic examiner would gleefully rub his hands on setting a particularly complex trick question.

"Eventually, from the whole of the *First Folio*"—C indicated the preliminary batch of the papers—"you will ascertain where the true nature of my problem lies." The Chief had said this during their second meeting in Northolt, which took place twenty-four hours after the first.

Now Naldo, with only a fraction of the evidence as yet at his disposal, had already uncovered some of the more sinister aspects of what was to be his case—his and Arnold's concerto: for C had given it a crypto. It was to be called *Symphony*—orchestrated by C, performed by Naldo and Arnie, with some solo playing by young Herbie Kruger, the child prodigy.

Naldo's mind became obsessed by the *First Folio,* not even wholly leaving it when he was with Barbara.

One night they went to see Olivier's film of Shakespeare's *Henry V*—Naldo had somehow missed it when it was first released. Afterward, all Barbara could talk of was the visual beauty and Walton's score: the language had failed to move her—"Shakespeare didn't write film scripts," she kept repeating.

All Naldo could recall was the scenes when the king, disguised in a cloak, spied on his soldiers on the night before Agincourt. While watching Olivier skulk in the shadows, exchanging words with those who could not recognize him, Naldo realized that he was now an observer of those who had been his colleagues—a shepherd watching the shepherds.

Later, he made tender love to Barbara. Afterward, he lay silent for a long time, thinking of Caspar and the responsibilities he bore with *Tarot*—particularly the guilt which had to be somewhere in his conscience in sending his nieces, cloaked, to act as agents.

Arnold Farthing arrived a fortnight after the telephone call that had brought Naldo leaping from beside Barbara on their day's lovemaking. There had been little chance to repeat such lengthy pleasure since the second visit to Northolt, though they dined often, went to the cinema or theater, and snatched moments to slake desire when they could.

"I'm on a job," Naldo had told her after Arnie had telephoned. "It's all I can tell you."

"And all I need know." She looked at him, her dark eyes still and deep as a Swiss lake viewed from under the heavy cloud of a brewing storm. "It's understood, darling. I'll ask no questions. That way I'm saved from worry."

It was then they made a decision. They would not break their news to their respective families until Naldo got some kind of a rest from the work in hand—and that might be some time now that Arnold had landed in England.

When he arrived, C asked that Arnold be brought to the Northolt house for what he called an "O Group"—using the tactical field jargon of infantry commanders. This took place on the day before the inquiry reconvened.

When they had gathered, he made a small speech outlining the situation, and briefed Arnie, saying he would have a great deal of reading to do as he must catch up with Naldo.

It was then, with the sudden craftiness of a skilled interrogator, that C turned to Naldo—"What," he asked blandly, "are the main clues in the *Tarot* crossword so far? Not the *answers*, but the *clues*."

Naldo stuttered for a moment, then gathered his thoughts. With some assistance from C they laid out three points.

First, there must have been a traitor within *Tarot* from a very early stage. This person's treachery had to be complex and double-edged—They decided to call the unidentified agent *Troy*—for not only had *Troy* betrayed certain operations to the Nazis, but also kept *Tarot* safe from the SS and SD wolves.

"You must remember the importance of this point." C stabbed the air with his finger. "Klaubert, the Devil of Orléans, had a mission in life: to rid his fiefdom of any members of the Resistance. You must recall that all units of the Maquis, in the Orléans area, together with anyone suspected of having dealings with the Resistance *réseaux*, were rolled up by Klaubert in short order. *But* Tarot *was allowed to coexist with the Nazis*. Given the man's record, this could only have been done by arrangement. *Tarot* stayed operational until five weeks after the Allied invasion of Normandy in June 1944."

Secondly, as Naldo had seen from the files, one of the reasons that Caspar was now under such pressure was the lack of information regarding the fate of *Maxine* and *Dédé*—Caroline Railton and Jo-Jo Grenot. All other members were accounted for—shot, either in Klaubert's headquarters or nearby. But the girls were a different matter. Certainly it was clear they had been arrested in St. Benoît-sur-Loire, and there were vague hints that they were last seen being driven, by two Gestapo officers, to the railway station. One report on file suggested their final destination had been Ravensbrück concentration camp—which was synonymous with death. But what few records remained in Allied Intelligence hands showed no firm information about what had happened to them.

"Obviously"—C gave each of them a darting look—"the prime candidate for treachery is the fellow Fenice—*Felix* as they called him. But you've yet to read the file on him, Railton."

"Nothing on him yet, no sir."

"I want you to hear his evidence at the Enquiry before you read the personal dossier and some additional credentials. However, there are reasons why we can discount him. I *do not* think he's our man. We'll see." He then started to speak of the third clue to *Tarot,* which needed a solution. It concerned Hans-Dieter Klaubert, the Devil of Orléans himself. "Simply, what happened to him? Where did he go? Is he alive or dead? We need to know exactly, because without Klaubert my own personal thesis on this whole business is shot down in flames." He looked at Naldo Railton, expecting a comment.

"Last seen walking out of the Rue de Bourgogne headquarters, carrying a briefcase." Naldo pointed to the heavy file he had started to read on the previous day. "I haven't got far with that, sir, but it appears he simply vanished—like so many. No signs of his death. Talk that he got out, via *Spinne,* the old SS network. South America?" He gave an uncertain shrug. "But he could be dead."

C sounded almost cross. "I believe Klaubert's also alive. What's more, I think I know where to look. Read on, Railton, and in the meantime the Jules Fenice evidence will be worth probing when he comes in front of the Enquiry—which should start again in a couple of days. They have to hear the GCHQ chap, the 'pianist,' and the OSS fellow who survived *Romarin.*"

Three clues which, once linked and answered, might provide enough evidence for them to follow C's long *Tarot* trail—his thesis—to the point where final answers had to be sought.

Three questions in need of three answers, before they could

really start work: The traitor? The girls? Klaubert?

C left the men alone, and they set to their study like a pair of students pressed on the brink of their finals.

ON THAT SAME evening, Caspar Railton returned to the house in Eccleston Square that had once belonged to his grandfather, Giles Railton, of whom there were many secrets—some under lock and key at Redhill Manor itself.

Caspar and Phoebe spent money on the place—redecorating and, more recently, dividing off some of the rooms to make a small flat for Caspar's mother, Charlotte.

In her day, Charlotte Railton had been a delicate, porcelainlike beauty, with a sharp, brittle wit. Now, at the age of seventy-one, her once night-black hair had turned white, but she remained slim and straight, while her sharp tongue echoed the quickness of her more youthful gift of repartee.

After an evening drink with Phoebe—during which she had learned not to ask questions, merely to read his face and manner —Caspar tried to spend half an hour or so with his mother.

This night he had hardly seated himself in her room overlooking the square below when she began: "This is a fine piece of betrayal, I must say. I've told him he should have flatly refused to appear. He's not *forced* to, is he? I mean it doesn't come directly under Admiralty Instructions and King's Regulations, does it?"

Caspar smiled, used to his mother's fast launching into a topic without first telling him the details. "What're we talking about?"

"Your own son." She almost barked. "*My* first grandson."

"Alex? What's he done now?" Alexander had followed a slightly different family tradition. Having proved to be a natural for signals, cryptography, and cryptanalysis, he worked for the Government Communications Headquarters, formerly the Government Code and Cipher School.

"What's he done?" Charlotte snapped. "Alex's done nothing as yet. But tomorrow he's going to give evidence at this damned Enquiry that seems to be set on nailing your hide, Caspar. Your own son!" She made a sound like a cross between spitting and swearing.

Caspar shook his head, smiling. "I don't think anyone's trying to nail my hide, as you put it, Ma."

"Hu!" She poured herself a stiff gin and went very easy on the tonic.

"Towards the end of the war, prior to D-Day and after, Alex was attached to a special department—monitoring the Nazi occupation forces. Whatever he has to say will be relevant." In British families connected with the secret world there is always what that trade calls interconsciousness. Wives—and husbands, where applicable—mothers, fathers, and sometimes children are made aware of the kind of job the officer does for his living, though never the details. So it was not out of the ordinary for Charlotte to speak to her son in this fashion. She had known when she married her young naval officer husband that part of his family dealt in the secret trade.

"You mean Alex *has* to give evidence against his father? He's *forced* to do it?"

Caspar smiled. "Ma, he's not going to blacken *my* reputation. It's not like that. I doubt if Alex has anything really new to tell us."

He did not know, then, that his nephew Naldo was at that moment reading Alexander's evidence. Nor did he know how dramatic the bare facts truly were.

Tomorrow he would hear for himself. Just as he would learn what the "pianist" had to say, though he had a fair idea. Caspar had spent the ten days of grace equipping himself for a kind of ordeal.

10

▼

ALEXANDER PERCIVAL RAILTON barely glanced at his father as he gave evidence in a polite, matter-of-fact manner. Reading it— and there was much more in the file than the bare essentials given to the Board of Enquiry—Naldo and Arnie both thought of coroner's courts they had attended. Alex's words read like the cold, scientific comment an autopsy surgeon would read out—bleak facts with no hint of the suffering contained within the words.

Early in 1944 Alex had been moved from Bletchley Park, home of GCHQ during the conflict, to an old house on the perimeter of the village of Arkley, near the London suburb of Barnet. This was the headquarters of the Radio Security Service, known as Box 25, Barnet.

The Radio Security Service was staffed by what were known as VIs—Voluntary Interceptors—who, sometimes working from their own homes, often without any special equipment and always in great secrecy, were initially responsible for detecting enemy traffic *from* Britain. After the Nazi occupation of Europe, however, they found to their surprise that they were able to intercept an almost incredible amount of enemy signals traffic. Their role changed, and RSS reached out, plucking Wehrmacht and Abwehr secret signals and orders from the dark invisible core of the new Nazi Empire.

By 1944 the RSS had become an enviable professional organization, with its VIs logging up to three hundred intercepts a day, all of which were sent to Barnet, where they were identified, sorted, and deciphered.

Alexander's job at Box 25 was, with others like him, to assist with the decrypting and analysis of German radio traffic prior to the D-Day landings. While doing this, the GCHQ experts gave full cooperation to those running *Operation Fortitude,* the huge deception plan devised to misdirect the German High Command into thinking the inevitable invasion would take place in the Pas de Calais area. Many devices were used, from "ghost" armies—which existed only on radio—to elaborate cloak-and-dagger disinformation operations.

"I was to deal with what we called 'new' or 'difficult' Wehrmacht signals," Alex told the Board. And more mischief besides, Naldo thought, reading it later.

"I have been given to understand that you require the details of what we called the Orléans Russians." He paused, and the chairman gave a slight nod.

"On February 3, 1944, I received an intercept from a V.HS/120, which was immediately identified as hand cipher. At first I thought it was one of SOE's people transmitting. The groups were not of the type used by German signals, though they were familiar to any of us who had heard signals from agents in place. I immediately copied the signal and asked for more details. The transmission went on for some two minutes. Later I attempted to decipher, using all known methods, but nothing made any sense. It was sent on to Bletchley Park for further investigation."

A few days later Alex received a similar intercept from the same source. "Again it made no sense, so we asked the direction-finding boys to pinpoint the signals and their strength. I then received permission to sweep the area myself."

"Would you give us the findings of the DF station," the chairman interrupted apologetically.

"It was the Orléans Sector." Alex all but threw away the information, anxious to continue what he considered a riveting story. He had quickly picked up two more signals. "Even on the second hearing I could recognize the sender's handwriting," he said, not in a boastful manner, but firmly—a man giving expert evidence. The decrypt made no sense, so he set to work trying all possible combinations.

Through February, March, April, and May, Alexander Railton listened to the signals on a regular basis. "The pattern soon became plain. He transmitted at one A.M. British Time, on every third day." Alex immediately reported the signals to both Baker Street and Broadway Buildings.

"I thought SOE or SIS might be able to snatch and identify him."

The chairman interrupted by saying they had copies of reports from two signal stations which confirmed the intercepts. They had heard them and reported they did not come from any known agent.

Alex continued. "On April 16, while sweeping the Orléans Sector, I picked up a receiving station. It was very faint, and, of course, we had no idea of the position—but the direction-finding stations judged it was far to the east. A long way off. There was no doubt that this station was responding to the operator whom we later called the Orléans Russian."

Alex was still working on a possible decrypt and got his break-through shortly after this faint trace of a mother station. The pattern of groups was identified by an officer of Signals Station 52A at Bicester who maintained they were those of an SOE radio operator coded *Descartes*. "We gave her the frequencies and got her to listen out. She heard one signal and was positive that it was *not Descartes'* fist. Not his handwriting. Someone had cleaned out *Descartes* and was using the cipher he had learned. We knew that from the pattern of groups, though they still made no sense when decrypted."

Three nights later, while receiving yet another signal, a senior colleague suddenly identified the mother station as Russian. "I should have known," Alex said with grave self-criticism. "It was a case of not seeing the obvious because I did not expect it. The mother station was clumsy, and kept inserting the letter R. That was an old, outdated, insecure spacing technique. We then went back to previous signals, decrypting with the *Descartes* cipher, and it all became very obvious. I felt foolish. Very foolish."

The outcome was that the distant operator and his mother station had translated his cipher from the original *Roman* alphabet into a revised form of *Cyrillic* alphabet. The resultant form produced a kind of bastard Russian if you used a straight decrypt from *Descartes'* original code.

"I believe you've been furnished with decrypts in English covering all the signals," Alex said.

The chairman nodded and asked if there were any questions from either the Board or Caspar.

To Naldo and Arnie, reading the heaps of paper in Northolt, the decrypts made little sense. The sender, originating some-where in the Orléans Sector, was known to his mother station as *Nikolai;* the mother station was *Sentinel*. As for the rest, they were the kind of thing that the British Broadcasting Corporation's Overseas Service had sent out every night during the four years of Occupation—messages that made sense if the receiver was already briefed regarding their meaning.

Some were repeated every couple of weeks or so: *The night will be dark next month* and *Tomorrow the dead will rise up* appeared to be the favorites.

"The thing of interest is that someone in the Orléans Sector was sending signals on a regular basis to a *Russian* controller, using the cipher learned by an SOE 'pianist' known as *Descartes*," C said later.

Naldo wondered if this was in reality the person they had coded *Troy*—the traitor within *Tarot*.

As for *Descartes*, they were to hear about him from the next subject brought in to give evidence—the SOE "pianist" who had worked for a short period within *Tarot*.

The real name of the "pianist" was Frederick Drake. He was a homosexual, but to his superiors this in no way counted against him—as, at that time, it did to so many of his sexual preference, particularly in military circles.

On Drake's first tour of duty he had been arrested with two other agents soon after landing in Vichy France. The Vichy police had put them in prison for three months.

After his release, Drake did two further tours, proving great courage and wit. On his final tour he became a senior SS officer's lover and then entrapped him with blackmail, sending back vital information regarding supplies and troop movements. His brush with *Tarot* had taken place during his second tour.

The thing everybody—both the Board and the unseen readers in Northolt—noticed about Drake was that he volunteered no information. It was as though the first experience in the field had proved a salutary lesson. He waited for the questions and then answered them in direct, simple terms.

"You were parachuted into occupied France on the night of November 7th/8th, 1943?"

"No." Direct; his English mellow with a no-messing-about undertone.

"That is on record." The chairman fiddled with his papers, flustered.

Drake gave a tired smile. "The record states I was landed in France on that night. I refused to parachute anywhere; it was much too dangerous."

To give him credit, even the chairman laughed before rephrasing the question. "You were *landed* in France on the night of 7th/8th November 1943. By what means?"

"I was taken in by a Lysander aircraft."

"Whereabouts did you land?"

"In a field." He paused, waiting for the chairman to indicate that he should give more details. The donnish man nodded and Drake went on: "In a field about twenty kilometers from Orléans."

"What was your field name?"

"Denis."

"And your orders were . . . ?"

"To link up with another radio operator on a bridge to the north of Orléans—near Meung."

"What was the field name of the other radio operator?"

Drake answered flatly. *"Descartes,"* he said.

There was silence for half a minute, then the SIS officer, who had not yet asked anything, coughed and opened his mouth, but the pompous legal man—the one with the striped suit and gold watchchain dangling in a double loop—got in first. "Wasn't that all rather insecure? Two radio operators meeting on a bridge?" the lawyer asked.

"It was see and be seen." Drake did not look at him. "He would have a girl with him. I was to make certain he was there. He had to be sure I was there. Both our first signals would confirm the other was in place."

"And you saw *Descartes?*"—the SOE man.

"Yes."

"What then?" Once more the pushy lawyer.

"I was to walk across the bridge—east to west. A girl would come towards me."

"You'd recognize her?"

"Yes."

"How?"

"Body signals. I would smile and embrace her."

"And all this happened? You made contact?"

"Like a bus hitting a pedestrian."

Finally the SIS man spoke. "In your own words will you tell us what occurred after contact? Give us everything: who you were supposed to be working for, what took place." He spoke as though, already knowing the evidence they were to hear, he wanted to get to some salient point.

Drake spoke quietly, using economical language. The girl had taken him to a safe house in the Rue Bannier. "I was supposed to be working for *Felix.* His *réseau* was known as *Tarot.* The girl said I could transmit my arrival message on 'sked,' but they probably wouldn't need me in the area. She said they already had a 'pianist,' and the place was getting crowded. I was furious—and a little frightened. It didn't smell right."

He asked to see *Felix* and she said she did not think that would be possible, so he insisted. "I said I would alert London and say I thought *Tarot* had been blown. I had my hand in my pocket, clutching the Welrod. I'd have shot her if she'd tried anything." The Welrod was a cheap, makeshift, near-silent pistol made for around $1.50 by the Americans especially for the OSS and SOE.

The girl said she would see what could be done, and Drake watched her leave. "I was distinctly anxious. To be honest I thought it might be a trap, so I waited for an hour watching from the window. There was a café across the street. It appeared to be used only by locals so in the end I left the wireless in the safe house and went to the café. I drank a glass of red—very slowly, sitting near the window so I could see the door to the safe house."

After another hour the girl came back with a man who Drake thought looked all right. "I was ready to kill if it was a trap, but *Felix* knew all the proper words. He said there had been a terrible cock-up—which wasn't unusual—and London had already been told one operator was enough. They had somebody working out of several houses in Orléans and the villages round about. *Felix* looked like a worried man. We were all worried. The SD and Gestapo had direction finders on the go all the time. A multitude of 'pianists' in one area doubled, trebled, quadrupled the chances of your getting snatched."

In the end they agreed to work Drake, on his normal "skeds" one week in three. "I wasn't happy about it and told London so at the end of the first week. Then, in my second week, *Felix* came to the house alone. He told me that he thought *Tarot* might have been infiltrated but he couldn't prove it. I asked after *Descartes* and he looked at me as though I was mad—asked me if the girl hadn't told me. I said no, so *he* told me. They had bagged *Descartes* on the first day."

"Did you report all this to London?" the SOE man asked.

"Of course. That night. I told them *Tarot* did not need me, that *Descartes* was in the bag, and that I was suspicious. I thought *Tarot* might have been infiltrated."

"They replied?"

"Moved me on. Sent me to Paris where I had a high old time for two months, rushing about the place, sending signals, and being pushed from pillar to post."

"And you heard no more about *Tarot?*"

"Not a peep. The Paris people seemed to think they were okay."

"Mr. Drake." The SOE man stood up. He held two photographs in his hand. "Do you recognize either of these girls?" He put the prints on the table in front of him. Drake looked closely and nodded, pointing. "That was the girl who looked after me. The other one was with *Descartes*."

The SOE officer handed each of the prints to Caspar. In the transcript it said, *The girl identified as Drake's contact was Jo-Jo*

*Grenot, known as Dédé. The other was Caroline Railton Far-
thing, known as Maxine. Both girls worked for réseau Tarot.*

Caspar's face gave nothing away. He got to his feet and asked
if he could cross-question Drake. The chairman nodded. When
Naldo and Arnie read the notes in the transcript they both realized
that it appeared as though *Maxine* and *Dédé* were, to use Arnie's
words, "working both sides of the street."

"You sent a signal to London, which said *Tarot* had no need of
you; that *Descartes* had been arrested, and that you were concerned the *réseau* was infiltrated?"

"I did."

"On your dating, that would be the signal sent at nine P.M. on
the night of November 22."

"I can't tell you the exact date but it would be a day or so
around then."

"That is the only date, around that time, that we have a record
of a signal from you. Can you recall the transmission—what did
it say?"

"As I remember it, the code for *Tarot* was *Bruno. Descartes*
was *PH*—for 'Philosopher' I suppose. 'Arrested' was rendered as
'invisible.' 'Suspect infiltration' was 'possibly has a fever.' It
would read something like PH INVISIBLE STOP BRUNO HAS NO
WORK FOR ME AND IS POSSIBLY FEVERISH STOP REQUEST MEDICAL
AID. 'Medical Aid' was the sign that it would be prudent to get
out quickly. I'd be asking for a new assignment."

Caspar picked up one of the papers spread across the table at
which he sat. "I've read all your signals for that period," he said
calmly. "I've also spoken to your case officer and seen his file.
The message you sent reads as follows: PH INVISIBLE STOP BRUNO
UNWELL STOP REQUEST MEDICAL AID. It starts with your normal
log-on sign and finishes with your security check."

Drake just looked at him.

"Do you agree that is the signal?"

"It could well be. It means the same."

"No." Caspar was firm. "That signal does *not* mean you are
concerned about *Tarot*. It is on record from your briefing that
UNWELL means UNSAFE TO TRANSMIT. So what you were saying
was, in fact, DESCARTES ARRESTED STOP WORKING FOR TAROT IS
UNSAFE STOP PLEASE MOVE ME ON. That is exactly how it was
decrypted. You made a slight technical error, I fear. You did not
say what you meant, and we had no hint of a warning from you
that you suspected *Tarot*. Merely that it was unsafe for you to
continue sending for them."

It was recorded that Drake shook his head and frowned. "If that's what I sent, then I did make an error. The signal was meant as a warning."

"It wasn't received as one," Caspar said. "It was acknowledged immediately and you were told to await instructions on the following night. The message sent to you, and presumably received, merely told you to move to Paris and gave you a contact time, place, and fallback. Correct?"

Drake nodded. Caspar sat down.

The SIS man shifted. "Had you any inkling as to who the regular 'pianist' for *Tarot* was?"

"I was given no hint, though I gathered it was one of them—by that I mean not a regular SOE 'pianist' sent in specially."

"Thank you, Mr. Drake."

The Board decided to break for lunch.

In Northolt it was the end of the transcripts delivered that morning. Naldo and Arnie continued reading some of the other files and discussing all the permutations so far. At five o'clock Naldo prepared to leave. He was in the hall when the doorbell rang in its clear sequence.

C had come with the transcripts from the previous afternoon's hearings. "I would like you to go through these tonight," he said crisply. "You'll need them before you get today's work—*Felix*'s evidence. It's been hard going but you're required to read this first."

Naldo had permission to use the telephone, and he alerted Barbara that their date for that evening was off.

C stayed as they opened up the transcript. It was the evidence of Tertius Newton, the OSS man who had survived operation *Romarin*—the plan to snatch Klaubert, the Devil of Orléans, with the help of *Tarot*.

They had flown Newton into London from the United States, especially for a detailed interrogation, and his appearance before the Board. His story took them all back to France four weeks after the Normandy landings, but it started in England.

11

▼

To use his own words, Tert Newton was "Fed up and far from home." Newton was in uniform, as he had been for the past month—battle dress, rubber-soled parachute boots, a camouflage jump-jacket. He was also armed to the teeth: an M-1 Winchester carbine, grenades, a large amount of ammunition, and a Colt .45 automatic, which hung from his webbing belt, the holster slung low, almost to his thigh, like a cowboy gunslinger. It was a new role for the OSS officer who had spent his war, until the last few months, skulking around in civilian clothes and helping to run a pair of SI agents in Greece and Portugal, where he had, inevitably, fallen over—or at least stepped on—the toes of the British Secret Intelligence Service. It appeared to be an occupational hazard of the OSS.

The reason behind his current depression lay in the fact that the bulk of his old friends in the Office of Strategic Services were already out there, in France and other occupied countries—many going via Algiers—assisting the various resistance movements and fighting the Germans from secret vantage points.

Newton and his team had all been told that they would be dropped, after D-Day, to back up the French Resistance fighters —viz., the one Frenchman who had also joined them: Antoine, known as Tony. Nobody bothered with the Frenchman's surname. But here he was, Tert Newton—trained, fit, and raring to go— with a fifteen-man OSS unit, stuck out in the wilds of Bedfordshire, England, at a place called Gibraltar Farm, on D-plus 28. Waiting.

It was hard to bear the fact that the team had a new commander—an English major by the name of Laurence Cartwright. They also had a new name—*Romarin*. What kind of name was that for a bunch of hard-bitten OSS thugs? French for the herb rosemary. Jesus, Tert Newton had known a girl back in San Jose,

California, called Rosemary who had legs like Betty Grable and tits bigger than Jane Russell's incredible knockers.

"We sat around that place for a whole month," Newton told the interrogators. "Nobody seemed in the least bit interested in us."

Of course he was quite wrong. On the morning of July 4, 1944, while the bitter fighting still continued in Normandy, Major Laurence Cartwright was called to the Intelligence Rooms in one of the rusty-looking old Nissen huts. The IO smiled at him and said, "Charlie says *Romarin* is 'go' tonight." Charlie was the OSS Signals Intelligence station at Poundon, Oxfordshire.

Cartwright, a short, breezy SAS officer, gave a sigh of relief. He was all too aware that the OSS team under his command was getting twitchy. Cartwright was more than a little twitchy himself. For the past four weeks he had been forced to keep the operational secret of *Romarin* inside his head. Now he could share it with the others an hour or so before they were due to leave.

Even the aircrew who would carry them in the big four-engined Liberator would not know about the mission. They would be briefed on the DZ and the ground signals that would mark it—probably grumbling because the French reception committee did not have the radio identity device, *Eureka*, from which they could pinpoint a truly accurate drop. Apart from that, they would not know any details.

When it came to the briefing, in a bare hut guarded by armed RAF Regiment men, Cartwright broke the news. They would not be going in anywhere near the fighting around Normandy, but far inland—and they would not be staying long.

The DZ was fifteen kilometers from the city of Orléans—there were details of how to make contact and form up once they had landed, together with maps and photographs of the entire area. A local Resistance circuit, *Tarot,* would be there to meet them with a truck and a stolen German staff car. Cartwright and an American called Dollhiem would be wearing German uniforms—Dollhiem and the Englishman both spoke good German.

The team was to be deployed in the truck. Cartwright and Dollhiem would drive in the staff car, and the Resistance people from *Tarot* were all set to cover them.

Plans of Orléans were produced, with a large-scale drawing of the area around Gestapo headquarters on the Rue de Bourgogne. They were also provided with a detailed drawing of the layout inside the headquarters.

"It was like something out of a movie," Newton was to say later. "They had this crazy plan to snatch the SS Chief—Klaubert—from his headquarters. We were to do it, if possible, without any fighting. The Englishman had a hypo full of some drug that would quieten him down, and he carried papers which requested him to go with them. Real cloak-and-dagger stuff with disguises and forged documents. It was unreal and scary."

Once this kidnap had taken place, Cartwright and Dollhiem would drive Klaubert back to the same field that had been their DZ. A Hudson aircraft from 161 Squadron would be waiting, and Klaubert was to be flown back to England.

The *Romarin* team was to be kept hidden for one day by the *Tarot* people. Joe—"Big Joe"—Farthing would assume command, and in the early hours of the following morning they were to split into groups of five, making their way across country to three different pickup points, where the Royal Air Force, which had a lot of experience in these matters, would collect them.

"I remember thinking," said Tert to a docile inquisitor, "if it all goes like clockwork, which was impossible, where would we be at the end of the day? Back at Gibraltar Friggin' Farm." The inquisitor allowed himself a smile.

They took off shortly after nine-thirty. It was still daylight and the lucky men who were near one of the few windows in the Liberator could see people working in the lazy English fields below them. Then cloud and darkness closed in.

Nobody could smoke, so Newton spent much of the time dismantling and reassembling his Colt, in the dark—"Just for practice."

It was almost one in the morning when the pilot signaled *DZ coming up*. They turned in a lazy circle with the engines throttled back for a glide across the DZ. Pilot, copilot, and navigator were all up front, craning into the blackness at around four hundred feet, trying to spot the diamond of flashlights that would indicate the dropping zone. It was bumpy and the machine pitched and yawed in the darkness. Behind them their passengers felt uncomfortable, rocking hard against each other. One man was sick. It was like a frightening fairground ride. The navigator saw the lights first, and the copilot yelled out the compass heading so that they could climb away and complete a circuit, to come in again across the DZ at seven hundred feet. The navigator had the stopwatch going as they performed the 90 degree turns. The markers came up right on the button. The height was good, and the pilot flicked the jump switch. At the debriefing the RAF dispatcher said the whole stick of seventeen men—the fifteen OSS, one British officer, and the French liaison man—were out in twenty-five seconds. He was suddenly alone in the aircraft's long belly with only the shrieking wind funneled in through the open hatch and the whipping canvas parachute static lines—hooked to the cable which ran the length of the fuselage—flapping and banging against the outside like shrapnel.

In training, Newton had never felt fear during a parachute drop; for him it had always been exhilarating—like leaping from some great high diving board into invisible water. That night, as he dropped into the darkness, feeling the familiar rush of air followed quickly by the crack of the parachute opening and the sudden wrench on the harness as he slowed down, Newton suddenly knew fear. It was as though he had waited for it all his life—or it had waited for him. The instinct, then the vivid picture of death in his mind.

He pulled sharply on the right-hand guideline to correct a slight oscillation, then, stabilized, peered into the blackness, knees up and body relaxed. There would only be a couple of seconds from seeing the ground to landing on it. Newton was concentrating so hard on the landing that he genuinely failed to understand what was happening around him. Just before hitting the ground everything fused, making contact between his mind and the events. He could hear the ripsaw noise of the Schmeisser machine pistols—below, right, left, and behind him. There were cracks of noise all around, and, seconds before he hit the ground, bullets came cutting into his canopy, tearing it to shreds. He rolled and pulled at the harness release, knowing that what was left of the canopy had fallen behind him. He was free, his carbine tucked into his shoulder, and his body trying to dig itself into the ground as burst after burst of fire came down around him.

Somebody to his right let out a ghastly scream, and there was an explosion behind him, as though a grenade had gone off. Something told him not to return fire—to use his carbine would reveal his position. Lie still.

The automatic fire went on for a long time, and his eyes slowly adjusted to the darkness. He seemed to be in a ditch, or gully, on what he figured was the western side of the field that formed the DZ. He pictured the map in his mind, and knew that there was a small wood at the north end of the field, too far away to be of comfort. The map's details had shown this ditch also. It was a deep dividing line between fields, and there was a track of sorts winding along the far side: also a sprinkling of deciduous trees. He felt around him. The ditch was full of bracken, fern, and undergrowth.

After a while the shooting died down. Newton did not have to put his thoughts into any cohesive form. The whole thing was there, a lump of fearsome knowledge within him—*Romarin* had been sold out. Instead of *réseau Tarot*, the reception committee had been the local heavies—Wehrmacht, SS, or Abwehr. It did not particularly matter which.

The air smelled of fresh grass, and, he thought, night-scented herbs and flowers, all mixed up with drifting smoke. Cordite.

He caught movement, low, on the side of the ditch, just behind him, so he gently turned, bringing the carbine to bear on the crouching figure that showed as a slightly darker mass against the night.

A voice whispered, "Natives."

Without thinking, Newton gave the password response, whispering, "Guard."

The figure dropped flat, rolled into the ditch, and crawled up to him. "Thank God. Who is it?"

"Newton. Tert Newton."

"Joe," whispered the figure. "Joe Farthing."

"You okay, Big Joe?"

"Guess so. Guess we're the only ones, though. Looked like most of the guys got hit in the air."

A single shot cracked in the night, somewhere to their right on the far side of the big field. Joe Farthing motioned Newton to stay down as he peered over the edge of the ditch.

"Shit," he muttered. "They've got flashlights. A whole line of them. Combing the field." He paused, and then peered out again. "The map showed cover up front—a small wood." His low voice was barely audible. "We should make for that cover, Tert. You want to try?"

Newton shook his head. He really just wanted to be left alone in the ditch, where he felt safe.

"You want to go? I'll cover you, then you can cover me."

"I'll cover you, Joe. But I'm staying where I am."

There was a pause as Farthing made up his mind. The silence went on for a long time. Farthing poked his head up again, then leaned back. "They're way over on the far side. I'm going. If you change your mind I'll be in that wood somewhere. Hide up until daybreak, then make for the road."

"I'll cover you, Joe," Newton whispered, levering himself up onto the parapet of the ditch. "You ready?"

Joe Farthing nodded.

"Okay. Go!"

Farthing rolled quietly over the side of the ditch and into the dew-soaked grass. For a couple of minutes he snake-crawled slowly to the left, then rose and began to move fast, in a low crouch.

Newton figured he had gone about twenty yards when a pair of flashlights with beams like long bright cones reached out—for a second they reminded him of the searchlights on the 20th Century–Fox credits. There was a shout in German. Then another, and the cones met, clamped on to Farthing's figure so that it looked like some strange humped animal, and the Schmeissers rattled.

Though he did not appear to falter, Farthing's whole body, still running, hit the ground. It looked as though pieces were flying from him as a burst of tracer curved from the shadows behind the flashlights—arcing over Joseph Burns Farthing's body.

Tert Newton slid down to the bottom of the ditch again. It took him a couple of minutes to realize that a stray bullet had caught him in the fleshy part of his right shoulder. Only now, at the bottom of the ditch, among bracken and fern, did he feel the pain. Groping with his left hand he touched his jacket. It was wet and sticky.

Newton's shoulder throbbed and he knew he had lost a lot of blood. He managed to get a field dressing out of his jump-jacket pocket and wedge it in place, pushing it up inside the jacket, over the wound. Then he pulled bracken over himself, put his face on his good arm, and lay still. "I guess I must have passed out," he told the interrogators—and the Board. "Next thing I heard was a shot, quite near to me."

It was day, quite late, he thought, because the sun was high and warm. He moved cautiously and found the blood was dry and caked through his jacket. The shoulder and arm were difficult to move. He hoped there was no infection. Then, remembering the shot, he slowly climbed up the side of the ditch. German soldiers were wandering about the field, some grouped around what he took to be a pile of equipment until, with a sense of nausea, he realized the pile was not just equipment but the bodies of his comrades. *Romarin* had become a mound of useless flesh in the middle of a French field.

Two soldiers came from the small wood for which Joe had been making. An officer followed them, tucking a pistol back into its holster. The men were dragging something, and gradually

it became visible as a body. So when they found him they would
shoot him. Now he knew.

But the soldiers appeared to have completed their search, for a
pair of trucks had been driven into the field—big Krupp six-
wheelers. There were three officers—one a tall man in SS uniform. They were giving orders and the soldiers loaded the pile of
shattered bodies into one truck, the equipment into the other.
Newton thought they treated the corpses of his friends like animals.

When they finished loading, the officers got into the front of
the trucks with the drivers while the enlisted men climbed in the
back of the truck with the equipment. He heard the trucks driving
away as he slid down into the ditch.

"I tried to figure out what I should do," he told the Board. "I
ate some of my K-rations and realized I was weak. When the
whispering began I thought I was hallucinating."

But the whispering was real. It was also in French and Newton whispered back, saying he did not speak the language. "I
could see these two guys on the other side of the ditch—away
from the field. One had a bicycle, the other was a priest."

The priest asked if he was American, and he told them. Then
the other man said, "Natives."

Newton automatically answered, "Guard," the operations
password.

The priest whispered that if it was safe they would come for
him after dark. The other Frenchman said they had saved one of
his companions.

"I hoped it would be Big Joe," Newton said later. "And even
though I knew it was impossible I still kept hoping."

The hours dragged by. Dusk came, and then the night. Newton thought he had dreamed the whole episode with the priest and
the Frenchman. The moon came up, then there were footsteps,
along the far side of the ditch. Footsteps and a rumbling noise.
Four men had come with a handcart—breaking the curfew regulations.

They took him to a house nearby, and a doctor was waiting.
The wound was tended, cleaned, and bandaged. The doctor told
him to rest, and Tert Newton asked where the other American had
got to. "You'll see him tomorrow," they said, then put him to
bed.

The next morning the Frenchman he had first seen with the
priest arrived with a dilapidated van that smelled of pigs. They

wrapped Newton up in blankets and hid him among straw and pig shit in the back of the van and drove him away.

The next stop was a pig farm—he knew by the all-pervading smell of pigs outside and the more pleasant aroma of ham being smoked in the kitchen. He was helped up a narrow flight of stairs to a small room. "They managed to squeeze two beds into the room. Dollhiem was in the other bed, unconscious. He looked very bad to me, but by the next day he was sitting up and talking."

Dollhiem had taken a bullet in the side as he parachuted in, but he was off course and landed in the little wooded area. By a near miracle he had time, and enough energy, to successfully bury his parachute and hole up on the far side of the wood, quite near the road. The Germans did not get to him during the night and he could not explain why, because someone else was groaning in agony nearby. In the night he heard the wounded man cry out and knew it was Cartwright.

On the next day, though he lost consciousness several times, Dollhiem managed to crawl across the road, undetected. He heard the shot from the woods and presumed they had put Cartwright out of his misery. He was very lucky because the Germans did not search any of the area across the road. The priest and the other Frenchman had come looking, though, and they risked a great deal by getting the badly wounded Dollhiem out in daylight. Newton figured it must have been shortly before they found him.

The Frenchman said they were part of the *Tarot réseau* and his name was *Felix*. Newton identified Jules Fenice from a photograph, and described the other members of the network—including *Maxine* and *Dédé*. In all, he accounted for the entire known membership of *Tarot*, which was interesting in the light of further information.

In a couple of days Newton was up and walking—quite fit again. *Felix* told them there was still heavy fighting in France, Belgium, and the Low Countries and Newton felt they should try to rejoin "The Outfit."

Dollhiem—who had also recovered quickly—was now very friendly with all the *Tarot* members, but Newton held back. "I asked some questions about how the massacre of *Romarin* had happened," he told both the initial interrogators and the Board. "They simply said it was one of those things. They had gone out to the DZ, ready to meet us, but were alerted that the SS and Wehrmacht had got there first. The girl they called *Maxine* ap-

parently bicycled back to the farm in an attempt to warn SOE and
OSS. But nobody acknowledged her signal."

(Note on the file: there was no incoming signal from Tarot *on
the night of July 4/5th, 1944, in spite of stand-by operators being
instructed to listen out on the usual* Tarot *frequencies.)*

"*Felix* seemed a good enough guy," Newton continued. "But I
wasn't certain about some of the others." In particular he cited a
fat man called *Albert,* identified as a local butcher; two young
men who were spoken of as *St. Christophe* and *le Teneur de
Livres,* the Bookkeeper. He was not completely happy about either *Maxine* or *Dédé,* and another French girl they called *Florence.*

Another note in the file stated that, regarding the women,
Newton's dislike should be regarded with suspicion, as he had
tried to have sex with each one of them. He admitted that to the
interrogators, just as he admitted there were no takers.

In the end he tried to get Dollhiem to join him and leave, but
the German-speaking American preferred to stay and told Newton he could probably be of help to the *réseau.* In any case, he
felt that he was not yet recovered enough. So Newton left in the
middle of the night and headed toward Paris. He told no one that
he was going, not even Dollhiem. On his fourth day a German
patrol arrested him. He gave them his name, rank, number, and
the name of a fictitious unit. "Those guys were jumpy," he said.
"Still and all, so was I. But I guess they were decent enough.
They took me to a temporary military POW stockade where they
did not even process me properly. The guards were old guys, and
when the British finally got into the area, they ran away and we
were liberated."

*(Note on file. Newton was captured three nights after the SS in
Orléans rolled up* Tarot.*)*

Newton, being fit enough, and with no unit, joined up with an
assorted band of British, French, and American troops who had
all somehow lost their original units. It was pretty chaotic in that
area at the time. He ended up with the U.S. Ninth Army early in
1945 and was with them at the Remagen Bridge and through the
rest of the campaign. In the end he rejoined his OSS colleagues
—who knew and approved of what he was doing—in Berlin,
from whence he was evacuated in the summer of 1945. A note
attached to the file stated that by the time Newton rejoined the
OSS he was a copybook case of battle fatigue, but pronounced fit
and well again by January 1946. The interrogators added the

comment that he appeared to be truthful, and, though questioned by several different teams, did not alter his story once. They were also "very impressed" by his attention to detail and attested that his memory could not be faulted on "matters of record."

Then the *Tarot* Board of Enquiry began to question him.

12

▼

LOOKING BACK ON the whole line of interrogation, Naldo realized that the Board went for Newton like a careful pack of wolves. First they circled him, sniffing with innocent-sounding questions, then, when they saw he had nothing with which to defend himself, they moved in and started to tear the man to pieces.

"Mr. Newton," the chairman began—and you did not have to hear him to know that he spoke softly, with no trace of guile— "Mr. Newton, this Tribunal—er, this Board—first requires to test your, how shall I put it? Your *bona fides*. You understand what I mean?"

"Sure." Innocence drifted from the line.

"You're a trained man, Mr. Newton. A trained covert operator. Am I correct?"

"Of course. Yes."

"Perhaps we should hear a little about your training, and your experiences *before* you joined the team known as *Romarin*."

"Okay." He waited for further questions but there were none. "I was invited into OSS—for training—in April '42—" He stopped again, as though needing help.

"How did that come about?" The chairman was so soft of speech that Newton had to crane forward to hear him.

"Pardon me?"

"How did you come to be interviewed?"

"Well . . . Well, I guess I was asked to see this officer in Washington."

The chairman would frown, Naldo thought, then fiddle with his papers. "We have a few—very few—of your details here . . ." A long, long pause while he seemed to be thinking over the next move. "I'm correct, aren't I? You were inducted into the United States Army in December 1941?"

"Yes. Fort Mead. Did my basic there as well. I couldn't wait to get in. Straight out of UCLA and I couldn't wait. They took me first time off. A-1."

"Yes. You were recommended for a commission?"

"That was after basic, yes. I did the officer-training course. Then they sent me to Fort Bragg to wait for a posting."

"You expected what?"

"To go to some infantry outfit."

"And what happened?" The chairman was patient, calm.

"They said a guy, an officer, wanted to talk with me in Washington."

"What officer was this?"

"Never knew his name. Never knew he was an officer, come to that. Just a guy. In the old Willard Hotel. Talked for about an hour. Then he said would I fancy working in secret; maybe behind enemy lines?"

"And you said yes?"—from the chairman.

"I was young. I'd achieved my dream since Pearl Harbor. I wanted to fight the Japs or the Nazis. It didn't matter which. The guy made it sound glamorous. Intriguing."

"What happened after you agreed?"

"He said I had the right qualities but I'd have to satisfy them regarding other things."

"What kind of things?"

"Well, they sent me off to jump school first. I guess they had to be sure I wasn't scared."

"And you *were* scared, Mr. Newton, like all of us."—The SOE officer.

"Oh, sure." He laughed.

"So you did a parachute course. Then what?"

"It seems a long time ago. Lifetime . . ."

"Several lifetimes," the SOE officer murmured.

"Let's see. I suppose I went to the Camp."

"Didn't you do a couple of months somewhere else before Camp X?"

"Yes, you're right. A couple of months near Washington."

"Wasn't it the U.S. Army School of Languages?"

"That's right. Yes, I did. I did a two months' refresher course."

"To brush up your French and German. Your knowledge of those languages was the main reason OSS recruited you in the first place. Am I right?"

"I guess so." Reading his curt answer, both Naldo Railton and Arnie Farthing sensed that Tertius Newton suddenly saw the trap into which he had fallen. He would be waiting, they thought, for the wolves to spring. But they only moved a fraction closer, as though they had not spotted the way in which his defenses had dropped. He must have braced himself for the next question.

"How did you like the Camp, Mr. Newton?" Naldo thought Newton must have breathed a sigh of relief—thinking they had missed his inconsistency.

"It was tough. Very absorbing, but tough."

It certainly was; Arnie had trained there. The picture came back into his mind. Oshawa, in Canada, forty miles from the main Toronto-Kingston freeway, perched on the edge of Lake Ontario: a sprawling old house and a large area of land, fenced and protected—on the south by the lake, on the north by treacherous and dense bush. The east and west perimeters had electrified wire as well as the constantly vigilant guards—British veterans of early raids on Europe. The huge area contained huts, disguised to look like barns, other odd structures, and varied kinds of terrain.

Arnie had been taken from the States—from New York to Roosevelt Beach, east of the Niagara Falls, on the U.S.A. side. Then across the lake into Canada, glimpsing blackened faces from the rubber boat as they stepped ashore. Like other OSS men trained there, Arnie got a medal for overseas service long before he came to Europe, because he trained at Camp X, Oshawa, Canada.

"Who did the silent killing—old Fairbairn?"—The SOE officer. Who else would have asked?

"A character. Yeah, Fairbairn. Taught us a lot of tricks."

"He taught many of us the same tricks when he was at Arisaig." —The SOE again. Arisaig was SOE's and SIS's school in Scotland. The syllabus there and at Oshawa was almost identical, and both SOE and OSS trained at the latter.

"Mr. Newton."—the chairman, whipping things back into line again. "Your comrade in arms, Dollhiem—wasn't he in your batch at the Camp?"

"Nat Dollhiem? Yes. Yes, he was there."

"Were you particular friends? Close at all?"

"I knew Nat. I think we were paired up in some night exercise while we were there. Blowing up a railroad line or something—"

The SIS officer broke in. "We're particularly interested in Dollhiem, Mr. Newton. You see, he's never been accounted for. A couple of days after you left the pig farm—after *Romarin*—

the local SS rolled up *Tarot*. We've accounted for everyone concerned except the two girls you knew as *Dédé* and *Maxine*—and Dollhiem. Mind you, the man called *Felix* has only recently been found, so anything could still happen. But Dollhiem was not pulled in with the others. Nor was he executed."

One of the lawyers spoke. "He flatly refused to leave with you, Mr. Newton? Leave the pig farm where the French took you?"

"It wasn't really like that. We didn't argue or anything. He just said he'd rather not come along. He wanted to stay at the farm."

"But he *was* fit enough to leave?"

"He was okay. He'd lost blood, yes. But it was really only an unpleasant flesh wound—through his side. He was moving about almost normally the day before I left."

"He could have gone with you? You have no doubts about that?"

"None at all. In fact he said he was okay, said he could come. But he chose to stay."

The pressure was being turned very slightly.

"He chose to stay? Did Dollhiem use those words?"

"It seems a long time ago. My memory's not as clear as it should be, but I recall him saying he felt he could be of use to the network. Yes, that's what he said: 'I can be of greater use here. There are ways I can help them.'"

The chairman began again. "Isn't it true that you knew Dollhiem *before* you got to the Camp?"

"I don't—"

"You knew him for the couple of months when you were brushing up your French and German, Mr. Newton. Isn't that so?" For the first time he stressed *French*.

There was a note in the transcript saying that Newton hesitated for some seconds. Then—

"Yes. Yes, I did. You know, I'd forgotten that. Yes, he was at the School of Languages."

"Brushing up his French, German . . . and Russian. Right, Mr. Newton?"

"Yeah. Yeah, he spoke all three. Unlike me." *(Transcript Note: Mr. Newton's mode of speech became less precise.)*

"That *is* a point, Mr. Newton." The most pompous of the lawyers, an interrogator by trade, moved into place. "When you told us the details of *Romarin* you claimed not to speak French."

"I don't," with a nervous laugh.

"But your record shows you were approached in the first instance because you spoke French and German. It also says you came through the courses with high ratings in both languages."

"That was a fix."

"A fix? What kind of a fix?"

"Oh, God, this is embarrassing. My German's good. Still is. But my French is schoolboy stuff. I can read it—translate on sight. But I don't speak French. I have no ability for the accent, and I can't follow it when it's spoken to me—I've some kind of block."

"There's no mention of that in your record."

"No."

"Why?"

"Because I talked to the instructors. Look, I was keen as mustard to get through. I came clean about the French to my instructor at the School of Languages. He passed me on sight translation. If there was any possibility of my having to speak French, they'd have pulled me from the op."

"But they didn't, Mr. Newton. They did *not* pull you from *Romarin,* did they? Did anyone really know? I mean anyone connected with *Romarin?*"

"I guess not."

"And you didn't own up to it?"

"I didn't think French would be required."

"You were jumping into France."

"I know."

"Why go into a French operation without the language, when everybody else must have thought you spoke it?"

"I wanted . . . Oh, hell. I wanted some action."

"You realize you could have caused trouble? Apart from Dollhiem, who was needed to speak German, you were the only other OSS officer down as a French speaker."

"We had Tony with us: Antoine, the French guy."

"Who was killed before he even touched his native soil."

"It all went wrong. You can't hold me responsible for that."

"Maybe not. Then again, maybe you were in part responsible."

"What the hell d'you mean by that?"

"You told us that nobody—*nobody* in the team—knew the extent of *Romarin* until a couple of hours before you left. Is that strictly true?"

"How could we know? Cartwright briefed us that evening. Before we left."

"Dollhiem knew, though, didn't he?"

"I don't know."

"Dollhiem was briefed, with Major Cartwright, a couple of weeks before the operation. He had to be briefed. He and Cartwright were both given a full rundown. They were even fitted with the SS uniforms. They both knew what was to happen long before the team got together at Gibraltar Farm. That's a matter of record, just as it's a matter of record that you and Dollhiem were close friends. Ever since the Language School you were close. Right?"

"Right." Softly. Caught.

"So when did Dollhiem tell you what *Romarin* was really all about?"

Newton's defenses were gone. "The day before."

"At last. The day before. He opened his mouth twenty-four hours before the operation got the green light?"

"Yes."

"He tell anyone else?"

"Not that I know of."

"Well, who did *you* pass it on to, Mr. Newton?"

"Nobody. I didn't breathe a word."

"Maybe. But we've already proved your evidence is tainted—and somebody passed it on. Probably in France, but it *was* passed on. Dollhiem and yourself survived, but they knew in Orléans. They knew you were coming."

Another of the lawyers asked if Dollhiem had access to a telephone. Newton said he couldn't be certain.

And they started going over it again, question by question. Then the same questions once more. Their queries rained down on Newton like cudgel blows.

The transcript went on for thirty pages and ended with the chairman suggesting that Newton should stay in England as they might need to hear more from him.

"Through the wringer," Arnie said, dropping his copy on the pink glass table, from which C scooped it up.

"And it's still going on." C smiled, reaching out for Naldo's copy. "I'm sorry you've been kept so late, but time's running short. You follow the line of my concern, Naldo?"

Naldo nodded.

"There's a little more that you won't learn from the Enquiry." He laid his body back in the easy chair. "Mr. Newton's offered to assist in any way he can. They have him in a quiet safe house with a pair of inquisitors. Just to be sure." He sighed, a weary man. "You see, it's not Newton who worries me. The missing Dollhiem is the true thorn in my side."

"Because he's a Russian speaker?" Naldo asked.

"Partly. That; the Orléans Russians; and one other thing."

They waited. C appeared to be making up his mind. Then—"This is family business, Naldo. You'll have to explain it to Farthing here. Are you aware of the cooperation between the Russian NKVD, our Service, SOE, and Farthing's former service, OSS?"

Naldo looked blank. Arnold shook his head.

"Well." C drew a deep breath. "We took it upon ourselves, rightly or wrongly, to allow the NKVD facilities into Europe—Germany itself—on a few occasions. They sent their men into London and we took them out via Gibraltar Farm." He turned toward Arnie. "Your former chief, General Donovan, was anxious to build on these operations. He wished to establish a permanent OSS mission in Moscow. The Russians, always our uneasy allies, agreed, but only if they could operate a similar NKVD team in Washington. I was against it, I can tell you that."

"I can imagine," Naldo murmured.

"So you can also imagine that many people almost went hairless at the idea." C smiled again.

"The plan was scotched, of course. But we *had* already received people from the Russian Service in London, and we had facilitated their entry—mainly by parachute—into Germany where, I must admit, they did better than my own people. Early in '44 we agreed to take three of them in. Donovan knew. We kept them in a safe house in London, and they came complete with their own dispatching officer." He paused, looking hard at Naldo. "That man was Rogov. Your Uncle Ramillies, Naldo. Gennadi Aleksandrovich Rogov." He saw Arnold Farthing's puzzled expression. "Explain it to Farthing at your leisure."

Naldo nodded.

C cleared his throat. "General Donovan knew we were about to infiltrate NKVD men into Germany, so he asked if his Service could be privy to the advance briefings. After all, SOE was doing the spadework, and we also had a representative with them—SIS, I mean. To cut a long story short, we agreed. The officer Donovan sent was Nathaniel Dollhiem, a good Russian speaker. He had several semiprivate conversations with Rogov."

"Jesus!" breathed Naldo.

"So"—C continued as though he had heard nothing—"that's

another piece of the jigsaw we are calling *Symphony*. The pieces get more numerous, not to mention more complex, each day." As he said it, the telephone rang. C picked it up and spoke quietly. Several exchanges took place before he cradled the receiver. "Well, time *is* running out. The school says that young Kruger's as ready as he'll ever be without more experience out in the cold. They've also narrowed the field of possible camps where Klaubert might be holed up—two in Germany and three in France. It's possible you'll have to get *Symphony* under way long before the Enquiry's heard all the witnesses. They've had a first session with *Felix* today. When they've finished with him, there's the all-important Buelow." He glanced at his watch. It was almost midnight.

"I suggest you both leave here. Take forty-eight hours off and come back around eighteen hours the day after tomorrow. I'll have transcripts up to date by then. You might have to read through the night, and I'll come over to give you my final briefing and, possibly, bring Kruger. You got a bed for Farthing, Naldo?"

"Yes. He can stay with me. No problem."

"Good. Don't forget it's imperative that we keep the whole thing silent as the grave—though I think a few words with Dick Farthing at Redhill Manor might not come amiss. If he's reluctant, tell him to telephone me, but for heaven's sake don't even give a hint that I'm running my private operation. *Nobody*, and I mean nobody, must know what we're at." He sucked in breath, almost through his teeth. An uncharacteristic action. "You know Richard Farthing worked at Oshawa on and off?"

"I had some idea he was there." Naldo tried to calculate the possibilities of getting to Redhill and back, plus entertaining Arnie *and* spending time with Barbara before he left. "Have my father and Uncle Caspar been told about Ramillies yet, sir?" he asked.

C gave a curt nod. "Your father was told this afternoon. He was instructed to break the news to Caspar when the Enquiry closed for the day. Caspar was going back to his office."

THAT AFTERNOON, CASPAR had returned to his office after listening to his old friend *Felix* giving evidence. Jules Fenice had been direct and believable. It was pouring with rain and Caspar had trouble getting a cab. James was waiting for him, and stood silently while he shook out his sodden raincoat and umbrella.

When the cousins had greeted one another, James told him about Ramillies, and his re-emergence as a senior officer of the NKVD.

Caspar, knowing who had set up his brother Ramillies' defection all those years ago, in 1918, walked over to the window and looked down onto the soaking streets. His mind seemed to be like a car in a skid. He thought of agents he had turned during his career—agents he had doubled.

Aloud, like any good Railton, he quoted Shakespeare, knowing James would understand.

"And is old Double dead?" he queried with terrible bitterness.

13

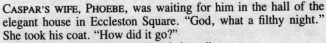

CASPAR'S WIFE, PHOEBE, was waiting for him in the hall of the elegant house in Eccleston Square. "God, what a filthy night." She took his coat. "How did it go?"

"Usual. Nothing to be bothered about."

"You know Alex is coming to dinner? Alex and Hester?"

"I'd forgotten. Sorry. Andrew couldn't make it?"

"No. He's working on a case. Some whore got herself murdered and he's briefing the defense. Murdered whores are more important than family dinner parties."

Caspar stood at the foot of the stairs. His head ached and he felt weary from the strain of the *Tarot* Enquiry: sick from the news about his long-lost brother Ramillies.

"Alex tried to cry off as well," Phoebe said, and Caspar gave her a blank look. "I told him he *had* to come."

"You can't go on treating him like a child." Caspar smiled but it held no warmth. "If he didn't want to come, you should have left it alone."

"The excuse didn't hold water. I told him we wanted no rifts in the family."

"You've been talking to my mother." Charlotte Railton's fury that Alexander was to give evidence flickered in his mind.

"Yes. I know he presented some information to the Board."

"Couldn't look me in the eyes, either. What he gave had no bearing on me at all." Caspar turned and began to climb the stairs. "I'll change. Be down in half an hour."

He went to the second floor, not to their bedroom. His study was on the second floor—practically the only room in the house that remained unchanged. It had been Giles Railton's study, and was known in the family as the Hide.

Caspar stood just inside the door, looking around the room with its big old military desk and the custom-crafted cabinet which took up one whole wall. The cabinet, made of polished oak, was lined with drawers of different sizes which contained his grandfather's maps, hand drawn and of almost every major battlefield, from the wars between Palestine and Syria, some 1100 years before the birth of Christ, to the Boxer Rebellion.

Other slim drawers held stacks of trays in which whole armies were stored—tiny, molded-lead replicas of fighting men and matériel—siege towers, ballistas, carts, early cannon, right up to Gatlings and French 3-inch field guns.

Here Giles had reenacted the great battles of history, using maps and models.

Now that he knew Ramillies was not dead, but working within the Soviet regime as an NKVD officer, Caspar wondered if he could ever use this room again. Here, his brother must have been briefed for the Russian adventure, and the seeds of treachery might even have blossomed in this very place. He closed the door, walking slowly to the bedroom and his dressing room where he began to change for dinner.

Over dinner, Caspar's daughter, Hester, was full of the social life she had begun to lead since demobilization from the WRNS. By nature she was a bubbly chatterbox of a girl, very attractive but, unlike most Railtons, not to be trusted with anything confidential. Nobody in the secret trade within the family would speak of it in front of Hester.

Alexander remained quiet during the meal, speaking only when the ladies retired, leaving father and son alone with the port. The Railtons would always maintain tradition.

"I gather Grandmama's angry because I had to appear before the Board," he said, pouring from the decanter. A couple of small drops of the wine fell to the white cloth like bloodstains.

"You mustn't be concerned about your grandmother," Caspar said. "She's got it into her head that I've been caught up in some witch-hunt."

"Well, haven't you, Dad?"

"No. I'm not under threat." He sipped his port. "Maybe I'll be hauled over the coals for not getting wind of the situation earlier. But I have no troubled conscience about running *Tarot*."

"Not even a conscience about recruiting the girls?"

"That's a different matter, and, yes, if you want to know, I feel like a murderer. Very guilty."

"It *was* a pretty cold-blooded thing to do." Alex looked away.

"I know," Caspar said quietly. "I *do* know."

"Do you also know that you're deluding yourself about the Board of Enquiry?"

"I don't think so."

"Dad, there were a hundred *réseaux* that went to the bad, were infiltrated by the Abwehr or got stuck with informers. Nobody's putting their British controllers on the rack. Nobody's been accused of lousing up *Prosper,* or the 'pianists' that were turned early on."

Caspar shrugged. "Let's see," he said, though in his heart he had long ago begun to worry. The Board was unnecessary when put against the other foulups that had gone on across Europe. C had ordered the Board of Enquiry and then said he wanted nothing to do with it. There had to be a deeper purpose. Something that mattered now.

In bed that night he thought to himself, No, this isn't just to do with *Tarot.* It's about something else, and the something else concerns C *at this moment.* He tried to think logically. What was it that mattered? Was Klaubert alive or dead? What had happened to Caroline, Jo-Jo, and the OSS man Dollhiem? What were the Orléans Russians' signals? Why? As he thought, certain pieces of the puzzle began to assemble themselves in his mind, just as they were being assembled by C so that Naldo and Arnie could take action and dig out the roots of truth.

As he drifted off into a troubled sleep, Caspar knew that the truth was important—not merely because in his profession people liked to know the truth, but because the truth about *Tarot* was essential to something that was going on in the here and now.

JUST AS CASPAR was easing himself toward sleep, Naldo was driving Arnold Farthing to Kensington. They had observed all the formalities: C going ahead on foot—though they knew he would have somebody trustworthy nearby—then Naldo leaving to walk a long route to his car and later picking up Arnold near Northolt underground station.

As they drove, Naldo gave Arnie a brief rundown on the complexities surrounding Ramillies—how he had been sent as an agent into Russia in 1918, disappearing almost immediately only to resurface—unrecognized by anybody, including Naldo—in the '30s while on a recruiting drive for the Soviets in Cambridge. Now he had been positively identified as an NKVD officer of some rank. "He's going to be part of our leverage for *Symphony.* I've no illusions about that," Naldo said.

When they arrived at the house near Kensington Gardens, Naldo checked to make certain Barbara was not there. He had provided her with a key so that she could come and go when she wished. "I'm not a free agent, if you'll forgive the pun," he told her, "but *you* are free. Always remember that." His father, James, had once told him that the best way to keep a woman was to give her a very long rein. Barbara had replied that she would certainly do as she pleased, but only as long as it pleased Naldo. Every meeting brought them closer together, and they spent twice as much time exploring each others' minds as they did enjoying each others' bodies.

Naldo offered Arnie a drink, pouring two stiff whiskies, excusing himself to go and make sure the spare bed was made up. He told Arnie they would probably be going to see his father tomorrow, "And somehow get up to Redhill Manor to see your illustrious Uncle Richard."

"*Our* illustrious uncle," Arnold reminded him. "That's good. Perhaps I'll get to see the famous Aunt Sara. I've seen Richard in the past five years of course, but only heard the fabled stories about Sara."

Naldo tossed back the whiskey and nodded. "In her day she was a great beauty." He paused, smiling almost secretively, then added, "And her day is far from over yet."

After a while Arnie took himself off to bed and Naldo dialed Barbara's number. She picked up after eight rings. Her voice was blurred with sleep, but she seemed to waken as soon as she heard his voice. "Shall I come to you now?" she asked. Naldo told her to go back to sleep but be ready for an early start in the morning. "I could well be away for a while," he said. "It might be a good time to break the news to my side of the family at least, otherwise the secret engagement'll go on forever."

Barbara groaned at the idea of having to get up at what she called "The crack of Doom." Apart from that, she sounded pleased at the prospect of being with him, even if only for a couple of days.

Naldo booked an alarm call with the telephone operator, then went to bed.

He had sexual dreams involving Barbara, but in the middle, his Uncle Ramillies came in, dressed as an SS officer. The SS officer kept ringing a bell. He woke to the shrill of his wake-up call. It was seven-thirty, and he dialed his parents' number at the Cheyne Walk house. A voice he didn't recognize answered and told him that Mr. Railton was away for the weekend.

"It's his son, Naldo . . . er, Donald. Where can I get hold of him?"

"Mr. and Mrs. Railton have gone to Redhill Manor for the weekend." It was only then that Naldo realized it was Saturday morning. They would be expected back at the Northolt house by six o'clock on Sunday evening.

Barbara arrived while Naldo and Arnie were drinking coffee. She wore a skirt and jumper, with pearls and brogues, her Windsmoor coat slung over her shoulders. "I've got one evening dress in the case." She pointed to the scuffed, battered old Revelation which had obviously seen her through the war. "Also what Mummy would call a 'sensible suit.' I thought as we're going to the great country house I should wear the right clothes."

She shook hands with Arnie, who said he knew all about her. "I think I broke in on your honeymoon." He smiled and she laughed. "Please don't tell anybody." Barbara actually blushed. "I don't know about Naldo's family, but sex isn't exactly considered the done thing with my people. I often wonder how Mummy and Daddy brought themselves to conceive Bertie and me."

"Sure, I know." Arnold grinned. "You do often wonder about your folks, don't you?"

"Never wonder about mine." Naldo snorted. "They look as though they'll never tire of rutting. Incredible."

Barbara draped herself around him, nibbling his ear and trying to make him laugh as he telephoned Redhill. Sara answered. "Naldo!" she said, her voice lifting in delight when he asked if he could come over for the night. "Of course—how wonderful! Your mother and father will be *so* pleased. James was saying only last night that it's been ages since they saw you."

He made certain Richard was at home before telling Sara he would not be coming alone, and she sounded happy again when he said Arnold would be with him. "And something of a surprise," he went on. "Don't breathe a word, because I haven't asked her parents yet, but I'd like to bring my future wife."

"Good grief, Naldo! Everybody had given up hope." When Sara laughed it was like being in a roomful of happy children. "Sara's laugh," Richard often said, "is not so much infectious as contagious."

"Don't tell my parents, please, Sara."

"My lips are sealed, Naldo." Then, just before she put down the phone, she added, "With butter."

"She sounds so bloody young." Barbara had her ear to the receiver.

"Looks bloody young as well." Naldo gave her a playful pat on her tight little bottom.

"My God, you're right!" Barbara muttered as Sara came out of the main door and walked briskly over the gravel to meet them when the car pulled up in front of Redhill Manor. "How old did you say she was?"

"I didn't. But I'll tell you later. Amazing lady, Sara."

Sara Railton Farthing's first marriage had been to James' father, John. After his death the Railtons had claimed her as one of their own. During the First War she had run the Redhill Estate and Farm almost single-handed. Even her marriage to Richard Farthing had changed nothing, except that Richard had added Railton to his own name as a mark of respect, binding the two families.

She embraced Barbara on their first meeting, hugging her, then holding the girl out at arm's length, her hands lightly on Barbara's shoulders, looking her up and down. "Well, well, well, Naldo, how did you manage to ensnare such a beauty." Then, quietly, "I've put you in rooms next to one another, in the West Wing." Unashamedly she winked at them.

"She's absolutely lovely," Naldo's mother—Margaret Mary—told him quietly over lunch. "And so full of fun. She'll make a great Railton. When's the happy day going to be?"

"I've to ask her family yet." Naldo looked slightly embarrassed.

"Well, get on with it, Nald," his father chuckled. They were very happy to see him.

"I can't just quite yet." Naldo gave his father a wary look. "I've been posted to Germany again."

"When?" James gave up any pretense of secrecy.

"Tomorrow night. I'll be away for a few weeks. Maybe months."

Margaret Mary sighed. "You're going to leave that beautiful creature with those big black eyes on her own? You men are mad."

At the far end of the table, Richard and Sara talked to Arnold, who had said he was only over for a brief private visit. Richard pumped him for news of the Farthing family as soon as he heard Arnold had just arrived from the United States: it was a necessary white lie.

Later in the afternoon, Naldo sought out Richard, finding him in what was forever known as The General's Study. The room was book-lined from floor to ceiling, but had a military flavor. Its windows opened out onto the rose garden.

"We have to talk, Richard."

Richard Farthing lifted his leathery face, one eyebrow raised in a quizzical fashion.

"I think, outside, sir, if you don't mind."

Richard nodded, took his favorite stick, and led the way through the rose garden to the tree-lined walk beyond.

"Well?" he asked, finally coming to a standstill.

"It's confidential." Naldo made it sound casual. "But C says you're to telephone him if you need confirmation. He'd rather you didn't."

"Your word's good enough." Richard was very still. Waiting. Naldo said that C had told him to ask about Camp X.

"But you know about Camp X, surely, Nald."

"I was never there. Just give me the general background, then I'll have a specific question. C seems to think you might have something to contribute."

"Right. Well, I suppose someone really ought to put it all on record now—but they won't. I suppose in the future so-called historians will argue the toss. You know about *Intrepid,* I presume?"

"Just fill it in."

"Bill Stephenson. Sir William Stephenson. I knew him very slightly in the First War. Canadian, small, wiry. Had the most penetrating blue eyes I've ever seen. He was gassed in the first show—Royal Canadian Engineers. Invalided back to England, then joined the Royal Flying Corps. That's when I knew him. Bagged twenty-six German aircraft. An Ace. Also an expert in wireless telegraphy. Invented the first machine for transmitting pictures by W/T. Made a fortune. Invested well. Scores of companies. Won the King's Cup air race in '34. Helped with the Spitfire—money, I mean. In 1940, Winston himself ordered Bill Stephenson to be his personal representative in the States. That *is* true. People will argue about that. But go and ask Winston."

Dick Farthing went on to outline Stephenson's work in America: the setting up of BSC—the British Security Co-ordination—in a couple of offices in Rockefeller Center, and how the organization became huge and of vital importance to Intelligence.

"Camp X was at first an extension of BSC in Manhattan. In the early days we called it the Farm. But 'Camp X' stuck. Two hundred and seventy-five acres of it. Nald, you know all this. The training was almost the same as you had for the field; and surely you know what a godsend *Intrepid*'s work was to the war effort. But you know all of this."

"Most of it. I didn't actually know that you spent a lot of time there until recently."

Richard nodded. "Yes, I worked for *Intrepid* on and off. Did some lecturing at the Camp."

"That's what C's interested in. He says you might recall someone who went through the Camp and came out the other side. An American. OSS. Name of Nathaniel Dollhiem."

Before leaving the Northolt house, C had given Naldo a photograph of Dollhiem taken when he was at the Camp. Now he showed it to Richard, who looked at it closely, then at Naldo. "Yes," he said softly. "Yes, I recall Nat Dollhiem. Spoke Russian and German, didn't he?"

"That's your man."

"Yes . . . We had a spot of bother with him . . ." Richard Farthing began to talk at length as he handed back the photograph.

Neither of them saw, or heard, Arnold Farthing, perched in one of the high windows of Redhill Manor, a camera with a long lens to his eyes. As the photograph changed hands again, he clicked off half a dozen photographs. If an American citizen was involved in *Tarot,* his superiors in Washington would expect him to give advance warning should there be any unpleasantness.

14

▼

DURING THE DRIVE from London to Northolt, late on Sunday afternoon, Naldo told Arnold Farthing exactly what Richard had said about Nat Dollhiem.

"Richard's given me something interesting," he began after they had dropped Barbara off and were alone in the safety of the car. "He has cause to remember Dollhiem, and he had some things to say about Newton as well."

Arnold waited, not asking anything, just letting Naldo do the talking.

It appeared that while Dollhiem was at Camp X, Richard was also there as a visiting lecturer—"He used to go over to talk about getting in and out of Europe by air."

It was true that Dollhiem and Newton had been very close friends. So close that a fight broke out one night in their hut. Another trainee accused Dollhiem of being a homosexual with a fancy for Newton. Nat Dollhiem had to be hauled off the man who had been taunting him. He broke the trainee's jaw and an arm. "So it didn't go unnoticed." Naldo slowed down slightly as a motorcycle policeman went past them. "The CO had him on the carpet, and for some reason Richard happened to be in the office at the same time. Dollhiem refused to apologize. Said the victim deserved all he had got. He lost his temper again and shouted something about what would happen to men like that when the Revolution came. It caused quite a rumpus and there was a genuine possibility that Dollhiem would be sent off the course. They weren't too worried about the political aspect, but Richard says he seems to remember that they checked up on Dollhiem and found he did have leanings to the far left. He couldn't recall the complete findings, but said he thought Dollhiem had been a card-carrying member of the Communist Party."

"And Newton?" It was the first time Arnold had spoken since Naldo started his story.

"Background figure. Made no fuss, but he and Dollhiem *were* very close indeed."

Arnold said that while C wanted nothing to do with the *Tarot* Enquiry officially, he presumed the Chief could organize special questions.

"You were thinking of what?"

"Getting Newton back in and asking more about Dollhiem— if he noticed anything during the drop? Was Dollhiem in a position to warn the troops on the ground so he wouldn't get his head blown off."

"We'll put it to him."

They separated near Northolt station and were both inside the house by six o'clock. Ten minutes later a GPO Telegram boy arrived on a bicycle and after an exchange of passwords handed over the transcripts of Jules Fenice's—*Felix*'s—evidence.

There was an initial note concerning his arrival in the room where the Board was sitting. He had gone straight to Caspar and embraced him, then presented himself to the other members of the Board. The first day was spent going over old ground—Caspar's first visit, the recruitment, his training and such matters.

Each member of the network was then identified by his or her name, the Board cross-referencing them with the information obtained from Newton.

Maxine and *Dédé* were already known by name; the fat man, whom Newton had spoken of as *Albert,* was the butcher, Henri Villar—the man Fenice had shown reluctance about recruiting during his final conversation with Caspar in 1940. Villar, Fenice now explained, had married his fancied widow, Mme. Debron; *St. Christophe* was Michel, Villar's son by his first marriage. The mysteriously named *le Teneur de Livres* was the son of another member of the *réseau,* the lawyer Jean Maury—himself cryptoed *l'Arbrisseau:* in English, "the Sapling," because of his slim, almost gaunt, build. The other girl, *Florence,* had been the local schoolmistress, Annabelle Sabatier, originally from the Roussillon area.

Those so far unmentioned to the Board included the doctor, Paul Clergue—*Immortel*—and the local *curé,* Ignace Fabrisse, whom they called *Céleste.* Of these last two, *Felix* said everyone thought the cryptonyms very funny: a doctor who was immortal and a priest called heavenly. The Board said nothing, though it was clear they felt the names were not amusing but very insecure.

The entire Board of Enquiry, and Caspar, of course, knew of

the eventual fate of each individual member of *Tarot*. *Albert*, the fat butcher, had been in Fenice's house at the time of the raid, and it was he who exchanged shots with the incoming troops and died riddled with bullets from a machine pistol. *Florence* had been raped at the Rue de Bourgogne SS headquarters. Later she was taken, together with *Immortel* and *Céleste*, to a wood near to St. Benoît-sur-Loire. All three were made to dig their own graves—the girl was too weak to do anything so the priest did it for her, hearing her confession at the same time and giving absolution to her and the doctor. The graves dug, they were shot and a few spadefuls of earth thrown over them.

This evidence was from several eyewitnesses who returned the following day and carried out a proper burial. The site was now marked and cared for by locals.

St. Christophe, together with *le Teneur de Livres* and *l'Arbrisseau*, was shot in a courtyard behind the SS headquarters in Orléans, but their bodies were taken to a mass grave south of the city. That was also now marked, and the evidence irrefutable.

Which left *Maxine* and *Dédé*, the OSS officer, Dollhiem, and *Felix* himself.

Maxine and *Dédé* had definitely been seen—by four unconnected persons—being driven from the Rue de Bourgogne accompanied by two SS officers. The written testaments were read again to the Board. One of them suggested that the girls were almost fraternizing with the SS. *They smoked cigarettes and were laughing and talking. I was only a few paces from the car, which had to slow down for a military convoy,* a witness had written.

The evidence on Dollhiem would come later. First, the Board started to examine Jules Fenice on his own movements, and the true reason for his flight and disguise in a DP camp.

He told them that on the evening before the raid he had gone into Orléans. "I went to make certain our radio was safe and try to send a message. It was after curfew when I finished, so I stayed the night. That's why I wasn't at the farm when the SS arrived."

"You sent a message?"

"Yes."

"From where?" It was the senior lawyer doing the questioning.

"We had two radios. One kept in Orléans, the other in St. Benoît. It was necessary to keep moving them around because the Nazis had detectors. They could locate a signal in five minutes. We used several places."

"And where was the radio on that night?"

"In the loft of a bistro near the Gare. I knew the lady who

owned the place: her husband was killed in 1940."

"*Knew* in the Biblical sense?" The lawyer did not sneer.

"I was sleeping with her, yes."

"And what message did you send?"

"A standard QSLIMI with our call sign for *Tarot*."

"You were asking for a reply to your last message, then?" The lawyer knew the Q-codes by heart.

"Yes. We had sent three messages since the massacre of the *Romarin* team. To let them know we had saved two men. There was no response."

The chairman broke in. "There is evidence of four transmissions after *Romarin*. All but one appeared to be jammed. The report is in front of you—pages fifty-six and fifty-seven, *Tarot Transmissions*. We had one report about the failure of *Romarin*, then these abortive transmissions, followed by silence. It was the primary indication that *Tarot* had been rolled up."

The lawyer acknowledged the information, then asked what happened on the morning of the raid.

"I was getting ready to leave when some Germans came into the bistro. Laure—the lady concerned—came up and told me. She had heard they'd been to my farm; that people were arrested, one already dead. There was an order out for me also."

"So what did you do?"

"She wanted me to stay at the bistro. Hidden upstairs. I did for a few days, then things became difficult. I reasoned with myself about the debacle of *Romarin* and what had happened to *Tarot*. I knew I would be blamed, accused, possibly shot when the British or Americans came. It was a panic, but I felt I must go. I went on foot—across country—heading toward Paris. When I finally got near the fighting I found a dead German soldier. I stole his paybook and a few other things. My German wasn't that bad. When they picked me up, I thought that maybe I would be given a new life—it was better than nothing; better than being shot by the Allies or the Germans."

"Why did you think you would be blamed?"

"Because I was guilty. It *was* my fault that *Romarin* went wrong. It *was* my fault that *Tarot* became a nothing—a pile of rubbish. *Merde!*"

"You're saying you betrayed *Tarot* and *Romarin?*"

"Only by bad leadership. We were betrayed by someone within *Tarot*. I don't know who that was, but I had known for some time that we were living charmed lives. Every other *réseau* and Maquis unit had been wiped out. It was logic that we were in some way protected. The SS in Orléans were good, so were the Abwehr. It was logic that we were—how you say it? Blown?"

"Who were your regular radio operators?" the SOE man asked, and there was a small space of silence as the whole room waited for this important information.

"The normal radio operators were myself, *Maxine,* and *Dédé.* We were the trained ones. Me in London. I trained *them.*"

Caspar's face screwed itself into a mask of pain. There was mention of a distinct reaction in a margin note to the transcript.

Both Naldo and Arnie had read to this point when there was a familiar Morse ring at the doorbell. Seconds later, C was in the pink room while the young Herbie Kruger's large frame filled the doorway.

C sat down, nodding at the transcripts, asking how far they had managed to get.

Naldo told him.

"There's a long way to go yet." C sounded somber. "And a great deal to do. You'll have to read the rest through the night—I have more with me. As for the German's evidence—Buelow's stuff—we'll have to work out something because I want you both out of here, with young Kruger. He must be run through those DP camps like hot salts. I need Klaubert, or at least a scent of him. I need him now." He went on to say that a 'Dakota' would fly them out of Northolt airfield at first light. "You'll do the German camps first, they're both quite close to Munich. I've a fellow there, he'll take care of things, but remember he has no details and must be given none. A trusted man will travel with you and return with these transcripts. You both know what I want, and I've put young Kruger in the picture. He'll obey you—either of you."

The smiling Kruger nodded enthusiastically.

"A word with you in private, Naldo. Just for a moment, then the two of you." He placed his arm on Naldo's shoulder and led him into the hall, where he gave some fast instructions before going back into the living room where, smiling at Kruger, he said, "Herbie, would you go into the hall, please."

The lad obeyed, still grinning, and C lowered his voice even as the door closed. "Whatever happens in Germany, I still want you to go into France—to Orléans. Now this is what I want from there. . . ." He spoke low and rapidly for the next fifteen minutes.

15

▼

Young Kruger sat in a corner as Naldo and Arnie tried to get on with the reading.

"They taught me everything," Kruger said. "Shooting, surveying, the tradeinkcraft." His English had improved slightly, but he was still inclined to substitute odd words, and occasional German. Receiving no replies from the two men, Kruger continued, "They even taught me another song about Piccadilly—

> *Oh, I don't wish to join der air force,*
> *I don't wish to go to war,*
> *I would rather hang around der Piccadilly underground,*
> *Liffing on the earnings of a high-born lady.*
> *Don't vant ein bullet up mein—"*

"*Herbie!*" Arnold shouted.

"*Ja?* I mean, Yes?"

"Shut up, Herbie."

"We've got work to do," added Naldo.

"Sorry."

But a couple of minutes later he was off again, humming the tune—a relic from the First War's "I don't want to join the army"—and fidgeting. It was unlike Kruger, who could sit very still, concentrating like a statue. Naldo presumed it was excitement.

"Look, Herb." Naldo stood up and walked over to the corner. "Look, there's an old gramophone here, and records. *Real* music I can stand." Next to the gramophone stood a stack of records, some big sets of up to twelve or fourteen sides of fragile 12-inch disks. Herbie rummaged among the collection. "Who is Gustav Mahler?" he asked, holding up a large thick folder which looked very new.

"A composer." Arnold looked up, irritated.

"Not the American, Glenn Mahler?"

"That was Miller, Herb! Glenn Miller!" Arnold gave a belch of laughter.

"A composer and a compatriot of yours, Herb." Naldo looked up and thought it must be a very recent recording. "Well, almost a compatriot."

"So. Never heard of him. In Germany we had Wagner. Wagner all the time. Breakfast, lunch, dinner—Wagner all the time. Here it says Second Symphony. The Resurrection. So. Symphony Number Two. The Minneapolis Symphony Orchestra and Choir. Conducted Eugene Ormandy. C. E. Bowen, Soprano; A. Gallogy, Contralto. So, this is good music, Naldo?"

"Just put it on, Herbie, and find out. We *must* read."

"Okay." There were eleven records. Twenty-two sides.

Scratchy, hissy, and clicky, the great solemn first chords leaped into the room. In all its romantic and death-ridden, nature-sodden beauty, Mahler's music filled the air, and Eberhardt Lucas Kruger sat, rock still. He spoke no more that night, and only moved to turn a record or put on the next. They must have heard the Mahler Second at least four times—but Naldo and Arnie were not counting, buried in the interrogation of Jules Fenice by the *Tarot* Board of Enquiry.

The Board bit hard on Fenice's self-accusation, prodding and probing, even stabbing at it like crazed dentists jabbing at an exposed nerve. But it soon became apparent that *Felix,* while holding himself guilty for not being a strong and true leader, was unlikely to have been the worm that caused decay in *Tarot* itself. The Frenchman was most convincing, and it was not hard to believe that this rising sense of guilt had been the mainspring of his flight from the oncoming American Third Army and his later disguise in a camp.

The Board changed its attack, taking each member of *Tarot* out in front of Fenice for his comments. They asked about politics—

"*Maxine* and *Dédé* were to the left, I suppose, but not Communists. The priest, well"—Fenice shrugged—"he was a priest. Of all of them, if I was asked for suspicion I would point to *Florence*." Fenice told them. "*Florence* was outspoken. I once asked her if she would have been happier with the Maquis. After all, that was where the Communists really were. She said no and I accepted it. The Communists were our brothers in arms then.

But even though she held a burning hatred for the Nazis, I was never truly comfortable with *Florence*."

"Why?" asked one of the lawyers.

"It is difficult. Sometimes she would disappear. She would be away for days at a time and never explained. I tried to give her as little responsibility as possible—"

"We have no photographs," the chairman butted in. "Can you describe her?"

"That is easy. Dark hair, small. She was very like *Maxine* to look at."

Naldo reflected that Caspar must have suddenly been filled with a tiny flame of hope. Could it have been Caroline who had died, horribly, after rape, and not the French girl? Any Railton like Caspar would hope for that rather than a betrayal.

They took him over each of the *Tarot* members again and again—there were pages of transcript—but, in Jules Fenice's estimation, *Florence* was the only oddity among them.

Next they went through the various "pianists" assigned to them. On the question of Drake, who had given evidence, the stories matched up. As for the others—captured and executed— Fenice could say little.

"Of course I was anxious when it happened twice. A third time was more than simply bad luck. To me it proved the Gestapo or Abwehr had inside knowledge. We were left alone—and it took me until early in 1944 to realize there was something decidedly strange about that. We lived on a tightrope of anxiety all the time, yet *we* were never arrested, while the 'pianists' were."

"Is that how you came to have two radios?"—one of the lawyers who had not asked many questions until now.

"Yes, we had one of the early ones—the old Mark XV, is that correct?"

It was.

"We kept that one at the farm, as it was too heavy to carry around. The other was one of the Parasets. That was the wireless we moved all over Orléans."

It transpired that at least three transmitters, brought in by "pianists" captured later, ended up in the hands of Klaubert's men. Naldo was slowly beginning to understand C's last orders given to them that night.

Painstakingly, the Board began to go back over every single operation conducted by *Tarot*, running through seemingly trivial details with *Felix*, trying to check and recheck dates and the names of those involved.

The picture that emerged was one bordering on farce. While some operations had gone surprisingly well, the bulk had been lash-ups from the beginning. They dwelt heavily on the supposed sabotage of Ju88 and ME110 G-4 aircraft at the Luftwaffe base near Orléans. They gave the dates and read the messages instructing action to be taken, together with the replies, which claimed aircraft had been destroyed.

"Yes, I sent all those signals—the replies stating action had been carried out," *Felix* admitted.

"Why, when you must have known the jobs were not done?"

"Until later—early 1944—I thought the jobs *had* been done. They were undertaken by *St. Christophe* and *le Teneur de Livres* —young Villar and Maury. I had personally instructed them in the handling of explosives, and how to set the right kind of charges. Those two went out on five separate occasions. We also *knew* aircraft had been destroyed. It was all over the place. Luftwaffe personnel talked about it in bars, restaurants, and bistros. In February '44 I discovered the errors." It was just about the time that Jules Fenice was starting to have grave misgivings about a lot of the work his people had done.

"And what was the cause of these—what did you call them? Errors?"—the senior lawyer at his most scathing.

"The wrong airfield was hit, therefore the wrong aircraft. The boys went to the satellite landing ground east of Orléans and destroyed twin-engined D-720s—captured French Dewoitines— the Luftwaffe were using for training. They were expendable airplanes. We expended them." Fenice tried a wry smile.

"And how could this happen? Didn't you do a thorough reconnaissance? Walk them over the ground?"

"Not personally. That was impossible. Near an airfield I would have been questioned. On the other hand, *Dédé,* in a short skirt on a bicycle, making sure the guards got a good view of her *petit*—er, her clothes underneath—" He shrugged again, holding his hands a few inches apart, forefingers extended, as if this explained everything.

"So *Dédé* did the reconnaissance and walked the lads through it on a map?"

"*Oui.* Yes. She merely got the wrong airfield."

"A mistake that could happen to anyone." The lawyer was still heavy on the sarcasm. "Was that the same problem when it came to the electricity pylons at Neuville-aux-Bois?"

"A similar misfortune. On that occasion it was *Florence*. She picked the correct pylons but gave the wrong map references. Foolish."

Again and again there were stories of wrong map references and mistaken identities. *Tarot* had even crippled a relatively harmless corporal, late at night in a dark alley, in mistake for his officer, whom they wanted out of the way for a time so that they could raid Wehrmacht stores.

It was six-thirty in the morning when Naldo and Arnie got to the *Romarin* operation—too late to go on reading at the house. C had told them to expect his man at seven.

They sent Herbie to make coffee, which he did reluctantly, not wanting to leave the beautiful sprawling masterpiece that was Mahler's Second Symphony. "Now that is a musician," the boy kept saying as he lumbered noisily toward the kitchen. "That is a real musician. A giant."

"What d'you think?" Naldo asked.

"I think it all fits perfectly well with C's *First Folio* and the main thrust of his theory." Arnold lit another cigarette. "They'll never get the full strength of it from the Enquiry. It really *is* up to us. *Tarot* was no go from the start, and I don't honestly believe *Felix* is as clean as C imagines."

At just before seven o'clock, the doorbell rang in sequence, and Naldo went to open it. He pulled the door back a few inches to ask who it was, and receive the password, "Clive Candy," to which he replied, "Blimp."

Naldo hardly opened the door any further. The figure that slid into the hall was short, very slim, dressed in a knee-length coat over cord trousers and a black turtleneck. On his feet he wore what were known then as gym shoes. He carried a briefcase and his slim frame had about it an aura of steel. The man felt like a trained killer. It was impossible for Naldo to analyze the feeling, but it was there, as though the man's body gave off vibrations of death and danger. It also showed in the eyes—pallid gray, the color of a dead plaice's skin.

Their visitor closed the door with his shoulder. "You're *D Major*, I presume," he said. There was no smile, just a quick up and down flicking of the eyes. The three men who formed C's *Symphony* team were using simple cryptonyms—D Major for Naldo; A Minor for Arnie; and, inevitably, E Flat for Kruger.

"The Chief calls me Cherub because I'm no Angel." In other voices the remark would have had camp undertones. With Cherub it was hard, matter-of-deadly-fact.

"I've come to take you to the aircraft. C said there would be some documents to bring back." He indicated the briefcase.

"We haven't finished with them yet." Naldo felt increasingly uncomfortable with the man.

"No matter. I'll travel with you. You'll finish them on the plane?"

"I should think so."

"Good. I'll return the papers. C says I'll be making trips to you with other documents." He opened the briefcase to display a pair of handcuffs inside. "I lock it to my wrist." He nodded, holding out his hand for the transcripts and saying they could have them back once they were airborne. He explained the procedure to them and they left, one by one, at five-minute intervals. A small van picked them up from different points near the Northolt shopping promenade, the station, and The Target public house. Cherub sat next to the driver, the briefcase handcuffed to his wrist.

They drove straight onto the airfield, over to a Nissen hut where Cherub told them to leave the van. He would stay outside.

WAAFs served breakfast to them in the Nissen hut—sausages, eggs, bacon, and beans washed down with thick dark tea served in enamel mugs. Arnold pulled a face when he tasted it, but Kruger ate as though he were never going to get a square meal again.

They traveled in a Dakota fitted with seats in the style of its pre-war brother, the American civil airliner, and immediately after takeoff, Cherub passed the transcripts back to Naldo, who handed one to Arnie. Herbie sat in the rear, eyes alert, enjoying the ride.

Naldo and Arnie worked their way toward the centerpiece of *Felix*'s evidence—the *Romarin* operation.

"The Americans dropped a lot of leaflets," Fenice began. "They had been doing it since '43, but now we knew the invasion was to be soon. I think it was American airplanes who did the *Carpetbagger* operations also—the dropping of more weapons and equipment. We only got hold of three or four canisters. The Germans gobbled them up. They seemed to know exactly where the stuff would be dropped."

"Advance information again?" queried the senior lawyer.

"They could have unbuttoned the codes we used, but that is doubtful. They were quite secure, and the speed at which they would have had to do it points to an informer, not a listener."

"So someone informed on *Romarin*?"

"This is difficult. *Romarin* was most secure. No radio traffic except for the one message we listened for. We took turns listening to the BBC messages each night. When we got the first part of the Verlaine poem on June 1, we were put into great spirits. When the second part of the poem was broadcast, some fools wanted to storm the German military installations. They did listen to me, though. It appeared they obeyed orders."

The BBC broadcast "personal messages" to occupied Europe after their nine P.M. news each night. Many of the messages were for individuals, or circuits like *Tarot*. The fragments of the Verlaine poem were for everyone—*Les sanglots longs des violons de l'automne*—"The long sobs of the violins of autumn,"—would be broadcast on the first or fifteenth of the month to signal the invasion of occupied Europe was imminent. The second line—"Wound my heart with a monotonous languor"—signified the operation would begin within twenty-four hours.

Romarin came four weeks later. "The code was contained in a personal message," Fenice told them again. "When we heard *Souffrons, mais souffrons sur les cimes*—'If we must suffer, let us suffer nobly'—*I* knew *Romarin* would take place on the following night." A note in the margin said that he thumped his chest hard with a balled fist when he said "*I*"—like a priest performing the *mea culpa*.

"You, and only you, knew the details?" the SIS officer asked.

"They were not radio messages—clandestine or otherwise. *Night Stock* brought the orders for *Romarin* directly to me."

Night Stock was the agent from Switzerland who had taken Caspar's first instructions, by word of mouth, to *Tarot* after the Fall of France in 1940. He had made regular tours of the various circuits throughout the whole of the Occupation, and now, it appeared, he came in after D-Day to carry messages and give instructions.

In his evidence, Caspar had spoken of the great work this agent was able to do throughout the war, and, in particular, during that period between D-Day and the final breakout and dash for the Liberation of France. When asked to produce *Night Stock*, however, Caspar was unable to do so. He had disappeared in the carnage and chaos of the battles.

"How much did *Night Stock* tell you?" one of the lawyers asked, and *Felix* was meticulous in his reply. *Night Stock* had given him the message sequence and said that when it was broadcast, the *réseau* was to steal a German staff car and a truck which they were to drive to the road nearest the dropping zone. "He said that parachutists would land. That it was a one-off special operation. He gave me the instructions, showed the layout of the DZ signals—an eight-man cross using the flashlights already in our possession. Time. Need for complete quiet—things like that. After the parachutists had landed we were to take orders from their leader."

"You did not know the objective of *Romarin?*"

"I have never known it. Though I could, of course, guess—from the need for a staff car and the truck—that it was some special operation mounted directly against the German authorities."

He was asked to take them through the events of that night—the night of *Romarin* but only after constant questioning to investigate whether or not *Felix* ever shared *Night Stock*'s instructions with any other member of *Tarot*. He denied talking to anyone before the night the message came through. Reading this part of the inquisition made Naldo and Arnold cringe, for the Board were, to a man, hostile, refusing to believe *Felix* had not talked. When he said he had only passed on the phrase for which the circuit had to listen—the passage from Victor Hugo about suffering—they pounced, yelping at the heels of the Frenchman's memory: trying to force some fissure which would turn into a crevasse through which a hidden truth would babble. Naldo felt they were pushing it very hard, considering the man had already been through the mill of SIS questioning.

They got nowhere. Jules Fenice stuck like a leech to his story. He gave details to nobody.

"So what happened once you received the 'Suffering' signal?" The transcript for once failed to identify the questioner.

"I gave instructions. *St. Christophe* and *le Teneur de Livres* knew where they could pick up the required transport. I told them to kill if necessary. You must realize we were all very, very buoyant since the Normandy landings. Everybody thought freedom would come overnight. It didn't, of course."

"So the lads, who had been spectacularly unsuccessful in blowing up aircraft and other things, were instructed to steal transport?"—the pompous lawyer again.

"Could I remind you, they had not been unsuccessful. They had done the jobs given to them. I was at fault for not checking and double-checking on the locations. Anyway, they stole the car and the truck. They showed great daring and skill. As far as we knew, the vehicles were never found."

"Really?"—The lawyer again.

"I had personally instructed them where to hide the vehicles.

Deep in a wood some two kilometers from the dropping zone. At about eleven o'clock that night I gave the other instructions. On a map, I showed everyone where to go and what to do. I also issued the flashlights and weapons."

"This was at your pig farm?"

"Yes. I called the whole circuit in. They were there until we broke curfew at just before midnight."

"And you went to the dropping zone?"

"We tried, but it was impossible. There were troops everywhere. The roads were sealed off. Nobody could get near. It was then we knew the operation was finished."

"So you went home to bed?"

"I passed orders that everyone should go back except for the doctor and Monsieur le Curé. *Immortel,* and *Céleste.*"

"You saw what happened?"

"Heard more than saw. The activity was enormous, so we got out when the real shooting began. The *Curé* and myself went back the next morning. We found the man called Dollhiem and managed to get him clear. Then, in the afternoon we went for another walk. The Nazis were moving the bodies. That's when we found the man Newton. Neither was very badly wounded. Dollhiem had lost a lot of blood, but he was a tough man."

"Let us turn to Dollhiem. *Tarot* was rolled up the following week—while you were in Orléans."—this last delivered with heavy suspicion by the SOE man. "We have accounted for everyone including yourself, except *Maxine* and *Dédé*—and Dollhiem. How do you think he got away? Or was he with you in Orléans?"

The transcript noted a long pause, then Fenice started again. "I have already told your investigators. Dollhiem went at the same time as Newton. Two days before the SS hit *Tarot.*"

"Newton says that he did not. That Dollhiem wanted to stay with *Tarot.* That he *did* stay with *Tarot.*"

"All I know is that I returned from seeing Villar, on the afternoon of the day they went. They were both there the night before. I saw neither of them in the morning. I went out—to see Villar. When I returned, *Dédé* told me they had gone."

"Did she say they had gone off together?"

"No, she just said they had gone. I presumed they left together. I asked no more questions."

"You didn't ask her how or why?"

"Why should I ask? They went. That was all. In their place I also would have gone."

"So you weren't surprised?"

"Not at Newton going, no. He obviously wanted to leave very quickly. He was jittery. But Dollhiem surprised me. He had said that he wished to stay and help us."

"And that was all there was to it? You didn't ask any further questions?"

"I've told you—no. It wasn't until I was brought to England that I knew they did not leave together."

With that, the current batch of transcripts came to an end. Naldo closed his eyes. The Dakota bucked slightly and the engines kept to their steady noise. He wondered what it must have felt like to be a man such as Jules Fenice, living that double secret life under the eyes of the occupying forces. A hall of mirrors, he thought. A fool's game, like a nightmare amusement-park ride with real fear on your shoulder. Glory and courage did not really enter into it. An unusual job in familiar surroundings. He stood up, steadying himself to the movement of the airplane, and walked forward to hand his transcript to Cherub.

Arnie had already finished. He dozed in his seat, thinking not of Fenice and *Tarot*, but of his own time at Camp X when he learned how to tell the difference between a Bren gun's bark and that of an MP38 or 40; how to handle any weapon; encode any message; blow up anything from a railway track to a warehouse; and how to kill, wound, or maim in silence.

When they got to the air base a few miles outside Munich, he had difficulty in adjusting to the landscape—both to the real and that which stuck as though glued to his mind.

Munich, he thought, had been through a fragment of hell.

16

▼

By DAY AND night, during the years between 1940 and 1945, Munich had felt the weight of both the Royal Air Force and the United States Eighth Army Air Force. Over 43 percent of its major buildings had been turned into rubble.

Then there followed more devastation in the vengeful battles as the Allied armies tightened their grip on Germany.

When it was over, a ragged force of civilians had crawled from the debris of war and in true German fashion begun to clear up the mess with their bare hands. As in Berlin, chains of black-clothed men and women piled bricks and shifted masonry, some-times making terrible discoveries beneath: whole families trapped and crushed to death; people caught together in cellars; individuals crammed into pockets of air which, for them, had eventually run out. Some were decaying corpses by the time they were found; others, because of air flow or cold, remained perfectly preserved, like wax effigies.

When the *Symphony* team arrived in the late spring of 1946, Munich was still a city of shattered buildings and makeshift living quarters.

Naldo and Arnie were given accommodation outside the city, on one of the American bases. They had passes and special ID, as did Kruger, whose papers were removed from him when he was taken to one of the camps.

C had told them to "run him through the camps." It took six days, with Herbie spending two days in each of the sprawling hutted and guarded places, only coming out for twenty-four-hour periods of rest and debriefing.

"More of a race than a run," Arnold said when they had finished. Arnie was moderately at ease in Munich, for it gave him the opportunity to see some of his own people and report to them. The Central Intelligence Group, who were still collating information—preparing a full assessment for President Truman—had a three-man team right there on the base. Arnie would slip away and talk with them. To his credit he did not advise them of their true target, but alerted them to a possible former OSS officer being implicated in treachery following the *Romarin* operation. One of the CIG men was called Fry, a tough, former Military Intelligence officer who now did his snooping in civilian clothes. Fry wore steel-rimmed glasses because, to use his own words, "SS guys feel at home when they sit across the table from me."

Fry was wooing Arnold Farthing. "Arnie," he said on the fourth day, "there'll be changes within the year. Plans're well advanced for setting up the most powerful Intelligence outfit in the world. Dulles himself is doing the spadework—he gave the okay on you liaising with the Brits on whatever you're up to. Play the right hand and you'll have a job for life."

In the second camp, Kruger caught a whiff of Klaubert, and that was a second-hand story which pointed them straight toward France. Of the three camps there, given to them by C, only two were now operating. They had not strictly been camps for displaced persons, but for displaced prisoners who were in the process of being sorted out: the relatively innocent going home; the suspects—SS, SD, and foreign collaborators—undergoing constant interrogation. "It's hell's crossroads for some of those men," C had told Naldo during the private briefing at the Northolt house.

France was exactly where Naldo wanted to be, if only to carry out C's special, most private, instructions.

They got Kruger's piece of information on the fifth evening. "It's a scent," the lad had said. "Just a tiny smell in my left nostril." He placed a long chubby forefinger beside his nose. "The man I talked to worked in Orléans. He came through DPW-14, one of the camps you mentioned—one in France. This man's name is Defoe—he made a joke about a book called *Gulliver's Travels*. I did not understand it." Herbie shrugged, his broad shoulders rippling. Naldo and Arnie sat waiting for more. "This Defoe worked as a cleaner, I think—"

"He was a cleaner at the SS HQ in Orléans? What nationality was he, Herb?"

"Difficult. Mixed blood. French and German. Father was French, I think."

"Sure it was Defoe? Not De Foe, or De Faux?" Naldo spelled out the variants.

"I didn't see it written down. He is displaced because of the two nationalities. The authorities cannot work out if he should be in France or Germany. He was originally brought from Germany, I think, to work in Orléans."

"I wonder?" Naldo said to nobody in particular.

"This is why he was trusted to clean around papers and things —you know how the SS and Abwehr were about locals working in their offices."

"What did he tell you, then, Herb?"—from Arnold.

"When he was in the French camp—DPW-14—this man said he was certain the former Orléans SS Commandant was there. Klaubert. Said he had dyed his hair black, but he was sure. Even spoke to him, and Klaubert said his name was Klausen. Told Defoe he was an *Unterscharführer* in the Norges Waffen SS—a Norwegian who had joined in 1941, like some of them did in occupied Europe. Defoe didn't believe him."

"I don't suppose he did." Naldo looked out of the window of the hut they called home. Lights burned along the regimented paths of the base. Shadows of men crossed and recrossed under the lights. In the distance was the city, almost unlit, just a few fires glowing in the streets where groups of men and women kept warm. The spring weather had not yet put heat into stones and pavements. "I think we should have a word with Defoe," he said. "If Herbie's correct, then it's off to France to find this Klausen."

Arnold sighed. "France isn't going to be that easy now the General's in charge. You never know who you're talking to." The BCRAM—Central Bureau for Information and Military Action —had been formed in London under General de Gaulle. Once France was liberated, the organization became top-heavy with agents and operators. It also became riddled with factions, both pro- and anti- British or American.

"It's okay. Nothing to worry about." Naldo cheerily left the hut, calm in the knowledge that C had given him at least six names, four in Orléans itself, who could be trusted to let them shuffle through the displaced and suspect prisoners and do the other job he had ordered.

Within the hour the man from the camp—whose name turned out to be Ernst de Faux—was seated in the *Symphony* team's hut, smiling happily after being fed sausages, potatoes, and a large glass of brandy. They gave him cigarettes as well and made the usual extravagant promises.

Yes, he said. Yes, the man claiming to be a Norwegian was Klaubert. He would stake his life on it. Of course he knew Klaubert, hadn't he seen him often enough? Hadn't he stood as close as this to him almost every day? The Norwegian was Klaubert, no doubt about it.

They took de Faux—a man of twenty-seven years who looked nearer forty-six—through his own story, testing his linguistic ability. He spoke both perfect French and German—the German with the singsong accent of Berlin. His mother was German, married to a French businessman who had offices in Berlin. Neither of them bothered much about politics—until it was too late. Charles de Faux had disappeared into the camps in 1939. His wife and son were given the chance to deny their French marital connections, and young Ernst was tested for a clerical job. "At heart I was French," he said. "I'm still French. All I want to do is be sent back there." In 1943 they told him there was an opening for a French-speaking clerk in Orléans. "I jumped at the chance, but what do you expect from those bastards? When I arrived they kept me in German barracks. I was employed as a cleaner. I dealt with the wastepaper from the offices and they told me to keep my ears open when locals were about and report back. I wasn't allowed to let anyone know I was half French."

Naldo asked the questions. Where was the headquarters? What did he know about the staff? Name some of the other officers? De Faux included Otto Buelow's name. Did the word *Romarin* mean anything to him? It did not. Could he recall an operation mounted against parachutists in the week of Sunday, 1st July 1944? He did—and gave the place and details. Did the name *Tarot* mean anything to him? It was a Resistance group. They were all caught and executed in the second week of July 1944. What did the man who called himself Klausen want? *Not* to be returned to Norway, that was for sure. Where *did* Klausen want to go? When de Faux told them, Naldo made up his mind.

It was all very pat, but certainly worth following up. They did not recommend that de Faux be returned to France for the time being, and the next day the three of them got a ride to the airfield nearest Orléans—on yet another Dakota.

THE SAFE HOUSE C had provided for them in the Rue Jeanne d'Arc, Orléans, was safe in name only. "They must call this a safe house because nobody's fool enough to come near it," Arnie said. The house was small—four rooms—set back from the street, which meant it had probably been in another street altogether. It leaned more drastically than the one Naldo had occupied in Berlin, and was surrounded by a clearing which sprouted old bricks and masonry.

Orléans had not only been subjected to the Royal Air Force raids but also to the thunder of shells from General Patton's advancing Third Army. Over a year later, the French—like their enemies in Munich—were picking up the pieces.

There was still a very small American presence in France—mainly Red Cross workers and Military Intelligence officers, helping those French who would accept their assistance. Through one of the Red Cross units, Naldo managed to telephone C in London and report progress, speaking in a double-talk he hoped C could follow, as the line was far from secure.

He returned to the Tower of Pisa, as they had christened the house, and gave Arnie instructions on how to get Herbie into the camp—which lay fifteen kilometers to the west. "You'll be taking a risk, Herb, but it's the only way," Arnold told the big German.

"All life is a risk. You take a risk being born; taking a crap, anything. It's all risk."

"Where's the risk in taking a crap, Herb?" Naldo asked.

"Like what I'm doing now." Herbie gave a huge boyish smile. "Dressing up in the rags of an SS officer and going in there is like taking a crap. You don't know who you're crapping on. The guy you crap on might be able to crap better on you. It's how life is."

Naldo turned away and smiled, covering his face. He went out, letting Arnold get on with the serious business of infiltrating Herbie into DPW-14.

At a quiet bistro he used the telephone and dialed one of the numbers C had given him. In his good French he asked for Inspecteur Joubert. They exchanged code words and Joubert set a time and place for a meeting. It was in four days' time. No, Joubert said, it could not be sooner. "We must be circumspect, my friend," he told Naldo, hanging up abruptly.

When Naldo got back to the safe house, Cherub was there, looking as deadly as ever and with Otto Buelow's evidence in the fat briefcase handcuffed to his wrist.

"The Chief says I have to sit with you like an invigilator until you've read it." He did not seem to have the usual muscles that would allow him to smile.

Arnold came in an hour later, nodding to Naldo. The nod implied that all had gone well. Herbie was now an inmate of the camp. Ways had been arranged so they could be told when he was ready to come out again.

Otto Buelow's evidence was straightforward and interesting. Both of them found it odd to read the transcripts so close to where the action had taken place.

A note, specially marked, said that Buelow had made an *exceptionally good impression* on the Board. *He gave evidence, and answered questions in a clear, concise manner; while the Service interrogators who had spent almost six weeks with him were of the opinion that he told the complete truth. Buelow is obviously a man of great intelligence.*

He began with a résumé of his life since the late 1930s, when he had first joined the Nazi Party. "I was a Nazi not out of conviction but from necessity," Buelow began. In the 1920s he had returned, with his wife-to-be, Mary Anne Railton—daughter of the late Charles Railton and therefore half sister to Jo-Jo Grenot. Back in Germany, they experienced the horrors shared by many of their contemporaries. "My country was financially bankrupt. One American dollar was worth two trillion Reichsmarks, so you can work matters out for yourselves. The Communist Party had a field day. I had returned to my country in the hope of helping to rebuild it. It was a losing battle. Many people like myself wanted some kind of stable democracy, but when Hitler came into power it was obvious the way things would go."

Either you joined the Party or took great risks if you wished to survive and live in some peace. Eventually Buelow applied for work within the Party—"With an English wife, it seemed more prudent to get into a job that would not keep me far from her side. But it was not long before our first separation, for I was posted to Munich."

Because he spoke English, Buelow found himself in the SD, that arm of the SS which became the Secret State Police, the Criminal Police, the Security Service, and the Secret Service. It was to the Secret Service that Otto Buelow was sent. "I worked directly under the orders of Reinhard Heydrich, who, of course, took his orders from Himmler."

Heydrich's Nazi Secret Service became a legend, as it was based mainly on British spy novels and the more sound principle of files and detail. "Heydrich's files were probably the most dangerous pieces of paper in the Reich," Buelow told them. "He had something on almost everybody. I believe that is why he was eventually given the prestigious appointment of Protector of Bohemia and Moravia—that, and the fact that certain people wanted him tucked away from the Führer's court. You must not forget that Heydrich was a true monster. A paradox. The man who wrote the draft plan for the extinction of the Jews; yet one who without doubt warned Jewish friends to get out of Germany in time—and, I suspect, often provided money and papers for them to make the exit across a frontier and not through one of the gas chambers." Buelow, the notes said, became very bitter. It was obvious that Heydrich had nauseated him.

"I saw him weep at music; heard him play music—beautifully; yet I also saw him condemn hundreds of people to death and chuckle over tidbits of information which could send a man to the gallows, or blackmail. He wanted me to go with him to Prague when he became Protector. I pleaded a need to stay in Berlin—which was where we worked by then. He was very kind to me, the monster. If I had gone with him, I could easily have been in his car on the morning of his assassination."

Heydrich was killed by a group sent into Czechoslovakia with the reluctant blessing of both SOE and the SIS. There was some talk that the team had originally gone in from England to bring an agent out, and when that failed they received permission to "execute" Heydrich. The SS were merciless to the Czechs after the assassination; at least one whole village—Lidice—was obliterated together with all its inhabitants.

"When Heydrich died, I was posted to Orléans in the January of 1944, after Mary Anne—after my wife—was killed by British bombers in Berlin. That was a terrible irony. I had taken such steps to protect her, and she died at the hands of her own countrymen. She was killed at a time when they were obviously moving anyone who had worked with Heydrich. As always in great bureaucracies, this takes a long while. They did not get around to moving me until the Christmas of 1943, and then it took only one day. Kaltenbrunner's adjutant came through the office, in which I worked with two other junior officers, and dropped some papers on my desk. I didn't look at them straightaway. When I did, I found I had been promoted to SS-*Sturmbannführer*—Major— and posted, as from 1st January 1944, to the small SD section directly responsible to Colonel Klaubert, head of the SS in Orléans. His reputation was known, even in my small office, in Berlin. The Devil of Orléans. I was sent on leave immediately. It was not the happiest Christmas I have spent."

On arrival in Orléans, Buelow found that Klaubert was on leave in Berlin. "I thought I had the authority to examine all the files," he told them. "What I found amazed me. Certainly, Klaubert had been ruthless—countless Jews had been sent away; a huge quota of men had gone to do labor service; Resistance groups and individuals appeared to have been wiped off the map. Then I came to this one file on a group known as *Tarot*. Klaubert's agents had all the evidence. Everything was there—codes, safe houses, leadership, and the names of all the members. He had all this, yet did nothing about it."

When Klaubert returned, Buelow asked him about the files. "Seldom have I seen a man so angry. He was furious with me. Said I should not have looked at any of the files and dossiers without his permission. I stood my ground and told him I found it odd that a known Resistance group was still allowed to operate in his area. He simply smiled and said, "I have a use for them all. Their time will come.""

"And their time *did* come," the SOE man said.

"Oh, yes. Yes. First we had the operation against the American parachutists. Then *Tarot*."

"Tell us about it."

Buelow added very little to what they already knew regarding *Romarin*, except for the advance warning. "We were informed of it during the afternoon. It happened that night. I was simply duty officer at headquarters. Klaubert went out with a section of Wehrmacht troops and some of his own people. They came back in triumph."

"And the following week you took *Tarot*?"

"Klaubert took *Tarot*. I was never involved. He said he would keep me in reserve."

"But you saw them?"

"Some of them. The men who were shot in the garden of headquarters. I knew other things were going on—there was a dreadful thing with one of the women, in the cells. They took her, the priest, and another man out of the town to execute them."

"And you had nothing to do with that?" the senior lawyer sneered.

"Of course. Of course I bear guilt, because I was there, with the SD. Some of my men actually took part in the rape. For some reason Klaubert kept me out of the way. But I'm not going to plead that I only obeyed orders, if that's what you think. Yes, I knew what was happening and it was horrible. Klaubert thought it necessary. I repeat, he also thought I should not be there. I cannot explain why."

"Two of the girls were taken from the headquarters in the Rue de Bourgogne by men described as SS officers."

"Yes. Klaubert gave the order that these two women were to go for what he termed 'special treatment' in Berlin. I did not see them and I don't know what the 'special treatment' was."

"Did you ask him?"

"Yes. He said they could be of use elsewhere."

"That's all?"

"That's all he said. When a man like Klaubert tells you something of that kind, you do not ask further questions."

"Did you see the officers again?"

"Oh, yes. They were two of the junior officers on our staff— Buchman and Stoltz. They merely handed the girls over to people who came from Berlin. They said the girls were friendly and had no fear—those were their words, 'The girls had no fear.' The men were at the railway station. Trains still went in and out even though the tracks were constantly being repaired because of the bombing. They were in civilian clothes, the men who took the girls away. I heard that."

"Mr. Buelow." The chairman did not use any military rank. "After the *Tarot* group had been dealt with, was there any significant change in Klaubert's routine?"

"Not that I recall. Except for the German-speaking informant."

"What was that about?"

"Until this Resistance group was liquidated, we all knew that Klaubert had his own special informers. He made jokes about it. He was a well-trained policeman really—always kept his informants out of the office. We knew he met them in secret—he met one on the afternoon before the parachutists came. There was a telephone call and he went out. When he returned he had all the information on the parachute landing. At first we thought it was part of some bigger strategic action connected to the landings in Normandy, but he said no, this was local, and to do with the Resistance. But after the group called *Tarot* was finished, one of the informants came to his office—many times he came."

"A local man?"

"I think not. He spoke German with an odd accent. He spoke French as well, but that was also with an unfamiliar accent."

"How often did he come?"

"Once, maybe twice a week. Klaubert said we should let him go straight to his office when he identified himself with a code word. The word was strange—'*Dreieck*.' In English this means a geometrical triangle."

"Can you describe the man?"

Buelow said he could, and when that was done, the chairman asked for a series of photographs to be passed to the witness.

"That's *Dreieck*—that's *Triangle*," Buelow said, pointing to one of the photographs with no hesitation.

A marginal note said, *The witness was positive. The photograph was that of Nathaniel Dollhiem of the Office of Strategic Services.*

17

▼

"I'LL HAVE TO tell my people about Dollhiem," Arnold said when they broke from reading. They were alone in the makeshift kitchen, boiling water for coffee on a primus stove. Cherub sat in the other room, curled like a spring and looking as though he was meditating on some new form of violence.

"*Your* people? Who the hell do you call *your* people, Arnie?" Naldo was usually a soft-spoken man, but now his voice rose as he turned, angry and taken by surprise.

"Strictly speaking I work for CIG—Central Intelligence Group."

"And C hired you from them. They're only a fucking committee, for Christ's sake! *This* you don't report to a committee."

Arnold looked at him bleakly. For the first time since they had worked on C's *First Folio* and *Symphony*, his eyes were cold and hostile. "They're more than a committee, Nald, and you know it. They've got a lot of men and women in the field. The job is to collate information, sure, but the old OSS order remains—case officers, agents in place, all the business of intelligence gathering, and a lot of the old tricks. They're running operations out there, Nald. Within the year Washington is going to sanction the birth of a very large intelligence service. It's going to make your SIS look like a Boy Scout troop."

"Washington has already turned down Wild Bill Donovan's plans. Wasn't that what *he* wanted—an all-seeing, all-hearing Service that would run a noose around the world—put a girdle round the earth? Wasn't that why he got sacked?"

"Partly. Empire building, they called it. Very heavy on the expenses. But he had enemies, you know. My guess is that CIG's going to whisper in the President's ear, and before you know it, Donovan's plans will be laid out and a new Service formed. In fact, I pretty well know that's what's going to happen."

"Well, it hasn't happened yet, and not a word of this should go back to your people—as you call them—until we've got more evidence. C hired you because of the U.S. involvement. C'll tell you when to talk. Until that day comes along, you keep silent, right?"

Arnie shrugged, unconvinced.

"C gives the orders. You may be with the CIG, but at the moment I gather you're being paid by SIS. I'd be grateful if you'd wait. Wait until we've got C's okay."

"As long as we *can* get his okay fast."

Back in the other room, with their coffee, they settled down to read the final pages of Buelow's transcript.

The Board had gone back, retracing the tortures and executions of those caught in the web of *Tarot*.

Then, out of the blue, the SIS officer asked, "What was he like? Klaubert, I mean."

"You have the photographs—tall, light hair, good-looking, scar on left temple, eyes—"

"No, Mr. Buelow. As a man. What was he like as a man?"

"A little like Heydrich. He could show immense charm, but beneath there was a most disturbing ruthlessness—not simply with prisoners, the Resistance, Jews, people to be sent to work in Germany. He was ruthless also with the men under him. A fairly minor misdemeanor was always treated with the maximum penalty. You could count on it."

"He showed no remorse?"

Buelow laughed, the transcript said. "He did not know the meaning of the word. Like Heydrich he signed death warrants and then went out and slept with the daughter of the family he had just condemned—I do not mean literally, of course."

"Sexual habits?" one of the junior lawyers asked.

"You know, I think he had a mistress."

"Yes. Hannalore Bauer—is that right?"

"It was right, yes. She had gone by the time I arrived in Orléans."

The chairman said they had no record of that.

"She went a year before the end. I never met her, and there were stories."

"What kind of stories?"

"The truth was difficult to discover. Also dangerous. I did not ask questions."

"What kind of stories?" the chairman repeated.

"One was unpleasant. Fräulein Bauer was supposed to have

followed him from Munich. He set her up in an apartment. It was said that he caught her there with a Frenchman, killed them both, and had the bodies taken care of."

"By his men?"

"It was a story, yes. Another was that she was killed in a daylight raid—an air raid; the Americans. Yet another was that they had a terrible fight and he killed her. The most popular was that he had her arrested and sent to the death camps—to Ravensbrück or Natzweiler. That was the favorite story."

The chairman said they would check what files they had on Ravensbrück and, for those who did not already know, Natzweiler was the first camp to be discovered—"By a Special Air Service team enquiring into the fate of some of their people. We also know that at least four women agents of SOE suffered truly terrible deaths at that awful place." He paused, as though reflecting on the fact that four young women had been virtually burned alive in the crematorium at Struthof-Natzweiler. Then, pulling himself together, he asked about Klaubert's sex life while Buelow was there.

"He had a woman, but she was kept well away—not like in the days of Fräulein Bauer. Nobody knew who she was, or where they met, but he disappeared sometimes for two days. She was French, we knew that. Some, of course, said she *was* the daughter of Resistance people who had been sent away. I think he fostered that rumor himself. He had a touch of the dramatic. As I say, like Heydrich he had contradictions. He would play gramophone records of the Mendelssohn violin concerto. As you know, Mendelssohn's music was banned because he was Jewish. Klaubert was a great contradiction."

Then they leaped forward to what the SIS man called "the last days."

The leading lawyer took up the questioning. "Mr. Buelow. This man you called *Triangle*. For how long did his visitations go on?"

"Quite a long time. Until about a week before our troops started to withdraw. Yes, about a week before."

"And the withdrawal, what about that?"

"We knew it was all over. The last-ditch offensive had failed. General Patton's Third Army was making incredible progress. It was like the Blitzkrieg in reverse. Some thought the Rhine would be a difficulty, but once the Allies started to roll, I knew it was the end."

"And you pulled out when the Wehrmacht withdrew?"

"Me in particular?"

"All of you—the whole shooting match—that's a reasonable description of your people."

"I stayed, as did two of my personal staff. Others broke and ran for it."

"Including Klaubert?"

"He left first. As soon as he had gone, they all drifted off— no, drifting's the wrong word. They dashed away."

"We have some evidence here that Klaubert just walked out one fine afternoon and did not return. Can you add to that?"

"I can add a great deal, yes. There had been Resistance fighters making a lot of trouble—troops machine-gunned from balconies, sporadic uprisings. They knew the end was in sight. Two days before the Americans arrived, I was ordered to burn all confidential files."

"And you did?"

"Naturally—it was an order."

"Then what?"

"That same afternoon—there was chaos, you must remember — Klaubert came into my office. He was in civilian clothes—"

"And that was unusual?"

"Very unusual." A marginal note said that Buelow smiled. "Klaubert was proud of his uniform. Most proud. Anyway, he told me that from now I was in charge. That I must stay at my post. 'You will fight to the end,' was what he said."

"And you didn't, Buelow, did you?"—from the OSS man.

"No. I disarmed everyone after I saw what Klaubert had done."

"And what was that?"

"He left the headquarters—in a gray suit, felt hat, and a thick overcoat—it was a very cold day. He carried a briefcase which looked heavy. I followed him to the corner of the street—at a distance, you must understand—and there was a car."

"What kind of car?"

"A French car. No plates. Dark blue. Klaubert got into the car and it drove away. I think it was the *Triangle* man at the wheel, and I had the impression there was a woman in the car, but I would not swear to it."

"And that was it?"

"The last I saw of Klaubert, yes. I surrendered, with dignity I hope, to the first American who came near. Already I had ordered white flags to be hung from the windows. The two men who stayed with me stood on either side and we surrendered correctly."

"And then?"

"Oh, marching many miles. Camps. Interrogations. More camps. Intensive interrogation, until someone told me I was to be taken to England."

"Were you badly treated?"

"No worse than I would have expected. To be truthful I expected to be shot immediately. Instead, I was fed and given warm clothing. Many of the interrogators were, naturally, hostile. Sometimes there was no food. Sometimes it was hard, but not as hard as I thought it would be."

They thanked him, saying he might well be recalled later.

Naldo and Arnold handed over the transcripts to Cherub, who nodded, leaving without a word to either of them, the briefcase locked and still chained to his wrist.

"Cheery little fellow, isn't he?" Arnold gave Naldo a wry smile, as though doing his best to repair whatever damage had been done by his confessed intention of passing on the Dollhiem connection to his American colleagues.

"Life and soul of the party." Naldo hesitated. Then—"Arnie, I know you've got to tell them, but later might be better than sooner. I've a job to do for C. Let me tell you about it—two, three days more, eh?"

"I'll wait for C's blessing."

"Good." If Arnie had wanted cheers and applause, Naldo wasn't giving any. "The enigma of Klaubert," the Englishman said. "Death on his shoulder and in his pen; a mistress who disappears; a man who might have been sleeping with a daughter of the Resistance; a lover of Mendelssohn; ruthless, but a breaker of laws by listening to the music of a Jew—music that was *verboten*—and who meets an informer who was part of *Romarin*."

"And drives away, maybe with him, and maybe with the mystery woman as well." Arnold spread his hands. "Then turns up as a Waffen SS man recruited in Norway. Sounds true to form, but I wonder what happened to *Triangle?* And the woman? If there ever was a woman."

"'A wilderness of monkeys,'" Naldo quoted.

"What?"

"Shakespeare. *Merchant of Venice*."

"You Railtons should have been in the business in Shakespeare's day." Arnold gave him a friendly punch on the shoulder.

Naldo looked serious. "We were," he said.

They had the use of a car, without driver, for a couple of hours each day, and took turns in going out to DPW-14 to look for the sign that Kruger wanted pulling out—a simple arrangement: a chalk mark on a wall.

There were no signs that Kruger wanted to get out by the time the fourth day arrived, and Naldo was ready for his meeting with Joubert, the police inspector.

He got to the bar where they had arranged to meet at five minutes after the appointed time. Joubert was a tall, thin, sad-looking man. He sat at a corner table with a newspaper laid exactly as their arrangements prescribed. At the moment Naldo arrived, he was balancing a piece of lump sugar on a fork and dribbling water through it into his Pernod.

"My old friend, how long has it been?" Naldo spoke the code in French and Joubert stood, letting his fork drop into the yellow cloudy mixture with a clatter.

"My God," he said. "You haven't changed at all. It must be six years—the entire war." This last meant everything was clear and there was nobody watching them.

Naldo ordered a Pernod for himself and followed Joubert's example with the sugar. "This is a great treat," the policeman said. "We now have sugar in quantity. When the Boche was here we had to hoard it—when we got any, which was not often."

They spoke in French, Naldo rapidly telling Joubert what he required.

"Yes." The inspector looked interested. "Yes, we found a few bits and pieces in the offices when we took over again. The entire place is to be renovated. You speak French with no English accent—more like someone from Paris. It's good."

"I had good teachers."

"I think you could pass for someone official—a civil engineer, come to survey the building. But the timing must be correct. If you come right at five minutes past one tomorrow afternoon, I shall be there, and the more senior officers will all be away. But it gives you half an hour, no more. Can you do that?"

Naldo nodded, and they discussed the minutiae, taking their time. At the end the Frenchman left first. "Give my regards to your Chief," he said, as though his relationship with C went back a long way—which it could well have done.

The following morning Naldo said he had things to do, would Arnie check DPW-14 for any signals? Arnold asked no questions.

At noon Naldo went looking around the shops that sold old

remnants left by families who had disappeared, or worse. In France you could buy a lot of second-hand goods in 1946.

Within half an hour he found the right thing—a very large, battered, and scuffed leather suitcase. At five past one he arrived at the Préfecture in the Rue de Bourgogne. A sergeant was at the desk, a cigarette stuck in the corner of his mouth.

"Yes?" The sergeant did not sound friendly.

Naldo explained that he was the civil engineer from Paris. "A preliminary survey," he said as though that explained it all.

"I know nothing about surveys." The sergeant eyed Naldo and the case which he carried as though it weighed a ton.

"I have had correspondence with an inspector..." Naldo carefully put down the case and took out a notebook, licking his finger and turning the pages briskly. "An Inspector Joubert."

"Then you're in luck, he's the only officer here." The sergeant cranked a large, old-fashioned telephone and got through to Joubert, who appeared in the entrance hall a minute or so later. Police in uniform came in and out—one with a suspect. Nobody paid any attention to Naldo, who greeted Joubert as a stranger, explaining his business.

Joubert looked at his watch. "Paris did not make it clear you were coming today." He spoke in a brusque manner as though there was no time for people from Paris.

"My boss comes next week," Naldo explained. "I need only a few minutes. I have to check the roof area."

"Nobody's been up there for years," the sergeant muttered. "There's a trapdoor on the fourth floor. I don't think they bothered when we took over again. You'll probably find skeletons, or SS officers hiding up there." He cackled as though this was a great joke.

"I'll have to risk it. You have a ladder?"

Joubert ordered the sergeant to see that a ladder was brought up to the fourth floor, then led the way, Naldo following, heaving the case as though it was almost too much for him.

A gendarme brought an old wooden ladder and propped it in the space between wall and trapdoor. Then Joubert sent him away. "You've got about fifteen minutes," he said softly. "No longer. I must get this ladder returned before anyone comes back."

Naldo nodded, asking him to steady the ladder for him. At the top the trapdoor was easily moved, as though it had been in regular use.

He looked down at Joubert and asked him to pass up the suitcase. "It's light. Nothing in it."

He pushed the suitcase up through the trap, slid a small flashlight from his pocket, and heaved himself into the low area under the roof of the building. The first thing he saw was a switch. He threw it, and three bulbs, hanging shadeless from the rafters, came on. Looking around, Naldo found he was in an Aladdin's cave. It took him ten minutes to load up the suitcase and another five to pass it down to Joubert, who had become edgy. Now the suitcase *was* very heavy.

As they went down the stairs again, Naldo talked loudly, saying it looked in reasonable condition up under the roof, and that he would submit his report. The real survey would be done during the following week—as Joubert had told him it would be, the day before in the bar.

It took Naldo almost an hour to get back to the Tower of Pisa.

Arnold sat in the main room with young Kruger.

"Missed him," Kruger offered. "The bird has flying."

"Has flown," Arnold corrected.

"Last night I saw him. Today, gone."

Naldo dumped the case on the floor. "Is it Klaubert?"

"No question. Like there's no question he's gone, and no question about where he's gone. We missed him by a week. The 'Norwegian' got his wish. They sent him to a camp in the Eastern Zone—the Russian Zone. Berlin." Kruger smiled and laughed. "They were really thinking the Russians would give him a very bad time of it. It was done with great malicious."

"Malice, Herb."

"Yes, done with great malice. They say that now he will be dead. Very slowly."

"I doubt it." Naldo sprang the locks on the case. Inside was a Paraset transmitter, used by SOE "pianists." "It was in the loft at what used to be SS headquarters," he explained. "And the 'one-time pads,' giving him and his 'home' operator a different cipher for each day. *Descartes*' pads, I believe."

"The Orléans Russians?" Arnie asked, expecting no answer. Then—"There's only one thing to do."

"Yes." Naldo was a long way ahead of him. "Herbie, how would you like a trip into the East? Into the Russian Zone—Berlin?"

"Depends on what I have to do."

"C will tell us and we'll tell you."

Kruger nodded his big head like a young Buddha. "Okay by me if the Chief says I go."

"Oh, he'll tell you to go." Naldo looked hard at Arnie, who also nodded and said, "We can only hope for a quick result."

But there was no quick result.

C closed down *Symphony* a few days after the team got back into London—on the day following a private interview with Naldo, who told him of Arnold Farthing's determination to report the Dollhiem business to his superiors.

"For the time being, Naldo, *Symphony's* finished—as far as young Farthing's concerned anyway." He gave Naldo a slow wink. "Let the Yanks do some of our work for us, eh?"

Naldo opened his mouth to speak, but C continued—

"You and Kruger'll carry on. If we need Arnold again I can tug at the odd string. In the meantime we brief the Kruger boy in a couple of days. He can be in the Eastern Zone next week. Then all we can hope for is that he'll hit his mark with some speed."

But Kruger's work in the Russian Zone took twelve months before it bore any fruit, and by that time many things had changed—for instance, the CIA was born, out of the CIG, by the OSS.

As was the reorganization of what was to become the KGB, out of blood, by the NKVD.

PART TWO

▼

THE GERMAN HOUSES

18

▼

By the summer of 1947 Arnold Farthing was well established as part of the embryo Central Intelligence Agency, based at that time in a confusion of offices scattered across Washington, D.C. The word "Central" was almost a joke with some operatives of the Agency, because people had trouble finding out who occupied which office, and where.

Arnie boasted a room only slightly larger than a walk-in closet, situated within one of the old prefabricated huts which had stood throughout the war near the Reflecting Pool and alongside the Lincoln Memorial. The view from the window was spectacular—part of the pool and the whole stone finger of the Washington Monument—but this did nothing to relieve Arnie's irritated feeling that his time was being wasted.

Technically Arnie was a field agent. Yet all he had done so far was sit in the little office studying confidential documents, or walk the streets and parks of Washington, being put through his paces by Roger Fry, the agent who had wooed him in Munich and was now his case officer, and who insisted on practicing all the arcane routines of tradecraft by staging meetings, running little surveillance operations, and acting out scenarios similar to the ones they had used in training during the war.

It was early June before Arnie found himself in tenuous touch with *Symphony* again, and almost July before he actually got back into the field.

For Arnie, the hanging around was more than normally frustrating, for he had been welcomed into the Agency with an open-armed, back-slapping show of pleasure and, in an attempt to cooperate, he had talked a great deal about Nathaniel Dollhiem and his suspicious part in the *Romarin*—and *Tarot*—business.

First he spoke, long and openly, to Fry; then to the tall, thin, academic-looking man who ran Counterintelligence. Together, the three of them went through the evidence—first in general, then later in great detail.

"And how did you come by all this interesting information, Arnie?" the head of Counterintelligence asked him.

"Family connections, mainly." Arnold explained his links with the Railtons and hinted that it had been "hard intelligence talk" within the Railton family.

James Xavier Fishman, head of Counterintelligence, nodded, giving him a sidelong look indicating he did not believe a word of it. "You picked it up when we loaned you to the Brits, didn't you, Arnold?" It did not even sound like a question; more a statement of fact. "There was an investigation into the *Romarin* debacle, wasn't there? You saw or heard it all, then some. Am I right, Arnold?"

Farthing heaved a sigh and nodded quickly, unwilling to tell too much.

"That wasn't hard, was it?" Fishman smiled. "No need to be shy. We appreciate your loyalty, particularly family loyalty. But we have to be sure of our ground."

Arnold nodded again, then began to talk. Altogether he thought he had probably helped them a great deal. Nat Dollhiem had been known to a lot of people in the old OSS ranks. Now, through Fishman, some of those people had verbal evidence that he was probably a Communist, and worse—he was a Communist who was somehow mixed up with a particularly brutal Nazi war criminal. All this added up to a great contradiction, but the head of Counterintelligence was used to such things in the labyrinth of mirrors that was his work. Somewhere, Arnie figured, there were people out tracing Nat Dollhiem's movements from the *Tarot* connection to Orléans and onward. They might even be looking for Dollhiem himself.

On the first Friday in June, Fry sent a coded message by courier to Arnold Farthing's little office. They would meet, that afternoon, at a prearranged spot—in East Potomac Park, near the Jefferson Memorial.

While Arnold was built like a football player, with a nose to match and a walk which could sometimes be called aggressive, Roger Fry was of a very different build: slim and lithe, with a manner that made you think of an unleashed charge of electricity. He was a good three inches shorter than Arnold, and favored a style of clothing which marked him as a dandy. He had long discarded the steel-rimmed spectacles sported in Germany, and this year he had taken to wearing colorful vests, even in the hottest weather. He was wearing a bright yellow one with brass buttons that afternoon as he waited in the park, one hand behind him, the fist clenched hard against the small of his back—the body language which told Arnold that he could be approached safely.

Arnie slid a hand into his right jacket pocket: his sign that he was not being followed.

"Let's walk," Fry said after they had gone through the formality of shaking hands—two friends bumping into one another by accident. Roger Fry set great store by these little rituals and, to tell the truth, Farthing was slightly in awe of him.

Though Fry was Farthing's senior by only three years, that trio of summers was important in the Agency's pecking order. Roger Fry was second-in-command within CA, which made him one of the "Knights Templar," as the top Agency brass were known. Most of the Knights Templar were also the "Founding Fathers." The Agency was already working hard to build its own mystique.

Fry had a leathery face with a small white scar running down his right cheek and another at the base of his chin, tracing down the throat, legacies of close combat while with a "Jedburgh" team of OSS guerrillas in Nazi-occupied Norway. His hair was short, brown, and curly close to the scalp, giving him an odd, womanish appearance from the back, but there was nothing feminine about him, as his current girlfriend—assistant to a high-powered legal adviser at State—could attest.

Now, as they walked along the path in the heat of the afternoon, Fry looked up at Farthing with cold gray eyes. "Jim Fishman's run friend Dollhiem to earth," he said quietly.

"*What?* Where?"

"Where do you look for an ear of corn, Arn? He's here."

"In Washington?"

"In Washington and in the Agency, both." Fry stopped talking as they passed some kids flying a kite.

"But he was reported missing—"

"Wrong." Fry's voice was dry, as though he was coming down with a throat infection, another permanent reminder of his wartime throat injuries.

"Everyone assumed he was missing." Fry spoke of Dollhiem again. "Fishman's run his eyes over the documents. Dollhiem's got a good story, Arnie. No wonder the politicians and the FBI have a beef about our security. The old OSS security was bad enough, and we've inherited it. Jim Fishman's doing a war dance; thinks he can shoot Dollhiem's story full of holes. He's convinced the guy's Red as they come; that he's a penetration agent."

"The story?" Arnold asked. He realized that he was sweating heavily in the heat. Fry, complete with vest, appeared cool and unruffled.

"He was liberated by the Russians, would you believe? Told all about *Romarin* and how he walked away from *Tarot*. Covered himself nicely—said he'd considered staying on at St. Benoît, then changed his mind."

Apparently Dollhiem claimed that he had worries about the security within *Tarot*—also wanted to go it alone, saying he mistrusted Tert Newton. He walked off and was captured by the Germans within two days. In the report he said that he had expected to be shot, but they thought he was worth interrogating when they looked at his dog tags.

"Should have been shot." Fry cleared his throat. "He was in civilian clothes. But they moved him East. Liberated in March '45 by the advancing Russians, who sent him back. If he *is* doubling, the cover's good. Medical reports show he was in a bad way. They broke his fingers during the interrogation, and his body was well bruised, undernourished, cracked ribs, the usual kind of thing. He was flown to Frankfurt, then home—repatriated, debriefed, and released from the Service. In January—this year—Administration recruited him again. He's been working in Special Support, on the German Desk, since then. Got a neat little house near Mount Vernon Square. Even brought his wife here. Nat Dollhiem's a little hero."

"And nobody thought to look under our noses?" Farthing's brow wrinkled, his eyes narrowing with anxiety.

"Nobody even tried to get corroboration. Nat's story is his own. No witnesses, no backup. They just accepted it, in Frankfurt and then here. He looked as if he'd been through hell and back, that was enough. No tears, no fuss, hooray for us."

"What do we do, sweat him?"

"No, we watch him. Fishman's had him coralled, so he sees nothing sensitive. But we watch him for possible contacts. That's going to be your job. Quiet surveillance. I'll point you and you do a report by the end of the month—habits, friends, chinks in the armor, all that stuff. He mustn't be frightened off. If he is what Fishman thinks, then it could be years before we can pin him down. There'll be a good safe team on him once you've done your report."

"Can I see his file?"

"It'll be with you tomorrow."

"What about the Brits?"

"What *about* the Brits? No cause to tell them anything. If he is a 'True Bill,' as the Brits would say, we don't want them screaming damnation or knowing that our security's screwed up."

Arnie nodded sadly. There were many things he did not like about the business. In the far reaches of his mind he had already decided they should lift Dollhiem as soon as possible: lift him and sweat him. To hell with trying to bait a trap for some Russian controller.

He was even more certain on the following day, after reading the heavily restricted file on Dollhiem—identified, on paper, only by the cryptonym *Screwtape*. The story seemed watertight, even down to naming the various German units that picked him up and passed him on; identifying his interrogators; detailing the questions they put to him—mainly concerning SOE and OSS operations in train following the D-Day invasion; the types and strength of units, and their orders regarding various Resistance groups.

His description of SS and Gestapo methods was vivid, but without actually saying it, Nat Dollhiem managed to convey that he had withstood the inquisitions and given nothing away. Certainly the medical evidence from those who treated him in Frankfurt was beyond doubt, but Arnie was intrigued to note that while he could give clear evidence of his captors, he made no mention of his saviors apart from the fact that they were Russian. No units, no names, nothing that could lead back in that direction.

At the end of the file he detected James Fishman's most recent work, a fast but profound dig into the subject's pre-OSS days. The head of Counterintelligence had turned over several stones, including the fact that Dollhiem had been a card-carrying member of the Communist Party during his last year at UCLA, and still apparently kept in touch with friends from those days.

So, Arnold thought, he was not going into the jungle blind. People from Counterintelligence had already been there before him: mail read before delivery, maybe they had even managed to listen in on his telephone conversations—after all, the technicians had come up with a number of small listening devices in the last few years.

Fry marked Dollhiem for Arnold—the two of them loitering near a bus stop as the stocky little man came out of his office on 6th Street. Naturally he now looked considerably older than the photograph. The face was puffy, while folds of flesh bagged under his eyes, and when he unbuttoned his jacket his gut hung over his belt in a sagging pot. Nobody would have taken Nat Dollhiem for an Office of Strategic Services hero. An out-of-town hick lawyer, possibly. He had a pasty dullness about his face, while the careless manner he appeared to adopt fingered him as a country boy trapped in error by a relentless city.

Dollhiem did not appear to use a car—cabs, buses, the railroad, but more often his feet, so Arnold Farthing found himself using street surveillance techniques. Within two weeks Arnie Farthing knew the strange outward pattern of the man's life. Dollhiem with his desk job at Special Support was like any ordinary government employee: he worked regular hours; left home the same time each morning, and returned at the same time most nights. But outside that working routine, the man observed what they called field rules.

Arnie was 99 percent certain that Nat Dollhiem had no idea that he was under surveillance, yet he behaved like someone who could well be the subject of scrutiny. Over the two-week period, Arnold established that he went out, after working hours or on weekends, five times a week—on Saturday and Sunday with his wife, and alone for three evenings during the week. Tuesdays, between eight and ten, he would visit the bar of the fashionable Shoreham Hotel, along Rock Creek Park. Thursdays he dined at a small French restaurant in Georgetown—arriving at seven-thirty and leaving around ten. Friday nights he haunted a bar in the downtown shopping area, usually leaving late. He was mean with tips, as well as in using public transport, and he drank the cheapest beer, sometimes laced with raspberry juice. "That's an old Berlin concoction," Fishman said when reading the report. "Nobody drinks it nowadays."

The pattern was there, but Dollhiem took immense pains to evade anyone likely to follow him. Arnold, equipped as he was with a CIA cab always near at hand, was able to keep up with his subject. But Dollhiem would play all the tricks, sometimes on foot, as often as not by cab, changing cabs three times or more for a relatively short journey; doubling back; entering a bar or restaurant, then leaving within five or ten minutes; changing his mind about which direction he wished to go. These rituals were always different, using an infinite variety of imaginative devices, yet he always ended up in the same places, on the same evenings, at the same time.

In short, as Arnold wrote in his report, *Screwtape behaves like an agent in place; we can only assume that is exactly what he is.*

There were no signs that he spotted me, but all the hallmarks are of a man taking great care.

Fry grunted at the report and said, "Old habits die hard."

"Not the way this joker goes about it." Arnold had peppered his paper with hints that Dollhiem should be given an enema straightaway—cleaned out with a short sharp shock. He was quite prepared to join the inquisition and put certain half-sure facts to the man—that he had been in constant touch with Klaubert in Orléans after *Tarot* had been blown; that he had driven Klaubert away on the day the SS man had left for the last time. He would even lie and say there was indisputable evidence in London.

Farthing said all this aloud to James Fishman and Roger Fry during the following week.

"You have nothing that'll really stick." Fishman drew in on a cigarette.

"If we go to the Brits we can sick it on him." Arnold was angry and out for blood. "They have at least one man—Buelow —who's willing to identify our subject as an informer who visited SS HQ in Orléans many times after the fall of *Tarot*. I think he'll also finger him as Klaubert's driver when he left."

Fishman gave a wry smile. "And you think we'll get a confession out of him? If he's the man I think he is, then it'll take more than a former Nazi officer's word to make him sing. This guy's got a lot of guts. If your theory, which is probably the Brits' theory as well, *is* correct, we're dealing with one hell of a tough cookie. Dollhiem's a man who allowed himself to be starved, beaten, have his ribs cracked and his fingers broken to establish *bona fides* and get back to America and into the Agency. You think he's just going to do an about-face when we hit him with what we've got? Or what you say we can get, Arnie."

"But we might have to wait for years—"

"So?" Roger Fry's voice sounded more arid than ever.

Fishman raised a hand in a gesture of protest. "You say there were no contacts while you watched him, Arnie?"

"None. I'm sorry, I guess I'm bushed after the past two weeks."

"Sure." Fishman nodded. "We've got a twenty-four-hour surveillance on him now, and to tell you the truth, those teams were filling in for you when you went off at night. Some of them even worked with you, watching your back. They tell me there have been several possibilities of contact."

"When? Not while I was on station."

"Yes. The same cab picked him up twice in your two weeks. You missed that, Arnie. There was also a girl he talked with at the Shoreham. Two minutes thirty-two seconds, my guys logged it. Nothing was passed, but they spoke. You came in a minute later—quite rightly giving him a chance to get settled. There'll be someone on his neck the whole time now."

"Take a couple of days' rest, Arn." Fry took on a protective tone. "I'll sign you out of the office and call you when we need you back."

Farthing's irritation was worse now that Fishman had caught him out in some sloppy surveillance. He left with a nod and a grunt, driving back to the little house in Georgetown that his family had owned for almost a century and passed on to him for use now that he was in Washington.

It was comfortable but lonely. He thought of Naldo in London with his Barbara, realizing he was jealous—not specifically of Naldo and Barbara, but of all lovers, irrespective of age or status. His last affair had been in London, before the D-Day invasion. She had been a Brit, a Women's Auxiliary Air Force officer. It had been a roaring, passionate business which started over a weekend and went on until he left London after the last German offensive—the Battle of the Bulge. Weekends, telephone calls, letters, one whole seven-day leave together. Then just the occasional letter. They had not broken it off in any formal sense, but events overtook them, severing whatever had held them together. Now, as he paced his cozy living room, Arnold had to think hard to remember her name, and in the remembering of it—Faith Kirk—he realized that if you had to do that after a year or so, there could not have been much in it after all.

Drunk with fatigue, he went up to bed and dropped so deeply into sleep that when the telephone rang he knew it had been calling to him for a long time.

Fry's dusty voice came into his ear. "Six o'clock at the Statler," Fry said.

Arnold nodded and almost replaced the receiver before he realized he had not even acknowledged. "I'll be there," he grunted. Six o'clock at the Statler really meant three o'clock at a chosen point on the old promenade along the Potomac in southwest Washington. His watch told him it was already one-thirty. Outside, the sun shone and all was well with the world.

Fry had changed his vest. This one was light blue and matched his tie. "The Brits want you again," he said as they stood looking out over the river.

"Who exactly?"

"Their Chief of Service—C."

"And do I go?"

"You go for us, Arnie. Jim Fishman and the Director want to brief you, and I'll be handling things if and when you need me."

"Will they know I'm there in a covert capacity?"

Fry paused. "We'll let them come to their own conclusions. You leave tomorrow and we start the briefings at six tonight."

"Can I refuse?"

"On what grounds?" Fry sounded startled.

"On the grounds that I'm still damned tired." Arnie laughed. "But don't worry, I'll go on any terms."

"Want to nail *Screwtape*, huh?"

"Yes, but there's a girl I know in England, name of Faith Kirk." Arnie smiled, and the long-forgotten lines of a poem—he thought it was Tennyson—came into his head—

> *The shackles of an old love straiten'd him,*
> *His honour rooted in dishonour stood,*
> *And faith unfaithful kept him falsely true.*

19

▼

A<small>RNOLD</small> F<small>ARTHING</small> <small>LIFTED</small> the hideous pink imitation-marble clock from the mantelpiece, cocked an eyebrow, and replaced the chunky elaborate timepiece dead center, under the beveled-edged pink-tinted mirror. "The old place hasn't changed one bit." He turned to Naldo, who nodded.

"So what brings us together?" Arnold was tired from the flight, in TWA's noisy, bumpy, and brand-new Lockheed Constellation. It had taken only sixteen hours from New York.

Naldo had met him and driven around for an hour before bringing him to the Northolt house. The door had been opened by a pretty young redhead, a girl of crisp efficiency who served him breakfast and showed him to a bedroom. Arnie slept for nine hours, waking to find Naldo and Herbie in the house. The redhead had disappeared.

"Wait for C," said Naldo.

In the corner, Herbie Kruger, who had remained silent after welcoming Arnold with a great bear hug, began to sing quietly, the voice extraordinarily well developed for a boy of sixteen, *"O glaube, mein Herz, es geht dir nichts verloren."*

"Herb?" Naldo queried.

"This is part of the final chorus in Mahler's Second Symphony." Herbie looked surprised, as though they should recognize both tune and words. "In English it means 'Have faith, my heart, for naught is lost to thee.'"

Naldo looked at Arnold and raised an eyebrow, inclining his head toward young Kruger.

"I have become very interested in the music of Mahler," Herbie continued. "In Berlin I have a winding gramophone—it is old and the music comes from a big green trumpet—but there are few records of Mahler's work available. I listen all the time to what I have. He was the greatest composer ever, I believe. The music helps me much. It helps me to remain calm—like a baby in the womb."

"In Berlin?" Arnold looked first at Naldo and then Herbie. "So you put him in, Naldo?"

"Wait for C, Arnie."

"Like hell. Come on, Naldo—what's going on?"

"Please wait for the Chief." Naldo sounded very British—the old school, trained for ruling an Empire which the Socialist Government appeared to be hell-bent on scattering to the four winds.

"Well, you can at least tell me what happened to your Uncle Caspar. Did they shoot him at dawn or drum him out of the regiment? What did that damned silly Board of Enquiry finally decide?"

"What did you expect it to decide? They did what everyone knew they'd do—left it all hanging in the air. The Board was dismissed until further evidence became available. Which means they didn't want to make up their minds. Poor old Caspar wanted to resign from the Service but can't do that now."

"Why? The dreaded finger of suspicion?"

"Exactly. If he resigns they'll all say, 'No smoke without fire.' Thought you'd have known that in your super, modern, and efficient Agency."

"Look, Nald, the Agency has its own problems—security, inexperience, and the FBI to name but eight of them. Come on now, what's going on here?"

Naldo Railton shrugged. "*Symphony*'s going on. C wants the whole team working together again."

"And you've been following up where we left off?"

Naldo nodded, a slow movement as if he was reluctant to admit anything.

"Tell me, then."

Silence reached out between them. Then—

"When you went back to the States we put Herbie into the Russian Zone. I shuttled between Berlin and London. Both Herb and myself were invisible as far as your people, and our own Berlin Station, were concerned. At least we managed to do that, thank heaven. It's not good over there. Things're deteriorating fast, Arnie. You know that."

"Sure I know it. The foreign ministers' conference in Moscow was just a long stream of stinking air. A fart. The Ivans and the West can't agree about the German problem. I guess the Ivans'll eventually draw a line somewhere."

"Or the shooting'll start all over again." Naldo was serious.

"Berlin is an island," Kruger said, but nobody took any notice, except perhaps Arnie who registered that the lad's English had improved and he was starting to fill out, looking healthy and well-nourished. It would be difficult to pin down the boy's exact age.

In London, Naldo had reported regularly to C. In Berlin he ran Herbie, who had been successfully infiltrated into the East and carried documents which allowed him to move from zone to zone with little difficulty. Between them they searched for clues that might lead to Klaubert.

"The Devil of Orléans could be in Russia by now, for all we know," Naldo said. "Only common sense tells C that they'll keep him near home, within East Germany—probably in Berlin. Me? I'm not so sure."

Herbie had played a complex game—giving the impression that he was working in the West and living in the East, or, at other times, vice versa. He had a room in both zones, under the same name, and facilities to set up crash meetings with Naldo. Apart from that they met regularly twice a week—always on different days and at irregular times. Herbie knew the many faces for which he was searching; he was also starting to make new friends in the East.

"Herb called for a crash meeting in early June. That's why C asked for you to come back. He doesn't want to bring anyone else into the circle. It's still very much his op, and he seems to trust few people these days."

Early June, Arnie thought. That's just about the time Counter-intelligence found Dollhiem in our midst. "He doesn't want anyone else in on *Symphony?* What about the redhead, the luscious lady who made my breakfast?"

"She's a housekeeper. Keeps the safe house fiction going when it's not in use. She's one of C's wise monkeys—hears nothing, sees nothing, says nothing. Answers to the name of Ophelia."

"So, about this crash meeting with Herb?"

"I was thoroughly shaken with what Herbie had to tell me." Naldo fidgeted. "I think C should talk about it, not me. I'm biased. I came back to London immediately, talked long with C, and then returned to Berlin. Arranged things so that Herbie could be temporarily unzipped from his routine without people paying much attention. You'll get the full picture from C, but there's a lot of danger ahead if C's going to continue pursuing Klaubert."

It was obvious that Naldo was not going further.

"Thanks." Arnold grinned. "I've got a bit of news for C myself. Don't know if my people want me to talk about it, but I will."

He told them about Dollhiem as soon as C arrived, before the head of SIS could begin talking about *Symphony*. When he got to the decision that Dollhiem should be left in place, as a stalking horse to cut out a larger prize, C flushed scarlet with anger.

"Why haven't your people told *me* anything about this?" It was a question delivered to the air, not specifically to Arnold Farthing, even though he was the only person who could answer it.

"Saving face, I guess. No intelligence service likes people to know it's got a penetration agent in place."

"I'll bet. Got him boxed in, have they?"

"Well boxed, sir."

"Small mercies, small mercies. Well, young Farthing, I suppose we'd better fill in the blanks for you, join up the dots, eh?"

"When I left, you were proposing to send Herbie into the Russian Zone—"

Naldo gave him a look of gratitude.

"So we were. Indeed we were. And what conclusions did you draw from that, Arnold?"

Arnie thought for a moment. "That you believed the brutal Klaubert had been playing both ends against the middle. That *Tarot* had a dedicated Communist on the inside who gave him information and led the *réseau* astray. That Klaubert was also an agent planted—maybe years before—within the SS. That Klaubert was one of the so-called Orléans Russians your listeners picked up. That, at the last, he spirited the Russian agent out of *Tarot*—either when he pulled them in, or after. That Dollhiem was an agent for the Russians inside the OSS. That Dollhiem helped Klaubert to get out and back to his masters—probably with the *Tarot* traitor—"

"Who was possibly a woman, yes. Well done, though it wasn't difficult once Naldo had found the wireless in the old SS HQ in Orléans. So where do we go from that point, Arnie?"

"If you're still thinking of finding Klaubert, you go East, I guess. Herbie was sent to look for him. Right?"

C nodded. "Him or anyone else with connections, yes."

"He found him?" Farthing asked.

"No." C clamped his lips together. "No, not him. But he found somebody."

•   •   •

It had been toward the end of May when young Kruger saw him first, and on that occasion he was uncertain whether it was him or not.

At that crash meeting in the first week of June, he had leaned forward, as though about to impart some great secret to Naldo.

"In the East it's worse than here, you must understand," he said. They were in a safe flat in one of the few streets left standing near the Ku-damm. Streets were still being cleared, unsafe walls brought down, rubble being sifted and carted away. Already building had begun, but water and electricity had not yet been fully restored throughout the whole of the city. There was dust everywhere, but that was true of the whole of Berlin at the time.

Dust and the thin tattered curtains blowing in the breeze through the open window of the safe flat, with its large old German furniture and an oil painting of somewhere that looked like the Wannsee hanging above the bed.

"I try often to walk somewhere near to the military headquarters—in Karlshorst," Herbie said. "This was where I first saw him. He was in uniform. A colonel. NKVD. I have done my learning well, Naldo, yes? I can tell ranks and know the uniforms. I thought it was him, but not for certain.

"So I keep my eyes open and wait." Herbie gave a big smile. "I know a girl who has work in the barracks—in Karlshorst. Typing she does. Typing for the Russian military police and NKVD. Maybe she'll give me a little something in time—who knows? I think I will get the name from her if necessary."

"That's good, Herbie."

Kruger smiled, very happy with the small praise. "Two days later I see him again. This time by accident. He is in a car—military car—sitting in back looking at papers. I get only a fleeing glips—"

"Fleeting glimpse, Herb."

"*Ja*, yes, so. A fleeting glimpse. This time I'm pretty sure. But still not certain. Not one-hundred-percent sure. I see the girl who works for them. We go for a walk together—it is Sunday—and I say if she wants chocolate or stockings or anything I can get them possibly. I let her know I have American friends. She likes this and we have a good time together, you understand? We— well, we. . . . In an old house scheduled for demolition—you understand?"

"You made love, Herb. Most natural thing in the world. No need to be shy about it."

"For me only the second time. For her, I don't know. It is good and she says she likes me a lot—her name is Helene Schtabelle. Her parents are dead from the Russians. I think her mother was raped and shot—maybe Helene also raped, so many were; but she is there and she must work, so she does good work for them. I ask her if there is any new NKVD officer arrived at headquarters—"

"And she told you?"

"No. She says she will discover it for me. So I keep watching and then I see him in daylight and with no uniform. He is in a car with the window open. The car is parked near where the zone changes from Russian to American—you know how sometimes they have sudden checks on people crossing one zone to the other?"

Naldo nodded but said nothing.

"He was watching as soldiers did the checking. He took much interest, as though looking for someone. Over there they arrest people often if they don't think the papers are in order."

"They do it in all the zones, Herb."

"But there it seems more—how do you say it—sinister? Yes, more sinister, like the Gestapo or the SS. In the war when they come and knock at the door you know it is someone's big trouble —well, usually."

"And you recognized him this time?"

"Oh, for sure, Naldo. For sure from the photographs it is him. And I see my Helene the next day. She tells me, so that settles it."

"Who?" Naldo Railton asked calmly.

"The Russian from England; from your family. He is Colonel Gennadi Aleksandrovich Rogov, second-in-command NKVD Russian Zone, Berlin. Your family, Naldo, your uncle's brother, yes?"

"Yes." Naldo's throat had become a desert and his hands trembled. Ramillies Railton, Caspar's long-missing brother, was so near to where they sat, yet a million miles away.

C allowed Naldo to tell at least a version of the Ramillies Railton story, to put Arnie in the picture. Now C spoke. "Rogov could be a little lever. He could be of use, Arnold. You follow me?"

"Oh, my God!" Arnold was genuinely concerned. "Don't tell me we're going to lift him."

"That's exactly what we're going to do." C's smile would have melted thick ice, yet nobody else in the room looked happy about it. "Yes, eventually we'll lift him, but we must have more on the man." Hardly pausing for breath, C asked Herbie to go and make some tea. "You make good tea, Herbie," he said, and the big youth smiled a daft smile that covered his own knowledge. Herbie knew they wanted to be alone, to talk about this Englishman, Ramillies Railton, whom he had spotted near what used to be the Unter den Linden. Odd that so many of the old linden trees had survived.

"We must make a new study of Ramillies Railton," C said, speaking softly. "Any ideas, Naldo?"

20

▼

"So HOW OLD is this asset of young Kruger's?" C looked at Naldo, his whole face softening, as though Naldo Railton was his nearest and dearest friend.

The old devil, Arnie thought, he's going to pull the strings and make Naldo do everything. Herbie and Naldo.

"Helene Schtabelle. Age twenty. Berlin born and bred. Orphan. She probably went through the mill, like all women in Berlin before the Yanks—begging your pardon, Arnie—and ourselves took over the other sectors." He did not even bother to mention the French, whose Berlin zone was small and did not count for much. Helene had stayed in the Russian Zone. She was already an efficient secretary. Naldo sketched it all for them. "She worked in Goebbels' Propaganda Ministry until the last days. No love for the Nazis, and certainly none for the Ivans. Clever, good looks—blonde, slim features, good figure. Has a room somewhere off the old Alexanderplatz. There are still some solid houses standing in that area. We've nothing on her. Looks clean as a whistle." It was all committed to memory, Arnold noticed; nothing on paper. The Agency would have had a dossier thick as a telephone directory.

"Mmmm," C mused. "What about Kruger? You think he's ready for it?"

"He'll need more than one asset if you're thinking of surveillance, sir."

"Yes, yes, of course he will. I'm thinking out loud."

"We need to know more—" Naldo began.

C sighed. "Of course we need to know more. Your Uncle Ramillies went into Russia on October 14, 1918, on instructions from the then C, and with guidance from his grandfather, Giles Railton. We had people there for a long time after that—it's all in the history books, Donald." The Chief was annoyed, nobody ever called Naldo by his proper name.

"What *isn't* in the history books, sir?" Naldo seem unperturbed.

"You know some of it yourself. You've never seen the file. *I* have, and when we got the sighting during the war—Rogov with the NKVD agents destined to be dropped into Germany—it wasn't much of a surprise. The file fills in some of the blanks. Your kinsman is a survivor, Naldo. He went in knowing he would not come out—not on our side anyway. He's served the Cheka —or the NKVD, OGPU, NKGB, MGB, MVD, or whatever they've called it over the years—since the end of 1918. That is no mean feat. He must be a very experienced and respected officer. He's really part of the history of the Revolution; served under the Cheka's founder, old Iron Felix Dzerzhinsky himself. That must make him a figure of some awe, especially as he's avoided the purges, worked under Yakov Peters, Menzhinsky, and now that bastard Beria—who must be a load of fun, especially as he appears to control the entire shooting match—Intelligence and Security."

Naldo nodded, as though agreeing with C. He had only a sketchy idea of the NKVD's history. Only the names of Dzerzhinsky and Beria were familiar to him. "We know he did a recruiting drive in the 1930s"—Naldo was talking of his Uncle Ramillies again—"and that he came over when SOE gave assistance to dropping their people into occupied Europe—"

"My dear fellow." C held up a hand. "We know pretty well what he's been up to throughout his career—until now, that is. Young Kruger's put his finger on the Russian Railton's latest appointment. What we need is dirt. Levers. Pressure points, Naldo, that's what we want."

"Should we talk to my Uncle Caspar?"

C gave a little nod and there was a rattling sound from the kitchen—Herbie testing to find out if he could yet return. "How long d'you think you'd last in the Russian Zone, Naldo?"

"A week, with luck. Passable German, not spectacular."

"If we could bait some kind of Beartrap . . ." C appeared to be speaking his thoughts aloud. Then: "Oh, I'm sure young Kruger could get a sympathetic team together, lure him, and get him into the West. No real problem there. But the fellow'd yell blue bloody murder. Wouldn't serve any purpose. Unless of course we can dig up some dirt."

"Our own Russian and Eastern networks, sir?"

"Oh, they're coming along nicely, I gather, but I'd like to keep this circle closed tight if we can. No office chitchat. Been our downfall before this." Another rattle from the kitchen, so C yelled at Herbie, "When's that bloody tea coming, Kruger?" Then, quietly, "I'd like you to sound out Caspar for me, Naldo. Then report. Right?"

Naldo nodded as Herbie lumbered in with a tray balanced precariously. "Tea is served," he intoned with a huge grin.

"DO YOU KNOW about the Railtons' dark horse?" Arnold asked Fry as they sat having a very old-fashioned tea at Brown's Hotel.

"The Dreaded Ramillies? Yes." Fry sipped his tea. To his surprise, Arnold noticed that he held his cup with the little finger of his right hand extended.

"I think they're on the verge of some op to lift him out of the Russian Sector. He's second-in-command, NKVD Berlin."

"Well, that's going to be a great help, isn't it?" Fry's face betrayed none of the petulance which encrusted his voice. "Just the kind of thing we want, some Russian NKVD bigwig screaming rape." He took hold of a tiny triangular sandwich and pushed it greedily into his mouth, an action at variance with the little-finger routine with his teacup. "Is this for real?"

"They seem serious."

"God in heaven. Berlin's difficult enough already—plunked in the middle of Russian-occupied Germany, with this four-way split in its military government." The Americans, British, and French could only get to their Berlin zones by using strictly defined roads, railways, and air corridors.

"There's talk of Beartraps. I guess what we'd call Honeytraps."

"Well, for God's sake try and dissuade them." He paused, as though in two minds whether to tell Arnold something weighing on his mind. Then: "There's still nothing on *Screwtape*. No contacts. Working normally . . ."

"And sticking to the same routine?" Arnie sounded smug.

Fry nodded and gave a dry affirmative. It almost made Arnold feel pain in his own throat when Fry had a particularly bad day.

"Fishman's acting oddly about him. Won't let us haul him in. It's gone on long enough, we're using a lot of manpower, and the longer it continues the more likely he is to spot the surveillance."

"You're beginning to sound like me." Farthing smiled. "I thought from the start that we should lift him and open him up."

Fry did not reply. Instead he altered the conversation in a quick curve. "What're you doing with your spare time? I presume you have spare time?"

"We're not meeting again for a week. Naldo's talking to his uncle, and they've put the lad Kruger out of play. Fattening him up for more action I guess, running him through more advanced training at that place they have near Warminster, as well as Ashford and Fort Monkton, for 'outdoor pursuits.'"

Fry gave an uncharacteristic grin. "B-movie stuff—Schools for Spies," he said in a dramatic tone.

"Nobody uses that word, Roger. Spies. You should know better."

Fry laughed aloud, then asked again what Farthing was doing with his time.

"I have a date tonight. Old flame. See where it leads."

"High time we got you married off, Arnold. Some nice Radcliffe graduate."

"Save me from the Cabots and Lowells, Roger. My old English flame is *very* high up the social ladder here. Let me find my own level."

That evening Arnold found it. The moment he saw Faith Kirk again he knew it was over for good. In uniform there had been something oddly vulnerable about her. In the severe tweed suit she wore that evening, combined with the painted mask of a face and hair that appeared to have been sculpted rather than styled, she was about as vulnerable as a python.

They ate at some little Italian restaurant which in spite of the food restrictions still in force had just reopened in Soho, and the conversation—after the first cool greeting—lapsed quickly into a monosyllabic round of questions and answers. Where are you now? Arnold wondered. Where's the lively laughing girl who gave off waves of passion as a crackling fire provided warmth? He was never to discover the real answer—though he supposed it had a lot to do with the British class system. Things were returning to normal in that tight little island where the wartime friendliness and we're-all-in-it-together attitude had quickly given way to a regrouping of the old unwritten rules. As an outsider, Arnold could see how much the new Socialist Government was to blame, taking sides, splitting people into categories. However, one clue to Faith's attitude appeared almost out of nowhere.

"Sorry I wasn't able to get in touch before," he said, trying hard to be charming. "After I left for the Continent it became difficult. Then Berlin; then back to the States. This is my first trip to England since I last saw you."

She looked up at him with a dead expression, as though she was speaking to someone on the telephone, miles away. "That's not quite true, is it, Arnold?"

"What?"

"You were in England a year ago."

Flustered, he made little swimming movements with his hands. "Oh, that? A quick in and out. No time for anything social."

"I found out quite by accident. You see, Sara Railton Farthing's a second cousin of mine, on her mother's side. She had dinner with us shortly after you'd spent the weekend at Redhill."

And that, thought Arnold, was that. The Railtons were real sons-of-bitches. Had relatives every which way. The hell with it. Her side of the conversation became rather stuffy. He just could not see through the layers of class she appeared to have spread over her real personality. Even the voice had assumed that pretentious singsong arrogance of the so-called upper classes. As she talked, Arnold began to switch off, seeing her lipsticked mouth moving, hearing nothing but picturing the girl he had once known, lying naked and laughing on the bed of a second-rate hotel room. He saw her home in a cab and went back to Kensington where Naldo had given him a room. On the way home, for the first time in his life, Arnold contemplated stopping the cab and approaching one of the whores pacing her beat in Knightsbridge.

So preoccupied was he that he failed to note the Daimler car following his cab, pulling up fifty yards or so in front of them to let out a passenger who sauntered back toward him, keeping to the shadows, walking silently past Naldo's house to be certain Arnold was safely in for the night.

NALDO WAS ALSO out on that night, dining with Caspar and showing off his bride-to-be. After dinner, Phoebe Railton led Barbara out of the dining room, to leave the two men alone with their port and, as she put it, "Your unsubtle dirty stories." Phoebe, like many women, had come to despise this old ritual of dividing the sexes after a pleasant meal. She said as much to Barbara, who kept her peace, knowing that they might have to wait for a long time before the men came to the drawing room.

Naldo had already hinted to her that there was "business" to discuss.

When the butler and maid had retired—Caspar and Phoebe still maintained a staff of two, though they knew it would only be a matter of time before that would also change—Naldo coughed apologetically. "I'm sorry, Caspar"—they had dispensed with the "uncle" some years ago—"I'm sorry, but I've misled you. I'm really here on business."

Caspar groaned and Naldo repeated his apology. "It really is essential, and it's on C's orders. He's asked me to say that this is highly sensitive. Not to be repeated in the office, if you follow."

Caspar nodded. "If it's C then I absolve you from all blame, Naldo. What's on the old man's mind—and why couldn't he ask me himself?"

"Better from someone in the family, I think. I've got to talk about your brother, Ramillies, I'm afraid."

"The Rammer? Oh, shit!"

"Why do you call him the Rammer?"

"Why? Oh, schooldays—the twins were younger than I. I mean Ramillies *is* much younger. Can't get used to him being alive. Schoolboy thing, though. Rupert was known as the Rupe, Ramillies as the Rammer. Oh?" He suddenly saw the point of Naldo's question. "'Rammer,' yes. No, sorry—it didn't have any sexual connotations."

"I need to have all your memories of him." Naldo felt uncommonly embarrassed. "Everything."

Caspar thought for a while. "To be honest with you, I didn't like him. Terrible thing to say about one's own brother, but he gave me the creeps."

"As a child, or . . . ?"

"Oh, later on. Hardly noticed him as a child. I was closer to your father—to James. We were more of an age. But later, when Ramillies was working with Grandfather Giles, I saw him off and on. You know I was the old C's Chief-of-Staff through most of the First War?"

"Yes."

"Ramillies used to come and see him now and again. Particularly just before he went off to Russia. He was in three or four times a week. Silent, creepy, made my flesh—well, you know."

Naldo nodded. "Any particular reason?"

"Nothing I could swear to. He was just—well, sinister."

"As a boy, an adolescent, any sexual leanings?"

"You mean was he queer?"

There was a pause through which Naldo counted fifteen and watched the light sparkling off the Georgian silver on the table.

"I can't swear to it," Caspar blurted, as though the whole business was unpleasant. "There were tales from the old school. I know that for sure. But I don't know how serious it was. You know exactly what I mean, Nald. Lord love us, there's always a bit of buggery—sodomy, call it what you will—going on at school. Part of life's rich pattern in the old days—buggery, bullying, and birching. Heard of a fellow the other day—fellow in public life: well-known—goes to whores to be flogged. Admitted it in the club. Said he'd got so used to it at school that he couldn't do without it. I suppose that happens to buggers, queers, as well. They're the few percent who go on with it; can't get it off with a woman."

"And you suspect Ramillies of being like that?"

Caspar sighed. "Not nice—even after what he's done." He swallowed, then put his lips together hard, as though willing them not to open. After a moment he said, "Yes, Naldo. Yes. Got to say it, I believe my young brother indulged in sodomy."

"Sorry to press you, Cas. Any hard evidence? Do you just base it on schoolboy stories and your observation of him, or . . . ?"

"Never had any interest in women. Not ever. Ramillies was a first-rate and dedicated watcher. When we had family gatherings at Redhill he always knew where everyone was at any time of the day. There was one incident . . ." Once more he was trying to close it out.

"It's okay, Caspar. If you can just—"

"I know we had some people over one Christmas. During the First War. I was in my wheelchair then and old Phoeb was my nurse. These people were neighbors. Two daughters, one of 'em a bit flighty. Took a fancy to Ramillies. Phoeb told me later she found the girl in tears. She'd made a fool of herself. Tried to make up to the Rammer and he'd pushed her away in disgust. I wondered then. Next day I saw him with one of the men who came up to help on the farm—older man, invalided out of the Army. Well-known queer in Haversage—what in the country we used to call a 'brown hatter.' Well, I saw 'em together. Saw the way Ram was lookin' at him . . ." Acutely embarrassed, Caspar came to a full stop.

"Apart from that subject—let's get off that—was there anything else?"

Caspar sipped at his port, then drained his glass, quickly

reaching for the decanter. "What's it all about?" he asked, looking flushed and solemn.

"Sorry. It's serious, Caspar. Serious and secret as the grave. The less you know, the better. Also, we've never discussed this, if you follow me." He stopped for a moment for Caspar to incline his head, acknowledging that he understood. "Now, anything else?" Naldo asked.

"Oh, God. Sly; too clever for his own good; secretive. We all are of course, but Ramillies was different. Yes, I knew he'd make a bloody good agent. Even as a child he always knew what we were all doing. Add that lot together and throw in the other business, and you have him. If I'd known C—old Mansfield Cumming—was sending him into Russia, I'd have advised against it. Enough?"

Naldo nodded. "Quite enough. You heard the one about the deb who became a Landgirl?" He changed the subject, taking them into the area men were supposed to inhabit once the ladies had withdrawn.

The rest of the evening went well, but Naldo was preoccupied in the cab on the way home. Barbara tried to talk, but he wasn't his usual self.

"You want me to stay tonight, Nald, darling?" she asked as they neared the house.

He looked at her and she thought she could detect pain deep in his eyes. "More than ever," he told her quietly and she smiled. "I hope we get the nuptials over soon. This is no way for lovers to carry on."

Like Arnie, Naldo had dropped his guard. He did not notice the dark Humber in their wake, nor the manner in which it pulled up for a second to let its passenger out, nor the way the passenger passed by in the shadows as they entered the house together.

"HOMOSEXUAL, ACCORDING TO Caspar," Naldo said, and C sat bolt upright in his chair.

There were just the three of them, Naldo, Arnold, and C, together in the Northolt house.

"Well, there's a pretty thing, a very pretty thing." C was smiling pleasantly. "As I recall it, Ivan's hot as mustard on sods and buggers."

Naldo winced. He had always held to the opinion that homosexuality—though he did not understand it—was best left alone.

"They're certainly a good deal hotter than us," C continued.

"High-ranking NKVD officer'd be in for the chop if *that* became public. Now, the only thing left is young Kruger's sexual education. I wonder if he knows about that side of the birds and bees?"

"Oh, I should imagine he knows more'n you or I, sir." —From Arnold. "Don't forget how he lived before I took him under my wing. Kids on the loose in Berlin when Ivan first arrived learned pretty near everything. Saw the lot as well— murder, rape, pillage, and doubtless a bit of sodomy on the side."

"Best give him a short course, though." C grinned like the proverbial Cheshire Cat. "Good news, Naldo. Those sort rarely change, and, from my experience, they can't go too long without it. I wonder if Herb and his Helene could mount a real Beartrap?" He paused as a car went past outside. For a second they all thought it was slowing down to stop. But it went on its way and C continued. "You know, I'm worried about Kruger. Should we really turn a blind eye to his sexual life? I mean, he's only sixteen."

"I guess it's too late to change it now, sir." Arnold hid his smile, then asked what was happening about Herbie.

"Happening? Nothing's happening!" C snapped tartly. "We're just giving him some further education."

"If you're educating him in Honeytraps and Beartraps, then *you're* assisting to corrupt his morals, sir." Arnold smiled in plain sight this time.

C grunted and said, yes, he supposed Arnold was right.

Two DAYS LATER they all went down to the big house, in its several acres of ground, near the garrison town of Warminster, in Wiltshire. They moved independently, Arnold going by rail, Naldo by car. Nobody asked how C got there, but he stressed the security. Arnold and Naldo went through all the rituals and were certain that neither trailed a tail with him.

Herbie looked very fit and was flush with new knowledge— "They teach me wonderful things," he told Naldo and Arnie as they walked in the grounds, shielded from roads by old walls and trees. "I learn of photographs that can be made in secret with very small cameras; and also how to steal voices onto wire. Many things. It is full of interest—here, in Kent, Hampshire, and London. Many devious things I learn."

"It's full of danger as well, Herb. You know that?" Naldo asked.

"I tell you a long time ago. All life is dangerous." Herbie

treated them to a big grin. "I have discovered some new Mahler music that is recorded—*Kindertotenlieder*. That is 'Songs on the Death of Children.' Sad, but enthralling. Listen to the songs and you know all life is a danger." He coughed loudly, looking much older than his years—more mature, strangely full of wisdom. He began to recite a verse from a poem in German—Naldo and Arnold translating it in their heads easily, for Herbie Kruger spoke slowly and with a deep emotion, once more a puzzling thing for a lad of his age. It was one of Mahler's Songs on the Death of Children:

> *"How often I think they're just out walking;*
> *They won't be much longer, they'll soon be returning.*
> *The day is fine, O never fear!*
> *They're only taking the long way back.*
> *They've only started out before us*
> *And won't come back home at all!*
> *We'll soon overtake them, up on the hills,*
> *In the sunshine! The day is fine upon the hills!"*

Naldo could have sworn he saw tears in Kruger's eyes, and Arnold was strangely silent.

They all lunched together, with a guard on the door and the food brought in on a trolley and left for them to help themselves.

C talked, giving a long and detailed description of what he required, stopping every now and then to query if Herbie understood. This was the start of a briefing that would go on all day, and when it was over Herbie spoke—quietly and with great confidence.

"How much time will I have for this?" he asked at one point.

"Not long, I'm afraid." C's voice was full of concern. "From the moment you go back in you'll have around four weeks."

"Ah?" Herbie shifted his large body in the chair. "Alone I must recruit, survey the target, and set it up in one month?"

"We daren't make it much longer." C's face took on the demeanor of his voice. "The time schedule is going to be very tight."

Naldo Railton leaned forward, eyes locking with Kruger. "Herbie, time is something we're going to be short of on this one. Look, if you've any serious doubts that you can't at least give it a good try, then tell us now."

C shot Railton a daggerlike look, then softened. "I suppose, yes," he muttered grudgingly. "Better to know now."

"How long before I go?" Herbie's head moved slowly, his eyes gazing in turn at each of the three faces.

"A week. Ten days. We have things to set up as well."—from C.

Herbie paused, but he did not seem to be making a decision. "I give it my best shot," he said, and the large face split into a massive grin. "I do it, don't have worries."

"We'll need to go through this very carefully, sir." Naldo was concerned. Very concerned. The Beartrap was complex and required a lot of people on the ground. In the furthest reaches of his heart, he thought Herbie was too innocent, too inexperienced, to carry it off. The boy knew nothing about agent-handling in the field; nothing about trawling for likely agents; nothing about auditioning them, let alone coordinating the whole thing. The timing had to be perfect. The whole little network must be unbreakable. "Look, why not let me go into the Ivans' zone and have a go at it."

"You said yourself that you'd last a week at the most." C was quite sharp in manner. "At least Kruger's got good cover, and the Ivans won't suspect him of devious complexities like this. You, Naldo, will go in for the one night. One night, see the last act through, and do the business. Like I said over lunch, you will scatter Kruger's team afterwards. If necessary you'll get rid of any weak links." He turned to Arnie. "And you know what I want from you and yours, Farthing."

"They'll want something in return."

"Oh, I know that. We'll do a deal. Tell your real masters that—and we'll cut them in on the product, if there is any product from the sodomite Railton."

"This all come under *Symphony?*" Naldo asked.

"*Symphony*'s the mother of it all." C turned sharply to Farthing, "And *Symphony*'s still *our* operation. No blabbing to your Agency about that."

"Don't worry, sir. Not a word."

"This op?" Naldo forced the subject again. "*Symphony?*"

"No, we'll give it a different crypto." C smiled pleasantly. "Let's call it *Brimstone*—didn't the Lord rain fire and brimstone upon Sodom?" He paused before adding, "And Gomorrah? Book of Genesis, wasn't it?"

They returned to London, each by his separate route. Naldo and Arnie got back to the Kensington house within an hour of each other. Neither saw the watchers in the shadows, who stood silent, as though waiting for them.

"THEY WANT A safe house in our zone. Unused by anyone else. New unlisted number. Their technicians'll service it." Arnold leaned over the Thames Embankment. To his right the statue of Boadicea in her chariot stood harsh on the corner of Westminster Bridge. Across the road the Palace of Westminster rose in all its wonder, the slender tower that was Big Ben pointing its finger at the evening sky.

"Sure that's all they want? A measly safe house in Berlin?" Fry grunted.

"They'll give something in return."

"Bet your ass they will." Fry's hand went to his mouth and he coughed hard three or four times. His slender body struggled under the strain. "This country's too damned damp for me. Even in summer."

"Do they get it?"

"Sure. A safe house is easy. And they pay. Jim Fishman's on a new track. *Screwtape*'s still clean as fresh sheets. He wants to talk to the German—Buelow. The guy who fingered *Screwtape*."

"They're not going to be happy if *I* ask for that."

"Why not? We've had legal access to the *Tarot* Enquiry file. Not the stuff you've told us about. Just the transcript of the Enquiry."

"I'd prefer it if someone else asked."

Fry shrugged. "We'll do it through one of the boys in the Embassy. You say there's a fee, and the Embassy'll request something. No need to let them see you know the price. We get Buelow. They get the safe house. How long they want it for?"

"Month, six weeks. Clean with nobody watching."

"Okay."

"Why does Fishman want Buelow?"

"He's going to pull in Tert Newton. Go over his story again. The Enquiry shot it full of holes. He wants to put them up against one another. See if there's been any disinformation. Any product comes straight back to the Brits, okay?"

"What's happened to Newton?" Arnie detected deception behind Fry's calculated manner.

"Oh, didn't you know? When the Brits finished drying him out, he went back to the States and applied for a new job. Got it.

Washington. He's a security officer at the Atomic Energy Commission's Headquarters. Sensitive, huh?" Fry gave a bleak smile, his eyes like pebbles in a frost.

"It's like a fucking Chinese box . . ."

"Or a *Matrioschka* doll, Arnold."

There was an unfriendly silence before Arnie replied, "I'll just give them word on the house. The Embassy can do the rest."

Fry nodded. "What's going on, Arnie?"

"When it's done I'll tell you. Best you shouldn't know yet."

Fry shrugged again as though he didn't care one way or another.

On the following day C announced that he had done the deal regarding the American safe house in Berlin.

NALDO BECAME AWARE of the watchers only two days before the final briefing for *Brimstone*. He spoke to C and Arnie. On the morning they left Kensington for the last briefing and the journey to Berlin, the two men let themselves out of the house within ten minutes of each other, both apparently heading for different destinations.

They spent two hours throwing the surveillance, and in that time Special Branch officers had the watchers in their sights. Losing their targets seemed to create some panic among the men who had watched Railton and Farthing. The lead watcher in each team made a fast telephone call from a public box. They were all still under Special Branch surveillance that night, and by then Naldo, Arnold, C, and Herbie Kruger were gathered together in the big house outside Warminster.

Brimstone was about to start running.

21

▼

IT TOOK THREE days to start up *Brimstone*. Arnold went out first, flying into Tempelhof airfield, the main base in the American Sector of Berlin. Naldo and Herbie went out on day two, traveling in a Dakota into the RAF base at Gatow in the British Zone. They all traveled under work names, and with papers to match. Later, in the safe house within the British Sector, they gave Herbie his complete sets of papers—the same ones he had used during his previous trips into the Russian Zone.

He was also to carry a hospital form which gave dates of admission and release, together with the scribbled details of a supposed stomach complaint for which he had been treated. The dates matched the time he had been absent from the Russian Zone and mentioned the sudden onset of the ailment.

Arnie lurked near Gatow and watched Naldo's and Herbie's backs while they got to the safe house. He then distanced himself, covering them until the first stage was completed.

"There's still time to say no, Herb," Naldo told the big German lad as they sat over a simple meal on the night before he was due to go.

Herbie just laughed. "When I say yes, I say yes. I also have found ways. I know Mahler's First and Second symphonies by heart. I can listen to them in my mind, like you can remember poetry and Shakespeare. They are my cover. I can retreat into them and hide."

Naldo knew what he meant but realized that Herbie had a lot to learn. Those kind of tricks were ones you didn't share with your controller—or case officer, as the Americans would have said. He continued to talk as though Herbie had told him nothing he did not know already. "Any problem—however small—get out fast. You come here or, if it's easier, to the address in the American Zone."

"You told me."

"Then I'm telling you again. The telephones will be rung in both houses every three hours. Two rings, then stop. Thirty seconds later it rings again. This will be every three hours, on the hour from midnight tonight. If there's trouble you answer, 'Fire.' If you've come out with everything set up you say 'Treacle.' On that word you wait and I'll be there in twenty-four hours. Okay?"

"You told me it all." Herbie grinned happily. "Nald, my good friend, don't worry. It will be well. But how you fix things so the telephones definitely work?"

"C's got it sewn up. You give a 'Fire' or a 'Treacle' and we'll know."

On the third day, Herbie left soon after five in the afternoon. He wore old working clothes and carried a battered document case containing food, cigarettes, and a bottle of cheap Schnapps. Hidden in a secret compartment were a camera, film, and a simple recording machine with accessories.

Arnie watched him all the way until he had mingled with the string of daily migrant workers who lived in the Russian Zone and worked in either the British or American sectors.

Only when Herbie was out of sight, clear and into the East, did Arnie leave to meet Naldo at one of the many makeshift clubs that had started up near the old Ku-damm.

The next day they both flew back—separately—to London and met C in the Northolt house.

"He's running," Naldo said, his voice uneven, for he liked nothing about the operation they called *Brimstone*.

"Good." C was brisk and workmanlike. "You know the form then. One of you here day and night with telephone access to the other within an hour. Shouldn't stop you having a pleasant time. If one of you goes out on the town he should call in every hour. If we get a 'Fire' or a 'Treacle' I want instant action." He looked at the two men. From their faces he could see they needed rest. "You'd better both stay here tonight. Then you can sleep. The telephone'll always waken you. We've had instruments fitted in the bedrooms."

"The telephone handling in Berlin *is* secure?" Naldo asked.

"Don't be stupid, of course it is. The Duty Officer here will get me as soon as Berlin comes on. Communications are the least of our worries."

"What's the worst?" Arnold was half joking.

"Well . . ." As C started to speak they both sat up and looked at him. There was a subtle change in his manner; something nasty in the woodshed of his larynx.

"Yes?" asked Naldo.

"What?"—from Arnie. They spoke in unison.

"I almost stopped the clock." C looked serious now. "But we'd gone a long way with *Brimstone*. I felt it was worth the risk. It concerns those jokers who had you under surveillance."

"We lost them, didn't we?" Naldo felt a spike of anxiety deep in his gut.

"Yes. Yes, you lost them. I told you it was perfectly all right when you got down to Warminster. But they were very good— good professionals. The Branch were on their backs. There was quite a to-do when they lost you."

"Who the hell were they? Ivans—?" Naldo began.

"We don't know who they were; only that they were professional." C's speech became very deliberate. "You see, the Branch lost them—both teams. We have excellent descriptions, but we can't tie them into any particular organization. They could even be old pros going private for someone else. Could even be your people, Arnie."

Farthing shook his head. "I'd know, I promise you that. If the Agency was working both sides of the street I'd know."

"Well, could be the Ivans, I suppose; or even 'Five.' They've been known to throw sand in the works before now. If anyone's got wind of my running a private operation—" He stopped. "You *have* kept it contained, the pair of you?"

Both of them acknowledged that *Symphony* and *Brimstone* had stayed within their small circle.

"It couldn't be my good Uncle Caspar getting trunky about what's going on?" Naldo's question held no conviction.

"Doubt it." C was certainly concerned. "We might have to put one of you up again. Tethered goat to flush them. We'll see."

"Great," muttered Arnie.

C's news did not make for peace of mind.

That night they tossed a coin to decide who took the first watch. Arnold lost. He would stay on through the next night and Naldo would take over from him at nine o'clock on the morning after. "I'll be away before nine tomorrow," he told Arnold. "Lot of time to make up with Barb."

"And the best of luck to you." Arnie still felt the need for female companionship.

They went to bed early and the telephone did not ring that night.

Arnold Farthing woke from a deep sleep to a tapping on his bedroom door. His watch showed it was after ten. "Come on in," he shouted loudly, assuming it to be Naldo. Instead, a vision appeared in the doorway, carrying a tray. It was C's lovely housekeeper—one of his wise monkeys, Naldo had said. The redhead called Ophelia.

"Golly," was all he could manage.

"And 'golly' to you." She smiled and a dimple showed on her right cheek. "Your colleague said you could probably do with breakfast." She came over and placed the tray on the bed—coffee, toast, bacon, and two eggs. Arnie noticed that her oval face was heavily freckled. She probably hated the freckles, but to Arnie they were like iron filings to a magnet.

"Well, thank you." He was still only half awake. "Ophelia, you needn't get thee to that nunnery, after all."

"Oh, not you, please!" she said. "My brothers, the girls at school, and even some of my old friends. My parents were crazy. Please don't call me Ophelia. I get really tired of the nunnery jokes, the 'been swimming?' jokes, and the 'Please don't get mad, Ophelia,' jokes." Her voice was firm and friendly—good-humored was how people would describe it. She certainly had none of that ghastly upper-crust drawl which so infected Faith Kirk's voice.

Arnie propped himself up in bed and pulled the tray toward him, glancing up at her again as though to make certain she was real. "I was only told that name. What else can I call you?" She wore a slim gray skirt, light blue blouse, gray shoes. There were no rings on her fingers, but a small, expensive-looking watch on her right wrist, and a tiny brooch in the shape of an O clasped to the neck of her blouse. He took it all in before blinking. For the first time since early puberty Arnie reflected on what she might be wearing underneath. Under the sheets his body responded to the adolescent thoughts.

She smiled. "I didn't realize you were American. Or is it Canadian?"

"American, ma'am. I'm—"

"No, please. I don't want to know names."

"Well, *I* do. You don't like Ophelia so I call you Miss—what?"

"Miss nothing. My friends, those I like, call me by my second name, Liz."

"As in Elizabeth?" Lordy but she had a smile that lit up the room—and those big round brown eyes looked like they could eat a man up.

"As in Liz."

"Great, Liz. Call me John—it's really St. John, *my* second name."

"That's settled. Enjoy your breakfast, I've got things to do." She made for the door.

"Er . . . Miss . . . er . . . hey . . . whoa . . . er . . . Liz."

"Is something not right with the breakfast?" She had the door half open.

"Looks great. I just wondered. . . . Well, look . . . I'm not your lewd and licentious soldiery, just a genuinely lonely Yank in London. Could we have dinner? Say tomorrow night?"

She smiled and shook her head slowly. She moves like a dancer, Arnie thought. Or maybe I just think she moves like a dancer because this is the first woman I've been close to in a long time. He did not count Faith Kirk.

"Against the rules?" He tried to smile, knowing it was simply some zany kind of grin.

"No, I'm not aware of any rules like that. It's, well, we *have* only just met."

"Oh, for Pete's sake, you aren't one of those, are you?"

"One of what?"

"I can't date you because our folks didn't introduce us." He mimicked her accent.

"Certainly not." Her smile really was terrific. When she moved her lips everything lit up—face, eyes, the full business.

"Well then, why no dinner tomorrow?"

"Why not?" She gave a laugh and disappeared. By the time Arnie had finished breakfast, bathed, and dressed, she had left the house. "Shit!" he said loudly to the walls.

He read for most of the day, listened to the radio—what the Brits insisted on calling the wireless—and generally moped. The telephone rang just after six.

"I've been home all day," said Naldo at the distant end, "but Barbara and I are going out to dinner. From around eight to ten we'll be at the Hungaria." He gave the number. "Home and in for the rest of the evening, okay?"

"Okay, but I expect you here, bright-eyed and bushy-tailed, first thing in the morning."

"Nine o'clock sharp." Naldo paused. "No news I suppose?"

"Not a jot. I think we're in for a long haul. Better get used to it, Nald."

He jumped when the telephone rang again shortly after eight.

"Hallo? John?" said the caller. He recognized her voice instantly.

"Well, Liz. You coming over to fix my dinner?"

"No, but I *will* have dinner tomorrow if the invitation's still valid."

"It's valid. Where and when, Liz? Oh, and why the change of heart?" Arnie tried not to sound excited, but knew that he had failed, the words tumbling over one another.

"I was supposed to see an old girlfriend. She's cried off, so I thought, why not?"

"Indeed, why not. You like Chinese?"

"Adore it."

"Choy's in Dean Street, then. Seven-thirty suit you?"

"Fine. Mind you, I don't usually take meals from strangers."

"I'm not a stranger, though, am I? I'm one of your gentlemen lodgers."

"Half past seven tomorrow, then. 'Bye." She hung up, and Arnie stretched back in his chair, eyes closed and a goofy smile on his battered face.

He was there at twenty after seven, having reserved a table using Naldo's telephone. She arrived at 7:48, full of apologies about not being able to get a cab, and all the usual feminine tales.

It was a very different kind of evening. They did not delve deeply into each others' lives or families. There *were* rules, and they both knew it. But she was fun, laughed a lot, a good talker, and nobody's fool. She ate, as well—a good sign. Arnold had long been used to women who merely picked at their food or pushed it around the plate. Wonton soup, ginger chicken, sweet and sour pork, noodles, egg rolls, special fried rice. "My family always say I've got hollow legs," she said. "I eat far too much. Wonder how these Chinese manage to get the pork, what with rationing and everything?"

"There are ways." Arnold liked the bit about "hollow legs."

"I'm an American." He looked her straight in the eye. "That means I hold the key to a dozen PXs in England. You want little extras—liquor, food, cigarettes, nylon stockings—I can get them for you." He remembered Herbie.

"I've heard all that before. I know the price for these things." She said it a shade too seriously, he thought.

"No strings." He lifted his hands, holding them apart in a gesture of capitulation.

Arnold took her home by cab—a block of flats off the Earl's

Court Road—but she shook his hand at the door, said thank you, and slid inside, leaving him looking at a solid piece of wood with an inlaid letterbox, number, and doorbell.

Arnold was hooked. She had red hair—with such a sheen that you could almost see your face in it—done up in a big French pleat at the back; a great figure which moved inside her clothes; a slightly crooked sense of humor, and something wild lurking behind the large brown eyes. He started to lay siege. Much good did it do him.

Even though most of Arnie's waking thoughts revolved around Miss Ophelia Liz No-Name, he remained conscious of the main task. Both he and Naldo confessed to moments during every day when their stomachs turned over at the thought of *Brimstone*.

"I wonder how he's coping?" Naldo said one morning during what they had come to think of as the changing of the guard. After a week they had heard nothing—not even from C.

"Yeah." Arnie let out a long sigh. "He's so damned young. Poor old Herbie. I wonder..."

They need not have worried. Herbie was managing very well indeed.

THOUGH HERBIE KRUGER was only sixteen years old, going on seventeen, he had spent the bulk of his life in Berlin. His first memories of this city came from his childhood. Berlin had become a great pile of rubble, but to Herbie, the city was not simply a place of façades behind which no substantial buildings stood, or mounds of bricks along what had once been streets. Herbie could follow the lines between the ruins, like someone placing a cellophane map over a drawing of scrawls, blotches, and whorls. The ruins became familiar byways to him, and by some strange childhood memory he could name streets and alleys, corners and squares, by their old names. His geographical bump led him to destinations some might have experienced great difficulty in finding among the odd jumbled cartography created by the British and American air forces, and the Russian tanks.

"Don't beat about the bush with Helene," they had told him. "Get straight to the point. If she's the girl you think she is, then she'll lead you to others." He did just that, not going toward Karlshorst, but heading straight for where the Alexanderplatz once stood. Here there were many skeletons which had once been well-remembered buildings, but some houses had stood firm. It was the same all over the city, for bomb and shell blast can do strange things. A whole section of houses, or even a single building, stood almost unscathed in the midst of ruin and desolation.

In the early evening of that first day back in the Russian Zone, Herbie waited quietly in a doorway, only a few steps from the house where Helene lived. He stood very still and calm, his eyes moving slowly but taking in everything. In his head he heard the "Huntsman's Funeral," based on the old French song *Frère Jacques,* from the Mahler First. Not one person escaped his notice, and he spotted Helene long before she detected him in the doorway.

"Eberhardt? What happened? I've been so worried." She hugged him, clinging tightly.

"A little illness," he whispered. "They kept me in hospital in the British Zone."

"Illness? How serious? Are you well now?" Concern blasted a stream of questions from her small pretty mouth. "I have soup and bread. Come home with me, you must eat."

Next to Herbie, Helene was small—around five feet six inches in her stocking feet—when she managed to get stockings. Her hair was short and almost blonde—not quite the real thing, for it was a very dark blonde. "Mama used to call me a blonde," she would say, "but I think she was being optimistic. I'm really only a kind of light mouse."

Herbie roared with laughter when she had first said this to him. "You are a very pretty mouse," he said as he engulfed her slight body in his huge arms.

Though slim—almost thin—Helene was neatly proportioned: good legs, breasts which were full though not too big, and a long face with an unusually small nose and striking gray eyes. She also had almost perfect buttocks, as Herbie knew. He could span the twin mounds of her rump with both hands.

Her room, to which she now took him, was not large but, as she often said, it contained everything she needed—bed, stove, washbasin, wardrobe, table, three chairs, and "The door locks from the inside. That is most important in these times."

"You see, nothing has changed." She threw open the door on that evening of Herbie's return, to reveal her room—spotless, clean, and tidy as ever. Helene Schtabelle prided herself on the cleanliness. "When you live in one small room, there must be a special place for everything, and everything must remain in its place," she often said, and Herbie, being astute, guessed that she had heard her mother reciting those same words to her during childhood.

"No, nothing has changed." He smiled his daft smile and moved slowly into the room. She closed and locked the door, turning to him. "You're sure you are well now?"

"You want me to show you?"

They faced each other, slightly apart for a moment, then as humans often do, they crossed the divide, snuggling into each other with Helene pressing and wriggling herself against Herbie as though she wanted to be magically swallowed into his large frame.

"Oh, yes," she whispered; and again, "Yes. Oh, yes."

The floor was strewn with clothes and the bed moved under the weight of their combined bodies. "I have missed you so much," she said afterward, and Herbie wondered at it, for they had made love only three times before.

"And I have missed you." His voice was soft with affection.

Later, they sat across the table from one another. Herbie had produced the bottle of Schnapps and the large piece of ham, together with the heel of bread he had brought with him. They drank her soup first and then ate the ham.

"It's a banquet," she said. "A feast for your return."

"We must save some." He looked into her gray eyes and saw a movement—maybe concern or just affection.

"Save? Yes? There is another mouth to feed?"

"Several, possibly. It depends on you. I have money and can bring food from the British and American zones if we need to feed more. But there is a most important job to do."

"Oh?"

Don't beat about the bush with Helene. Get straight to the point—she can lead you to others.

"I have a secret." Herbie still locked eyes with her. "It must become your secret also, and, if you love me, then you will keep it our secret. If you cannot lock it away in your mind, then you hold my life captive."

She looked frightened, but was intrigued by this talk of secrets. "Go on"—she swallowed—"darling Eberhardt, tell me."

"I have not been ill. I have not been in the hospital. What I have to say concerns the Russian I asked you about—the officer of their NKVD. The Russian called Rogov."

"Aha." The noise from her throat was neutral—part surprise, part fear, part excitement.

"You do not like the Russians?"

She gave a little shrug. "They pay me to work."

"But you do not like them. What did they do to your parents? What did they do to *you,* Helene?"

She flushed, and he repeated, "I must know how you feel. If you are willing to take revenge for what they did to you and your family. You like them or you do not like them? Which?"

She had turned very red, and he saw that the movement in her eyes was one of anger. Then, after what seemed a lifetime, Helene Schtabelle nodded. "It is not a question of liking or disliking. If you are a Russian informer then I put my life in your hands. I hate them."

Herbie slapped the table. "Good! For that answer you get British cigarettes." He produced a tin box of Players Navy Cut. Her eyes widened. It was a box of fifty. "You could buy almost anything with that in some parts of the city." Her voice quivered, and Herbie smiled. "Then I could probably buy the entire city," he said. "I have three boxes of these and I can get more."

She looked frightened again. "Some would kill you for these." Her thin hand hovered over the box. "There are Russian soldiers in Karlshorst who would cut your throat."

"Yes," he said simply, lighting a cigarette and offering them to her. Helene's hand shook as she took one, inhaling the strong tobacco, then coughing.

"I hope to pay for some services, yes." Herbie gave her a conspiratorial smile. "But I hope to find people who will do what I wish for no payment at all. People who hate as you hate. I will tell you everything now." He started to talk, but of course told her only a part of it, for if things went wrong it was better that she did not know too much.

"Can you find me people who will help?" he asked at the end.

"Plenty." This time she looked at him in a different way. She embraced him with her gray eyes which spoke of reverence and not a fragment of fear. "I can name you four people who would help you tomorrow. I can invite them here."

"Good."

"You don't know——" she began.

"I think I do."

"No, you cannot know how deeply so many of us hate these people. We never talked of it before, Eberhardt, but I have longed for some opportunity. . . . You don't know the humiliation of having to work for them, after . . . after what they have done." She lowered her head, as though she could no longer look at him. "I have told you about my mother—how she was raped—but I never told everything."

"I can guess."

"Can you?" Her blurred eyes flitted up and then away again. "It killed my mother. Me it did not kill, even though twenty of them took me and left me for dead. I was bleeding for nearly a month. Until then I was a virgin. In the house where I was born, Eberhardt. On the stairs. Twenty of them." She raised her head and he saw the tears making great deltas down her cheeks. "I have never told anyone about it properly. They came at night. A squad of big Russian men. They stank of sweat and guns, oil and spirits. Some of them were drunk. My father said we should humor them . . ."

Helene talked it away between bursts of tears and anguish. How the soldiers had bludgeoned her father to death in their little parlor and then dragged her mother upstairs. "I still hear her screams. She was always such a gentle person, *Mutti* . . . Oh, my God, *Mutti!*" It was as though she called for her murdered mother. Herbie went over to her, putting an arm around her, comforting, drawing her close to his massive chest. She told how they stripped her and gang-raped her, some coming straight from her mother to her. Then how they left and she pulled herself upstairs to find her mother's body and see the indignities of their last horrific acts.

"You have been the only other man—ever; ever in my life, and I thought I might hate you also. But I love you, Eberhardt. You've given me respect again. You *cannot* know what hatred for those pigs burns in women like me."

"Then you must show me." He held her very close, and presently they went to bed, not to make love, but to be near each other. Helene clung to him like a child and sobbed even after she had fallen into a deep sleep. Even after all this, the boy Kruger sensed she had not told him everything.

The next morning she said that she would bring some people back with her in the evening. She could contact them during the day.

Herbie went out, into the American Zone, where he walked about a lot, listened to Mahler's Second Symphony in his head, looked at the ruins and the building work, and used his special papers to buy more ham, bread, and Schnapps—they had given him a fortune in paper money that could be spent in the American or British zones.

At five-thirty he returned to the one small room near the Alexanderplatz and laid out the food. Helene came in an hour later. She was followed—at intervals—by two young men and two girls. So Herbie first met the team who would make *Brimstone* possible. Their names were Willy Blenden, Gertrude Müller, Kurt Kutte, and Ingrid Mann. Not one was over twenty years of age.

They ate, drank, and smoked the cigarettes. Then Herbie questioned each one of them in turn, getting to know them. It was risky, but the only way he knew, so he began to talk. "This concerns a Russian officer—a high-ranking man of their secret police. We will have to identify him, and Helene will help us with that. Then we shall have to find some way of following him—watching him, especially seeing what he does in the evenings and in his off-duty periods. This is not going to be a simple business. It will also be dangerous, so if any of you think you haven't the stomach, it would be best to leave now."

He looked at each in turn, praying they would all stay, because if one left he would personally have to seek out him—or her—and kill.

They all looked back at Herbie, their eyes glowing with interest. He thought—blasphemously, he considered later—that this was what the disciples must have looked like when they listened to Jesus preaching.

22

▼

LIKE MOST YOUNG people in Berlin they were all scruffy. Clothes were not easy to come by. Willy himself was a big lad, not as large as Herbie but strong in the limbs and with obviously muscular shoulders. He was the best-dressed of the team, sporting a leather jacket and thick field-gray trousers.

Certainly he possessed a relaxed manner—what today would be called "laid-back"—and a quick-witted tongue. Herbie always felt he might become a liability to the team, unlike Kurt Kutte, who was small and inoffensive-looking, a definite asset, for he possessed a very sharp intelligence and that particular way some people have of becoming almost completely invisible, even in a small group.

All of them were, thankfully, able to blend into any given background. Only Herbie felt his size was against him in matters of surveillance. "My body does not suit this job; someone sees me and never forgets," he would say sadly. Yet he was soon able to turn this to an advantage by cultivating the slow, dull, and unreliable style that would in later years make him such an asset to the Secret Intelligence Service.

On the first night—when Herbie gave them the rough outline of what was to happen—it was agreed that Helene would try to discover Rogov's general pattern of movements—when he had free time and, if possible, what he did with it. Until they had some idea of how Rogov occupied his off-duty hours, there was no point in starting any watching operation.

To keep surveillance on the NKVD man with only a team of four young people would be difficult enough—at Warminster they had told Herbie that this kind of job really required several interchangeable teams, and he knew that made sense, just as he knew there was no way for him to recruit any large teams at short notice. In the field you had to improvise. It was one of the first, lasting, lessons he learned.

Herbie had only one option regarding how he spent his days —keeping up the already established fiction of going off to work in the British Zone and returning each evening.

It took two days for Helene to make any progress. On the third night she came to Herbie's own room, in a battered old apartment house overlooking the river, near what had been the Markus-strasse—now an area containing little more than rubble which was gradually being cleared into neat piles.

"Eberhardt, when're you going to do something about this place?" Helene had asked this ever since her very first visit.

Kruger gave a giant shrug and a foolish grin. "Oh, I'm looking for a better place. What's the use of doing anything to this?" A large hand swept slowly around the room as if he were proud of the cracked and dirty walls, the small iron bedstead, the packing cases that served for chairs and tables, and the one electric bulb that burned dully overhead. "They'll soon pull this place down for sure." Another of his grins. "Anyhow, it's cozy."

"It's as cozy as a rat's nest." Helene wrinkled her nose. "Come to my place, Eberhardt. Please, at least it's clean."

Herbie gave his most stupid grin and nodded slowly. In truth he needed no bidding to get out of this dump. "You've got news?" he asked, as though this was the last thing that mattered.

She gave a nod of pleasure. "Yes, but I'll tell you at home. Why don't you move in with me properly, Eberhardt? It would make life less complicated."

"Less and more complicated, *Liebling*." He rose from the packing case on which he had been sitting. "I have to keep a little bolt-hole for myself. You understand?"

Back in Helene's room he sat in one of her old chairs while she talked and prepared a simple meal for them. "The gossip is that he has a lady friend. An illegal lady, because they're not really allowed to mix with the German population."

Herbie's eyebrows shot up at the thought of there being a woman involved. "But they all mix with the local girls." He allowed the bemused expression to remain on his face and in his eyes. "I have seen them."

"True, but NKVD must use great care. Anyway, he is off duty every Wednesday afternoon, from one o'clock until curfew. He takes one of the cars from the officers' garages and drives out of Karlshorst. Nobody knows where he goes, but when they have jokes with him, the other officers say he visits a lady. He just smiles and looks like a sheep. This proves it, they say."

"Does he always use the same car?" Already Herbie could see

difficulties. Even bicycles would not be easy to procure for his team; while trying to follow a car on a bicycle was an almost impossible task.

"Yes, he has a car for private use. German, of course, one of the old VWs—the little one, *you* know."

"Yes. Color?"

"What d'you think? Dull green, like all of them."

"Does it have a registration plate?"

"Just numbers: 85942." She looked at him with great pride. "There, I should get a prize. I learned everything—"

"Everything except where he goes."

"Ah." She gave a secret smile.

"You know where he goes?"

"No, but I know he drives west."

"Into one of the other zones?" He heard the alarm in his own voice.

"No." She shook her head a number of times. "He drives west inside the Russian Zone and uses what streets are available to bring him to the western end of the Unter den Linden—along the Friedrichstrasse. Then turns right. One of the other secretaries has seen him repeatedly. She also has Wednesday afternoons off duty."

"Perhaps this other secretary meets him?" Herbie thought of the consternation it would cause if the English Russian really was meeting a woman.

"I hardly think so." Helene giggled. "You don't know Berta!" She puffed out her cheeks and prescribed a great circle around her body, with her hands. "The other girls call her Brünnhilde."

"So." Herbie became lost in thought. After a while, when Helene brought soup and bread to the table, he told her he would bring food back from the British or American zones tomorrow. She was to arrange for the whole group to gather at her room, just as before.

On the following night he told them that it was important they should do exactly as he instructed. He drew a little map, showing each of the team where they should station themselves so they could get a picture of Rogov's exact movements—at least from the Karlshorst barracks to the Unter den Linden. He stationed Willy on the Linden itself, near its intersection with the Friedrichstrasse, in the hope that he would be able to spot the little car and track it for at least some of the way. Everything was set for next Wednesday. They would hold another meeting on Thursday evening.

For once Herbie altered his rules. The days were slipping past, and Naldo had told him time was important. So on Wednesday

Herbie did not go into the British Zone. Instead he made his own way up the Unter den Linden at a little after eleven-thirty in the morning.

The sun was weak and watery—it had rained the previous evening and Berlin smelled of smoke and carnage. Rain brought this smoldering smell out of the ruins and the earth. If there was thunder with the rain, people could easily imagine the Russian assault was here once more, or the Amis were bombing them, haunting the present with the horror of the past.

The almost undamaged Brandenburger Tor stood out, black and sharp, at the western end of what had once been a great wide thoroughfare—Berlin's answer to London's Bond Street or Paris' Champs-Elysées. Herbie turned right, going east and walking slowly, lumbering but looking as though he was on important business and knew exactly what he was doing—which indeed he did. In the past twenty-four hours he had made discreet inquiries —mainly from those who inhabited the twilight world of illegal drinking dens or lived rough among the ruins. Some were not eager to talk, but Herbie had money, which was a key to the city's other world.

Along the Unter den Linden, structures were starting to rise awkwardly from the ruins—some of which seemed to form a kind of cloister along the pavement. A few makeshift shops had been opened, but appeared to be very short of things to sell; women stood in line for a pile of half-rotten cabbages and beetroot. Yet civilians crowded the restructured sidewalks, and some of the women even wore hats of the latest fashion from the Western zones. Russian soldiers also moved among the people, occasionally stopping to check papers or give orders to building workers. There was very little traffic—mainly Russian transport, which blasted innocent cyclists out of their way with constantly blaring horns.

Herbie recognized the gaps where streets had once emptied onto the wide thoroughfare. With terrible nostalgia he recognized a metal sign which hung awkwardly from a blackened wall. *Zigarren. Lotterie* it said, taking Kruger back to childhood, for he knew exactly where he was and could recall his father's strong hand holding his, leading him into the shop smelling of spicy tobacco. The memory brought tears to his eyes and the longing for some magic power which could reverse time. He heard Mahler in his head, and the words, sung from the Second Symphony—

Was entstanden ist, das muss vergehen—

All that arose must perish
All that perished, rise again!
Cease thy trembling!
Prepare thyself to live!

Then, almost before he realized it, he was at the point where the Unter den Linden opened up onto the Platz am Opernhaus and the Platz am Zeughaus. Domes had become skeletal structures, walls remained with their windows now blank unglazed eyes. What had once been glory was now a dark and terrifying monument of man's folly.

He stood for a moment and then chose his route, leading through the piles of masonry and half-broken walls until he found what he had been looking for—a side street with some houses still standing. There, in the protection of the remaining buildings, in doorways and by the curbsides, he saw them.

There were about half a dozen, crouched in the shadows or loitering on the pavement. Young men—all of whom seemed to have taken care with their appearance, for they looked reasonably, if garishly, dressed, and neat; their hair longish but clean and thick. When they walked they did so with a kind of arrogance, a bounce, even a sway.

As Herbie proceeded, one young man detached himself from a half-ruined doorway and asked if he had a cigarette. Herbie's hand went to his pocket, passing a whole pack to the boy, who smiled as though to lure him, asking if he could do anything for him. "I have a room. Not far away," the boy said, coming closer so that, with a shock, Herbie realized he had rouge on his cheeks and his lips were painted scarlet.

Herbie shook his head, giving a sharp "No!" followed by "Take care. If the Russians catch you—"

The boy shrugged and moved away, muttering that he could lead the Russians a dance if he wanted to.

At the end of the road, Herbie turned, looking back, trying to find a vantage point from where he could observe the scene. Finally he came across a tall pile of uncleared rubble. He made a circuit and then began to climb it from the back. If he lay on the hard bricks at the top, he had an unrestricted view of this little street where the boys paraded, appearing and vanishing as men came into view.

He saw a short, well-dressed, middle-aged man stroll slowly down the pavement. One by one the boys came out to speak to him. Three times he shook his head, but when he was approached by the fourth, they stood together, near a wall, talking. He saw the boy's hand come up to caress the man's cheek, and then the pair walked away, cutting through an alleyway which had once been a building, now reduced to a pair of walls and weed-encrusted masonry.

At around one-thirty a car turned the corner. Other vehicles had come that way, but they drove at normal speed. This one was a drab-colored little Volkswagen. He could clearly see the numbers on its registration plate—85942.

The car seemed to falter, and, instead of driving straight through, it began to crawl, first up one side of the street, turning just below the point where Herbie lay, to go back down the other side, still moving slowly. As it passed, young men would appear from their hiding places, showing themselves and retreating again as the car passed by. Finally it stopped near one tall youth who wore what appeared to be a spotless white shirt and dark trousers which were tucked into boots, stolen no doubt from some hapless officer during the last days of battle in Berlin.

The boy moved quickly to the car. There was a short conversation, then the door opened and he seated himself beside the driver. The VW did not linger, drawing away at top speed.

Herbie smiled grimly and nodded to himself. As the car had come toward him, he had clearly seen the driver. It was Gennadi Aleksandrovich Rogov.

ONE WAY OR another, the whole team had sighted the NKVD officer. Herbie sat calm and quiet, his large hands, fingers spread, over his knees, listening to each of their stories, one at a time, never interrupting, so that they all felt important.

When it was over and they sat back full of their own pride and excitement, Herbie began to talk. "Through you, I know where this man now goes on his Wednesday afternoon jaunts." He beamed at them, making them feel irreplaceable. "He has no secret woman here in Berlin. In fact just the opposite." Herbie held the pause, dropping his voice to keep their attention. "None of this would have been possible to discover without your assistance." Always give your agents a sense of their own importance, they had taught him at Warminster. Always flatter them.

"You will be well rewarded, but the most difficult part of this operation has yet to come—next Wednesday." Again the pause, counting to ten in his mind. "For this we need one more actor to play a leading role. It is up to you to find him for me."

They bent their heads closer, eyes raised expectantly—the muscular Willy; dark, angular Gertrude; the insignificant-looking Kurt; and the scruffy blonde Ingrid.

"You must find me a very pretty boy," he said slowly. "The most pretty boy in the Russian Zone. Very beautiful—and not one who usually flaunts his body on the streets near the Platz am Opernhaus."

The girls both gave a sharp intake of breath. Willy laughed. "You want a *bum bandit*," he said, using an untranslatable slang word.

"Quite."

Kurt said, "You mean this man is a queer?"

"Exactly."

"He picks up those boys off the Platz am Opernhaus?"—from a wide-eyed Ingrid.

"So it would seem."

Willy sniggered. "Good God! He's a windjammer."

Herbie gave him a stern look. "Do not mock, Willy. Don't ever do that. There but for the grace of God goes you."

They looked at one another shiftily, as though each was reluctant to allow the others to know they could name such a person. At last it was Ingrid who spoke.

"I think I know someone."

"Yes?"

"He is beautiful, one cannot deny it—strong, good muscles, the face of a woman, with lovely blond hair. He also hates the Russians, but is afraid of them."

"Then you will have to bring him here and we will teach him not to be afraid." Herbie gave her a wonderful smile. "His name?"

"Just call him Nikolas."

"Good. Can you persuade him to come here tomorrow night?"

"I think so."

"Make sure of it."

When they had gone, Herbie turned to Helene. "What has to be done will be done here," he said. "It will be quite safe when it's finished. I shall have help from the British Zone. And when we do it—which should be next Wednesday—I hope to provide this Colonel Rogov with Nikolas as bait." In the far corner of his mind he prayed that Nikolas would find the strength to go through with what would be asked of him.

"He must bring the Colonel here, and we will have to remove certain things from this room." His eyes moved toward Helene's wardrobe. "If your clothes are taken from there, do you think I would fit inside?"

She gave a nervous laugh. "You are to hide in my wardrobe, Eberhardt? Like a husband trying to catch his wife with her lover?"

"Something like that. I will have a small camera—the shutter makes little noise. We will have to make a small hole in the wardrobe door, I fear, but you will be compensated for that. The pictures will not be good—dark and grainy, I think. But they will serve their purpose." He looked about him, brow creased. "I shall also require somewhere to place the recording apparatus."

"Recording . . . ?"

He gave her his most innocent smile, which was really full of guile, and began to pace around the room, peering inside the wardrobe, looking under the bed. At last he finished. "Good. Next Wednesday, when you come home from work, it will be finished. Silence, though. No speaking of this to anybody. You understand?"

Somehow, in his words and actions, Herbie appeared to have taken on a new authority. Helene did not know if she liked it. However, she understood.

On the following evening Ingrid brought Nikolas to the room. He was tall and slim, walked with a firm masculine stride, but, once seated, gave himself away by his effeminate movements and the way in which he spoke. To begin with, these things were not noticeable, but as he relaxed, realizing he was among friends, so his sexual predilection became apparent.

After a while Herbie began to speak to him of what would be required. Nikolas was frightened at first, then started to gain strength from Herbie's own confidence. At last the only remaining worry was that of going into the street off the Platz am Opernhaus. "They know each other there. I have a friend who was so short of money that he tried his luck on the street. They beat him up and sent him packing."

Herbie told him that he would be protected. Finally he agreed.

"We must dress you superbly, and you have to be placed at the most favorable vantage point," Herbie said. "It is essential that he choose you—and only you. The trick has to be like the way a conjurer forces one of his audience to take a certain card from the pack." He was glad Willy was not there. Willy would have said something about making the Colonel take the Queen of Hearts.

It was finally arranged, and Herbie gave the boy his instructions. He must keep out of sight until the following Tuesday night. On that evening he would be brought, by Ingrid, to this room. He would stay in the room, with Herbie and Helene, until Wednesday, when Willy and Kurt would take him to the Platz am Opernhaus.

He agreed, and Herbie then gave instructions to Helene. She would tell the others what to do—Willy and Kurt were to go and spy out the lie of the land around the Platz am Opernhaus. All would meet again—here—next Tuesday night.

When the boy had left, Herbie produced a brace and bit from the bag he always carried to and from "work" and started to bore the hole in the wardrobe door. He made many tests to check its correct position before making the first small hole.

The following morning he crossed into the British Zone as usual, but this time he went straight to the safe house he had last shared with Naldo. There he sat and waited until the telephone rang at twelve noon. It rang twice, then stopped. Thirty seconds later it rang again.

Herbie picked up the instrument and spoke—

"Treacle," he said.

IN LONDON, NALDO and Arnie went about their business, doing turn and turn about in the Northolt house.

As the days went by, their inner tension increased. Neither would admit it, but they both worried about the Kruger boy. Naldo thought he was really too young to go into the field and run an operation like this; Arnie did not so much think of his age, he was more concerned with Herbie's experience. He knew from his first days of handling the lad that he was naturally streetwise. But this was something else—working close to the Russians on their home ground.

Never once did they discuss their fears, but as time began to stretch, they also worried about hearing nothing from C. For all they knew, the whole of *Brimstone* could have been blown sky high.

Only once did Arnie meet Fry, who called a crash meeting five days after it started.

They met in the Reptile House of the Regent's Park Zoo. Fry was engrossed in watching the cobras through their thick protective glass. During the war all of the dangerous creatures had been moved out of London to places of greater safety. It would not have done for cobras, rattlers, or even tarantulas to have been released by a Nazi bomb shattering their warm glass boxes.

"The cobra is a beautiful creature," Fry said, as if to nobody.

"We should have agents with that kind of hypnotic power—or interrogators at least."

"If you like that kind of thing." Speaking for himself, Arnie did not care for snakes.

"Washington wants to know what's going on." Fry had taken to speaking out of the corner of his mouth, like Cagney or Bogart in convict movies. He seemed to have become conscious of his own irreplaceable position in the grand strategy of worldwide political actions. Like many intelligence officers, before and after him, Fry's view of things had warped his perception, making him subject to *folie des grandeurs*.

"I fear Washington'll have to wait."

"Arnie, you're under discipline," Fry reminded him.

"I know. You ever heard of an Italian play called *The Servant of Two Masters*?"

"Theater isn't my thing."

"Well, I'm under discipline twice over." Arnie spoke gruffly. "And if you want to blow everything, and put a lot of people's lives at risk, you get Washington to give me a direct order."

"They might have to."

"You'll know when I have the full story. At this moment I could only give you half-baked information," Arnie lied. "Just leave it be, Roger. As soon as I'm able, you'll have everything. You *are* going to be cut in after all."

Arnold stayed for a few more minutes, listening to Fry make threats of the "there'll be trouble if we're not cut in" variety.

He left feeling quite happy. It was his free day and he would be seeing the redhead Liz No-Name that night. They were going to the theater—a farce called *Worm's Eye View* at the Whitehall. He knew there would be a lot of British jokes which he would not understand, but that did not matter. He would be with Liz and they would have dinner afterward, somewhere in Soho. He did not care that she would only shake hands with him at the door to her apartment block afterward. Arnold had reached the stage of feeling it was enough—for the time being—just to be with her. He had, in fact, been with her—in cinemas, theaters, and restaurants—practically every other night since their first date. He had once reached for her hand in the cinema, and, on the last occasion, she had allowed him to hold it until their palms became damp with sweat and she had taken her hand away, pointedly drying it off with her handkerchief.

It was all a bit adolescent, he knew that, but it did not worry him.

In the end, that night turned out to be different. He quite enjoyed the play, and they had excellent Spaghetti Neapolitan in Gennaro's. When the cab stopped outside the block of flats off the Earl's Court Road, Liz leaned across to him and whispered, "Why not send the cab away."

Slightly bemused, he did so, and allowed Liz to lead him into her flat, where she gave herself to him with eager passion. Two hours later he realized that he must call Naldo and report the number where he could be reached. He did so, and as soon as the receiver was back on its rests, Liz reached for him again. She was insatiable once roused.

Arnold did not complain.

Meanwhile, Naldo was not as lucky as Arnie. Barbara Burville, not to mention her parents, was putting the pressure on. "Look, darling," she said, all wide-eyed and innocent. "You know I don't mind, but the Ma and Pa are getting pretty restless. They go on and on about setting a date."

Naldo would sigh and tell her there was no possibility as yet, unless she wanted to fix a time that might have to be changed later.

"Can't you speak to your wretched boss?"

"At the moment, no. But I'll do it as soon as possible. Barb, I want to get it legalized as well. I also have more than a suspicion that my mother and father know exactly what's going on and want things put on a proper footing—not to mention my grandmama once removed, or whatever Sara is."

Barbara gave a mock pout. "I want to be Mrs. Railton, Nald. Really I do."

"I'll talk to . . . to my Chief as soon as I hear from him."

In fact he heard from him on the following afternoon when the telephone rang in the Northolt house and C said, "It's on. He's waiting at our place for you now."

Naldo telephoned Arnie and within two hours they were both heading—by separate routes—toward Berlin.

In the safe house within the British Zone, Herbie all but crushed Naldo's ribs with his bear hug.

"Well?" Naldo asked.

"Wednesday afternoon, Nald. On Wednesday afternoon I'll have Colonel G. A. Rogov all trussed up for you like a Christmas pudding. Okay?"

"Turkey, Herb. Trussed up like a turkey." Naldo Railton grinned.

23

▼

THE FINAL PHASE of *Brimstone* began on Tuesday night. In the few days available to them, Naldo went through the details with Herbie, who continued to move between the Russian and British zones. This time he brought more items back from the British Sector.

During the two days preceding Tuesday, Helene grudgingly helped move most of her clothes from the room off the Alexanderplatz to Herbie's hovel near the river.

"There must be no traces that a woman has ever been here," young Kruger said, repeating what Naldo had already told him. On Tuesday night, with most of her more intimate belongings gone, Helene tacked up a poster showing a red flag which backed the faces of Lenin, a Russian soldier, and an obviously Germanic family all linked together in harmony. "Just to make Rogov feel at home," Kruger said.

An hour before curfew, Ingrid brought Nikolas, whose face bore the strain of one awaiting execution, to the apartment. When Ingrid left, Helene and Herbie began the slow job of putting the boy at ease.

Helene washed his hair, using a good shampoo Herbie had brought from the West. Then they showed him the clothes, which made him feel even better. He changed behind a makeshift screen they had put up by hanging a blanket over a string stretched across the room. When Nikolas emerged he did so looking much happier. He had been given fresh cotton underclothes, stout woolen socks, a blue shirt, some nicely cut cavalry-twill slacks, and black leather shoes which matched the short leather jacket that was in much better condition than the one proudly worn by Willy.

Scrubbed and with his light hair clean and bouncing with

body, Nikolas paraded up and down the room to the praise of both Helene and Herbie.

They ate a good meal and, before retiring to their respective sides of the blanket screen, Herbie sat down with the boy and went over the moves again—like a coach rehearsing his team in the changing room.

"There will be no danger," Kruger repeated for the umpteenth time. "The only danger will come from yourself. Show no fear. A man like this will be nervous about what he is doing. Like an animal he'll pick up the scent of any anxiety from you. Just do it." He gave a small laugh. "Lie back and think of Germany if you have to, and don't forget the only time you'll really be alone with him will be in his car. In the street Willy and Kurt will be near, and once you've reached this place you won't be alone. But for God's sake take care—don't draw attention to the wardrobe or the door. He can panic easily."

Nikolas nodded and gave a weak smile. Herbie continued, forcing confidence into him.

Later, when they were behind their separate sides of the blanket, Helene whispered, "You will be going when this is over, yes?"

"We'll see. If I go, it won't be for long, *Liebling*. I'll be back." Herbie lied easily, knowing that he could well be out of the Russian Zone for a long time.

"Please promise you will return. That you'll come back to me, Eberhardt. Please."

"I promise." He fondled her, realizing that he would miss some of the comforts she provided. He stayed awake long after Helene had dropped into quiet sleep.

Herbie thought about life and the multitude of things he had already done. In England they had pointed out some boys to him—they were in the uniform of some very privileged school. "Those kids are just your age, Herbie," one of the instructors told him. "How'd you like to go to a school with kids like that?"

He had shaken his head, and afterward looked at himself in the long mirror which hung on the wall of his room at Warminster. Compared to those boys he looked an old man—thirty almost. He had grown up in a different kind of school. Yes, he remembered his parents—particularly his father—with love and regret; but his life had been one of incident and a different kind of learning. He knew the ways of the street, the ways of deception and death. Having learned all this, he was bound to look older. He would not change it for . . . what was it they said in English?

For a king's ransack—or something. No, Eberhardt Lucas Kruger would not want it any other way.

In the morning—the Wednesday morning—Helene behaved herself and held back tears until she was out of the room. Herbie had warned her not to show anxiety in front of Nikolas. She was good, he considered. He would use her again.

Together, Herbie and Nikolas tidied up the room—Herbie throwing open the window to disperse any female smells that might remain. It was overcast outside, with dark clouds moving across a lighter gray sky like shadows on a wall at night. Suddenly Herbie felt a stab of panic. What if the NKVD man did not go to the street that afternoon? What if his duty roster had been altered or if he suddenly changed his mind? What? If? Herbie pulled himself together. "It'll go like clockwork," he told Nikolas, who had washed, dressed himself in his new finery, and now waited impatiently with great nervousness, like someone early at the airport for his plane—someone who had never flown before, worrying and with time to pass.

At noon Herbie looked at his watch. Naldo would be crossing into the Russian Zone about now. Another quick attack of panic. *What if?* There for a moment, then controlled. "It'll be fine, Herb." That was what both Naldo and Arnie had said.

Willy and Kurt arrived shortly after twelve-thirty and took Nikolas away quickly. "I want you here on the dot," Herbie had instructed them. "In and out. No hanging about with him. It'll only make him nervous—you also."

His final words to them had been, "You make certain, now, that he chooses *our* boy and none of the others."

When they had gone and he was left alone, Herbie locked the door—Nikolas had a key. "You must be seen to open the place," Kruger had told him. "He must really *believe* it's your place."

He did not close the window—there was plenty of time for that—but he opened the wardrobe, for the hundredth time, to check all was well. The aperture in the door was quite large, bigger than he had intended, so he had covered it on the inside with cellophane. Through the cellophane he could make out blurred figures in the room, and he was able to remove the little transparent square with one pull that made no noise. Again and again he had practiced getting the camera up to the hole and centering on the bed through the viewfinder. This was the smallest camera he had ever seen, and they had tested it on the previous Friday on Naldo's orders. Helene swore she heard nothing when he pressed the shutter release. He used a whole roll of film, taking it back to Naldo, who pronounced it good. "Much better than I thought, but if you could manage a little more light it would help."

So Herbie had replaced the dull overhead bulb with one of 100 watts—unheard of, and far above the regulation allowance. It was a risk he was prepared to take, and one to which Naldo gave his blessing.

One o'clock. Naldo would be here now—and Arnie as well, if he was to come. Nikolas would be with Willy and Kurt in the street near the Platz am Opernhaus. In about forty-five minutes, Herbie knew he had to be in the wardrobe. For the last time he checked the wire recorder, which was under the bed, shielded by two old suitcases, the microphone lead disguised and running up to the little bowl of flowers on the bedside table. The microphone itself was buried among the flowers. That had also been tested. It worked.

Herbie looked at his watch again. One-fifteen. As though he was far away, outside his own body, Herbie noticed that his hands were trembling. He closed the window and thought of Nikolas.

WHEN THEY REACHED the place, Willy gently pushed Nikolas into the position they had chosen—a doorway a little distance up the street. There was another boy near the corner, and a second in a broken archway several yards away, which meant their target would see two boys—ones he probably already knew—before he set eyes on Nikolas. There had been much discussion about this, and Herbie had taken advice from Naldo. "Third," Naldo had cautioned. "Did you know that if you deal out four cards in a row and ask someone to point to one of them, nine times out of ten they'll pick the one third from their left? If the boy is as good-looking and as fresh as you say, then he'll go for him—providing he's the third possibility. I'd put my shirt on it."

Nikolas stood for a moment, looking up the street toward the Platz am Opernhaus, then stepped back into the lee of the building. Already Willy and Kurt seemed to have disappeared, but he knew they would be very close—hidden in a doorway or behind one of the cracked walls.

The two boys higher up the street saw Nikolas, nodded to one another, turned, and walked down toward him. They were both tall, well-built lads who could take care of themselves—heaven knew, you had to be able to do that on these streets.

"What you think you're doing? Our patch, this." One of the

boys spoke quietly to Nikolas, coming close to him. The other performed a flanking movement, arriving on Nikolas' right side.

"Clear off," said this second youth. "We don't want mystery talent. Here it's like a union. You have to belong. You don't belong—so fuck off."

"Why don't you look behind you?" Suddenly Nikolas was very much in control of himself.

"We don't—" The first boy started, then made a little sobbing noise of pain. Willy had come up behind him, grabbed his wrist, and hooked his right arm into the small of his back, twisting the arm up to his victim's shoulder blades. Kurt silently performed the same move on the second boy. "Live and let live, eh?" Willy said. "Live and let live, otherwise we'll put you in the hospital for several weeks—and what'll you do then?"

By now they were twisting the arms harder. The boys both cried out.

"Shut your poxy mouths, the two of you. Understand?"

"It's only—" one of them started to say.

"It's only a warning," Willy growled. "Tell us you'll behave yourselves and go back to your pitches. Just nod. None of us want trouble."

The two boys nodded vigorously. Willy and Kurt let them go and they scuttled back to their beats, massaging their arms.

A moment later a prospective client rounded the corner. He was short, fat, and had a mincing walk. He passed the first two boys, who went out of their way to proposition him. Nikolas stayed in the shadows, but the little fat man spotted him.

The little man moved toward Nikolas and spoke. "You want some good company?"

"I'm waiting for a friend."

"Aren't we all, dear? I'll pay well. Very well." He took a step closer, and Willy came silently up behind him. "On your way," Willy said.

The little man turned, looked as though he was going to argue, then Willy spoke again: "You heard what he said, freak. On your way. Go!"

There was no argument. The little man tried not to look flustered, flashed a weak smile at Nikolas, and trundled on down the street to where a fourth boy emerged from the shadows.

Ten minutes later the Volkswagen came slowly into the street. "Wait," Kurt hissed from his doorway. "Wait! I'll tell you when to move."

The VW went slowly past the second boy, the driver peering

out of his window. *"Now,"* Kurt whispered loud enough for Nikolas to hear.

Nikolas stepped onto the pavement and the car slowed, then came to a halt. The driver leaned close to the window and beckoned.

"You want a friend for a while?" Nikolas asked, looking straight into the man's face.

"That depends. You got somewhere to go?"

"Yes. A little way from here, near the Alexanderplatz."

"You're new. I haven't seen you before."

"I'm new, but not to the game. I'll give you the time of your life."

The driver seemed to hesitate. "The Alexanderplatz is too far. . ." Another hesitation as he took in Nikolas' looks and build.

"It's very private." Nikolas spoke steadily, no fear in his voice. "I'm really looking for a permanent friend. I won't cheat you."

"How much?"

Nikolas named the price Herbie had told him to offer.

Again the driver paused. Then—"Okay. Come in and tell me how to get there. I want to walk the last bit, don't want the car seen near your place, okay?"

"Naturally." Nikolas gave him a dazzling smile, thinking to himself that if this man was a Russian he spoke very good German. Inside the car he could see, for the first time, that the man was tall—too tall for a car like this. He sat bunched up over the wheel.

Nikolas put a hand tentatively on his knee, smiled up at him, and began to give directions. "Don't worry"—he amazed himself by the way he was able to handle things—"don't worry, I'm not like the usual street boys. I come from a good family. I'll make you proud to know me—to be my friend."

"We'll see about that," the driver said, pushing in the clutch.

"Yes, we'll see. You all say you're different. What do I call you?"

"Klaus," Nikolas lied as he had been told.

"Well, Klaus, we'll see. It's usually I who turn out to be different."

Nikolas gave the driver very precise instructions. Once more, Herbie, at Naldo's instigation, had told him the exact route he should take. "I don't want him being caught out by his own people," Naldo said. "On something like this there's always a chance in a million that they've had an eye on him and know what he's up to."

Both Gertrude and Ingrid had been stationed along the proposed route, with instructions to alert Herbie as best they could should the Volkswagen have a tail.

Nobody followed. The driver did not talk during the journey except to ask Nikolas to say when they were within about a quarter of a kilometer of the place where he lived. Nikolas obeyed him, and the NKVD officer found a side street in which to park. "Right. Get out here," he said, and as he climbed from the car Nikolas saw that the man was indeed tall, a little over six feet. He certainly did not look Russian either, more French or even English. He had a very distinctive nose and what Nikolas thought of as an aristocratic bearing, even in the badly tailored Russian civilian suit he wore. The suit was the only thing Russian about him.

"You go ahead," the NKVD officer said as he locked the car. "I'll follow you." For a moment he seemed to soften and smile. "It's better to be very careful, my dear Klaus. I wouldn't want to see a nice boy like you get into any trouble on my account."

Nikolas walked slowly—"Don't hurry *anything*," Herbie had told him. Already he found himself enjoying the game. (It was Herbie who had said, "Treat it like a kids' game." How was Nikolas to know Naldo had demanded that Herbie should say this?)

For a moment he loitered outside the house as though pausing to check a nonexistent wristwatch. He would be able to afford a wristwatch after this. The man he had picked up did not even look at him. Inside the hallway, Nikolas hesitated again, and was making a show of searching for his key as the client followed him through the door.

"Upstairs?" the man asked. Nikolas nodded and began to climb the creaking stairs. "Third floor." He looked back with a smile, praying that Herbie was already in place.

Across the road, standing well back so he would not be seen through a window, bomb-stripped of its glass, Naldo Railton watched. He did not smile.

HERBIE HAD BEEN in the wardrobe for almost five minutes when he heard the key in the door. There was over an hour's wire in the recording machine, and he had set it going just before clambering into the confined space, the little camera hanging from its short strap and bouncing against his chest. He took the camera in both his big hands, lifting it as far as his chin, then remained still as a statue. He seemed so quiet that he appeared to have stopped breathing.

What happened in the room could only be viewed as a blur of movement, through the cellophane, though Herbie heard every word. He became detached; nothing appeared real; he found nothing shocked him, and felt no guilt at being a hidden listener. First the tentative words, then the more overt bodily approaches, the exchange of money and the undressing.

Then the two blurs were on the bed and there was movement. Quietly Herbie's hand stole up to peel away the cellophane. Neither the man nor the boy on the bed heard it. They were, as he could see, thoroughly occupied with each other.

He looked through the viewfinder and took the first in a series of twenty shots that covered almost thirty minutes.

At last it was over. The couple lay, naked, side by side. Herbie adjusted the camera for one last shot and his hand slipped, banging the camera onto the inside of the door.

"What . . . ?" The man shot bolt upright.

"It's the plumbing," Nikolas said with great control. "It makes the walls rattle, the furniture also."

"Oh, yes?" He was naked, making directly for the wardrobe. Herbie allowed the camera to drop, preparing himself for the assault to come.

"You shits!" The NKVD man heaved the wardrobe door open, so hard that it was almost ripped from its hinges. The whole structure swayed, nearly throwing Herbie off balance. He saw the nakedness, and the fury on the face, then the man turned and flung himself toward his clothes, piled neatly on one of the chairs. Distantly Herbie thought, He's going for a gun. He has a gun there. But he did nothing.

The man had reached the clothes when the main door opened with very little noise.

"I should just stand up and stay very still if I were you." Naldo had a pistol in his hand. This time he *was* smiling. "Hallo, Uncle Ramillies," he said. "Nice to see you after all these years."

24

▼

THAT NIGHT NALDO, armed with unimpeachable documentation, took his long-lost Uncle Ramillies into the British Zone. True, Ramillies was drugged and covered with old sacking, tucked into the trunk of the matt-gray Humber in which Naldo had entered the Russian Zone that morning. Also, the documentation was unimpeachable as long as nobody checked thoroughly with the British Military Governor's Office, or, come to that, the Foreign Office.

From the moment Naldo walked into Helene's room near the Alexanderplatz, things began to move.

"Please don't do anything stupid, Uncle Ramillies." Naldo had the Browning automatic pointed at Ramillies, using the two-handed grip. "Herb, get his gun. It's somewhere among the clothes, I should imagine. And you"—flicking his eyes toward Nikolas—"you get dressed."

"I protest," Ramillies said in Russian. "I am a colonel of the Red Army. You are in the Russian Zone. We have the jurisdiction here." It was a shade halfhearted.

"At the moment"—Naldo smiled at his uncle—"by virtue of the power invested in me by this nine-millimeter Browning automatic pistol, *I* have the jurisdiction."

Herbie went over to the clothes and rummaged for the gun tucked neatly under the folded jacket while Naldo told Ramillies that he also had better get dressed. He sounded very happy about everything. In his mind, as he watched his uncle, he saw the man's height and manner of bearing was distinctively that of a Railton, as were his features: the strong jawline, high forehead, clear blue eyes, and long patrician nose which flared slightly at the nostrils—the Railton nose.

Ramillies continued to mutter threats as he dressed, then sat down on the edge of the bed and changed his language to German—*"Ihr Penner! Ihr Scheisskerle!"*—"You bums! You shits!"

"Please, no flattering," Herbie said with a big grin. "What we do now, Naldo? Look"—holding up Ramillies' weapon—"he has American fucking gun."

"Lease-lend, I guess." Naldo could not dampen his own feeling of elation. This was a moment of history for his family—the return of a treacherous son and the opening of that hidden cupboard which had contained the ghastly Railton skeleton since the end of World War I.

"What we do, though, Nald?"

"We get him out of here, first. Handcuffs in my right pocket, Herb."

Ramillies did not even struggle as Herbie handcuffed him.

Shortly after this the remainder of the team returned. When they saw their quarry, all four of them burst into excited chatter, even some applause. Ingrid actually kissed Herbie, and everyone patted Naldo, as though he was some strange creature from another planet. In the end, there was a lot of noise and Naldo was forced to bring the self-congratulations and general hubbub to order. "Which of you can drive?" he asked loudly over the noise.

Willy raised a hand.

"Okay—Herbie, give this one the keys to our friend's car." Again he looked at Nikolas. "You show him where it's parked. At dusk drive it to some good spot near the river and push it in—and for God's sake don't get caught or even seen."

They nodded, very seriously.

"And do as you're told," Herbie added. "No tricks, Willy. The car will be on every Russian wanted list by late tonight. Don't get tempted, eh."

Willy shrugged, then told Herbie, okay.

"Before you go, we might need a bit of brute force." Naldo looked toward his uncle. "A small injection. I have the stuff here."

They held the NKVD man down on the bed while he struggled and kicked, as Naldo gave him the injection—a rather crude anesthetic which would keep him quiet for around eight hours.

When Ramillies was unconscious, Naldo dismissed everyone. The girls were to head off Helene and bring her back just after dusk, but leaving themselves time to get home before curfew. Kurt was sent downstairs to keep an eye on the front of the building. Willy and Nikolas went off to stand guard over the VW until it was time to dispose of it.

"You all come here early tomorrow," Herbie told them. "Your

pay will be ready for you. Come before Helene leaves for work."

"They all okay?" Naldo asked as soon as they were left alone with their sleeping beauty.

"They're very good. I think, though, they should all get work, like Helene. They'll be picked up and forced into labor if they remain leaning against walls. But they're better than me. I nearly fucked it up for you, Naldo."

"Watch the fucking language, Herb."

"Okay. But we can probably use them again—the team, I mean—if we have to. I shall put fear of God into them tomorrow. Make them stop being lie-abouts. Make them get work. For the Russians if possible. They come in very useful one of these days."

"And tomorrow you'll bring the gubbins to the house in the British Zone."

"What is gubbins?"

"The pretty pictures and the recording."

"You not taking them?"

"No. Just in case anything goes wrong."

And that was it. Nothing did go wrong. "It seemed almost too easy," Naldo said to Arnold later.

"Ops that run smoothly *always* seem too easy. Question yourself again after they've started to dry out your uncle. If there *are* problems, it *will* have been too easy." They were in the British Zone's safe house by then, and Naldo was winding down from the stress of the last hours.

He had left Herbie alone with their prisoner while he walked a kilometer to the cleared bomb site where he had parked the Humber, hidden away behind a broken wall.

Carefully, he drove back to the Alexanderplatz house and drew up directly outside. Then he helped Herbie carry Ramillies to the door. He opened the trunk, and they chose a minute when the street was empty, in the gathering gloom, to dump their captive, covering him with sacks. Naldo drove carefully until he reached one of the many streets that divided the zones, when he put his foot down and—to use his own words—went "Split-arse into safety."

Now, in the safe house, with Ramillies still asleep in one of the bedrooms, he asked Arnold what arrangements C had made to get their man to England.

Arnold looked at his feet. "I have news." He looked up, and Naldo saw something had gone wrong. "In his infinite wisdom, our lord and master has decided we should keep your uncle here."

"What? Here? Here—in Berlin?"

"Not necessarily Berlin. He came over for the day. Called me in this morning." Arnold grimaced. "Lots of cloak-and-dagger stuff—telephone calls; a bodyguard, and an ultra-safe house near the airfield—near Gatow."

"And he doesn't want my uncle back in the land of his fore-bears?"

"His op, Nald. He's obsessive about it—*his op*. He keeps repeating it, and what he says goes. He feels, and I quote, *It would be unwise to bring Ramillies into the UK—for a while at least*. I can understand it. The Ivans're going to get themselves really screwed up. NKVD officer missing. Is he dead or was he filched? Do the Brits know where he is? Stiff notes to the Military Governor, telephones ringing at midnight in Whitehall . . ."

"You mean he wishes to be able to say he has no idea where the missing Russian colonel has gone? None of his business?"

Arnold said that was the way he had read it. "He suggested we take him to the big safe house in Munich for a start. Says we should avoid military bases if possible."

"Interrogation?"

"We know what it's all about. We sort him—oh, we do get some help. By the devious methods he's going to get your Uncle Caspar into the act. Said Caspar'd know how to do it."

"That's what I figured."

Ramillies was awake, but looking ill by the time Herbie turned up.

"I fix them all," Herbie told Naldo. "No trouble there. I have trouble with Helene. Doesn't want me to leave and all that stuff. You know women?"

Yes, Naldo said he knew women, and marveled at Kruger's maturity. They had made their own arrangements for processing the film right there in the safe house, and while Naldo waited for the prints to dry, he played the wires, which were perfect. He grinned at Arnie. "Snaps're fairly dramatic as well."

They gave breakfast to Ramillies, who refused to eat and de-manded to see a senior Russian officer. "No Russian officers here," they told him. Then Naldo took a turn around the block—to be certain there was no "iffy surveillance," while Arnold and Herbie baby-sat their prisoner.

"We going back to England, Arnie?" Herbie asked, and Arnold gave him a watered-down version of what he had told Naldo.

They left that evening without really saying much to Ramillies. There was a Dakota at Gatow, and Naldo drove them onto the base, with Ramillies again well sedated. They had genuine papers for the trip, but did not attempt to get their captive on board until they were certain nobody had hidden eyes on them, apart from the two ground crew, who were RAF types and knew how to zipper their mouths.

Naldo had used the Munich house before, and could see why C suggested it. It lay about three kilometers out of the city, set on two acres, surrounded by trees, and fitted with security locks throughout. There were even several Service hoods permanently based there to patrol the grounds with a pair of evil-tempered German shepherd dogs. The Service hoods were of the kind who asked no questions and talked to nobody as long as the paperwork was genuine. C had given Arnold very good paperwork.

They dumped Ramillies in the most secure room, reserved for people like him or agents out for a day or two of debriefing. Over dinner, after explaining the situation to Herbie, they started planning strategy.

"Go in hard, I think," Naldo decided. "Hit him with the lot, dangle the carrot, then get straight down to the nitty-gritty— Klaubert, the Orléans Russians, Klaubert's escape, and who went with him."

"Promise him immunity?" Arnie asked.

"Anything—so long as it's not recorded or written down. Promise him the earth, a place in the sun, and as many young boys as he requires, for the rest of his life. If he doesn't cooperate, we use the first stick: pretty pictures and the recording." In the basement they had more sophisticated equipment, which could transfer the wire sound to twelve-inch acetate discs. They were also equipped with both wire and cylinder recording apparatus. The more simple magnetic tape would not come into use until the 1950s.

No things are that easy—particularly in Naldo's and Arnie's line of business.

Ramillies did more than just not cooperate. "I am a Russian citizen, an officer of the Red Army. You hold me here against my wishes. There will be a diplomatic incident when it becomes known. My name is Gennadi Aleksandrovich Rogov. I am not this Ramillies you claim."

Naldo sighed and tried again. "Look, we *know* who you are

—an officer of NKVD; a former officer of the British Secret Intelligence Service who defected to the revolutionary forces in Russia in 1918. October to be exact. Under the cover name of Vladimir Khristianovich Galinsky, if you want the details. We can prove who you are. Let's make it easier on you, Uncle Ramillies. Christ, you met me in Cambridge in 1935 when I had some half-baked ideas about Communism. *I* remember you. Let's talk properly."

But Ramillies recited only his Russian name, rank, and number.

The day afterward, both Naldo and Arnie went in, leaving Herbie by the door, outside.

"Okay, Colonel Rogov, we're convinced. What do you want?"

"I wish to be returned to the Russian Sector, where I shall make a full report. Then we shall see where the explosions come from."

"You want to take the photographs with you?" Arnold asked.

"And the recordings?" Naldo added.

"Recordings?" The Colonel had probably worked out how to get around embarrassing photographs by saying he had been drugged and set up for the camera—after all, had he not directed such operations himself? Recordings were another thing entirely.

"Recordings," Naldo repeated. "You didn't think we'd rely on photographs alone, did you? We have every word that you and the boy said from the moment you entered the room. *Everything,* including his price. We told him he particularly had to say the price aloud. He did. So, all the conversation plus the, ah, sound effects."

Ramillies went a shade lighter in color. "You bluff." He laughed unconvincingly.

"It's a good recording," Arnie said brightly. "We're thinking of giving it to the Voice of America—your people listen to our programs, I presume."

Ramillies shrugged. "If you have this recording, then play it."

"You want to hear it first?" Naldo asked.

"I—" There was a tap at the door and Herbie put his head into the room, inclining it toward Naldo, who excused himself.

"Man says he's your uncle on the telephone." Herbie pointed to the hall.

It was Caspar. "Our mutual principal suggested I call this number. Says you have a surprise package waiting for me."

Naldo thought, Christ, he hasn't even told Caspar. Into the telephone he asked where Caspar was.

"Here."

"We'll pick you up. You know the Three Rs?"

"Yes, very well." Caspar indicated that he realized his nephew would give him a time three hours later than any proposed meeting time.

"Okay, go there at three this afternoon. I'll drive in and pick you up at the ladies' entrance. Got it?"

For "ladies' entrance" read the imposing Frauenkirche, in the Marienplatz, which had escaped serious damage in the Allied bombings. Naldo hoped his uncle was quick off the mark.

"Got it." Caspar was very quick off the mark. "Look forward to seeing you." He hung up abruptly and Naldo went back into the interrogation, immediately seeing that Ramillies looked more than a little shaken. Arnie had been playing some of the more salacious passages of the recording.

"SO WHAT'S ALL the mystery? Your father sends his best, by the way." Caspar settled into the Humber next to Naldo.

"You mean you *really* don't know?" Naldo negotiated the streets out of the Marienplatz.

"Not a clue. The Old Man simply said you would have a surprise, and that I was sailing under sealed orders." He tapped the breast pocket of his coat. "You know what he can be like. I have a sealed envelope, not to be opened until I've seen what you've got." He paused for a second too long. "Says you can tell me everything you've been up to."

"Really?" They always warned you about being obsessive, of seeing agents everywhere and becoming overly suspicious of everyone, but Naldo just did not believe his uncle. "The Old Man didn't tell me that, Caspar. Mind if I check on it?"

"Well . . ." Caspar laughed, caught by his own devious words. "Well, I'd rather you didn't, really."

I'll bet, Naldo thought. Caspar was a cunning old fox, but he had been out of the field a long time. "You a trained inquisitor, Cas?" he asked.

"Done all the courses, yes. Had a go at a couple of probables. One was a definite. Yes, I'm a fully fledged interrogator. Why?"

"One of the reasons the Old Man's sent you, then." Keep it in the family, he thought to himself.

Caspar asked if anyone he knew was working with Naldo. "Arnie Farthing and the German lad, Kruger." He did not elaborate, and Caspar grunted.

Naldo slowed the car to show his face to the hoods who opened the gates to the safe house. The garden was walled, topped by great shards of broken glass and barbed wire thick enough to make even a professional think twice. Trees ran inside all the walls, and a great stretch of open lawn was floodlit during the night, from dawn to dusk. A gravel drive swept down in a series of S-bends to the circle in front of the house—ornate, very Bavarian, with distinctive wooden eaves.

"Been here before." Caspar almost shuddered. "We cornered an SS general in this house. Bastard shot his lady friend and bit the old L pill before we could get at him. Made a nasty mess all over the carpet as I recall. Yes, I suppose I liberated this property for the Service."

"Good for you, Uncle Caspar." Naldo brought the car to a stop with a swerving flourish of gravel.

"Oversaw some of the refurbishing as well." Caspar seemed to be off in a world of his own. "Expect that's one of the reasons the Chief wanted me here. We built one or two little surprises into this place. Extra-interrogatory devices."

"Maybe that's one reason. The other's a little closer to your heart. Come on in and meet the subject."

Caspar swung his artificial leg onto the gravel. As he stood up, his face underwent a strange change. "Oh, Christ!" He looked Naldo straight in the eyes. "It's the Rammer, isn't it? You've snatched Ramillies from the Ivans?"

Naldo took his arm, speaking briefly, giving him a shortened version of how they had entrapped Ramillies, adding details of the recordings and photographs. "Come and meet your brother, Cas. He's being a bit bolshie at the moment."

"Well, he would be, wouldn't he? That's what he is." But the smile on Caspar's face did not speak of humor. After almost thirty years, he was about to come face to face with his own flesh and blood. A Railton traitor he had come to hate, since he learned that he was alive and a shade too well. After all, had not C given him all the secret intelligence they had on Colonel Rogov—a thick dossier containing times, dates, places, names, analysts' reports? It was an incomplete, fragmented map of Ramillies' life since he had first gone into Russia for the Secret Intelligence Service. A lot of the topography was substantial, though some sections were only half-explored, and others guessed at from makeshift readings.

In later years, when they were able to talk more freely to people in the trade, both Naldo and Arnie heaped praise on the way Caspar handled things. "It was the most ruthless, determined, and well-timed breaking of a subject I ever saw," Naldo would say. But, of course, Caspar was the ideal choice—the suspect's elder brother, and also a man of great experience in the business, as well as one who had studied what was known of Ramillies' secret life backward, forwards, and almost sideways since he had been given access to the files. He wasted no time, walking into the room, his face set, eyes rimed with frost. You could almost feel the cold.

"Hallo, Ramillies," he said, as though he was empty of any emotion. "Our mother does not send her best wishes. She would rather that you were dead—which of course will probably be the end of it, soon. They've shown you the pictures." He looked at Arnie. "Played him the words?"

"The best bits."

"Well, let him hear the lot, then package up three copies with three sets of the photographs. I'll dictate the covering letters. One set to Marshal Stalin; one to L. V. Beria, who has overall control of the Russian Intelligence and Security Services; one copy to L. F. Raykhman, Chief of NKVD Executive Action Department. You know how to get them delivered."

"Wait!" There was nothing weak or pleading about Ramillies' voice.

"Why should we wait? You've been shitting on us for years. You think we snatched you to have a show trial or an international incident? Or did you imagine we'd subject you to some sort of interrogation—like your people do in those unhealthy cellars behind Dzerzhinsky Square, in the Lubyanka? You think we'd prise secrets out of you, Ram? Think we'd use electricity and pincers? You think your crony Beria is going to show you mercy?"

Ramillies looked white but in control of himself.

"There's nothing to ask, brother. We know it all. But the family—I mean in its broadest sense—felt it was time we had you scraped away, like surgeons scour infected tissue. It hurts, old son, and most of us here are real family.

"No. No secrets. We post this stuff back. Then we put you in a registered package to Moscow. It's as good as done." Caspar turned to Arnold again. "Play him the whole recording, now—all of it. Make him listen. Goodbye, brother!" And he turned toward the door and walked away.

Naldo caught up with him in the hall. "Cas? Caspar—you've got him on the run! Go back and blaze away." He stopped short as his uncle slumped against the wall. There were tears pouring down his cheeks.

"Cas?" Naldo put a hand on the older man's shoulders.

"Don't." There was no sob in his voice, only a hardness he had never heard from his uncle before this. "That little shit in there's *my* brother—*your* uncle. We should do what I suggested. *I* have to face my mother—his mother; and *I* have to live with the memories of what the little bastard's done."

"But, Caspar..."

Caspar flapped his artificial arm. "It's okay, Nald. No, of course we're going to dry him out. But this is the best way to soften him up. Give him time to think about what would happen to him in Moscow. Then he might just start to plead, and even if he doesn't, we'll find a way."

They did not let him sleep—Naldo, Arnie, and Herbie exchanging watches, talking to him the whole time. They asked no questions, but followed Caspar's explicit brief. Both Naldo and Arnie were amazed that Ramillies' brother knew so much about the traitor's secret life, and even more dazzled by the detail he managed to keep in his head. He was able to recite whole chunks of the NKVD man's personal history—recruiting in English universities during the 1930s; his contacts with known Russian agents in occupied Europe during the war; his prime job within the First Directorate, or Foreign Department as it was known during what the Russians called the Great Patriotic War; and his close relationship with the beast Beria, a delicate friendship forged by Ramillies to preserve his own survival during the purges and reorganization within the NKVD during the late 1930s and early 1940s. He even knew the names of some of Ramillies' agents in the field: admittedly most of them were blown agents, but Caspar had chapter and verse on them.

"You've got one hell of a lot on him," Arnie said.

"That's what it looks like to you." Caspar smiled. "I hope it's going to seem the same to him. If we give him too much time to think, he'll see that we really don't know about anything that matters. Mind you, he *has* to see that in due course, otherwise we don't win the golden chalice from him." He chuckled. "If anyone knows about Klaubert of Orléans, and what's happened to my nieces, that bastard does. They're *his* nieces as well, don't forget." He gave a weak smile. "The Old Man didn't have to put it in words to me, but he's allowed you to risk your necks pulling the Rammer out of the Russian Zone, so that I can put him to the question about Klaubert and the girls. I presume that's why the whole of this business is tied up so tightly—I mean, nobody else knows, do they, Arnie?"

"No. Only Naldo and myself—and Herbie of course, but he's really only a spear carrier. I think the Chief sent him along for the experience."

Caspar nodded. Herbie was told to talk to Ramillies about anything under the sun, and use his common sense. "Pretend you know more than you really do, Herb," Naldo counseled.

It was from Herbie Kruger that they first realized, the following morning, that Ramillies Railton was starting to crack. They had left Arnie with him while the three of them had breakfast, looking heavy-eyed after snatched odd hours of sleep.

"That fellow is one frightened man. Leave him longer and he'll need change of underpants." Herbie spoke in such a normal tone that the other two—Caspar and Naldo—did not at first realize the meaning of what he had said.

"Herb?" Naldo looked up from his coffee. "Why do you say that?"

Herbie gave a grunt. "We speak German to each other. Every time I go in he gets cozy—you know, like I'm different to you crowd. I am German. He asks the whole time about if you're serious."

"Serious?"

"Serious about sending him back to Moscow."

"And you said?"

"I spoke the truth." Herbie gave the grin of a monster. "I said, yes, of course; why not? It would be good for him to go back to Moscow. In Moscow he would see his life in—how do you say it?—in perspex?"

"In perspective?" Caspar tried.

"*Ja*. Perspex-tive."

"Perspective, Herb," Naldo said as though on auto pilot.

"The best was last time. He cry, that one in there. He think I'm more on his side, and he weep tears. Not in front of you, but with me. I sing him a little Mahler."

Naldo grunted. "That would make anyone weep."

"Well, I have not yet properly learned the music of *Kindertotenlieder*—Dead Children Songs. But I have the words. I tell him words. Tell him he is going back to Moscow. Tell him more words, like '*In diesem Wetter, in diesem Braus*'—

> "*In this grim weather, this storm,*
> *I'd never have sent the children outside!*

*But they've taken them out of the house.
I had no say in the matter."*

"And he wept at that?" Naldo frowned.

Caspar nodded slowly. "I think I understand." He pushed his
chair back. "My dear brother, whose own twin was driven out of
his mind by battle at sea, has been reflecting on his youth. People
do that when faced with the kind of horror he must know waits
for him in Moscow." He gave an enormous sigh. "I think it's time
I laid some more news on my shit of a brother. It's time to go for
the bastard's jugular."

Naldo followed as Caspar strode—showing no sign of his one
artificial leg—down the passage to where Arnie continued to talk
to Ramillies about his secret life.

25

▼

So now, on that first of many mornings when he began to win his brother back, to see justice done and take vengeance for the whole of his family, Caspar went to him with the same cold lack of humor that he would maintain over the next weeks and months.

"Well, brother Ramillies, have my people looked after you? Do you want for anything?"

Fatigue creased Ramillies' face, making him look like a man in his late sixties, rather than his fifty-two years. His eyes were bloodshot, his stubble gray, and his thinning hair dirty and disheveled. "They haven't let me sleep," he said, his voice surly and hoarse.

"Good practice." Caspar spoke sharply, with no sympathy. "Good practice for what you will undoubtedly go through when they get you back to Moscow."

Ramillies appeared to sag within his own body, his head giving a tiny nod that could be taken as tacit agreement.

Caspar continued. "The three packages—the photographs and records—are ready to be sent covertly into the East. I await final instructions from my superiors." He sat, looking maliciously at his brother for almost three full minutes. Then Caspar drew in a deep and tired breath. "I hold out no hope, Ram. No hope at all, but God knows why, I have put some proposals to my Chief."

"You shouldn't have bothered. I shall go back and face what has to be faced."

"Certain death?"

Ramillies nodded.

"Very well. I'll get on to London now." He stood, turning toward the door. Ramillies spoke again as Caspar's hand touched the knob.

"Cas?" It was the first time in three decades that Ramillies had spoken to Caspar on the equal terms of their brotherhood. "Cas ... What are the alternatives to Moscow?"

Caspar stayed by the door, then took a step back into the room. He asked Naldo and Arnie to leave him alone with Ramillies and they both gave signs of reluctance, as though following Caspar's lead as good dancers will follow a partner.

"Please," Caspar said very quietly. "Please leave me alone with him."

Finally they left the room. Herbie was outside and Caspar went back toward the table separating him from Ramillies. He hesitated but did not sit down.

In reality he was playing for time. On the previous evening he had given Naldo and Arnie a guided tour of the safe house to show them some of what he had called the extra-interrogatory devices: the listening and recording devices in the basement— each linked to a main room or particular area of the house. Caspar had checked on the one covering the room in which the primary interrogation would take place—even though, as yet, Ramillies had no idea he was to be interrogated. Possibly he had prepared himself for it, and then with Caspar's arrival the preparation had become ragged.

When he judged that Naldo and Arnie had activated the hidden microphone, Caspar seated himself again. "There's little I *can* offer, Ram. Very little. You had better know that this whole operation was mounted solely to get rid of you. I was sent over to give positive identification, that's all. Just like the Coroner's Office has to have identification of a body. The word was no deals, no interrogation, nothing. Identify him as your brother and throw him back—with the evidence. Let the dead bury the dead."

Ramillies, so devoid of humor, gave a thin smile. "Talk'st thou to me of 'ifs'? Thou art a traitor; Off with his head!" he said.

"Ah, still a Shakespearean, Ram? Thought Chekov would have lured you from the Railton habit."

"He has his moments." Ramillies' voice was as dry as a bone and the hint of a smile had long gone from his lips. "Right at the end of *The Cherry Orchard* the bourgeois family leave old Firs, the family retainer upon whom they have all relied for years, locked in the house. He tries the door and says, 'Locked. They've gone. They forgot about me. . . . My life's gone as if I'd never lived. . . .' Then, from offstage, comes a distant sound, like that of a string snapping, slowly—sadly—dying away. Then silence broken by the sound of an ax striking a tree in the orchard outside. Is this what I've come to, Caspar? Was the little game in the Alexanderplatz the sound of the string snapping? Because that's how I feel—that my life's gone as if I'd never lived." He looked up, his eyes full of deep thoughts and concern. Then—"Alternatives?"

"I've told you. I don't think there are any, but I just might be able to give you a few more years. It depends."

"On whether I'm traitor enough to double myself. Tell you all I know. Policy; some names; possible strategy."

"Oh, I don't think you could tell us *that* much. Long and costly business as well, Ram, now the Socialists are in power. We're accountable for every penny these days." He leaned back in his chair, eyes closed for a fraction as though in deep contemplation.

"You *did* say you *had* put forward some proposals." Ramillies said it softly, as though fearing he might break in on Caspar's thoughts.

"Only a small idea or two. Orders are that you should be returned unopened—without interrogation. London sees you as a very committed member of the Soviet regime. They all know that you were manipulated before and after you were first sent into Russia. But you're a part of Revolutionary history now, aren't you? Still a believer. Or have you become just another disillusioned Party hack?"

"What are your small ideas?" Ramillies either did not wish to answer his questions or could not.

"I might just make out a case for you to be taken back to England and subjected to a thorough interrogation."

"Well?"

"That would end up with a trial for treason, and one bright morning you'd take a walk with the public hangman." He tapped the table lightly. "But I suppose even that would be better than the things your good friend Comrade Beria will do to you."

Ramillies did not answer.

"There's another possibility, of course, but not much hope at the end of that one either."

"Tell me."

"That we have a long talk. You answer certain questions—there must be *some* queries London wants to clarify. If the answers come out right, we could possibly get the okay to lose you. You might run and take your chances. No." He saw the doubt on Ramillies' face. "No, you're quite right. That's a non-starter.

They'll never buy that." Another endless pause, then—"Was it really worth your life, Ram?"

Ramillies put his head in his hands, making motions as though washing his face. "I really do not know. To me, Communism is similar to Catholicism. The ideal, the faith, always remains true, though some members of the body politic can be corrupt and misleading. The truth remains in spite of human frailty."

"And there's a lot of human frailty within the ideal now?"

Ramillies nodded. "Stalin doesn't care a fig for the Revolution or the Party. Sometimes I think he even despises it. He's a thug. Tell London I can give them certain things—some hard intelligence. Some—I must stress *some* only. Not all I might know. It's time I was honest with somebody. Tell them I'm still joined by the hip to the ideology that made me become what they see as a traitor. I see myself as a man who has remained true to his faith. I believe in a political destiny, and I cannot carry the Party message—the message of the Revolution—unless I am alive. So I will exchange some intelligence for my life."

Caspar sighed. "Lot to ask, Ram. They'd hold no brief for that kind of talk in London."

"Would you try it anyway?"

"Let's see." Finally Caspar left the room.

"Of course it's a load of double-talk," he said to Naldo later. "It's possible that my brother's guilty of the worst sin—of really believing all that business of staying alive to further the cause. My guess is that he doesn't give a damn about anything but his own skin; and that's our strength. We can play along with him, and so milk him dry. Who knows, we might even get him to face the real facts of life."

So it began, the long trail through Ramillies' memories. Caspar went to him later that day and told him, "London's bought it—but only up to a point. You are not to be allowed back into the U.K. We keep you in Germany at least until we see how positive you are—which means we keep you here until they're satisfied of your full cooperation. I have to stress *full* cooperation. I shall send back daily reports. If you fall below what they think is the line of truth, then back you go, Ram, and I shan't have any say in it. In fact I'll even dump you in the Russian Zone myself. Now, will you cooperate?"

Ramillies only nodded his head, and a memory from childhood stirred in Caspar's mind. Ramillies tended to be truthful. If he wanted to avoid direct lies he would nod or shake his head without speaking.

"Will you cooperate?" he repeated.

Ramillies opened his mouth, closed it again, looked down, and then seemed to regain strength from somewhere. "Yes." The voice was firm. "Yes, Caspar. Yes, I shall cooperate fully and without reservation."

"Good." He did not allow himself to look either happy or relieved. "Good. Then we'll begin."

In all it took nearly six months to bring Ramillies Railton to the true point of their questioning—the problem of Klaubert, Jo-Jo Grenot, and Caroline Railton Farthing. The approach had to be made obliquely, through the tall grass and undergrowth of a lifetime of deception that lay deep, encasing Ramillies' history. Nobody—least of all Caspar—wanted him to even suspect the main object of the questioning.

During those months, many things happened.

To start with there was the incident which became known as "Herbie's trouble."

While Naldo and Arnie exchanged wry smiles when it occurred, it was really no laughing matter. It was discovered when they decided a doctor should give Ramillies a thorough checkup. Caspar was not happy about going into a long, and possibly arduous, interrogation unless they were medically sure Ramillies would stand up to the physical strain. He had lost weight, was not sleeping, and appeared to get genuinely exhausted after even short sessions with Caspar, who quickly realized that if he was ever going to get the real answers to the important questions, it would be necessary to backtrack through the years, digging all possible details of Ramillies' career in the Russian Service, right from the very beginning.

So, because the circle of knowledge was so closed, Naldo was dispatched to London, under a passport which fingered him as Mr. David Rathbone. Once there he met C in the Northolt house to talk about getting medical opinion.

C said he would arrange matters. It would be a military doctor who had signed the Official Secrets Act, and was, to use C's own words, "As discreet as a one-time pad."

Naldo was with C for the best part of an hour, and as he was not due out again until the following day, spent the remainder of the time with Barbara, who met him at the Kensington house, wrapped her arms around him, led him to the bedroom, and gave him her all. Naldo returned to Germany feeling happy and tired. In his mind he considered the experience had been like drinking the most satisfying alcohol in the world and then being dragged through a warm and magic pool that produced the kind of pleasures you only imagined in adolescence.

Back in Munich, the doctor arrived—in darkness with a large member of the Military Police SIB, in civilian clothes.

While the doctor was examining Ramillies, Herbie went to Arnold, looking very embarrassed, and haltingly asked if he could possibly have a word with the visiting physician.

"What's up, Herb?" Arnie was concerned at the anxiety in the big German boy's eyes.

Young Kruger looked away. "I think I catch a little cold, Arnie. Maybe I need—what you call it?—a pick-you-up?"

"Yeah. Pick-me-up, Herb."

"That's it. If I could see the doctor perhaps for five minutes . . ."

"See what I can do, Herb." And Arnie went in search of Naldo, who at that moment was with Caspar and the doctor.

"Basically the man's exhausted." The doctor—a young major—was speaking of Ramillies. "He's obviously under stress, but tired."

"Heart okay?" Caspar asked.

"Sound as the proverbial bell. Heart, lungs, all the organs seem fine. Just tired. Shouldn't be under too much stress."

"Pity." There was no anxiety in Caspar's voice. "'Fraid he's going to be under a bit of stress, Doc. Will it kill him?"

The doctor shook his head. "No. No, it won't kill him, but he might collapse on you. If he could be allowed to go a bit easy—"

"Sorry, Doc. Do what we can, but he's got to work quite hard."

The doctor shrugged. "I'm told you're in charge. Up to you."

"Yes, it is really, isn't it."

During this last exchange, Arnie whispered to Naldo, who stepped in, asking the doctor if he would mind giving another member of their unit a quick going over.

The doctor went off into one of the other rooms with a distinctly crestfallen Herbie.

He reappeared fifteen minutes later, asking for Caspar. "You *are* the senior officer here?"

"Yes." Caspar was wary.

"Rules of the game at the moment. I'm duty bound to report a self-inflicted wound."

"What?"

"Your man, Kruger. Medical ethics concerning confidentiality go by the board in the occupied zones, I'm afraid. If this is a military unit, I have to report a self-inflicted illness."

Caspar looked up sharply. "In a strict sense this is *not* a military unit. Will Kruger be okay?"

"Long as he has no alcohol for a month and takes the pills as instructed."

Caspar nodded. "Give him the pills, Doc. I'll see to the rest."

"That girl, that Helene," Herbie fumed later. "She was all bees—is that right?—all bees?"

"Honey?" Naldo suggested.

"Bitter wouldn't melt in her mouth."

"Butter, Herb."

"Well, only one thing melts in her mouth—I know! But she must have been making fuckings with other people. I felt she was not telling me whole truth!" He gave a histrionic sigh. "*Ach*, I feel uncleanly."

"The Doc says it's just a dose of the clap," Naldo said.

Arnold grinned. "Keep taking the pills."

"No laughing thing!" Herbie almost shouted back. "That doctor say I should always take preventions."

"Good rule, old son." Naldo felt a bit of a hypocrite, reflecting on his own sex life, but he had one partner only, and that, as far as he could see, would be for the rest of his life.

"Preventions are like swimming with all clothes on," Herbie grumbled.

"You could get something much worse." Arnold had straightened his face. It was true enough. He had an old friend whose father had caught syphilis which was never detected. The man had died in an asylum. "Just take care, Herbie. Okay?"

"Okay." He frowned. "When I go back to Russian Zone, Nald?"

"Don't know, Herbie. Maybe not for a long time."

Herbie slowly nodded his large head. "Okay. I only hope she give a lot of Ivans this uncleanness. I give her bloody nose when I see again."

They had to break it up at that point. Caspar wanted to get on with the serious work.

It was not so much an interrogation to begin with, for Caspar contributed little to his brother's monologue. Ramillies began with his infiltration into Russia in 1918 and a meeting with the now infamous Felix Edmundovich Dzerzhinsky—the founder of what was to become the very engine of Soviet power. It was as though Ramillies was obsessed by the man. "He was the High Priest of the Revolution," he said. "You see, he understood Revolutionary power like no one before him and nobody since. The Vecheka, which was the father of NKVD, became the power base and the bullet fired by the Revolution. Everyone realized the dangers of 'counterrevolutionaries.' Only Felix understood that there was only one way to contain them."

"And what part did you play, Ram?"

"Me? You'll laugh. I was the diplomat as far as the family was concerned. The military wasn't for me. Oh, no. But Felix Dzerzhinsky made me a soldier. I went into the Army."

Ramillies had been a Political Commissar urging the Army to march to the beat of the Party drum. The Civil War was in full horror, and in battle the commissars urged men forward with pistols, not held toward the enemies of the people, but aimed at the backs of Red Army troops who lagged behind. His baptism of fire had been to act as immediate judge, jury, and executioner on the field of battle.

"It made a man of me, and a zealot, Caspar. Oh, yes, one zealous enough to be sent later into a different sort of field."

When the powerful émigrés fled from Russia, both Lenin and Dzerzhinsky saw them as dangerous elements, strong enough to seduce Russian emigrants to turn, form power bases in the West, and launch counterattacks on the Bolsheviks, who now held the country in thrall. Ramillies—mainly because of his knowledge of the West and his fluency in languages—was sent into the Counterespionage Department, the KRO, the *Kontrarazvedyvatelnyi Otdel*.

"Nowadays you would say we ran surveillance on important émigrés in the West. But to begin with our job was to try and persuade the princes, generals, former men of influence, to return home. 'Come back to Mother Russia, she needs you as she has never needed you,' we would say. To get them back would mean they could be disposed of in private. Only when that failed did we do the job on foreign soil."

"You killed for the KRO, Ram?"

He nodded. "Three times. In Paris all of them." He gave the names, dates, and method. Caspar sent the information back to London. It was all accurate. Now they could trust Ramillies a little more. He was baring his soul, for the KRO eventually became the network of foreign surveillance—the nest of agents in the field, ready to further the Revolution throughout the world when the moment came.

They were over a month into the interrogation before they got to Ramillies' visits to England in the late 1930s.

"I did some auditions in Oxford and Cambridge. But I was not alone, there were many who went out as apostles, and we gathered a good crop. Caspar, do you realize how deeply we've eaten into the upper echelons of your society? We have agents everywhere, in your Foreign Office, even in your own Service." He could give no names, for he knew none—or claimed that he knew none.

What Caspar did get out of that long, rambling, often anguished, always self-serving story which gushed from Ramillies was a two-hundred-page manual on the history and activities of the Soviet Intelligence Service. This was distributed in 1949 as classified material within his own Service and the CIA.

Later, when everything was over, Naldo said, "At least Ramillies made Caspar a hero by giving him the facts with which to write one version of secret history."

But Caspar wanted more—not just the bare bones of organization, the bloodletting and internal squabbles, or the personalities and tradecraft of the NKVD, so soon to become the more universally known KGB. Caspar required three nuggets of truth which he thought were buried within the day-to-day dealings of the Russian Intelligence community. So he plodded on, allowing Ramillies his moment of ironic triumph—for by now his brother was carried forward by his desire for immortality within his old family. He wanted to show them what he had accomplished, and the means with which he had written the pages in blood, stealth, and deception.

The next incident came after three months. With little warning they were suddenly moved.

The team never learned where the tipoff came from, but there was no doubt that the Soviets had tracked them down. Orders came through, in a Flash cable, in cipher, one Friday night. They were to be ready at four o'clock on Saturday morning. Five cars collected them and they were driven, by long and devious routes, to another well-equipped safe house ten kilometers west of Frankfurt. By chance Naldo heard later that on Saturday night three men—all of them German—were killed while attempting to breach the security of the Munich house. When Caspar was told he said, "Then we might be running out of time."

He still had a long haul ahead, but at least he could see the dim light of Klaubert and the girls at the end of the maze which was Ramillies' evidence.

26

▼

THE HOUSE NEAR Frankfurt was not as large as the Munich place, but it stood on rising ground, with a good commanding view. Somehow C had managed to have a squad of hoods there, ready to guard it day and night.

The only problem which first seemed to face the team was the interrogation room. It was large with a great solid glass window —rare in Europe in those days. There was only one set of recording equipment, and that was linked by a complex series of cables embedded in the walls to this one room.

"After what's happened in Munich you're wide open." Naldo stood with Caspar, looking at the great view from the interrogation room's window. Lawns went down in terraced steps—orderly as a battalion on parade. Below the lawns were clumps of bushes, then a half circle of trees which marked the boundary with the road. Even the paving stones on the straight drive up from the road appeared to be set at identical intervals. The flowers obeyed some order to bloom. Caspar said it was all prick-neat, which Naldo took to mean piss-elegant.

"Put one good man down there with a sniper's rifle and you're dead meat."

Caspar gave his nephew what used to be called an "old-fashioned" look. "Nip outside, Nald—take a peek at it from the terraces."

Naldo did as he asked. The window was invisible, like a great black shield. When he returned, Caspar was still in the room, but he had somehow got hold of a very heavy hammer. He walked over to the window and gave it a ferocious blow, using all his strength. The hammer simply bounced back, not even leaving a chip in the glass. "It's bulletproof, one-way, and all that. This'll be safe enough."

Caspar did another three weeks of finely tuned interrogation before he struck the first oil.

It happened on a Wednesday afternoon. As is the way of these things, the morning's work had been almost barren. He was coaxing Ramillies to the moment when the demon king of Russian Intelligence first came on the scene—Lavrenti Pavlovich Beria. Beria, the man who still stood at the head of Stalin's Intelligence and Security agencies now, in 1947.

"Stalin brought in Beria as Yezhov's assistant, and soon Comrade Yezhov was pronounced insane and carted off in the dead of night—the old knock on the door, Caspar—and taken to the Serbskii Institute, where he promptly hanged himself. He was in a straitjacket, but he hanged himself and nobody asked questions.

"So we had Beria, the magician who made almost all of the old guard disappear and weeded out my own department, the KRO."

"But not you, Ramillies. Not you."

No, Ramillies said, not him, for he was too useful. "And I also agreed with all things Comrade Beria said. Yes, Comrade Beria; no, Comrade Beria; lick your arse, Comrade Beria."

Ramillies was especially useful because of his great knowledge of languages, and experience in the West. For Beria's first great reform—apart from disposing of hundreds of officers—was the institution of the so-called Spy Academy at Bykovo, forty miles from Moscow.

Ramillies was there as an instructor for three and a half years, and it was from his description of Bykovo that Caspar took the bulk of his chapters on tradecraft when he came to write the Classified Manual for the SIS.

The description of training at Bykovo was long and full of picturesque detail. Ramillies' eyes blazed with the fervor and joy of it all as he spoke about it—the training in surveillance, ciphers, combat, silent killing, radio, contacts in the field. They were meat and drink to him, but only an hors d'oeuvre to the main course in which he participated—"legends and linguistics," he called them, which in plain language meant turning intelligent Russians into foreigners—"illegals" to work in the field and become, in all senses, another person, born and bred in the country chosen for him.

Their long, faked lives—documented and finely engraved—

were their "legends." The language part was almost as complicated.

Not only did they have to master the language of their target country, but also the true vernacular—accents, slang and, hardest of all, the kinesics—so they could, with ease, imitate the body language and facial expressions which were part of the people's heritage in that country.

"You know we even have a whole town in Bykovo, built as an American small town—'Little Chicago' they call it. Incredible, but it's true. Trainees live there for weeks, just going about the routine of a small American town. At Bykovo our agents learned like actors. They learned to play roles; to live new lives. Stanislavsky would have been proud of them. That is how we were able to send so many convincing people abroad." For the first time since it had begun, Ramillies laughed with a little pleasure. "Can you believe we had agents learning to jitterbug, and listen to the radio serials, on which we tested them. I personally prepared a test for 'The Lone Ranger.' This is true, Caspar. We made them into Americans, Italians, French, Belgians, Portuguese, Spaniards, Dutch, good Nazi Party members as Germans. And they were all—to a man and woman—great Stalinists."

"And what did *you* do in the war, Ramillies, apart from train your super 'illegals'?" Caspar felt a twinge, a sudden clarity—he *knew* that he was nearing the real killing ground.

"Me?" The cold smile returned. "Me? I *ran* illegals, Caspar. I ran three in the United States at long range; and six in Germany and Austria."

Often, Caspar had taught in his lectures at Warminster, there are moments when instinct must rule. He had reached an instinctive moment now, and he plunged in. "You ever come up against an SS officer called Klaubert?" He realized that he could hear his own heart beating. "Hans-Dieter Klaubert—SS-*Standartenführer*."

In slow motion he saw Ramillies nod. "Of course. I helped train him—you know my German is good, and I'd visited Germany a great deal. He was never at Bykovo, of course. Klaubert was German born; tried to defect to us, for his political beliefs, in the late 1930s—'37 or '38, I think. He was persuaded to remain in place; in Germany. To be a good Nazi in order to remain an even better Stalinist. I did on-the-ground training with him. A very good agent. Yes, of course, Hans-Dieter Klaubert was one of mine. Orléans, wasn't it?"

Within himself, Caspar let out a long and relieved sigh. Somewhere in the back of his head he could hear his own voice saying, "Got you!"

And from far away there came a sudden and sad sound. It was like the prolonged snapping of a string.

27

▼

BY THE TIME Caspar reached the most sensitive part of Ramillies' interrogation in Germany, so Otto Buelow, miles away in Washington, was beginning to collaborate with the Agency.

The deal was that in return for the use of the safe house in the American zone of Berlin the Agency would be allowed full access to Buelow in person. Two skilled inquisitors—with FBI backgrounds—came to London, did an on-the-spot analysis, talked with other people on the ground who had a good knowledge of the *Tarot* Enquiry, and decided that "the Otter"—as he was known in Railton circles—should return to Washington with them.

For the first two and a half weeks Buelow went through what they called the fattening-up process. He was given a pleasant apartment, allowed certain freedom, though watched over by Agency bodyguards, and generally treated well. He had good food, entertainment, and sightseeing. He was even offered female companionship, which he turned down. It was felt that Buelow should be at ease before they went through his *Tarot* Enquiry evidence in detail, and allowed him to look at Dollhiem —the man he had fingered as Klaubert's contact *Triangle*—in the flesh. Generally, for security reasons, they still talked of Dollhiem as *Screwtape;* just as Tert Newton was *Screwdriver.*

The two Agency men took Otto out to restaurants, wined and dined him; went with him to stores where he marveled at the comparative luxury, and dug deep into the money allotted to them, having him measured for new suits, buying shirts, ties, shoes, and other delights.

By the third week Otto Buelow looked a different man. He regained weight and color, was well-dressed and relaxed, and appeared at peace with his surroundings. There was even talk of his being allowed to settle in the United States—heaven knew there were plenty of former Nazis with truly evil pasts being quietly infiltrated into the United States with the covert assistance of Military Intelligence, the Agency, and State. Most of these had their papers sanitized so they could bring their knowledge and experience—of rocketry, atomic, and connected subjects—to bear on the various military programs designed to put the United States in the global lead as far as missile and atomic weaponry was concerned.

Otto Buelow knew nothing of this, so did not question the reasons for his newfound American friends showing such open-handedness toward him. In the middle of the third week they began the interrogation—a calm, slow business conducted mainly in a beautiful little house on O Street which had been in one of the Agency men's family for years.

There were three interrogators and no tricks. It would be better, it had been decided, to go through things with Otto in a straightforward manner. So the trio, usually together, began a normal question-and-answer routine.

They took Otto back through the early ground covered in his *Tarot* evidence—his return to Germany, marriage, the years of unrest followed by his own admission that he had joined the Nazi Party "out of necessity, not conviction." They were all impressed with their subject's attitude. He added little to what they already knew about the Nazi Intelligence Service and the part Heydrich had played in its formation, but his refusal to dodge the main issues of responsibility had a refreshing candor about it. Like the *Tarot* Board of Enquiry they warmed to this uncomplicated German who admitted his own knowledge of atrocities just as he had done during the original hearing. They had all done service in Germany and were used to former Nazis using the most common of excuses: "I did these things under orders."—"I was only obeying orders."

"I knew what was happening. How could I not know, during the time with Heydrich? It is to my shame that I did nothing about it. A man should have the intelligence and courage to disobey orders when he knows them to be outrageous or unjust. I had the intelligence, but, alas, not the courage."

Slowly they moved on to his posting to Orléans and relationship with Klaubert. Finally, after some weeks, they came to the OSS operation known as *Romarin*, the breaking of *Tarot* and his identification of Klaubert's informant known as *Dreieck—Triangle*.

"You say the man came to the Rue de Bourgogne headquarters many times?" they asked him.

"I think two or three times a week."

"And not until *after* the raid by parachutists?"

"After that. Also after the *réseau* known as *Tarot* had been rolled up and liquidated."

"Can you remember the very first time you saw the man—this *Triangle?*"

Buelow's brow creased. "I told them in London that it was at headquarters. I have given this much thought, and I might have been wrong. It is possible—just possible—I saw him before that first visit to the headquarters on the Rue de Bourgogne."

Mentally the three interrogators sat up and took notice. Was Buelow about to change his story? Gently, they urged him on. "You saw him *before* the parachutists, or before Klaubert ordered members of *Tarot* to be called in?"

"No," Buelow said firmly. "I should have kept a diary. Made notes. No, it was certainly after July 5—the parachutists were taken in the early hours of that day. The bodies were disposed of on the sixth. I am certain of that. You see, July 6 is the anniversary of my marriage. I always spend a few moments thinking about Mary Anne on that day, and have done ever since she died. So I *do* know what happened on July 6, and I *do* know that I had not set eyes on the man Klaubert called *Triangle* before then. But we all got used to seeing him regularly after that—certainly after the members of *Tarot* were arrested and killed."

"But you might have seen him before the day they took *Tarot* apart?"

"Yes." Confident now. "Yes, I think so, and it would have been a couple of days before the *Tarot* arrests, only I cannot remember the complete circumstances."

"Try, Otto. Please try. It's very important."

On the following day, during the afternoon session, Buelow volunteered that, if he had seen *Triangle* earlier, it was in a small bistro used almost exclusively by German officers. "You see, I have this memory that shortly before the hideous business with the *Tarot* people, I saw Klaubert in this place. It was called La Vache Grise, the Gray Cow, a silly name but very popular among the officers."

"And you think you saw the man *Triangle* there with Klaubert?"

Buelow hesitated. "I saw Klaubert there. Once. Once only, after July 6. . . ."

"And before *Tarot?* You're certain?"

"Absolutely. I visited the place twice during my whole time in Orléans. Once soon after I arrived and once after July 6, 1944. Almost a week after, but before *Tarot*. I know I saw Klaubert there on that second occasion, and there was something unusual about it. I have gone over it many times in my mind. He was there with other people, and I believe the odd thing was that they were in civilian clothes. I think perhaps that *Triangle* was one of them."

"Let it be," the senior interrogator counseled the others in private. "He's either playing some game with us—unlikely because of his frankness—or he's buried the incident deep. If that's true we'll trigger it out of him at some point."

So they dropped this possible first sighting of the man they called *Screwtape*—Nathaniel Dollhiem—and Otto knew as *Triangle*, informer to Hans-Dieter Klaubert. Instead, they began to zero in on one of the other mysteries: Hannalore Bauer, one-time mistress of Klaubert.

Otto could add little to what he had already told the *Tarot* Enquiry. Fräulein Bauer had disappeared before his arrival in Orléans, but gossip had it that she had been replaced by a Frenchwoman. There were many rumors running around the Rue de Bourgogne—that she was one of his informants; that she was a wealthy woman, a countess some said, who planned to marry Klaubert when it was all over.

Some stories had him meeting her in a château nearby—on the Paris road—but that was not likely, for the château was used as a convalescent hospital for troops back from the Eastern Front. Certainly Klaubert's official car had been seen there. But it was also often seen parked in another street—the Rue Bannier. All three inquisitors had heard that name before, but at first could not put the finger of their minds on the context.

The whole thing came together, with startling—almost shocking—clarity during the following week, when they drove Otto Buelow out to look at Dollhiem and Tertius Newton.

They took Otto in the back of an unmarked van. There were small windows in the sides and rear—one-way so they could observe without anyone seeing into the van, which was also equipped with recordings, radio, and the usual paraphernalia of surveillance. For an hour they sat quietly almost directly opposite the entrance to Dollhiem's office on 6th Street.

"That's him!" Otto almost shouted when the man appeared. "Older, fatter, but that's *Triangle*. I'd know him anywhere."

Two of the interrogation team in the back of the van with him nodded and smiled. "We want you to take a quick look at some-one else, Otto. Just a guy. You probably haven't ever set eyes on him before, but it's best to be sure about these things."

Newton would be leaving his apartment building near Dupont Circle to start the late-afternoon shift at the Atomic Energy Com-mission's headquarters. Two teams had been keeping watch on him, and they had discovered nothing as yet sinister about him. In fact, unlike Dollhiem, he kept to a very regular routine and used no antisurveillance techniques.

The van stopped where there was a good view of the parking lot nearest to Newton's building. The man's car was there, plainly in sight—a gray Chevy—and they pointed it out to Otto. "Very soon a man will come out of the building over there and go to that car," one of the Agency men said. "Just tell us if he rings any bells. We'll let you know the minute he appears."

Tertius Newton came out a little after five o'clock in the after-noon. The weather had changed to a light drizzle and he was wearing a raincoat and a snap-brimmed hat which did not bode well for any clear identification. But, on the sidewalk, just out-side the building, Newton hesitated, stopping to turn up the collar of his coat. In that moment he appeared to look directly toward the van and they all heard Otto Buelow's sharp intake of breath and the muttered, "*Mein Gott!*"

"What is it?"—from one of the agents.

"He was there. That's the one. Now it's clear. Now I re-member." Seeing the former OSS man, Tert Newton—aka *Screwdriver*—appeared to have demolished a huge wall in Otto Buelow's memory.

They allowed the German to continue watching Newton as he walked to his car and drove away. Otto's face was a map of incredulity mixed with fear, which caused one of the agents to ask if he was frightened.

"Only for my own sanity. How could I have forgotten?"

"Tell us about it now, while you've got it fresh in your mem-ory."

As the van drove back to the main Agency Technical Branch, the recordings were switched on and Otto Buelow talked.

Yes, he had seen Klaubert on an unspecified date, but between the *Romarin* disaster and the harvesting of *Tarot*. It had been on his second and last visit to the restaurant called La Vache Grise.

"I can even remember what I ate. It's so clear now. God knows why I could completely forget a detail like this."

They told him it was perfectly normal. So much went on at that time—and afterward. "Memory is a selective thing. You recognized the guy we call *Screwtape* right away when they showed you his picture in London. You told them you'd seen him many times at the Rue de Bourgogne office; you knew he was Klaubert's informer. You simply told them what you knew. Your mind buried the other guy."

Buelow had eaten simply—a potato soup, some lamb cutlets, and a mousse. He did not notice Klaubert until he had paid his bill and was about to leave.

"I remember the waitress asked me, rather archly, if there was anything else she could get me. I shook my head, left a tip, then asked if I could have another coffee—you must understand the coffee was *not* the real thing; even the army of occupation could not get real coffee. It was the stuff we called *Muckefuck—Ersatz*. I smoked a cigarette and drank the coffee slowly to digest the meal."

He paused, then shrugged, the incredulous look coming back into his eyes. "I looked around—the place was crowded: mainly with Wehrmacht officers. Then I saw Klaubert. He was in uniform, with his back to me. How could I forget this? Two men were with him, in civilian clothes. I couldn't understand that—the civilian clothes. I must have known then that they were either undercover Gestapo, collaborators, or informers. Later, of course, I *knew* one of them was an informer, the man *Triangle*. But the other I have not seen until today."

"You did not see the one we call *Screwdriver* in London?"

He shook his head almost violently, "No. Never. Since that night three years or so ago I have not seen him. Until today. The one you call *Screwdriver* was with Klaubert and *Triangle—Ach*, why play games? He was with Klaubert and Dollhiem at La Vache Grise on that night."

"You're absolutely positive?"

"Otto, you're one hundred percent sure about this?"

The men spoke in unison. The van slowed for a red light and the recorders went on turning.

"I first saw the man Dollhiem with SS-*Standartenführer* Hans-Dieter Klaubert at La Vache Grise in Orléans on one evening after the debacle of what I now know was an OSS operation code named *Romarin*, and before the arrests and deaths of members of the *réseau* known as *Tarot*. On that occasion Dollhiem and Klaubert were with another man who I have seen this afternoon. The man you call *Screwdriver*. I am positive about this. Certain."

One of the agents nodded, the other asked how they were behaving.

"They laughed a lot. All three of them seemed pleased with themselves. They also appeared to be having a good time. As I left, the waitress was taking two of the bar girls over to the table. As far as I know none of them saw me."

The agents looked happy, and one of them spoke the date, names, and a code word into the microphones. Then he stopped the recorders, removed the spool, and placed it in its box, marking the label with time, date, and destination. When they arrived at the car pool of the Technical Branch he had a messenger sign for the box, writing out an authorization slip for the recording to be taken immediately to the senior agent handling the case—his name was Marty Forman and he worked under James Xavier Fishman.

It had been a good afternoon's work, and the agents drove Otto back to his own apartment building. They both lived out in Alexandria and were sharing the ride home, but first they came up to Otto's apartment where one of them asked to use the telephone.

He spoke directly to Forman, who had received the recording but not yet listened to it. They had five minutes of telephone double-talk, which contained a great deal of self-congratulation. After this, both men told Otto he had done very well and was there anything he would like to do that evening? They were both prepared to come back into town for a night out, but Otto said he would like a quiet evening. A few minutes later, the agents left him.

Twenty minutes after this, in the now pouring rain which had superseded the drizzle, the agents' car, heading out toward Alexandria, was deliberately sideswiped twice by a heavy truck. On the second hit, the car overturned, catching fire and exploding. The emergency services pulled out only blackened and twisted remains. The two agents were eventually identified by dental evidence.

Otto Buelow heard about the "accident" on the radio but naturally did not link it to the men who had been with him.

Just after nine o'clock that evening, as he finished his lonely dinner, the doorbell rang in Otto's apartment.

There was a strict routine about callers. Otto was under instructions not to open up to anyone he did not recognize or connect with the Agency, which now kept only a light—logging—surveillance on the apartment block.

He called, asking who it was, and his visitor replied in a manner which, for Otto Buelow, constructed a bridge back over the years of his life. He peeped through the little glass eye they had installed in the door. The person standing there immediately registered in both eye and mind. He knew his caller was telling the truth, just after one tiny glance.

Otto unchained and unlocked the door. "Good gracious," he said. "Is it really you? What are you doing here? How did you find me?" Such was his excitement that he did not see the curious long barrel of the weapon rise up from under the visitor's coat. He was conscious of a thump, and then the blinding pain in his eyes, nostrils, and throat as the cloud of hydrocyanide wreathed for a second about his head. The burning went down into his chest and there was great pain.

As he fell back into eternal darkness, he croaked half a word.

"Ott—" he said, and died.

His caller put a gloved hand on the door and pulled it almost closed, then ran, dropping the weapon in panic, for the telephone had begun to ring in Buelow's apartment.

28

▼

OUTSIDE THE HUGE one-way mirror that was the window of the interrogation room of the house near Frankfurt, the sun blazed down on the neat terraces, drying the earth and creating cracked brown patches on the lawns.

Inside, Caspar was gently bringing his brother toward the moment for which they had all worked and waited. In the bowels of the house Naldo and Arnie sat watching the recorders turning, straining their ears enclosed by the heavy padded earphones.

Herbie sat outside the interrogation room door, his mind replaying the Mahler Second Symphony.

Caspar had taken Ramillies through his career a dozen times, always stopping short of the agent-handling during the war. Now he had reached the point again. Offering his brother a cigarette, he lit one himself and paused, as though dreading the moment and so delaying it a little longer.

"Now we come to your agent Klaubert." Caspar looked hard at his notes, speaking as though this was an unimportant aspect. "You've told me a great deal about him already—how he offered himself in the 1930s, how you helped train him and persuaded him to stay in place. Now I'd like to hear about communications and the kind of intelligence he passed on to you."

Ramillies gave a smile which seemed almost as secret as the grave. "I wondered when we'd get back to *Lightning*."

"Your agent, Klaubert, was *Lightning?*"

Ramillies nodded. "We never mentioned it in the signals. I presume you have all those, Cas. Personally I considered the method very unsafe."

"And what was the method?"

"Oh, come on, Caspar. You must know what happened."

"I'm asking *you*. Just as they will ask you again in London if we're ever allowed to take you there. Tell me."

So Ramillies confirmed the method of what had become, during the *Tarot* Enquiry, the Orléans Russians—how the SOE "pianist" coded *Descartes* had been captured, together with his radio and supply of one-time pads. "Klaubert spoke reasonable Russian," Ramillies said. "It was his idea to transmit on regular schedules, translating the one-time pads into Russian. I felt someone in England would pick it up very quickly. Did they?"

"Not as fast as you might imagine."

Ramillies raised his eyebrows.

"Was he an assistance? A help to you?" Caspar continued to put on pressure. Over the weeks they had broken down many barriers. A bond was slowly being built between interrogator and subject. Caspar was almost desperately trying to turn this into a full relationship of trust—occasionally offering Ramillies morsels of intelligence from his side of the barrier. Deep inside, Caspar knew the dangers of this, just as he was all too aware of the razor's edge he was walking in trying to speed up the whole business.

Ramillies cleared his throat before speaking. It had become a habit and Caspar wondered if it was done to give him time to come up with plausible answers. "Excellent on the state of play in Berlin, with the top brass, when he went back there to receive personal briefings. Twice he gave us magnificent résumés on Hitler's physical and mental condition and some interesting inside intelligence on Himmler. Pity he wasn't called back to Berlin more often. Apart from that, he was very good on troop movements and the like. A little bit of stuff on supply and economics. Kept us abreast of the situation generally in his area."

"More than that, surely? He held his cover together exceptionally well."

"Yes—ruthless bugger. Did his SS job with what one might call enthusiasm. But he concentrated mainly on Jews, and you know the Russian attitude on that subject."

"London will want a lot of detail, you realize that? What, for instance, are the chances of us getting to him?"

Ramillies looked genuinely puzzled. "What d'you mean, getting to him?"

"Just what I say. London, Washington—and Paris, come to that—could well ask you to produce him for us. Or, if not produce him, point us along the route. They would like him in the flesh."

Ramillies looked startled now, and Caspar felt his stomach churn.

"But you've got him, haven't you? You *must* have him somewhere. It was on my list of priorities—find him, they told me in Moscow. Find Klaubert. The Allies have him and we can use him."

Caspar felt the onset of what appeared to be great fatigue. "You're joking, Ram. Klaubert's a priority of ours. *We* need him, so cut the rubbish and give me some solid facts. Apart from anything else, he's wanted for war crimes—he wasn't called the Devil of Orléans for nothing. But we also want to get to the bottom of some other matters. So where is he, Ram?"

Ramillies spread his long fingers wide, turning his palms upward, like a magician showing that his hands were empty. It was an obvious gesture of truth. "My people're just as anxious to get hold of him." His eyes only betrayed concern. He did not display any signs of being an accomplished liar—the constant denials, the eyes clear, locking into those of his interrogator, and the voice a shade too steady. In the time he had already spent with his brother, Caspar thought he had learned the man's deceptive tricks. He had even caught him out twice. Now Ramillies gave nothing: his whole manner was of a man in anxious shock, his eyes darting to Caspar's face and then away, like some animal who fears the unknown.

"Truly, Cas. We wanted to bring him in. We searched for him. In the end it was assumed that you, or the Americans, had him."

"Truly, Cas"—that had the ring of falsehood about it. Caspar coughed and asked, "Did he have an exit plan? Was he set up for a fast escape to your people?"

"Nothing in detail. All our people in place had passwords, and the senior officers knew the words." He gave a cynical shrug. "Not that passwords would have helped them much, knowing some of the Red Army officers. There was a scorched-earth policy. The only good German was dead, if you follow. Personally, I had advised him what to do."

Caspar nodded, then started to press the point. For two hours he pushed Ramillies about Klaubert. It was impossible to accept his brother's word first time around, so his questioning changed—the queries designed to dazzle and confuse, then return again to Klaubert, like large-scale military feints which turned into attacks from some unexpected quarter.

He went through the tradecraft Ramillies had used with Klaubert, the signals and infrequent meetings, trying to catch his brother on the wrong foot and so lead him into error.

"You ever meet Hannalore Bauer?" Caspar asked.

Ramillies raised his eyebrows, smiling. "The thorn in *Lightning*'s flesh? Yes, I met her once, when he first went to Orléans. I was in for a day or so. He introduced me as a senior SS investigator. At that time he seemed to be genuinely fond of her. It changed when she caught him out."

"How?"

"How did it change? Or how did she catch him out?"

"Both."

"She suspected his game. Hannalore was an ardent Nazi—a fan of Hitler's, and an old friend of Eva Braun. I don't know the exact circumstances, but she either saw him with somebody and put two and two together, or she got a glimpse of his notes before he had a chance to destroy them. Whatever it was, she threatened to expose him to the Party—to the High Command, I suppose."

"And Klaubert did away with her?" It went through Caspar's mind—not for the first time—that, right up to the OSS *Romarin* operation, their information was that Hannalore Bauer was still in Orléans, acting as Klaubert's hostess.

"She disappeared." Ramillies spoke as though this was the most natural thing in the world. "I really don't know what happened, but, when you are about to be exposed by your lover, survival comes first. The loved one is of secondary importance. In any case I suspect he was already deeply into his affair with our plant in the local Resistance."

"Ah!" Now Caspar smiled. "Your plant was within the *réseau* known as *Tarot,* I presume?"

Ramillies merely nodded.

"Let's talk about that." Caspar put his notes to one side. By now he had no idea whether Ramillies was telling the truth or not. Was Klaubert really missing? Was he dead? Was he in the East? His brother was tricky—tricky as a cheap fairground huckster and twice as professional.

"You want to talk about *Tarot?*" There appeared to be genuine surprise from Ramillies.

"Why not?"

"Wasn't it all obvious? Klaubert's cover demanded that he should wipe out all Resistance networks in his area of operations. He allowed the one called *Tarot* to survive—"

"Until the end—or almost the end."

Once more Ramillies nodded.

"Your people penetrated *Tarot* early on?" In his mind, Caspar concentrated on pulling the truth, painlessly, from his brother.

"From the beginning. Even though we had a nonaggression

pact with the Nazis, the NKVD were ninety-nine percent sure that the pact would be broken. Yet nobody expected Hitler to invade Russia with the brutality and ferocity he finally showed. Even our most skilled military analysts had no idea that the Nazis would commit themselves to total war on two fronts. Strategically it was downright folly."

Caspar let his brother go on in the same vein for some time before he asked, "And you, naturally, ran your asset within *Tarot*." It was not even a question.

"I serviced the asset, yes. One of many, you must understand."

"And met him?"

"Once. It was a her, not a him."

"Of course. You said Klaubert had an affair with her. Put me out of my misery, Ram. That was my *réseau*. I was responsible for it."

"Yes, I know." Ramillies was calm, quiet.

"So who was she?"

"You really didn't know?"

Caspar shook his head.

"Her street name was *Florence*. I never knew her real name, and I only met her once—in a safe house they had in the Rue Bannier, Orléans."

Caspar's mind was a sudden whirlwind—*Florence*, the girl whom Jules Fenice himself suspected. The schoolteacher, Annabelle Sabatier, who had been so violently treated—gang-raped in the cellars of the Rue de Bourgogne, then shot with the priest and the doctor, *Céleste* and *Immortel*.

"She was Klaubert's mistress?"

"Of course. Didn't you know that?"

"No." Caspar said it quietly, in full realization that he was giving information to his own subject. "Then Klaubert really was a monster."

"I should imagine he was not averse to carrying out his duty as he saw it—for the best."

"He had one mistress done away with because she found out about his work for you. That, even *I* understand. I don't see why he should sacrifice his second mistress, who was also his contact within *Tarot*."

"Did he do that?" Ramillies leaned forward. His face and eyes showed interest. "How did he sacrifice *Florence*?"

Caspar shrugged and told him what had happened. "The

graves have now been properly marked and are tended," he said at the end.

"They were close." Ramillies frowned again, as though it was his turn to disbelieve. "If Klaubert were capable of love, I'd have said he loved *Florence*. If it became necessary to show he had no links with *Tarot* or the Resistance, I suppose he might have done this thing. But it's terrible." Again he shook his head in disbelief. It was like a dog shaking off rain. "This is truly shocking. You're sure of it?"

"Certain. Now, Ram, now you've heard that—and I can bring you proofs—tell me what happened to Klaubert. Where is he? Moscow? Or tucked away in East Berlin, in your zone?"

Ramillies all but snarled, "I've told you—he's missing. My information is that the Allies are holding him."

They went on until very late that night, and Caspar still got the same answers. "I just don't know," he said to the others over an evening meal. "I'm working in the dark and much too fast. At this moment my intellect tells me to believe him, but my instinct tells me to beware."

"You mean you believe we *have* got him?" Naldo asked.

"If young Kruger was right, we did have him, didn't we? Posing as a Norge Waffen SS officer."

"But they sent him East at his own request. Assuming that was Klaubert, he would have got to his masters long ago. Ramillies would have known." Arnold took a mouthful of food from his fork and chewed methodically.

"We'd know, wouldn't we?" Naldo asked. "We'd know if any of our people were holding on to Klaubert?"

"C would know." Caspar's mind was on the information Ramillies had given to him.

"So *we* would know." Naldo stopped his mouth abruptly. Caspar was there as an interrogator, not as a member of C's operation *Symphony*.

"Unless he's gone to ground," Arnie ventured. "Maybe I should have a look around the Frankfurt Compound."

They all knew exactly what Arnold Farthing meant, but none would speak openly of it. The Frankfurt Compound, originally the OSS HQ in Frankfurt, contained what was probably the most sensitive Intelligence organization in postwar Europe—the Gehlen Organization.

General Reinhard Gehlen was in command of the German Army Intelligence East during the closing years of the war. An almost intuitive Intelligence officer, the General appeared to some to have an uncanny insight into the Russian grand strategy. He ran many agents behind the Russian lines and in Moscow itself. He also turned Russians to fight secretly against their country, and was concerned not only with espionage, but also subversion and sabotage.

Gehlen took a very long view of life and espionage, to the extent that he finally delivered the whole of his organization, complete with agents in place, documents, and dossiers, into the hands of the Americans. After a complex series of meetings, Gehlen made a deal. His organization and expertise would be placed at the Americans' disposal until such time as a new German government was set up in the West. It would then become the main Intelligence agency for a reconstituted West Germany.

At the moment, the whole Gehlen Organization, with its access to vast quantities of intelligence on Russian aims and intentions in the postwar world, occupied the Frankfurt Compound. Even wives and children had been brought in. While highly secret, many thought the very presence of the Gehlen Organization was a time bomb.

"You have access to the compound, Arnie?" Caspar asked.

"Shouldn't be difficult. I have to see our liaison man from time to time." He could ask Fry if there was a real possibility that Klaubert was in hiding among the Intelligence personnel, he might be flushed out. Yet he did not like seeing Fry while he was working with the *Symphony* team.

Caspar nodded. "It's a long shot, but—maybe. Maybe. Let's see."

"Arnie"—Naldo stretched out in his chair—"is there any real chance that your folk have Klaubert under wraps and just aren't telling us?"

"Unlikely." Arnold weighed the chances. "It's not as though the guy's connected with Intelligence—"

"He was connected with Russian Intelligence."

"True, but we're not looking for him in that context." He closed his mouth, realizing that he could say too much in front of Caspar. "You want me to ask about the compound—"

Naldo broke in quickly. "Give it a day or so, Arnie. Least said the better at this moment."

Young Kruger was baby-sitting Ramillies, and Naldo suggested they should change watches now so that Herbie could eat.

"He's big enough already." Arnie smiled. "That kid's gonna be a giant by the time he's full grown."

"He still—" Naldo was cut short by the ringing of the telephone. He nodded, leaving the room to answer it. He seemed to be out a long time. When he returned, he looked dazed.

"Cas." He sat opposite his uncle. "Cas, I've got bad news."

"Phoebe!" Caspar was always convinced his wife would be stricken or die suddenly when he was away.

"No." Naldo shook his head. "The Otter's dead."

"What?"—both Caspar and Arnie in shocked unison.

"In Washington. Under your people's protection, Arn. The Otter was apparently murdered."

The telephone had started to ring again. Naldo hurried away. It was going to be a busy night.

Though they had no details, they all knew that unless it was some crazy accident, Otto Buelow's murder was somehow tied in with the whole maze which surrounded the Farthing and Railton families.

Maybe they should have asked Gehlen to start looking in the first place. But they had no idea of the full extent of the events which were shaping in Washington.

IN WASHINGTON, MARTY Forman had just listened to the recording in which Buelow fingered both Nat Dollhiem and Tert Newton when he heard of the deaths of his other two colleagues.

The Duty Officer had been told to pass on the facts. Question marks poured quietly into Forman's ear.

"The cops're out there now," the DO said. "I gather that two witnesses say it appeared not to be accidental. They were in cars behind the truck, and they say he just veered over, hit the car broadside, then pulled back and did it again, smashing them off the road. The witnesses say it was cold-blooded."

Marty said nothing. He always found he got his best results by staying silent—particularly when hearing something bad.

The Duty Officer continued. "There are other people who were on the same stretch of road—ahead of the truck. They say they just got the hell out of the driver's way. They were scared shitless."

Again a silence.

"The truck turned off at the next exit. Nobody got its number. One fellow claims the plates were covered by some kind of fabric. Said it looked like sacking."

This time the silence stretched on. "That it?" Marty Forman finally asked.

"That's all for now, sir."

"Okay. Keep me posted. Right?" He cradled the receiver.

Marty Forman had not come into the Agency by the scenic route of Harvard, Yale, or military officer material. He had been a hoodlum and did not care who knew it.

Thickset, short, and with muscles everywhere that counted, Marty had once been a Brooklyn street fighter. If the war had not intervened, he would almost certainly have ended up in jail. After Pearl Harbor he had enlisted, and during his basic training an OSS officer, doing the rounds and trying to spot talent, had seen him fight in the intersquad championship. The OSS man knew Marty Forman could not box to the tune of the Queensbury rules, but he saw the way in which this stocky young boy with a bull-neck could handle himself.

Marty was interviewed and found to be intelligent—in those days the Army considered an enlisted man to be intelligent if he knew where London, England, was, and Forman knew a good deal more than that. The OSS needed hoods like Marty, so he was taken away and trained. When he finally got to Europe he was not only disciplined, but also a natural as far as covert action was concerned.

By the war's end, Marty Forman had learned a great deal more about the work. His combination of brawn, brains, and shrewd instinct put him in line for a good job with the CIA when it had finally been formed earlier in the year. The Buelow business was his first major assignment with the Agency.

He had listened to the recording of Buelow's evidence with mounting pleasure. Got the sons-of-bitches, he thought to himself. He also thought he would like to tear the balls off Dollhiem and Newton with his bare hands. Marty Forman possessed many interrogation techniques which the Agency would not be happy about using.

He was just considering the next move when the telephone rang and he got the news about Herbert and King—the names of his two colleagues on the Buelow interrogation.

Now, having digested the facts, he picked up the telephone again and asked to be patched through to B28—the surveillance unit on duty outside Buelow's apartment building. All was quiet there. Four men and one woman had gone in since Buelow had been delivered. Two men had come out. Nothing was out of the ordinary. Later he cursed himself for leaving things as they were. But he telephoned his superior and gave him the latest news—which included a fairly detailed report on Buelow's evidence.

The result of this conversation was that he did not get to call Buelow himself for almost an hour.

The distant bell rang and rang, and certain warnings began to go off in Marty Forman's head. He had the line tested, and when the Agency operator told him it was okay he did not even stop to alert B28. He crashed from his office and sprinted for his car, taking off like a racecar driver.

He reached Buelow's building in eight minutes flat and did not contact the B28 unit, whose van he saw plainly across the street.

Alone, in the elevator, Marty felt the butt of his .38 revolver, which gave him the same kind of comfort a rosary does to a devout Roman Catholic.

He saw immediately that Buelow's door was open a fraction. Drawing the revolver from its holster, Marty pushed the door open with the heel of his left hand, stepping over a metal object in the hallway. Buelow was sprawled on his back, his face only slightly contorted into a grimace, but enough for Marty Forman to know he was dead.

He went through the small apartment at top speed, kicking open doors, crouching, holding the pistol in front of him in the two-handed grip. There was nobody there, so he went back into the passage to retrieve the piece of metal.

It looked like a malformed air pistol—a tube around seven inches in length, with a trigger and what looked like a firing pin at one end. The barrel was too small to take the end of a pencil, so Marty broke all the rules and inserted his silver ballpoint pen behind the trigger. It was something you just did not do. Marty had known men who had got a bullet in the foot—or, worse, the balls—through picking up a weapon like that; but there was no alternative.

Gently he carried the object back into Buelow's apartment, gingerly setting it down on a table.

He took out his handkerchief, wrapped it around his right-hand index finger, and dialed Field Support.

They were there within ten minutes—ambulance, disguised as a building-supply-company van, and men who, at one time or another, had worked with the FBI. Nobody wanted the Police Department in on this one. Once the cops came in, they would not only draw stupid conclusions but also give it all to the Press.

By the following morning they had no leads, but a certain amount of information about the weapon. The barrel was really a tube made in three sections. When all the reports were in—traces of cyanide in Buelow's body and faint traces among the glass and

on the inside of the tube—they came to the conclusion that the
trigger and firing pin operated a striker in the first tube which in
turn ignited a small powder charge in the middle tube, crushing a
glass phial in the third. The phial probably contained about 5cc of
hydrocyanide, which would vaporize as soon as it hit the air,
killing the victim almost instantly. It was a weapon they would all
see again in the early 1950s, for it remained in vogue with the
Soviet Service for a few years.

"Wouldn't that take out the guy who pulled the trigger?"
Marty Forman asked when the experts came to deliver their ver-
dict.

Not necessarily, they said. There was an antidote that could be
taken before firing, and another, just to be safe, afterward.

"Wasn't Buelow under discipline not to open the door to
strangers?" Fishman later asked of Forman.

"No way would he open up unless it was one of my guys."

"And your guys can be accounted for?"

"Two were already dead, out on the Jefferson Davis Express-
way. Two were in front of the building. One was in back, but
never out of contact for more than thirty seconds—he's okay
anyhow. I've known him a long time."

"And the men Buelow had fingered?"

"Both accounted for. They're still under surveillance."

"It strikes me." Fishman looked out of his window and into
the far distance. "It strikes me that our teams have also been
under surveillance. I gather from sources in Europe that Klaubert
certainly worked for the Russians. Therefore Klaubert's friends,
who are now within this Agency and the Atomic Energy Commission, also worked—and still work—for the Russians. The
only conclusion is that we have a Russian hit team here in Washington. Maybe they spotted Buelow. Maybe they were afraid
about who he could recognize—"

"Like Dollhiem and Newton?"

James Xavier Fishman nodded. "Yes, like them. Or perhaps
like someone else we've yet to tie in. They probably thought they
were eliminating all possibilities by killing your colleagues Herbert and King; then taking Buelow out. Happily we have the
Buelow recordings. So we can go on keeping close surveillance
on Dollhiem and Newton—good, invisible street men, Forman.
All you can muster." It was an order and Marty Forman nodded
acknowledgment.

"Which leaves the problem of the person who killed Buelow
—who must have known his murderer and trusted him. I pre-

sume your watchers have photographs of all people going in and out of that building?"

"I've got the blow-ups here, sir." Marty delved into his brief-case and spread a dozen grainy matt black-and-whites across the desk. "If I've read everything correctly, there are two here that bear looking at in detail."

He had ringed one photograph of a tall, bareheaded man entering the building. Even in the grainy photo the man appeared to walk erect, with a military bearing. His head was thrown back slightly and the hair looked light-colored. The second blow-up showed the same man leaving. The photographer had zoomed in to show the face.

Fishman looked at the pair of pictures for a moment, nodded, then scanned the others. Seconds later his arm shot out toward one of them. "Now that's a pretty girl." He smiled. "A very pretty girl. I've seen her before somewhere. You carry on, Marty. I have to make a call to Europe."

Within the next half hour he was speaking fast and confidently to Roger Fry, who had already set up a meeting with Arnie Farthing.

THEY MET IN the lobby of the Frankfurter Hof—an old hotel near the Kaiser Platz—surrounded by suspicious waiters and thinly disguised whores.

"I need the okay to talk to people in the Compound," Arnie said.

"They have plans?" Fry did not smile as he asked.

"I think they might need to speak with someone high in the Gehlen Organization. After that, if it happens, the whole circus is going back to London."

"Ah—then you'll probably be able to combine things. Washington's either gone paranoid or they're onto something. They seem to think there's a Sov hit team operating under their noses."

"In Washington?"

"So it would seem. Buelow's down to the Sovs, it appears, after fingering Dollhiem and Newton."

"So?"

"So I get you into the Compound. You fire off your questions —I'm not even asking you what they are. And then Washington wants you to do some research in London and other places."

"What kind of research?"

"Political. Views, attachments, and backgrounds."

"Whose backgrounds?"

"Relatives of yours, Arnie. Washington wants everything on Caroline Nellie Railton Farthing and Josephine Grenot. Relatives and one-time members of *Tarot*."

"Probably dead relatives." Arnold did not look happy.

"Washington wants it finished yesterday. I said you'd get it done in two weeks. They say ten days tops. Political educations, political literacy, societies, habits, beliefs, right down to the color of their souls, via the color of their underwear. Got it?"

"Get me into the Compound and I'll try."

"Oh, you'll do more than try." Fry took off the clear glass spectacles and for a moment looked human. "You'll do more than try, Arnie. You'll do it all. That's what you're paid to do."

"Money doesn't enter into it."

"Really? We'll see. But, as we're on the subject of death, there is something else you should know—and possibly pass on." Fry then quietly told him of the way the Otter had fingered Dollhiem and Newton before his murder.

Neither Fry nor Arnie even saw Herbie Kruger who sat, a newspaper raised to cover his face, at the far end of the lobby.

When Fry and Arnold left, the big German lad quietly got up and followed Roger Fry, carefully and at a distance. He followed him all the way home and reported the results, later, to Naldo Railton.

29

▼

"IT'S TIME FOR the truth game, Arnie." Naldo Railton sat across the dining room table from Arnold Farthing. It was two in the afternoon, they had lunched on *Zwiebelsuppe* and *Frankfurter Würstchen*—the spectacular onion soup and smoked pork sausage of which there now seemed to be no shortage. It had been their staple diet since arriving at this particular safe house. Along the hall, Caspar was having another session with Ramillies. He had not mentioned to anyone that the *Frankfurter Würstchen* constantly carried him back to the Fenice pig farm at St. Benoît. He even dreamed about it. In nightmares he saw the bodies of Caroline and Jo-Jo lying among the pigs.

Arnie smiled pleasantly. "What truth game would that be?"

"The same one you're playing with your case officer." There was no warmth in Naldo's voice.

"I'm just trying to do us all a favor."

"With your case officer?" Naldo's voice rose, moving up the scale with incredulity.

"What is all this, Naldo?"

"You're on loan to us, Arnie. You and I've been working as a closed-shop team for C on and off since last year. Right?"

"Yes, but—"

"No buts, Arnie. C is not a happy man. He's been on the scrambler to me this morning—angry would be a good word. Anyhow, he wants some answers."

"About me?"

"Among other things, Arnold. Yes—about you. About you and Mr. Roger Fry."

"But you knew I was—"

"Seeing someone from Liaison, yes. We've known it was Fry for some time. He follows you around like a dog. Your meeting with him at the Frankfurter Hof was monitored, and London's run

Fry through their card index. Roger J. Fry, aged thirty-four, un-married but has prospects with a Miss Gloria Van Gent who works in State and has a rich daddy. Fry is CIA Covert Action—just as you are when you're at home. Served with OSS from its inception; awarded CMH for ops with a Jedburgh team in Nor-way, where he was wounded. One wonders if he came up against any of the Norge Waffen SS. We know he's running two—*two*, mind you—CA agents in Europe. You, Arnie, are one of them."

"So? The product is to be shared from *Symphony*."

"*After* C's had it all. How much have you given your people, Arn? The works? Every move? If you have, then you're out; finished; probably put through the wringer."

"No. I've been discreet." Arnie sounded very calm. His con-science was all but clear. "Okay, so I *have* been seeing my case officer. What d'you expect, Naldo? I work for them."

"You work for *us* at the moment. I repeat—how much have you given them?"

Arnie let out a long sigh. "As little as I reasonably could. They have no idea—no idea at all—about what's at the heart of *Symphony*. *That* I promise."

"But they know the general brief?"

"Not if you mean C's brief—they knew nothing of that. They knew from the outset that we were out to find Klaubert, but they've always thought we wanted him for the *Diable d'Orléans* thing. It was difficult, Nald. Especially once they got the Central Intelligence Agency off the ground. Putting me in Covert Ops—well, they expected me to pass on intelligence. I suspect they know we were also trying to get at the truth about Caroline and Jo-Jo. They *have* seen the *Tarot* Enquiry transcripts, on C's say-so."

"But they haven't seen—or heard—any of C's suspicions?"

"I can promise you, Naldo, that all C's classified stuff has stayed locked in my brain. Even when *Symphony* went on hold, and I was back in Washington, I gave them only the minimum. None of the stuff we've read. Certainly nothing from C's *First Folio*."

Naldo nodded. "I believe you, Arn, but C was in a panic. He sees it as an important line we have to draw—which means if we come up with answers he'll be able to trade with your people. You know what he's like. He's had the whiff of something big, so he wants it in a safe deposit account."

"You really believe it? C, I mean."

Naldo gave a shrug. They seldom talked openly about the

weird and complex web which C had woven together in the series of documents they spoke of as the *First Folio*.

"I don't know. With C it's hard to tell. Yet he could be right, Arnie. You know that."

"I know we should draw your Uncle Caspar in. Last night he said he was working in the dark. If we could—"

"Not a word!" Naldo snapped. "I damned near pleaded with C this morning. No go. It's almost as though he thinks Caspar's a conspirator."

"When you think about it," Arnold said, "the silence *is* necessary. Caspar's personally involved. If all this was normal, C wouldn't let him near his brother."

Naldo grunted again. It was difficult to tell whether he agreed or not. Then: "Okay, Arnie, what did you tell Mr. Fry this morning?"

"I've applied to get us into the Compound."

"We decided to wait that one out." Naldo did not sound angry.

"I know, but it's there if we want it."

"Doesn't surprise me. You knew of course that your Roger Fry's living in the Compound?"

"No, but it's in character." Arnold paused. "My turn to be indiscreet now. Fry got heavy this morning. Following the Otter's death, Washington wants me to do an in-depth analysis of Caroline and Jo-Jo. Political in-depth. I said we were probably going back to London."

"We're almost certainly going back, and taking Rogov-Sodoff-Ramillies with us. It appears that notes have been exchanged. The Sovs are hopping mad: asking what's happened to their boy. We've denied all knowledge—at least the Foreign Office has denied it." He gave an evil smile. "They don't know we have him, of course."

"And the Russians do?" Arnie looked serious. "Hence the move from Munich to here, and, I presume, the return to your green and pleasant land."

"Particularly after what's happened to the Otter."

Arnold paused, then said Fry had told him something else.

"Important?"

"I think so. I'm giving it to you as a sign of good faith." And he went on to tell Naldo about the fingering of Dollhiem and Newton.

When he had finished, Naldo said it fitted—meaning that if Dollhiem and Newton were Russian penetration agents, within the wartime Office of Strategic Services, it fitted C's complex theory.

"As does the killing of *Florence,* which seems to have upset friend Ramillies so much. You think that bastard's got any suspicions?"

"Hard to tell. I really would like to see him sweated by the hard men at Warminster. You're right, of course, Caspar's too close—too personally involved."

After a moment of silence, as though wrapped in thought and grave decision-making, Naldo said they should go and listen in on the present session.

In the sterile room that had once been the wine cellars, the recording machines turned steadily. Through the earphones came the relaxed voices of Caspar and his treacherous brother. Caspar was again leading him through the dance of questions, still trying to catch Ramillies off guard.

"Can we not pinpoint the date when Klaubert first made approaches to your people?" Caspar asked as Naldo put on his headphones.

"We've been over it, Cas."

Patiently, Caspar said he would like to go over it again. "The shape of the picture is there; now I want the detail."

"He made the pass in Berlin. I know that."

"When exactly?"

"I'm pretty sure it was '39. The spring of '39."

In the cellar Naldo muttered, "Come on, Ramillies. You know when, right up to the day, hour, and minute."

"Was it after Molotov became the Russian Foreign Minister?" Caspar was off again.

"Yes." Unequivocal.

"That was in early May 1939. Right?"

"Yes."

"Ah. So when did he make his pass at your people?"

"I don't know if I was even told."

"But you were his control, for God's sake. What rank was he when you first met him?"

"SS-*Sturmbannführer.* A major."

"And he was working in Berlin?"

"He was on Himmler's staff."

"So he must have made his pass towards the end of April."

"Possibly."

"But I thought you were sent to advise him to stay in place. That's what you said before."

A longer pause.

"That's true. I was told to *make* him stay in place."

"Then it's reasonable to assume that you were sent to Berlin pretty sharply, Ram."

"I suppose I was."

In the cellar, Naldo pulled one phone away from his ear, raising an eyebrow at Arnie, who followed suit. "We know." He gave a grim smile. "We know the exact date, so why's he playing silly buggers, Arn?"

"Did you go fast, Ram?" Caspar asked upstairs. "I mean did the instructions come out of the blue?"

"Everything happened quickly in my line of business." He was not giving an inch.

And so it went on. "Ever-decreasing circles," Caspar said over dinner. "My dear brother'll end up spinning into his own arse."

"He's turned particularly evasive." Naldo spoke as though this was the most natural thing in the world.

"They do that—defectors do it. And Ramillies is no willing defector. He spewed everything out about the long past pretty quickly. When he was frightened. Now the fear's off, he's become difficult. It was like pulling teeth trying to establish when Klaubert made his pass at the Russians."

"So we noticed." Arnie was distracted.

"Picked up one of the Russian Legation people, we gathered in the end. Mid-April 1939, right?"

"That's what he says now. Ramillies was sent as soon as they realized the man was serious."

"And it took them the best part of a month to establish that." Naldo smiled to himself. Those dates were probably correct, for they fitted perfectly with the documents in C's *First Folio*. Tomorrow he would have another go at C. It was time for Caspar to be pulled off and Ramillies exposed to a taste of danger. He would get that at Warminster.

The radio was on, tuned to the AFN. Vera Lynne sang "There'll be bluebirds over the white cliffs of Dover."

"We could get your brother Ramillies a job from her." Arnie grinned.

"Oh?" Caspar still preoccupied with his subject's prevarication.

"Yeah." Arnie's grin widened. "He'd be just right for it."

"For what, Arnie?" Naldo joined in the game, playing straightman, for it was already an old joke.

"For cleaning all that bluebird crap off the white cliffs of Dover."

Early the next morning, after speaking to London, Naldo told Arnie he could go and fish in the Frankfurt Compound.

THE MEMBERS OF the Gehlen Organization, seen by Arnold Farthing, were very correct and strictly professional. "They're like a bloody detective agency," he told Naldo afterward. "It's as though they're going out of their way not to take sides. The first guy who saw me said it wasn't really his province, but he'd put me onto the right man."

"And he did?" asked Naldo.

"Yes and no. They specialize in Russia—'We are only really familiar with the Eastern areas of operation,' the guy told me. Interesting, though. Knew Rogov without batting an eyelid. Knew what he did, who he worked for. Didn't know his agents, but they understood exactly who he was." Arnold did a passable impression of an impassive German officer: "'This Rogov, he has gone astray, I think, yes?' 'Yes,' says I. And he is not Russian-born according to our sources.' 'Really?' says I, looking shocked to my colonial core. The guy gives me one of those smiles—you know, half-a-mouth and no eyes. 'You should examine his background, Herr Farthing. He could be of special interest to you.'"

"Good luck. Get your kit together, Arn. We go late tonight. I've yet to break the news to Herbie and Caspar."

"Which means I'm confined to barracks and not allowed to use the phone. Herr Fry must not hear of this, yes?"

"Jawohl. For you, Herr Fry is over—until he figures we've gone."

THEY GAVE RAMILLIES no warning. In fact even Caspar was not told until ten o'clock. They were scheduled to move out just after midnight. SIS hoods appeared to come out from under stones. The night was alive with them, shadowy figures moving outside the house—cordoning off the area for a radius of ten miles: some could be detected only by the crackle of their big walkie-talkies. They were all young ex-officers who enjoyed the games of glamour and asked no questions except what weapons they could carry and whom they could kill.

Naldo had spent two hours on the telephone talking to C, and during the late afternoon a very young man in blazer, cavalry-twill slacks, and sporting an Etonian tie, turned up and spent another hour with Naldo. His name was Curry Shepherd—"New, but bright. Good on organization. He's just twenty years old and looks younger than Herbie," Naldo told Caspar and Arnie.

The convoy was made up of four cars, the van- and rear-guard cars were specially stripped-down vehicles with reinforced bumpers, bulletproof glass, and no rear windows, for these had been removed to take the mountings for Bren guns. The hoods in the back sat on swivel gunners' seats facing outward.

A shaken and white-faced Ramillies was put into the car behind the armed lead vehicle, flanked by Herbie and Shepherd. Arnie sat up front with the driver, his hand resting on the Thompson clipped under the dash on the passenger side.

Caspar and Naldo were in the next car, while the other special vehicle brought up the rear.

They drove west, to an unused airstrip around ten kilometers away. One runway was still usable—the two others were pockmarked with bomb craters. An RAF team had rigged up emergency lighting and there was a yellow control van parked to the right of the runway about halfway down.

The cars pulled up beside an Avro York, one of the many transport aircraft derived from the Lancaster bomber, its Rolls-Royce Merlins clattering.

Herbie and Shepherd hustled Ramillies aboard. The others followed.

The takeoff was bumpy and noisy and, once airborne, they had to shout to converse. The whole aircraft was alive, trembling from the engine power and shaking in the air that was flung against its wings and fuselage.

"Are we going in to Northolt?" Arnie shouted.

"Lyneham actually." Naldo gave his colleague a long slow smile as he cupped his hands near to Arnold's head. "Wiltshire," he explained. "It'll be easier for the boys to take Ramillies off to Warminster. That should put the fear of God into him. We're to go to the Northolt house." Naldo paused, then cupped his hand again. "C's seen the sense of things. Caspar's to come with us. He's joining the *Symphony* team. Going to be initiated with a couple of days' reading—the *First Folio*. One of us'll have to be with him."

"I've got to fit in this bit of research for the Agency. Can you cover, or will Barbara never speak to me again?"

"Herb'll cover. He comes with us. Young Shepherd and a team are taking friend Ramillies to his incarceration. I'm going to ask how long we've really got—a marriage has been arranged, remember?"

After a silence broken only by the thrashing engines and quivering air, Arnie asked Naldo's advice. "How would you go about looking into their pasts—Caroline and Jo-Jo, I mean?"

Naldo shrugged. "I personally wouldn't, but—as you're under discipline—why not talk to Richard? Better still, sit down with Sara. She knows everything."

Arnold nodded and lapsed into silence—the shouting was too difficult. Yes, he would go and talk to Sara and Dick. He also wanted to spend a lot of time with Liz No-Name, if she was willing.

It was still dark, a good two hours before dawn, when the York tilted its wings, leveled out, dropped its gear, and began a bumpy descent into Lyneham, the engine pitch rising and falling and the airframe grumbling when the flaps were lowered.

They all stood on the asphalt apron as two cars and a van drew up alongside the aircraft. Two large men, gentle as wild bulls, came from the van and escorted Ramillies into the back. Naldo had seen men go like this before. The men would sit very close to their prisoner during the bone-shaking drive, saying nothing and refusing any rights. Curry Shepherd, after giving them a merry "Cheerio!" climbed in next to the driver, and the van went off fast, its taillights disappearing into the darkness.

"You're to come with us, Cas." Naldo nodded toward his uncle.

"For what?" Caspar was obviously out of sorts because his errant brother was being removed from him. He probably thought it reflected on his methods.

"For a talk with C. He's got a nice fat file for you to read."

They reached the Northolt house in time for breakfast. Liz served them but purposefully ignored Arnold, only speaking to him in a whisper when he managed to slip from the table and caught her in the kitchen. She said yes, he could call her, and Arnie returned to his bacon and eggs, feeling that all was well with the world. He even tolerated Herbie, who had spent most of the journey, and now most of breakfast, practicing his English.

Later, when C arrived with Cherub almost yapping at his heels, the room was cleared and they sat in a semicircle—like a Bible class, Arnie thought.

Cherub stayed in the hall and they heard the outer door close as Liz left the house.

"Right," C began brightly. "We have a couple of days' work

for you, Caspar. The others know all about it, as they are completely familiar with a theory of mine which has bearing on you, *Tarot*, Klaubert, the whole shooting match. My collateral—my proof—is here." He slapped his hand on the thick, flagged file at his elbow. "I compiled this, and only Naldo and Arnie know what's in it. Herbie, old dear, would you join the good Cherub in the hall?"

Herbie went like a lamb, but as he reached for the door he turned. "You call him good Cherub. I think he's a shit, Chief."

"Nevertheless." C glared at the big German, who grinned at him and went out quietly.

"Right, Caspar, as your friends and relatives here will tell you, the nub of our theory is that Klaubert was indeed working for the NKVD." He paused to make it more dramatic—as he had done when first revealing the information to Naldo and Arnie. "He was working for the Russians because *we* told him to. You see, he came to us first and there's nobody left around to tell us about it. But the files contain all the essential facts. Now let me go through them for your benefit."

As he talked, Caspar's face assumed a picture of disbelief— just as Naldo's and Arnie's had done when they first heard it.

Naldo watched his uncle, thinking, You wait until you've read the file, Caspar. Then you'll see what fools we mortals be.

30

▼

"You MIGHT WELL ask, how can this be?" C spread his hands, a brief smile entering and exiting his face like a flash from a signal lamp. His speech had taken on an almost Churchillian timbre. "Yet you, Caspar, of all people, should understand. You know of the trials, tribulations, blood, sweat, tears and toil that went on in those fifteen years prior to the war. The constant battles with the Treasury, the rows with the Foreign Office over diplomatic status, scandals over missing funds, officers in sensitive positions long after they should have been put out to grass, simply because our late Chief couldn't get his hands on decent Treasury allowances."

Caspar nodded, but C did not pause for breath—"Then the gradual loss of networks—not to mention stations: Vienna Head of Station arrested; Berlin closed down. Then that ghastly final year, with dear old C so ill that I had to do his job for him half the time, and run Section Two into the bargain. *You* know what a godawful cock-up it all was, Caspar. You even went to the Chief and asked—what? He told me your exact words, but—"

"I asked to be sent into the highways and byways of Europe and compel them to come in. To set up networks. To take up arms against a sea of troubles."

"And he replied?"

"By all means."

"And you did well, Cas. Very well. But 1939 was about the most ghastly year in my life. You realize that by 1940 I was left with only Berne, Lisbon, and Stockholm, while our depleted networks were going out all over Europe. There were moments when I never thought they would be lit again in our lifetime."

"But they did come on again, sir." Naldo felt sorry for his Chief, who had now lapsed into brooding silence.

"Oh, yes. Yes, indeed. But it was a close-run thing, young

Railton." He took a noisy breath and fixed Caspar with his small eyes. "We had one agent within the Abwehr but he went dead in '42." He spoke of Paul Thummel, a senior Nazi Intelligence Service officer. "And we viewed *him* with some grave disbelief until he delivered the goods." He tapped the dossier they called the *First Folio*. "To understand this, you must be aware of two things. First, that I was foolish not to have caught on to the truth earlier than I did. Second, that any offer from a person inside the Nazi hierarchy was looked at with great care. We always showed immense caution where the Gestapo and the Abwehr were concerned."

He pushed the heavy dossier toward Caspar. "It *is* all there now. I just hope to God it's not too late."

For a full minute he sat, staring at the folder as though it was some kind of bomb—which, in a way, it was. Then, pulling himself together, he looked around the crowded pink room. "Herbie'll baby-sit you, Caspar. My Cherub will maintain contact. You'll need two days minimum—"

"Probably three, sir."—Naldo, anxious to get as much time as possible.

C nodded, turning back toward Caspar. "If you need to talk, use the secure line to my office. Or, better still, tell Cherub, via Herbie, and I'll be with you in an hour or so. As for the rest of you"—he stared around grimly—"don't stray too far away. Let my office know where you can be found." His eyes finally rested on Arnold. "I've an intuition that they'll be expecting you back in Washington soon. Things are apparently hotting up over there. Who knows, we might even find our prodigal son, Klaubert, romping around the Reflecting Pool."

BECAUSE C HAD given them a lift back to central London—making them leave the house separately and walk to appointed pickup locations—Naldo and Arnie did not feel secure enough to speak with one another until they were safely back in Naldo's house near Exhibition Road in Kensington. Herbie, having no such inhibitions, had mumbled something about it being "Good luck for some. The wine, the women, and the singing, I suppose," as they left the Northolt house.

Now Arnie repeated it—"The wine, the women, and the singing for you, Nald?"

"I couldn't care less about the wine and the singing, actually."

He lunged for the telephone. Barbara's phone double-burped eighteen times before he gave up.

"Off with another guy, I shouldn't wonder." Arnie shook his head. "Might I use the instrument?"

"Fixing up a visit to Redhill?"

"Second on my list. Trying to arrange a night of lewd lust and abandoned passion first."

Liz No-Name was in and agreed to meet him for lunch. Arnie made straight for his bedroom, where Naldo allowed him to keep his things. Arnold had so arranged matters to give himself a permanent excuse to return to Washington via London if recalled quickly. He was out of the house within the half hour.

As for Naldo, he sat and waited it out, dialing Barbara's number every five minutes. He finally got through at three in the afternoon.

"Oh, my God, if I'd known!" she shrieked. "You're really back? Back for some time?"

"Where the hell've you been?" Naldo knew his patience had worn thin, just as he knew his attitude was unreasonable.

"Out to lunch with Vi."

"Vi?"

"Vi Short. You've met her. School chum. *Lady* Vivienne Short."

"Oh, her."

"Yes, her, Nald. What d'you expect? D'you really want me to sit at home all day just waiting for you to get back into London?" Her voice had become shrieky with hostility. "Because if that's what you want, you can bloody well think again."

"Barb, look, I'm—"

"I only hope to heaven you're back for a reasonable amount of time. My people're getting very difficult. They really *do* have to start making plans for the wedding."

"I'm sorry." He could think of nothing else to say.

"Sorry about what? Your bloody-minded attitude? Or are you trying to tell me this is just another wham-bang-thank-you-ma'am interlude?"

There was a long silence, then Naldo said, "Both actually."

"Both actually," she mimicked. "Well, if it's *both actually,* you can bloody well fuck off." And she banged down the receiver. Naldo dialed five times, but she had obviously taken the phone off the hook.

"Oh, Lord," he sighed, then went slowly to take a shower and change. He could be at her flat within the hour.

OVER LUNCH, LIZ appeared perfectly normal—she joked and chatted, looked happily into Arnie's eyes, and even reached out to caress his sleeve.

While they sipped their coffee, Arnie asked how she would like to spend the afternoon. She glanced away, then said, "I have to leave to go back to you-know-where around five. But, if you're really asking, then I have to tell you. I'd like it very much if we could spend the rest of the afternoon in bed."

Arnie felt free, much as a prisoner might feel as he leaves jail, or a man who rises from a severe illness of which he thought he was likely to die.

They made love with inventive tenderness for almost two hours. Then, at around four-thirty, as they lay on their backs, Liz suddenly clasped his hand tightly. It was a movement he found vaguely unnerving.

"Liz?" he asked, turning his head to see she was crying—silently, without a shaking of her body or sobs in her throat. With Liz it was a hail of tears flooding her cheeks from the wellspring of her eyes.

"Liz, what's wrong?" He propped himself on one elbow and looked down into her face as she swallowed and took a deep breath.

"Arnie . . ." She paused. "I have to tell you."

"What?"

She struggled. "We can't meet again. That was it. It's over now."

"Liz—but why?"

A long silence, then he repeated, "Why, Liz?"

"Because I've been warned off."

"Warned?"

"Wait." She placed a hand over his mouth. "My Section Head told me you were coming back to the house last night. She was nice enough about it, but apparently we've been spotted."

"So? You said it wasn't against the rules."

"It's not." She tried to give a little laugh. "I know a girl with 'Five' who's been having an affair with her Head of Department since the war began—or at least everybody presumes she is. Stays with him and all that."

"So what's the problem?"

"Arnie." She took another deep breath, more in control now. "Arnie, I've got too fond of you in a very short time. It isn't fair on either of us."

"Why the hell not?" He felt the first twinge of anger, and a nasty little warning voice in his mind.

"Because you'll be going away again soon. Back to the States. I've thought about it, truly I have. My Head of Section advised me to give it a lot of thought. She said she didn't want to see me hurt; knew I was becoming involved with you, and it's true, Arnie. In a few more days I might not be able to let go, and I don't want to get hurt. Not again."

"Someone before?"

"We all have our wartime stories, Arn. You know that. I have mine. You'll go back to the States, and—well, maybe I'd never see you again."

"So nobody's *ordered* you to stop seeing me?"

She shook her head. "But it's the sensible thing, isn't it?"

Arnold thought for about twenty seconds before saying, yes he supposed it was the most sensible thing. He did not feel happy about saying it, but—having a suspicious nature, probably nurtured by his work—Arnie knew the ways of these things. He had no reason to think that Liz was lying, but she was right. He might well be on his way back to Washington in a couple of days. He might not return to England for a very long time. On the other hand, the girl could quite easily be trying to force the pace, and so lead him into a commitment. Arnie was not one to be hurried down that slippery path.

"Okay, Liz." He nodded, unhappy and disappointed. "Okay, if that's the way you think it should be."

She seemed very preoccupied, even worried, as they dressed.

Arnie did not kiss her as he left. She would have allowed it, but he was not taking any chances. As he walked up the street, looking for a cab, a voice in his mind said, "Arnie, you're a shit." And another voice answered, "Yes, I know. Sometimes you have to be in order to survive."

Returning to Naldo's house, he put in a long-distance call to Redhill Manor. Both Dick and Sara seemed excited at the prospect of even a short visit.

ON THE OTHER side of London an even more melodramatic scene was being played out by Naldo and Barbara.

They were close together, half naked on her bed, now. But for the best part of two hours they had shouted and clawed at each other like animals.

Barbara accused Naldo of being insensitive.

Naldo, with equal vehemence, told her she did not even begin to understand the kind of discipline under which he worked.

She threw her engagement ring at him, cutting him slightly on the cheek.

Naldo said that if she really wanted out, then she could go— and good riddance to her.

Barbara said she did not want to speak to him or see him ever again.

Okay, that was fine, but could she return his copy of *Forever Amber*?

That made Barbara say he was nothing but a sex maniac. "You only want me for my body," she said, throwing back her head, an act which she knew displayed her breasts to their best advantage.

Love thirty.

Love forty.

In the end they faced each other, flushed and angry, then, suddenly, the squall was over and they started to laugh.

"I'll talk to my Chief in the morning," Naldo said. "Maybe he can give me some idea, and we can tell your family a definite date. I'll talk with him tomorrow, I promise. Where in hell did your ring get to?"

Barbara grinned. "Oh, shut up, Nald. Undress me. We've wasted enough time as it is."

Naldo decided he must ask his father about women sometime. James Railton had never broached the subject with his son.

IN THE NORTHOLT house, Herbie Kruger had asked Caspar's permission to take the gramophone into what had once been the dining room. Caspar had no objections, and Herbie was as happy as a child. Carefully padded with clothing, in his luggage, he had brought back a whole set of Mahler's Third Symphony, which he had picked up in a Berlin shop. It was a work he had yet to hear.

Years later, when it was all over, Caspar could never explain how, when he thought of the Klaubert business he always seemed to hear great brass chords made slightly discordant, distorted and reedy instead of full, as if ushering in a new season.

Alone in the pink room, Caspar took up the heavy dossier and flicked through it. It was bulky with files, most of them original and culled from dozens of sources within the SIS Registry. There were signals, together with their decrypts; long summaries; reports; analyses. These were interleaved with pages of more recent date upon which C had made annotations in his neat hand. He also made marginal notes, not so neat, on certain papers.

The first document was a signal from Munich on September 28, 1938. It had been sent via the diplomatic bag—nothing sensitive went out of Germany by telegram anymore.

It was marked CX—which meant For Chief of Secret Service Only—and signed *Hornet*. In the margin C had noted that *Hornet* was a young officer called Nigel Mannus, who had been sent to Munich in order to help cover for the local Head of Station while the diplomatic circus was in town.

Decrypted it read:

APPROACHED AT LEGATION TONIGHT BY SS OFFICER STOP I AM CIPHERING HAWK IF YOU CLEAR STOP WISHES TO MEET ME PRIVATELY ON MATTER OF STRICT SECRECY STOP CLAIMS HE HAS INTELLIGENCE WHICH COULD BE OF USE TO OUR SERVICE STOP BUT WILL ONLY ANSWER TO CSS DIRECT STOP NO OTHER OFFICER WILL DO STOP PLEASE ADVISE STOP.

There was a decrypted reply with a notation from C which read, *This, and the following signals, were seen by the CSS only. So Nota Bene: only CSS and Hornet were involved.* The reply signal read:

TAKE GREATEST CARE IN HANDLING HAWK STOP USE ABSOLUTE SECURITY AND CAUTION STOP ADVISE HIS POSITION AND REASONS FOR WISHING TO ASSIST STOP CSS STOP.

On the following page was *Hornet*'s reply to the then C:

MET HAWK IN PUBLIC ONLY STOP TALKED FOR FIFTEEN MINUTES STOP HE IS ON RSH'S STAFF STOP CLAIMS TO BE DISENCHANTED WITH NAZI POLICY AND IDEALS STOP WISHES TO COME ENGLAND AND TAKE BRITISH NATIONALITY STOP ALSO CLAIMS HE HAS SEVERAL PROOFS DOCUMENTS AND PHOTOGRAPHS OF SPECIAL CAMPS AND PLANS FOR EXTERMINATION OF ALL GERMAN JEWS STOP WILL STILL ONLY HAND MATERIAL PERSONALLY TO CSS STOP.

Under the signal C had written, *RSH stands for Reichsführer*

Himmler. If only I had seen this, or if C had shown it to me. What suffering could have been averted?

The next page contained a third signal from *Hornet:*

CONVINCED HAWK IS SINCERE STOP HAS LEAVE IN EARLY OC-
TOBER STOP WISHES TO PROCEED LONDON TO MEET WITH CSS
STOP.

C's reply was to the point:

WILL MEET YOUR POSSIBLE ASSET IN BASLE OCTOBER FOUR-
TEENTH AT NOON STOP RV HOLBEIN ROOMS IN KUNSTMUSEUM
STOP HE WILL CARRY A COPY OF BAEDEKER STOP I SHALL
CARRY COPY OF THE TIMES OF THIRTEENTH OCTOBER STOP I
SHALL APPROACH HIM AND ASK QUOTE DO YOU ADMIRE HOL-
BEIN END QUOTE STOP HE WILL RESPOND I PREFER THE ELDER
TO THE YOUNGER STOP HAVE TODAY POSTED YOU HORNET AS
ASSISTANT PCO MUNICH UNTIL FURTHER NOTICE STOP YOU WILL
TRAVEL TO BASLE AND STAND OFF WHILE I MAKE CONTACT
STOP IF HAWK FAILS TO ATTEND THIS RV SEVER ALL REPEAT ALL
CONTACT STOP CSS STOP.

Caspar turned the page. What followed was a long report
flagged *CSS only.* It turned out to be the previous, long-dead C's
personal report on what occurred on October 14, 1938 in the
Holbein rooms of Basle's famous Fine Arts Museum.

As Caspar read, so the years slipped back. He could even see
his old Chief, looking drawn and slightly haggard as he had done
in the last autumn of his years.

31

▼

EVEN IN THE passage of less than a decade, the style of the document seemed almost clumsily outdated. It was certainly genuine —Caspar would have known the neat hand of his old Chief anywhere. He paused, reminding himself that he must be suspicious at all times. So it was either genuine—as he believed—or a very good forgery.

The date stamp, faded from a worn ink pad, was October 23, 1938, and, from the prefix, the papers appeared to have been filed under a miscellaneous batch of classified documents in the Foreign Office Central Registry.

The cover was flagged red, while the number and heading showed that the series of files, from which this had been taken, would never be released to the Public Records Office. The fact that they had been moved under a Foreign Office heading indicated that they were knowingly tucked away, far from the reach of prying eyes. Certainly no passing historian or researcher could have easily laid his hands on these dozen or so sheets of folio.

The whole thing was handwritten, showing that the author had made certain no typist would see the pages, which were headed "*Most Secret,* Private Report by C regarding Operation Antennae." It began with a brief preamble in which the then head of MI6 stated he had destroyed an original sealed letter left in his safe, giving instructions should he meet with an accident—deliberate or otherwise—during his journey to Switzerland.

As his eyes raked the pages, Caspar still smiled. His one-time Chief's report read almost like a Boy's Own tale of derring-do, the broad object of which was made plain in the first sentences— the detail clear only if you had studied the series of cables passed between *Hornet* and the CSS. Even then, there was no mention of *Hornet*'s real name. Caspar had only the current C's word that the man was one Nigel Mannus.

"I set forth on this operation, which I have dubbed *Antennae* for obvious reasons, without speaking to any other serving officer or committing notes to paper," it began. "There are three reasons for this. First, it is not seemly for the CSS to be involved, alone, operationally in the field. Second, we are in profound need of another reliable source of intelligence within the Nazi camp. Third, I have an intuition that *Hornet*'s possible source will become useful. This last reason is probably why I have not confided in another soul. Intuition, I have learned over the years, should never be a guiding force in matters of intelligence or strategy. So no harm will have been done if I return empty-handed. I refuse to become a laughingstock in those areas of Whitehall which, of late, appear to have become a slough of despond."

So it started, followed up with a crisp statement of what precautions he *had* taken—"Being of reasonably sound mind, and knowing the devious ways of the Nazi Secret Service, and their Gestapo, I realised this might well be a method of entrapment. This is why I made certain the meeting with *Hawk* was to take place in the open. For the more private consultation I had in mind, Berne was alerted and instructed to leave their safe house ready for use from 15th onwards. The Head of Station, and his deputy, in Berne, had no idea who would be using their premises, and they were ordered to stay clear.

"On 14th, as arranged with *Hornet*, I presented myself at the Museum and was in the Holbein Rooms on the dot of noon. Alas, *Hawk* did not appear until almost quarter past the hour. He was obviously being very careful, but carried his Baedeker prominently.

"I waited a few moments to assure myself that he was not being followed, and was pleased to catch a brief glimpse of *Hornet*. All seemed to be clear so I finally approached *Hawk* in front of Holbein the Younger's *Christ in the Tomb*. We exchanged the arranged greeting, and I was glad to see he gave me only one quick glance.

"*Hawk* is a tall man—six feet or so—well proportioned and very much the old-style Prussian in manner and bearing—right down to the duelling scar stitched along his right cheek. He, naturally, wore civilian clothes and was very definitely edgy. At first I did not know whether to take this as a good or bad omen, but made my little speech as quickly as possible, ordering him to be in the station buffet on Platform One at Berne Station at ten the following morning.

"The next morning I stood off until I saw *Hawk* arrive on

Platform One at the Berne Bahnhof, and waited for fifteen minutes to observe any suspicious movement among the usual throng
of travellers. *Hornet* went into the buffet shortly after *Hawk*. This
was a good move on his part, as it would not only give the man
confidence, but also make certain I was safe.

"I made my approach as soon as *Hawk* was alone at his table.
I went over and sat down, ordering coffee. Then I quietly told
him to follow me when I left. He proved to be no fool, merely
nodding, as though I had asked him if I was on the correct platform.

"By noon we were together at the safe house.

"Almost immediately it was clear that the man had his mind
set on coming to England as quickly as possible. Unless he is a
consummate liar, he regards the Nazi Party with great contempt.
'They are fanatics, followed by hoodlums,' he told me. 'The
German people have been betrayed and will be dragged into a
march of folly. We live in a country run by arrogant, ruthless men
who see themselves as Germany's saviours.'

"He said he hoped that I was not taken in by the so-called
Munich treaty. There will be war within the year. It appears that
he was in Munich during the meetings and recounted to me a
story he heard from one of his brother officers who was in the
company of Herr Hitler and the porcine Goering after Chamber-
lain had left. Goering, it appears, asked his leader why he had
signed such a stupid piece of paper, to which Hitler replied,
'Well, he seemed such a nice old gentleman, I thought I would
give him my autograph as a souvenir.' I tend to believe the story.

"For the first hour he almost pleaded with me to take him
straightway to London, so I knew it would prove to be a difficult
piece of work to persuade him to stay on as our man. Eventually I
cut him off short, subjecting him to a long, though friendly, interrogation concerning his background and present situation.

"He gave me positive proofs that he held the rank of *Haupt-
sturmführer* in the SS—which is roughly the rank of Captain,
going by Army equivalents—and is on Himmler's staff. He also
brought some of the documents he had promised.

"They make grim reading. Already the SS has set up several
camps—Concentration Camps, they call them. I presume they
had the idea from us, for I recall reading of the Concentration
Camps we set up in South Africa during the business with the
Boers. The Nazi versions are supposed to be places of correction
for those who are criminals. Yet the term criminal appears to go
further than theft, fraud, murder and the like. Most of the un-

happy inmates have either spoken out against the Party or are members of some minority group. He showed me a photograph of one of these camps, high barbed-wire fences, guards, dogs, and a sign in ironwork over the gate saying *Arbeit Macht Frei*—'Freedom through Work.' Yet I cannot believe that many of those incarcerated in these places will ever see freedom again. They belong, in the main, to classes unacceptable to the regime —gipsies, homosexuals, some religious sects, certainly many Jews.

"The wretches who are imprisoned suffer greatly at the hands of their guards, and are used as slave labour. The punishments are apparently brutal, and the photographs and papers are enough to show this is true.

"As for his claim that there is a plot to enslave, and possibly murder all Jews in Germany or annexed countries, there is no proof. *Hawk* claims that he has heard it spoken of, but, I suspect, only in abstract terms. Certainly there has been strong anti-Semitic feeling in Germany for some years, and evidence of unjust oppression, but I really cannot accept the idea that the Nazis would even attempt a kind of genocide. After all, we are in Europe, it is the twentieth century, and society has long freed itself from barbarism.

"I asked *Hawk* about his prospects in the SS, and he became very alarmed at this hint that I might leave him in Germany. I boxed mighty cleverly, for he is on leave in Switzerland and could easily make a run for it—France is so close. For right or wrong I persisted, and he said he dreaded the thought of where the SS would take him. He is frightened of being put in charge of one of these camps, I fear, so I changed the subject and asked about his own connections within the Party he sought to betray.

"He has what appears to be a mistress—a Fräulein Bauer who is a personal friend of Hitler, and almost part of his court. He then told me certain things which have not been passed on by any of our own people. It seems that the picture we have of Hitler the ascetic political man with high moral ideals, is simply an image fostered by propaganda. I was amazed, almost shocked, to hear there was a scandal in the late '20s concerning his niece, a girl called Geli Raubal, with whom he had a long—possibly incestuous—relationship, and who committed suicide because of him. There have also been many love affairs, and he has a mistress, a Fräulein Eva Braun. Why have our own sources not reported this? *Hawk* says it is common knowledge within the SS and among Hitler's circle. *We* should have been apprised of this information through our embassy officers long ago.

"I pressed harder and discovered that, because of *Hawk*'s attachment to this Fräulein Bauer, he has a stepping stone into the circus which surrounds the German leader. I decided to sleep on this and ponder.

"*Hawk* stayed in the house with me, for we talked until late, resuming again after we had cooked ourselves breakfast the next morning. By this time a plan had formed in my mind and I went for him like a bull at a gate.

"First I asked him what his motives were in wanting to come to England. He replied that he could not stand the Nazi regime and wished to fight it, which played straight into my hands. 'If you really wish to fight Hitler and the Nazis, then you must fight from within,' I told him.

"He seemed taken aback at this, asking how he, a mere Captain in the SS, could fight back? I then explained. He was silent for some time—most of the morning in fact. Later he came to me and said of course I was right. To flee was cowardly. If I really thought he could help, then he would assist in any way I suggested. It then became all too obvious that he is a very frightened man, for he immediately stipulated a watertight private circle of knowledge regarding the gathering and passing on of intelligence by him.

"He will work to me alone, at the moment, though I have explained he must do it through *Hornet,* who will act as a cutout. It took some time to convince him this was the only way it could be achieved. But I have given my word that *no other person* will be informed of his true identity.

"We talked together at great length, and it appears that—as he has already indicated—he is gravely concerned in case he is posted to some SS Unit which calls upon him to show ruthless brutality. I told him that, if he is determined to assist us, he must at all costs keep his cover as a loyal SS Officer. I must admit that my blood ran cold when I heard of the oath he had taken upon joining this, so-called, elite force. The form of words is as follows—

> *I swear to thee, Adolf Hitler,*
> *As Führer and Chancellor of the*
> *German Reich*
> *Loyalty and Bravery.*
> *I vow to thee and to the superiors*
> *whom thou shalt appoint*

Obedience unto death
So help me God.

"*Hawk* also described other ceremonies which appear to show the SS as almost a religious society—there is even a form of catechism, their songs are like hymns, rituals abound and there are other binding oaths. The whole business smacks of a warped Jesuitical training, in which God and Hitler are mingled as one. It is blasphemous. I said as much to *Hawk*. He nodded, remarking that Himmler had been brought up as a strict Roman Catholic. Does the *Reichsführer* see himself as a kind of cardinal to Hitler's Pope?

"When talking of *Hawk*'s cover, I could only counsel him that, if he was to escape detection, he would have to do as he was ordered. 'If they demand ruthlessness of you,' I said, 'then you must show it. In fact you have to appear to be one of the most ruthless officers within the SS.'

"He blanched at this, but I convinced him.

"That night I put out a prearranged sign for *Hornet* to approach. He arrived at ten:thirty, and together we worked out a method of communication. I told *Hawk* that we required anything he could get hold of—particularly advance notice of Order of Battle; War Plans etc. Also any details—however trivial—of Hitler's life and state of mind, plus those of other members of the Nazi hierarchy, especially his own chief, Himmler—*Hawk* calls Himmler the 'chicken farmer.'

"He asked what he should do if he was posted away from Berlin, or taken off Himmler's personal staff. I instructed him that he should go on sending whatever intelligence he could. Then, as an afterthought, I said, 'It might be interesting for you to tap into the Russians.' He had mentioned that he was on good terms with two officers from the Soviet Legation. *Hawk* asked if I really meant this, and when I told him, yes, he admitted that he had already been approached by members of the NKVD. The thought of working with the Soviets is really as repugnant to him as his present situation, but I see great opportunities here. He has agreed to appear interested if they make any further overtures, though I cannot understand why he did not report the earlier passes to his superiors, and said so. He answered that he was prompted by fear. 'You do not seem to understand what horrors could be heaped on me,' he said. 'If I reported the Russian approaches, the Gestapo would not think twice about investigating me—and that could truly mean a slow death, even though I was behaving with loyalty.'

"We have agreed the following—

"That *Hawk* shall be known under the code name *Harold* and will, until such time as it becomes difficult, send information on a twice-monthly basis. *Hornet* has arranged dead letter boxes for him—both in Berlin and Munich. I have placed *Hornet* in sole charge and made many reassurances that *Harold*'s intelligence will be seen only by me. *Hornet* will send it CX by the diplomatic bag, or King's Messenger. We spent a day with him on the kind of cipher he should use, and he proved an able pupil.

"*Harold,* as he is now named, will be my private source, and I write this simply for the use of any successor."

The document was signed in C's full name, followed by his title—CSS: Chief of the Secret Service.

Caspar glanced through the pages again.

So, he thought, by the end of 1938 the weakening C had a private agent within the Nazi SS and a young member of the SIS acting solely as his controller and cutout.

In the distance he heard the scratchy sound of Herbie's records on the gramophone.

Caspar turned to the following pages, neatly divided into dossiers or sets of specific documents. The next one came directly from the SIS Registry, and was C's personal analysis of intelligence which came, as he put it, "from a very delicate source." Some of these pages of intelligence analysis had obviously been sent on to C's Deputy during times when C himself was either at home or in the hospital during 1939.

Caspar was about to read on when Herbie knocked at the door to tell him the evening meal was ready.

"Come in, Herbie." Caspar beckoned the big German.

"You are wishing to speak?"

"Yes. How much do you know about all this business?" He indicated the files.

Herbie shrugged. "I am office boy only. I fetch and carry. Arnie calls me a gofer, which is funny, yes? He say I gofer this and gofer that."

"You haven't read these files, then?"

"Me? No. I go blind, deaf, and dumb with files. I am like the four wise monkeys, *ja?*"

"Three, I think."

"Four. I see no evil thing; I hear no evil thing; I speak no evil thing; and I screw no evil thing. So?"

Caspar allowed him a small smile.

"There is food," Herbie said. "The girl who looks after us has made good meal. You want to go on reading or do some eating?"

Reluctantly, Caspar dumped the file into the large document case where it was usually kept. He locked it and carried it through to the dining room where the attractive redheaded girl was waiting to serve the meal.

For an odd reason, Caspar got the impression that she had been crying.

SUMMER HAD GONE without the *Symphony* team even noticing. Arnold took the first possible train to Haversage the following morning, arriving at noon. He had telephoned ahead, from Paddington, so Sara waited for him with the car and told him the latest news as she drove the mile into the small market town, passing through the square with its statue of King Alfred—minus his ax which, it was said, had been taken by the Americans and carried by one of them onto the bullet-raked *Juno* beach during the Normandy landings on D-Day.

Sara chatted on as she maneuvered the Daimler out of the town and up Red Hill to the gates of Redhill Manor. It was as Arnold got out of the car that he realized autumn was almost upon them. A breeze hit a pile of dry brown leaves, which whirled and rustled, reminding him of Roger Fry's voice. There was something he should do about Fry, he thought.

"Great surprise, Arnie." Sara came around to him and linked an arm comfortably through his. He felt the side of her body against him and thought, God, she's over sixty yet feels as soft as a young girl. Looking down, he saw her eyes sparkling. "Naldo's bringing his intended down later."

"Oh?" Arnie felt a twinge of worry. He had really wanted Sara and his Uncle Dick alone for the day. "When's later?"

"Early evening. They say they've all but fixed the wedding date."

"Great. Mind if I use the phone, Sara?"

"Not at all. Here, leave your case and use the General's Study. Dick's taken one of the horses out, so you won't be disturbed." She propelled him toward the study door where he put a call through to Naldo in London. Barbara answered.

"I'm here doing the packing. We'll see you later." She sounded extraordinarily happy, and Arnie felt a real stab of regret. For a second he wondered if he had been right to push Liz away without putting up even a token resistance.

"Okay, Barb, can you do me a very confidential favor?"

"Try me."

"Tell Nald that I don't want anyone to know where I am—the Chief, my people, *anyone*."

"Your command is my word. It's as good as done, unless Nald's already spilled the beans."

Sara waited in the breakfast room with coffee.

"You wanted to talk to Dick?" she queried once they were settled.

"Both of you, really. And I'm sorry, Sara, it isn't easy."

A shadow crossed her face. "Caroline and Jo-Jo?"

He nodded. "How did you know?"

Her voice was flat. "Oh, it's what they all say—Cas, Naldo, everyone who knows about it. You're all the same. You start the conversation by announcing, 'This isn't going to be easy.' They've been traced?" The question presupposed that the girls were dead.

Arnie shook his head. "No. But, between us, I think we're a little nearer. It's possible we'll find out soon enough."

She looked out the window and he realized there were tears in her eyes. "No, it isn't easy, Arnold. We've more or less given up all hope of ever knowing. Accepted their deaths, of course." A long pause. "What did you want to know?"

"That's the least easy part, Sara. I've got to ask about their politics."

Sara gave a long sigh. "Oh, lord." Another sigh. "What are the politics of the young, Arnie? They all think they've found a new way of changing the world, and they all think it's better. . . . You know about Jo-Jo's background, don't you, Arnold?"

He nodded a "Yes." In his mind he thought of the stories he had heard—Jo-Jo, the orphan bastard of a Railton, brought up by another Railton.

"I treated her like my own daughter, and she was an elder sister to Caro. It was odd to see them as children, they were so alike. They had everything. Then, when they had been formally educated, Jo-Jo wanted Paris—the Sorbonne, which was her right, and where she did very well. Caro naturally demanded the same. Even with the age difference they always had to be the same, do the same things. Caro would've been twenty-eight years old now. Jo-Jo thirty-one."

"Sara, their politics are what I'm asking about."

She gave him a dazzling smile. "Of course. I don't know—not for certain, Arnie. But Dick'll probably say the same. We both saw them in '38, and again in '39. Pleaded with them to come back if things got difficult. To be honest, they appeared to have moved slightly to the left of Lenin. I don't know if they were actually card-carrying members of the Communist International—the Comintern—but Dick might tell you. Dick has a tendency to know just about everything. Sometimes he shields me."

She looked away, out the window again onto the view she had loved and known almost from her own childhood, for she had been barely an adult when John Railton first brought her here. Once more the weary sigh. "As for Caro and Jo-Jo, like others we tried to ignore it. Thought it would go away. Their revolution had nothing to do with manning the barricades or throwing bombs. They wanted to cut through class. All men and women were equal to them." Her face suddenly underwent a small change, as though deep inside her she had long digested something very bitter. "I think they carried that message to others. It's totally out of proportion, I know, but I think both of those girls gave their bodies to anyone they believed to be in need of them; and what money and intelligence they possessed they passed on to similar people." She gave her smile again, lacking in dazzle now: laced with wormwood. "Ask Dick, Arnie. I think he probably knows more than I do."

"Sure, Sara. I'm sorry."

Sara's trick in life, Arnie thought, was that she did not allow moods to hold her for long. Over lunch she was as bright and sparkling as ever. The smile she gave him as she left the room afterward was as flirtatious as some golden summer girl up to her knees in long grass and lust.

"Sara's told me what you want." Dick said it the moment the door was closed. "I have to ask you why."

"And I can't tell you, Dick. There must be a reason, but I am simply instructed to do some research into their political backgrounds. Both Naldo and myself—well, we thought it best to start here, with you. To be truthful, Naldo suggested it."

Dick nodded. His leathery face had taken on a fast and solemn look, as though he had received several injections of novocaine and could not move a muscle.

"Okay," he said at last. "In Paris, they were fashionably left wing. I have my own reasons for believing it went further than that, rich spoiled babies that they were. Always the trouble with the privileged, there comes a point when they discover the whole world is not like them. When that moment comes they either go on just as before, or they despise their families and feel guilty about their own good fortune. There was a bit of both in Caro and Jo-Jo. Enough to worry me."

"You saw them last—"

"In '39. Actually they promised that should things become really bad, if war overtook them, they would come home. I think they meant it." He paused, as though about to weigh his words. "I should tell you that I know for a fact Caspar had no knowledge of their political leanings. I've never spoken to him about it, but I'm as certain as I can be that both of those girls were members of the Comintern. They wanted to change the world. They couldn't understand why so many people didn't want the kind of world they offered. They starved themselves, mixed with dubious people, did good works—like Sara, only their good works were for a very uncertain ideal."

"No more than that?"

"If you want the truth I can give you a few names. Some addresses." He glanced away. "Actually, you'd be doing me a favor, Arnie. I've checked on certain of their old acquaintants from the Paris days. Found out where they are now—the ones that lived. But I've never had the guts to go and ask the right questions. I'll give you the names if you'll bring me the answers —the true answers, mind. I don't bruise that easily."

Arnold promised, and made arrangements to leave for Paris the next afternoon.

At a little after six o'clock that evening Naldo and Barbara arrived in Naldo's Humber. "Your shadow's been looking for you, Arn," Naldo told him. "I said I thought you were still in Germany. Seemed a bit put out."

"Thanks. I need some time to do his dirty work. Keep him at bay, will you, Nald?"

"Naturally."

"Could you brief Sara and Dick as well?"

Naldo nodded. Then—"We must be closer to the end than I thought. The Chief's given me the go-ahead for a Christmas wedding."

"Isn't it wonderful?" Sara appeared from the General's Study, her arm wrapped around Barbara's shoulders. "Dick and I were married from here at Christmas."

"I'm afraid it has to be Surrey for us." Naldo gave an uncharacteristic little grimace.

"Honeymoon here then, Nald." Sara was serious.

"With the whole family around? I know Redhill at Christmas."

"That's exactly why you should spend it here. We're family; we'll leave you alone like proper lovebirds and laugh if you don't come down for meals, but it *would* be fun."

To his surprise, Arnie saw the look pass between Barbara and Naldo, and the honeymoon at Redhill Manor arranged between them without a word crossing either's lips.

As THEY WERE all sitting down to dinner that night talking of weddings and happiness, Caspar opened the next batch of papers in the ghastly pink Northolt cave.

The first private report of the meeting with the SS officer remained in his head. He could hear the trams of Basle and smell the new-baked bread and strong aroma of coffee in the Berne safe house, which he also knew well.

They covered exactly the period between the former C's return to London after his adventure in Switzerland, and his death. Mainly there were decrypted letters and telegrams—from *Harold* as well as *Hornet*—mixed up with the intelligence analysis from C, which he had already briefly examined.

First came the initial product. The first messages from the newly recruited *Harold* of the SS.

32

▼

THE MESSAGES FROM C's fledgling agent—*Harold*—began on
November 13, 1938. The first was short and bitter. The decrypt
read:

> You will see that I told you the truth. The whole world now
> knows something of what has here been called Crystal Night.
> Yet I suspect the news outside Germany gives only a fraction
> of the truth. I was involved, naturally, and am heavy with
> guilt. Hundreds, possibly thousands of Jewish shops and busi-
> nesses have had their windows broken; while Jewish Temples
> have been burned. Looting and brutality are ripe with horror
> and, bearing in mind my original warning to you, the scale of
> this terror is great—Jews murdered, clubbed to death;
> hundreds, maybe thousands taken into the Camps. Again I
> must warn you—this is only the beginning. *Harold*.

Between this message and March 1939 there were a number of
short pieces of intelligence, some of it of interest—order-of-bat-
tle for both the Wehrmacht and the Luftwaffe. There were special
reports on the Panzer divisions, and one message drew attention
to what was later to become known as Blitzkrieg.

Caspar shook his head sadly over a particular passage:

> You should caution your military men to read a book by a
> young French colonel called de Gaulle—*Vers l'Armée de Mé-
> tier*. Also one by a senior German officer, Erwin Rommel,
> *Infanterie Greift An*. The latter was written two years ago.
> Both books are required reading for *all* our officers, and will
> show your people the way German strategy is changing. There
> will be new mobility, with tanks and bombers crushing for-

ward positions, while infantry will leapfrog with the tanks. *Harold*.

Caspar wondered how much use had been made of this advice, and of further information which poured in. On March 1, *Harold* predicted the move into Prague and the takeover of Bohemia and Moravia. A week later he sent a long letter which gave almost the entire text of Hitler's speech declaring that Czechoslovakia had ceased to exist.

Most of the reports were in the form of lengthy letters, which must have taken hours to encrypt. All were both accurate and could have been of great use.

Late in March, *Harold* reported his promotion to *Sturmbannführer*—Major—together with his concern that this elevation would lead to a posting as a staff officer in one of the camps.

But it was a report from the first week of April that made Caspar sit up as though stung.

An opportunity has come for me to take your advice regarding the Russian business. There has been much coming and going here. Do not be surprised if you hear suddenly of a pact between my country and the Russians. I realise it sounds impossible, but it becomes increasingly likely as each day passes. AH appears to have set his heart on it. There is, of course, plenty of opportunity to speak with members of the Soviet Legation, and visiting Russian diplomatic people. In terms of great secrecy I have made an approach to a man named Baleikev who I suspect to be one of their Intelligence officers. He has responded well. I do not know how to describe my feelings. I seem to boil with a mixture of hatred for those who lead my country, and a sea of guilt at what I am doing. Pray for me. *Harold*.

Caspar wondered how much praying the old Chief was doing at that time. If at all, it was probably for himself. The next message was simple, but told Caspar all he needed to know. He had suspected it from page one of C's *First Folio*, but it still made him catch his breath.

It is done. The Russians have accepted me and worked out a series of codes and similar instructions. Once they had questioned me, in great detail, four times in all, they told me to be prepared for a visit from my controller. I returned home late on Thursday night, having been dining with my brother officers. Hannalore is away, visiting her aunt in Austria. I went to my study and switched on the lights. There, sitting in a chair, was my man. He is to be known by me as *Thunder*. No clue to his true name. A tall man who does not look like a Russian. He speaks German well, also English like a native. To hear him you would think he was born of your country. First I am to give them mainly military and economic details. I am to use the code name *Lightning*. Please give me instructions of what I should *not* tell them. *Harold*.

So, *Lightning! Lightning* equaled Hans-Dieter Klaubert. Hans-Dieter Klaubert also equaled *Harold*, C's inside, private source within the SS. During the interrogation of Ramillies, outside Frankfurt, he had asked his brother about code names. Much earlier, Ramillies had given him *Lightning;* during a sultry, sticky afternoon, a low rumble of thunder had precursed a downpour. "God's playing with my crypto," Ramillies had said, with almost a sneer. When Caspar had queried the remark, Ramillies volunteered the information that he had been *Thunder* to Klaubert's *Lightning*.

Now Caspar turned the pages rapidly. Most of the information was about troop and weapons buildups and reorganization. Early in August, *Harold* once more predicted a Soviet-German peace treaty, and then, in mid-August, he was moved to an active unit—"In preparation for war. I have several officers and many clerks and experienced NCOs under me. We are to be a field unit, ready to take military control in occupied townships," he wrote. "I am still in Berlin and we are training, mainly on how to treat local people of countries overrun by our armies. I am afraid for my soul. There will be need for many arrests of able-bodied men and women to act as labour. Foreign Jews are to be shown no mercy. I hope God will have mercy on what *I* might have to do."

Interleaved with these messages were C's replies, which mainly thanked Klaubert for his invaluable work and pointed him toward other targets. There were also instructions on what to give to the Russians, and—more to the point—what *not* to give. C was controlling this asset through *Hornet* and clearly holding him close to his chest. By August, Caspar knew, C was already bedridden.

The last week of August explained much of what was later to occur. By now it was certain that war could not be averted. The dossier included signals sent directly from the Foreign Office warning embassy diplomats to prepare to evacuate. *Hornet* issued information two days in advance of the signing of the peace treaty between Russia and Germany—a piece of news that rocked the world, for Britain appeared to be about to sign a similar document. *Harold* calmed any fears. "Do not take the treaty seriously. My controller, *Thunder*, still wishes me to feed them with a lot of information. Neither side trusts the other. War is a week or so away."

Then came a long message from *Hornet*:

Because I have to prepare for evacuation, I have given *Harold* fresh instructions. He realises that he can no longer rely on the system which has worked so well until now. He understands perfectly what must be done, and I have arranged, without giving any details, for our people to clean out two letter-boxes in Switzerland. *Harold* will communicate regularly by letter to one of two Poste Restante addresses—in Berne and Zurich. He will write to a distant relation called variously Anna Flemart (an aunt); Ingrid Stoltz (a second cousin); Karl Mulders (a great-uncle); Peter Diester (another second cousin); and Paul Dopft (a family friend). All will appear pro-Nazi and I have taught *Harold* a simple checkerboard cipher. This is the best I can do at such short notice but it should arouse no suspicions among the German military censors who will see the letters. The decrypt will be done on the basis of the second letter to the right at the beginning of each line up to line twenty, when it will become the first letter. Also the first letter to the far right for the first twenty lines, and the penultimate letter at the end of each line thereafter. The letters should be taken in rotation—left, right, etc. I enclose the checkerboard, and his letters will all include the initials RKT in some form of order attached to his name. Once we begin to operate him directly from London a further, and safer, method can be used. I trust this is satisfactory for the interim period. *Hornet*.

There followed an *en clair* telegram from the Embassy in Paris to the Foreign Office. It was dated August 28, 1939, and read:

REGRET TO INFORM YOU THAT NIGEL RICHARD MANNUS FORMERLY DPCO MUNICH KILLED IN MOTOR ACCIDENT NEAR AMIENS WHILE RETURNING TO ENGLAND BY CAR ON YOUR IN-

STRUCTIONS PLEASE ADVISE NECESSARY DEPARTMENTS AND
RELATIVES STOP BODY WILL BE RELEASED FOR ONWARD JOUR-
NEY AS SOON AS FRENCH POLICE WILL ALLOW STOP ENDS.

There followed a tightly written note by the present C which
said that, while Mannus was on the SIS books, there was no
record of his being operational regarding any current agents. Of
course C had technically broken all the rules of agent-handling in
keeping this asset to the closely restricted knowledge of only two
people, but who could have known these two would die within a
few months of one another? *It is difficult to understand,* C wrote,
*how my predecessor could have entrusted his secretary with a
letter naming me as his successor, yet making no provision for
his agent, Harold.* He did not even know if C, who was quite ill
by this time, was even informed of the young officer's death. It
did, however, explain the bewilderment of various people when
decrypts came in from Switzerland. There they had been decrypted on Mannus' instructions only, then transmitted in a more
secure cipher to London. In England there was, naturally, certain
suspicion in dealing with an agent, not on the books, called *Harold.* C noted, *In the first months I had no time to investigate what
was a small matter, but it did cause great alarm.*

"I'll bet it did," muttered Caspar, closing the file. It was late
and he was not yet halfway through the *First Folio,* although C's
research already made terrible sense. It was interesting to see that
all these messages had come from three quite separate files—one
an outdated SIS Registry folder marked "Dead Ciphers"; another
from "Defunct Cases: Germany"; while the facts of Mannus'
death were in a pensions file from the Foreign Office.

ARNOLD FARTHING, TRAVELING on a Canadian passport as Adrian
Fox from Toronto, took the early BEA flight to Paris the following morning. He checked in at the modest Hôtel Moderne near
the Place de la République. It was far from *moderne,* but suited
his needs, for Arnie expected to be in the city for only twenty-
four hours.

It was a fine, warm autumn day, and Arnold walked toward
the Place de la République, stopping by a café where he sat at a
sidewalk table, drank coffee, and ate a roll stuffed with ham and
mustard. Paris was almost its old self again and smelled of strong
coffee and that particularly pungent French tobacco. He collected
a handful of 25c pieces at the café counter, then walked—in

Paris he liked walking, and on this occasion he had the added reason to check in case he was being followed. Arnie was still hungover by the people who had shadowed Naldo and himself in London; and then the night dash they had been forced to make from Munich to Frankfurt. It was also possible that Roger Fry was taking an extra interest in his movements.

All seemed clear. He spent half an hour "walking the doubles" and came up with nothing unusual. At last he went into a public phone booth, which allowed him an almost all-round view as he dialed several numbers.

He had come armed with the list of names and addresses given to him by Richard. There were also some telephone numbers. He dialed three, only to find that, with the Occupation and return to normality, they had been changed. On the fourth call he got lucky. The man he wanted would meet him on the Rive Gauche —in a particular *bar-tabac* within the hour. At last he was able to start his quiet investigation into the lives of Caroline Railton Farthing and Josephine Grenot, who had once lived in a tiny flat in the Rue de la Huchette.

The man he was about to see had been a leading name in the Maquis, which made it an even bet that he held left-wing views, if not actually a member of the Communist Party—Stalin had dissolved the International, the Comintern, during the war. Also, the man Arnie had just spoken to had been Caroline's and Jo-Jo's landlord during the few years they had lived in Paris.

The bar was crowded, even in the middle of the afternoon, and the person Arnie sought did not appear to have arrived—they had arranged a very simple recognition code, *Paris-Soir* opened at page 4 and folded in Arnie's left hand. The contact would have a paper packet of Gauloises stuck into his breast pocket, bottom up.

Arnie stood at the bar and ordered a *cassis*. Ten minutes later a small man wearing a battered beret elbowed in next to him and asked the barman for a packet of Gauloises, which he took, carefully placing them bottom up in the breast pocket of his somewhat ancient jacket. He then turned toward Arnie and grinned.

"Are you English?" he asked in French.

"No, Canadian." Arnie studied the man's face. He was someone who would go quite unrecognized in a crowd, having the kind of features which, once seen, were immediately forgotten. An ideal face for a crook or an agent.

"Let's take a walk." The Frenchman spoke good English.

In the clear sunshine they strolled down toward the river.

Arnie leaned against a wall and gave the Frenchman a quick glimpse of his Communist Party card—an excellent facsimile run up in Washington under the name of Fox.

"You are close to the cause, I understand," he said, going out on a precarious limb.

The Frenchman nodded, then put out a hand. His name was Claude Manceau and he had a tight firm grip. He asked how he could help.

"Just before the war you rented a small apartment in the Rue de la Huchette to two English girls."

"Of course."

"You know what happened to them?"

"They left. Just before Paris was occupied by the Boche. They were good girls, they left the rent for me. I don't know where they went. Maybe England."

"No, they joined a *réseau* near Orléans. I have been asked to try and find them. You see, they went missing from there soon after the invasion—after D-Day."

Manceau gave a little nod, as though to say this was the most natural thing for them to do. Then he asked if they had been captured. "Are you looking for them alive, or just for the graves?"

"We don't know." Arnie put on a solemn face. It was what a Frenchman would expect. "What I need is some corroboration regarding their political situation."

The pause was short, but Manceau locked eyes with Arnie so that the silence appeared to go on forever. "In those days many of us belonged to the Comintern." Manceau did not break the eye contact and Arnie thought he saw a worm of uncertainty move deep behind the brown irises of his eyes.

"Yes." Arnold stepped in quickly. "I was a member, as were you, I believe."

Manceau gave a hint of a nod. "Possibly," he said a little sharply. Then—"As for the girls, they were not fully committed as far as I know. How did you call them in your country? Journeying friends?"

"Fellow travelers."

"*Oui,* fellow travelers. This was what they were. Of course after the Occupation—who knows?"

It was Arnold's turn to nod. "Who knows?" he repeated. "Perhaps a man called Jean Gardien? You know him?"

Manceau gave a short laugh. "I know his real name. Gardien was his *nom de guerre.*"

Arnold gave a pleasant smile. "Yes. The real name is Jean Faveron, correct?"

Manceau inclined his head. "Yes. Yes, Jean was a senior Comintern organizer. He could well have known."

"He still lives in St. Germain?" The trick question Dick Farthing had given to him.

The Frenchman cocked an eyebrow. "Faveron lives beyond our reach, Monsieur Fox. He died in the final days of the Occupation. In the cellars of the Avenue Foch." During the years of Nazi tyranny, Gestapo headquarters in Paris had been in the Avenue Foch. Arnold was immediately on his guard. Manceau's reply had been too smooth. If he was to the far left, he would know the real truth about Jean Faveron.

Arnold frowned. "Then I must try in Orléans." Behind Manceau two barges passed sedately, heading downriver, low in the water.

"I've told you all I can." Manceau held out his hand.

"Yes. Yes, thank you." They shook hands and Arnie thought he could detect a little more sweat on the man's palm. Stress? Or merely the warmth of the afternoon?

They said their farewells, and as Arnold walked away he had a distinct sensation of nervousness, as though the Frenchman was still watching him. Out of the corner of his eye he saw two men, wearing corduroy trousers, rollneck sweaters, and heavy, military-style boots come out of an alley to his right.

He crossed the Seine again by the Pont Saint-Michel. When he reached the Rue de Rivoli—where he hoped to find his next contact—the men were still with him, holding back about fifty yards, but definitely there. He tried a few doubles, then ducked into the Métro at the Hôtel de Ville and out again just as quickly.

He reached the Rue de Rivoli fairly sure that he had lost the pair of watchers. They were not very good, and you do not wear heavy boots if carrying out a street surveillance.

The old apartment block he was looking for was almost opposite the intersection with the Rue St. Martin. The area was replete with new construction work—noise clogged the ears and scaffolding reached across the sidewalks.

An aged concierge nodded to him, muttering to herself as he asked for M. Tiraque.

Tiraque had been especially recommended by Dick Farthing. "Not the most pleasant man in the world, but he knows a great deal about what went on among the various political factions. For an American he makes a very good Frenchman." Dick had given him an amused, somewhat conspiratorial look.

Arnold asked why Dick had not gone to him. "It's a long story and has about the same number of twists as a corkscrew. Basically I'm too old. He's trouble, that one. But it would be embarrassing to risk my neck on him."

"Embarrassing, when the truth about your daughter's at stake?" Arnold suspected there was far more than age involved.

"I've been looking for someone like you—I presume you have cover—to do the job for me."

"If he can throw light, couldn't you have sent someone before?"

Dick had spread his hands in a great Gallic shrug. "Arnold, there's a time and a season for all things. I know a great deal about Tiraque. More than I can even tell you. The time and the season are here. See him for me. Please. Ask directly about Caroline and see what his reaction is—and watch your back."

Arnold had said he would see Tiraque if he could. If he had time. Now he found himself standing in the hall of an apartment that smelled of success and money. There was an undoubted Fragonard wash drawing on one wall, and a piece of sculpture Arnie could not place set on a gilded lacquer cabinet. He priced the lot at around half a million dollars.

"The spoils of war." Tiraque was in his late sixties, Arnie guessed, and looked like a retired prizefighter who had taken lessons in style and grooming. Yet he still seemed out of place among the objets d'art in his hallway. "You said your name was . . . ?"

"Fox, sir. Adrian Fox. I have absolutely no authority, or right, to bother you." Arnold showed him a second piece of fabricated card, set behind clear plastic in a wallet. It claimed he was from the War Graves Commission.

"You probably haven't." Tiraque had a gruff accent which could have originated from the streets of Brooklyn, and made Arnold wonder why a voice like this had a name like Tiraque. "Come in anyway."

He ushered Arnold into a large room at the rear of the apartment with windows looking out on a remarkable view over the rooftops, across the river to the Ile de la Cité. Notre-Dame seemed to rise up with its towers within touching distance—a trick of the eye, for it remained a long way off. Two great crystal chandeliers hung from the ceiling, and the room was fabulously decorated and furnished—a Cézanne on one wall, a Seurat on another, while the third wall was adorned with an incredible English carpet, a coat of arms in its center—but Arnold's attention was taken by the most beautiful thing of all: a young woman, who could not have yet reached thirty, sitting on a comfortable and very large settee. She had long blonde hair hanging almost to her waist, an elfin face which, while still young and beautiful, had a strength of character marked on it, as though some hard experience in her young life had left a print on her features.

"Meet my wife, Mr. Fox." Tiraque gestured. "Jacquie, darling, this is Mr. Fox from the War Graves Commission."

"Good lord, what do they want with us?" Her voice was low and seemed to smile. When she spoke the sun must have come out, for Marcel Tiraque, just as it did for Arnold. Jacquie Tiraque did not get up. Her skirt was arranged in a circle, completely surrounding her on the settee, so it would have been a hazard for this lovely girl to change the pose.

"A wild-goose chase, I suspect." Arnold could not take his eyes from Jacquie Tiraque.

"Sit down, Mr. Fox. You'd like tea or something?" Madame Tiraque's long, slim arm reached out, as if toward a bell.

Arnold lifted both his hands as though pushing at an invisible wall. "No. No, thank you very much. Your name came to us from an odd source . . ."

"It would be odd." Tiraque chuckled at what seemed to be a private joke. "Please go on."

"Well, we're trying to trace the burial places of a number of people connected with SOE and the Resistance. Some—many—have eluded us." Arnold realized that he was going to have to improvise. There was wealth in this room. Wealth and power. You could feel the power coming off Tiraque like heat from a stove. Make a wrong move—touch him—and you would get burned.

"Well, I knew a lot of Resistance people—and some SOE also." Tiraque had an odd trick of seeming to be just a comfortable, friendly middle-aged man, yet danger hung around him like poison ivy among harmless flowers.

"Jean Faveron? Also known as Jean Gardien?" Arnold thought, Try that for size.

Tiraque had taken a silver case from his pocket and was in the act of removing a cigarette. It stayed, poised between thumb and forefinger for a fraction longer than it should have done. "Forgive me." Tiraque held the case toward Arnold, who refused. "Darling?" He offered the case to his wife, who took a cigarette. Tiraque leaned over and lit it for her. Did Arnold imagine it or was the man's hand shaking slightly?

Tiraque lit his own cigarette, inhaled deeply, and blew out a long stream of smoke. "Jean Faveron," he said calmly, "died in Gestapo headquarters here in Paris, one week after the Normandy landings."

"Yes, I know."

"Then you must also know that people who died there were usually dumped—God knows where."

"Yes, but some bodies have been identified."

Tiraque's manner had become cold. "Not Faveron's body, though. I would have thought you knew his body was burned. Covered in gasoline and burned in the garden. Has nobody told you that? I thought every department of the military had dossiers high as the Eiffel Tower on Faveron. He was a much-respected, highly decorated hero."

"I didn't know that. I'm sorry, you see I'm rather new to this."

"Why," Tiraque asked with increasing iciness, "should an American be interested in Faveron?"

In fact, Arnold Farthing knew very well why a thousand Americans should be interested. Faveron was a name given to him by Dick. "Test people with it," his uncle had told him. "Faveron was a Communist as far as the Resistance was concerned. In fact he worked with several of the OSS teams—and betrayed them. He was, in plain words, a double: a Nazi, put in to flush out the easy targets. There're plenty of people still looking for him. A story was put out that he died under interrogation in the Avenue Foch, after which his body was burned. In fact, he's almost certainly still alive."

Back in the sumptuous room, with its beautiful furniture and crystal chandeliers, Arnold replied that he was not an American. "I'm Canadian," he lied. "Canadian and not long out of the Service. I needed a job, had some contacts, so I'm doing this until something better comes along."

"And who did you say gave you my name?" Tiraque stood up—suddenly, somewhat threateningly. Arnold braced himself for anything to happen. He did not like this sense of tension which seemed to have come into the room with Faveron's name.

In with both feet, he thought, then calmly answered, "A guy called Railton. Donald Railton." Dick had told him to use Naldo. "Don't even mention me," he had cautioned.

He was side on to Jacquie Tiraque, but swore he detected a long sharp intake of breath.

"You have the wrong people, friend." Tiraque stood over him. The man's body seemed to say, "It's time you left, buddy, and if you don't go of your own accord, then you'll end up with your nose sticking out the back of your neck."

"I'm sorry. I didn't realize . . ." He stood, making sure he was square on his feet, and well balanced, as he took a step toward the door. "Please forgive me, Madame Tiraque." His hands flapped wildly, gesturing a kind of apology.

"It's all right, Mr. Fox. Nothing to worry about." She had remained calm in spite of the intake of breath.

As he got to the door, Arnold hesitated. "Might I mention one other name?"

"Go ahead." Tiraque's eyes had turned to glass. He seemed to be really saying, "Go ahead and see what happens to you."

"Caroline Farthing. She worked—" He stopped as Jacquie Tiraque's jaw sagged, her face losing all color, eyes staring.

"I think we've had enough questions for one day, Mr. Fox. Time to go now."

Tiraque, with his heavy pugilist's build, did not lay a finger on him, yet Arnold felt he had been bodily propelled toward the door.

On the third turning of the stairs, the two men who had earlier followed him launched themselves from above and below, falling upon him like skilled assassins. As he rolled with the first punch, Arnold had a picture of Jacquie Tiraque firmly in his head, and he knew where he had seen her before.

THE ONE WHO had been hiding on the stairs above threw the first punch. It caught Arnie on the right shoulder and he rode with it, his own arms coming up, hands flat and straightening, ready to chop, maim, or kill if necessary.

The hood attacking from below signaled his move too quickly, the right foot, shod in the studded military boot, swinging back to kick, aimed dead center at the apex of Arnie's thighs.

Arnold, who had trained with the best street fighters in the world, chopped at the man who had thrown the punch, turned, then jackknifed his own right leg—high, so that his heel caught the kicking man in the chest. The blow took all the wind out of him—possibly breaking some ribs in the bargain—and, in his off-balance, uncompleted kicking stance, the attacker keeled over backward.

The stairs to the apartments were not carpeted—just hard

stone with sharp, angled risers. The would-be kicker gave one great grunt and hit the stairs hard. Arnie thought he had broken the man's back, and the idea did not worry him as he turned to deal with the second thug, moving in close, the cutting edges of his hands hard as steel, and chopping viciously at his target's upper arms. After the sixth blow his opponent would feel only numbness in the arms. He felt nothing at all as Arnie chopped both hands, simultaneously, against each side of his neck in a terrible scissors blow. Silently he thanked those leathery little men who had trained him so well for the OSS. All the agony he had suffered at their hands was now being paid back in gold.

The hood went limp, pitching forward on the stairway, his head lolling over the top riser.

Arnie Farthing just ran, taking the stairs two at a time and jumping the last three. In the comparative safety of the street he hailed the first cab to come in sight, telling the driver to go to the Moderne, stay while he paid his bill, then take him on to the airport.

Arnie could not wait to get back and tell Naldo what, and who, he had seen in the Rue de Rivoli.

33

▼

EVER SINCE HIS return to England, during the previous year—at the beginning of operation *Symphony*—Naldo Railton had been trying to make time to see his sister, Sara Elizabeth.

As children they had been very close, and Naldo looked back on his early years as a time of great happiness within his family. He could recall quite clearly the long period when his father was away—during the First World War, when he was tiny—and the romps and laughter he had shared with his mother and sister.

Sara Elizabeth was always called Elizabeth, or Liza, to avoid confusion with the great Sara of Redhill Manor. With the passing years she grew into a more serious child whose main preoccupation was music—inheriting her mother's gift for the piano, and even dabbling in small compositions which were not without merit.

Serious though she was, Elizabeth could never be accused of being solemn, for her acute sense of humor usually prevailed over all things, even after she found religion to be her life's mainstay.

The Haversage Sisters, as members of the Community of St. Mary the Virgin were generally known, had their Mother House a mile from the center of the small town—a Victorian Gothic building which overlooked Haversage from the north, almost as Redhill Manor did from the west. Sara Elizabeth Railton first met members of this sisterhood during visits to Redhill Manor, and at nineteen she had already made up her mind to devote her life to God within the Community.

But the older nuns, together with at least two priests, bade her wait. With the coming of the war, she became stronger than ever in her conviction and, in 1942, at the age of twenty-five, Sara Elizabeth Railton became a novice.

Naldo was overseas at the time his sister was admitted fully into the Order—as Sister Elizabeth Mary—in 1945. He had seen little of her since, though they corresponded frequently. Now, Naldo, together with his future bride, took the opportunity to visit her, before the pair went on to see Barbara's parents in Surrey to give them the news of a fixed wedding date—they had mutually decided on December 23.

Just as they were leaving the Manor for the arranged meeting with Sister Elizabeth Mary, the telephone rang. Naldo answered, expecting it to be some friend of Sara's. A dusty, dry American voice was at the distant end. "Might I speak to Arnold Farthing?"

"Not here, I'm afraid. This is Redhill Manor." Naldo knew immediately who was calling.

"That's the number I dialed." There was no hint of humor in Arnie's case officer's voice: "I believe he's on his way to the Manor now."

"First I've heard of it." Naldo frowned.

What he said was true enough. Naldo was not to know how Arnie had arrived at Le Bourget airfield to see the last London flight of the day steaming down the runway on takeoff; nor how he had sweated out the night, positioning himself for a good view of the main small concourse doors, so he would have the advantage if new assailants came looking for him. By morning he had a seat on the nine-thirty DC-3 which would take him into the temporary London airport—a collection of huts, tents, and connecting duckboards, formerly the Fairey Aviation Company's aerodrome called Heathrow.

On arrival, Arnie took an airport bus straight into London, headed for Paddington Station—where Roger Fry finally picked up his spoor in the shape of a ticket office clerk—and the first train that would take him to Haversage Halt.

Fry hung up quietly, leaving Naldo standing with the receiver in his hand. He shrugged and told Barbara that it looked like Arnie had problems.

"We're going to have problems as well if we don't get a move on." Barbara kept looking at her watch. "Didn't you say they were very strict about visiting this monastery?"

"Convent, Barb. Monasteries are for monks."

"Lord, I'm jumpy. Why does your sister have to be a holy woman? Nuns look like black crows or rooks to me. They scare the—"

"Yes, I know—"

"I was going to say—if you would listen—they scare the pants off me."

"Oh." Naldo looked crestfallen. "I thought *I* did that."

She chased him to the car and within half an hour they were pulling up in the large forecourt of the convent which, Naldo admitted, looked to be the ideal place to shoot a horror movie.

A silent novice, in white habit and with downcast eyes, led them along passages and through carved Norman arches, erected in the 19th century. Everything sparkled, as though dust was Satan's work and had to be driven out daily. The quarry-tiled floors shone, as did the woodwork and a life-sized crucifix set into an arched and gilded embrasure. The air was filled with the mingled scent of wax polish, well-kept wood, flowers, and incense. Finally, the novice tapped on a heavy wooden door and opened it to reveal a pleasant room with easy chairs, a nice watercolor of the downland above Haversage, and a table on which sat a tray with coffee and cups. The red and black quarry tiles of the passages continued into the room. Barbara was later to remark that the place must be "bloody cold in winter with all those tiled floors and hardly a carpet in sight."

The novice whispered that Sister would be with them soon. She left the door open, as did Elizabeth when she arrived.

"Oh, but you're lovely." She held Barbara by the shoulders, her arms fully outstretched. "Naldo, I hope you realize what a lucky man you are to be taking such a bride." Sister Elizabeth Mary was almost unrecognizable to her brother—her face framed in the white oval of a wimple and long black veil, while her body, full and shapely as he remembered it, was hidden by the long black habit, gathered at the waist by a slim white knotted cord. He knew it was his sister only by voice, laugh, and the incredible smile which had brightened many days of his adolescence.

Barbara relaxed in the young nun's presence, for she was taken off-guard by Sister Elizabeth Mary's almost vibrant attitude to life. In the Convent Guest Room, they drank coffee and nibbled digestive biscuits.

"What on earth do you find to do with yourself all day?" Barbara asked ingenuously.

Elizabeth flicked at her black veil with one hand, threw her head back, and laughed. "There are not enough hours in the day for us. You have no idea, Barbara—Mass at six o'clock, the singing of the office, chores around the house. I teach in the local school—music of course—and there's the garden to keep up, and the wood carving, and executive work for our other houses. We have two in Africa and three more here in England. One is a hospital for people addicted to alcohol and drugs. Between ourselves, I prefer my teaching. I deal with very small children, and it's quite touching how they show their affection. I've a sneaking feeling that, at heart, they think I'm a penguin."

Barbara giggled. "And what else do you penguins do?"

"All the time, we serve God. In every way—work, prayer, and play." She saw Naldo's slightly uncomfortable look, and the way he glanced at his watch—this was after an hour's cheerful conversation—"It's all right, dear brother, I've long since given up any hope of converting you."

Naldo made a face at her. "You'd be surprised. Sometimes my work brings me nearer to God than you'd imagine."

His sister sighed. "Well, brother, it's never too late. Remember what Saint Augustine said, and he found himself wrong in saying it: 'Too late came I to love thee, O thou Beauty both so ancient and so fresh, yea too late came I to love thee. And behold, thou wert within me, and I out of myself, where I made search for thee.' Oh, dear, I'm showing off. I've been studying the *Confessions*." She looked straight at her brother. "You all right, Naldo?"

From down the passageway, slick with polish, came the rise and fall of voices, so strong, yet paradoxically so frail—nuns singing words almost as old as time in the silver beauty that is plainsong.

> *Come Holy Ghost our souls inspire,*
> *And lighten with celestial fire . . .*

Naldo stood silent, unknowingly swaying to the simplicity of the rhythms, his eyes glued to the chessboard pattern of the tiled floor. His mind drew back two years, for in Saint Augustine's words, just quoted by his devout sister, he thought he had found the way to Hans-Dieter Klaubert; the Devil of Orléans; *Lightning* to the Russian NKVD; *Harold* to the British Secret Intelligence Service.

The last time he had read those words of Augustine was in the pink house in Northolt—land of commuters, trains, businessmen and women who left their homes to work in central London and slept each night, safe now from the bombs, in this little clutch of beehive dormitories.

He could not know that his Uncle Caspar was, almost at this very moment, reading the same words, and making the same connection, in the same pink room.

THE PRESENT C had written a long explanation of the general reaction of the Secret Intelligence Service to their mystery agent *Harold*. "In retrospect, there was no sense of urgency," he said, the green ink spilling across the pages in his small, almost copperplate, hand. "You will appreciate that I took over in a full capacity in November 1939, and I had already been doing C's job and my own for several months.

"I was aware of these signals coming in from Berne, and the crypto of an asset coded *Harold*. I suppose it was not until January or February 1940 that a real investigation began. I queried Berne regarding the source and they, in turn, gave me the bare facts. *Hornet* had advised them of someone operating out of Germany who would, for a while, be using the very simple checkerboard cipher. He had told them that the source was top grade, and the material would be CX—C's Eyes Only.

"Naturally I instituted a check on *Hornet,* and found him to be unavailable, for the reasons you now know. As I have already written, it was exceptionally difficult for me to believe that *Harold* was the late C's personal source. It was too dangerous to take the reports at more than face value.

"To be honest, now the facts are known, I cannot think of any officer in the Service who would not, at that point, have accepted the intelligence input from *Harold* with anything but scepticism.

"I alone instructed the decrypts to be examined and assessed, and ordered that not too much reliance should be placed on them.

"When the war ended, in the light of the investigation regarding *Tarot* and the OSS operation *Romarin*, I made it my business to collect every single item in this dossier. They come from many files, and have not been easy to trace. There is no reason to be in any way suspicious about this, as our dead files are, by the very nature of secrecy, spread over a wide area in our Registry, the Central Foreign Office Registry, and the Treasury. This is for security only.

"However, my feelings now are that we ran an asset inside the Nazi SS to *his* detriment, and our own grave loss. You will see that we were dealing with a man who remained completely loyal to us without us giving him assistance, even though we should have known, from his later terrible and emotional turmoil, that we had a true bill of sale on our hands.

"I carry the blame for not having *Harold* serviced properly, and must take responsibility for what has happened to him. Indeed, there are times when I feel I am responsible for the dreadful things he was forced to inflict upon good French, American, and British men, women, and children in order to keep his cover. This is a hard burden to carry, but heaven knows how much harder it must have been for him."

Red-eyed, and muzzy through lack of sleep, Caspar closed the heavy folder and stretched back in his chair. He had stayed awake throughout the night, fascinated and almost incredulous of what he read.

Herbie had shown concern for him—staying awake also and bringing him coffee at regular intervals.

"Why not you have a little rest, Mr. Caspar? No good this staying up through the night."

Caspar had replied sharply, "Get off to bed yourself, Herb. Don't stay up on my account. There's work I must do."

"This I am knowing. It is you I think of." And Herbie retired looking pained and hurt.

Caspar, by the time he reached the final pages of the *First Folio,* was not just tired, but angry and frustrated. It stretched his credulity when faced by what appeared to be the obvious conclusion—that *le Diable d'Orléans* was in reality a British asset; and that he had provided possibly the most accurate intelligence available to the Secret Intelligence Service throughout the whole war. The anger boiled inside his mind and brain as he riffled back through the decrypts, knowing none of them had been taken seriously. If only someone with an ounce of true ability had put *Harold*'s decrypts alongside the facts, as they emerged after the events, they would have seen that the asset—even though they had no knowledge of who the man was—had been Grade A Plus. He was a supermole the like of which had not been in place anywhere else through those days of carnage and massacre between 1939 and 1945.

Twice a month, regular as clockwork, letters had come into Berne or Zurich from private soldiers, NCOs, and officers of the Wehrmacht; men of the Luftwaffe; even officers and men from the Kriegsmarine. They had been posted from places as far apart as Paris, Calais, Berlin, Hamburg, Brussels, and Prague. How in heaven's name the man had managed it was beyond Caspar, but the originals, with copies of date-and-place stamps, were all there, preserved in cellophane slipcases, with the decrypts next to them, plus the more secure encryptions for onward transmission to London.

They all brought precise greetings to *Aunt Anna* (Flemart); *Cousin Ingrid* (Stoltz), between whom the sender, on one occasion at least, suggested there had been a lot more than should have been the case, even with second cousins; *Great-Uncle Karl* (Mulders); *Cousin Peter* (Diester); and *Paul* (Dopft), the old family friend. They had all come from people whose name and initials were variations of the three letters RKT—Kurt Thomas Ruchart; Rikard Theodore Kulle; R.K. Tannen. How in God's name had the censors missed that one? After all, the Germans were methodical to say the least. Yet, it seemed, they *had* missed it.

The letters were almost an art form in themselves—gossipy, joke-ridden, wildly pro-Nazi with constant references to the gallant Führer or the writer's brave comrades-in-arms. They were also long, and incredibly painstaking, for it took ingenuity to write naturally and remain bound by the conventions of the almost childish checkerboard cipher.

Hornet had obviously devised that particular checkerboard with great care. On graph paper the whole thing ran 52 squares by 52, making a board that could take four entire alphabets—two across the top and two down the left-hand side—the letters jumbled and set at random. In the main checkerboard there was therefore room for nearly three thousand further jumbled characters—over a hundred alphabets. To decrypt the letters you followed the instructions given by *Hornet*, writing down alternately the second letter from the left of a line, then the first on the right of the same line, changing the order every twenty lines or so.

Then you simply used the letters thus taken as you would use a map reference—the first A across coupled with the first A down would bring you to the true letter, wherever it lay within the grid.

It was wholly insecure, for a sharp wrangler could soon exhaust all mathematical possibilities and so construct the checkerboard grid himself. *Yet nobody had questioned the letters,* while the intelligence they carried was vital and exceptional.

Harold had given a good week's warning before *Plan Yellow* —the Nazi assault into Holland, Belgium, Luxembourg, and France—together with full details of the strategy, which, if it had been taken seriously, could not only have saved thousands of lives but also possibly prevented the Nazi occupation of Europe.

He had also revealed the date, together with the strategy of *Barbarossa*, the invasion of Russia, over a month before it took place. Some letters contained most secret specifications of arms —including minor details of work progressing on the V1 and V2 weapons, the specifications on new armor and design of tanks. Others gave hints on the morale of the Wehrmacht, the Luftwaffe, and the Kriegsmarine, especially where it applied to the submarine packs working out of the French ports. After his visits to Berlin, when he was often in the company of Hitler's court, *Harold* would report on the leading figures of the regime, even political analysis of the interaction between Hitler and his generals. *Harold* was the first to covertly give an alert to a growing plot among high-ranking officers—the plot which led to the attempted assassination on July 20, 1944—but by that time *Harold*'s own mind appeared to have become unhinged. If anyone had taken his intelligence seriously in the first place, they would have realized by that point that they had an unstable agent in place.

Now, with the knowledge that *Harold* was Klaubert, Caspar's fury grew. Soon after the D-Day landings, *Harold*'s letters became almost unintelligible, full of self-pity and remorse.

"How can I atone for the sins I have committed against my fellow human beings? Can I ever seek forgiveness, or find peace?" This was the constant theme, intermingled with quotations from scripture or the saints.

Indeed, Caspar thought, how could the man live with himself? Mentally he made plus and minus columns. Klaubert-*Harold* had stuck to his word and given British Intelligence the best information of any asset in place. The minus to that lay firmly on the consciences of those officers—C included—who did not make any deep examination—or correctly analyze the quality of the information.

Having seen the "Orléans Russians" transcripts, Caspar knew that Klaubert-*Lightning* had fed them only low-grade intelligence, except at moments when he felt it would further the cause of the Allies as a whole. A large plus there.

But the huge, overpowering minus was the ruthless way Klaubert had maintained his cover—the hundreds sent to the slave-labor and death camps; the Resistance groups smashed and their members executed after bloody torture; and finally the family matter—*Tarot*, Caspar's own people, and his two relatives, Caroline Railton Farthing and Jo-Jo Grenot. Were they dead? Was Klaubert dead, or still seeking his forgiveness?

Certainly he had been forced to consort with two Russian doubles, Dollhiem and Tert Newton, both of whom were carrying on the Soviet secret war, trying like so many to get their hands on the most precious possessions of the postwar Allies: the secrets of the atom bomb. Had Dollhiem or Newton been behind the death of Buelow in Washington? What more was there to be extracted from Ramillies? Certainly Caspar's own interrogation of his brother had fallen short of the mark, for Ramillies had dodged issues, misled, and taken him down dead-end alleys.

Day came. The milkman called. Herbie brought more coffee, with bacon and eggs, which Caspar devoured greedily, his mind still searching for more facts thrown up by this extraordinary pile of fudged secrets.

By midmorning, in his rheumy-eyed state of fatigue, Caspar was aware that his mind was in no state to deal with these complexities. Yet, as he riffled through the decrypts for the last time, his eyes fell upon one of Klaubert's last letters.

"God save me," he wrote. "Soon I must leave this hell—both the hell of the place itself, and the hell which burns my mind and, therefore, my soul. Lord, now lettest thou Thy servant depart in peace—but where can I find peace, with the lives of so many weighing down my soul? I shall burn for eternity, like those I alone have sent to the chambers and fires, or—worse—the living tortures. Is it too late? Saint Augustine thought it was too late. I have of recent days taken to reading his *Confessions* in secret, just as last year I read Saint Ignatius Loyola's *Spiritual Exercises*. It was not too late for him. Yet, like myself, he thought it so. Lord, help me to peace. I fear death—am terrified of it—more than anything. For I would leave this world unabsolved—no priest in the confessional could absolve me from what I have done, particularly my complicity, and duplicity, in the last weeks. Do I know where to go? Is there a place that will give me refuge so that I can make full atonement? I read now what Augustine wrote—

> 'Too late came I to love thee
> O thou Beauty both so ancient and so fresh
> Yea too late came I to love thee
> And behold thou wert within me
> And I out of myself
> Where I made search for thee.' "

Why? Caspar thought. Why had he split these lines so oddly? Caspar Railton knew little about Saint Augustine, but he was almost certain that this was a passage of prose, not split as though it was some kind of blank verse.

He took the note pad he had used while reading the *First Folio,* and uncapped his pen. Carefully he counted the letters, jotting them down until they read—

O-E-T-H-E-E-N-E-N-F-H-E

Then, Caspar reached to the back of the file and opened out the large piece of graph paper which held the copy of the long-dead young *Hornet's* checkerboard cipher.

In the kitchen, where he was preparing a meal, Herbie Kruger heard what sounded like a huge war-whoop.

"I told him," Herbie muttered. "He should not have worked all night. His brain is creaked. He is unhung. *Ach,* these Railtons, they are all crazy." Then he smiled. "The Farthings also."

Almost at this same moment, in the polish- and incense-laden air of the convent, Caspar's nephew, Naldo, looked at the checkerboard floor as he heard his sister recite the passage from Saint Augustine. He also saw how the Devil of Orléans had laid out those words, and wondered if perhaps, at the end in those last days, the SS man had left a clue, marked an arrow on a piece of paper to draw them to him so that retribution or forgiveness might follow.

NALDO WAS PREOCCUPIED as they drove back, through Haversage and up Red Hill to the Manor. As they slowed, signaling for the left turn into the drive, one of the local taxis crept through the gates.

"Arnie, do you think?" Barbara asked tentatively. She knew enough, now, to stay silent when some obvious work problem had intruded, pulling Naldo's mind from her.

"Mmm." Naldo nodded. "Yes, probably. Hope the bloody telephone doesn't ring for him."

"Ask not for whom the bell . . ." Barbara began, then saw, as they approached the house up the long elm-flanked drive, Arnold Farthing battering on the door.

They reached the turning circle just as Vera Crook, one of the servants, opened up to Arnie, who plunged past her, shouting with his voice at full power: *"Dick! Uncle Richard! Dick, you bastard! Where are you?"*

Naldo came up the steps, and saw Vera's shocked face, and

the look of anger in Arnie's eyes as he went on shouting.

During the journey back to England, Arnold had realized that it was Dick Farthing he must question before even giving his news to Naldo.

"Dick . . . ?" he shouted again, his voice echoing around the old hall that had seen so many moments of drama.

The door to the General's Study opened and Dick Railton Farthing came out, his brow creased with annoyance. He saw Arnie, and Naldo with Barbara coming in behind him.

The two men—uncle and nephew—faced each other for a moment.

"Well?" Dick asked quietly. "What is it, Arnie?"

"Tiraque. That bastard Tiraque, Dick. Who *is* he?"

"Ah." Dick showed no emotion. "You saw him, then?"

"I saw him. Who in God's name is he?"

Dick's eyes flicked from Naldo and Barbara back to Arnie. "You ever hear of a courier called *Night Stock?*" he asked when Vera had closed the door and disappeared belowstairs.

"Caspar's *Night Stock?* The one who operated out of Switzerland?"

"The same."

Naldo, not knowing what was at stake, said, "Then Caspar's perjured himself. He told the Enquiry that they'd lost sight of *Night Stock* in the final battles—in France."

"Yes." Dick gave the hint of a nod. "You'd better come in and hear the truth." He held the door of the study back. Barbara hesitated and Naldo muttered for her to seek out Sara.

Inside the study, Dick went behind the big old military desk. The sun filtered in through the rose garden, though the flowers were now gone and the bushes had been tied back for pruning.

"I should tell you first"—he spoke very slowly—"that this is more a family matter than a Service one. Yes, Caspar lied at the Enquiry. There was a furious row at his last meeting with *Night Stock*—who has a strange history of his own. Tiraque's his real name, by the way. He accused Caspar of a number of things. Caspar accused him back. I . . ." He stopped, for Arnie had taken a photograph from Dick's desk. It showed two girls, both pretty —one with short, dark hair; the other blonde. "Arnie?" Dick asked, puzzled.

"I was sure." Arnold did not appear to be speaking to anybody in the room. "Now I'm absolutely certain." He looked up at Dick, then Naldo. "This is a photograph of the missing Caro and Jo-Jo, yes?"

Dick nodded.

"Why?" Naldo asked.

"Do you know anything of Tiraque's circumstances in France? His manner of living?" He looked into Dick's eyes.

"He's a very wealthy man. Always was. Likes style. He always regarded *Night Stock* as a stylish name. He'll be living well, Arn. Why?"

"Married?" Arnold raised his eyebrows questioningly.

"Not that I know of."

Arnold smiled. He looked very happy. "Then I might just have solved one of the problems, though I don't understand it." He indicated the photograph. "Jo-Jo's turned into a very beautiful woman, Dick. I met her yesterday. With Marcel Tiraque. He introduced her to me as his wife, Jacquie."

There was a second's fury which crossed Dick's face like a sudden squall. Then, with an oath which damned Tiraque, his hand leaped out for the telephone.

34

▼

NALDO WAS QUIET, while Arnie could scarcely disguise his impatience as Dick dialed the exchange and booked two calls to different Paris numbers.

"They should come through within the hour if we're lucky," he said, replacing the receiver.

"I've been bloody lucky on your account, Dick." Arnie could not hold back his anger. "You give me names so that I can investigate Caroline's and Jo-Jo's political leanings, and a pair of thugs try to kill me."

Dick looked startled. "Where? Where did they try this?"

"You okay, Arn?" Naldo seemed concerned.

"I might just have killed one of them and maimed the other. Yes, I'm fine now—except for Tiraque, whose balls I'd like on a plate."

"Where, Arnie?" Dick's tone was more demanding, and—Naldo thought—more authoritative. He wondered how much Dick Farthing really knew about the inside of *Symphony*.

"As I was leaving Tiraque's flat. The one you gave me, the one in the Rue de Rivoli."

"I gave you several names." Dick was definitely on the attack. Naldo knew him well enough to see, and feel, the tension. Dick Railton did not take kindly to younger officers—nephews or no —calling him a bastard. "Several names—among them Tiraque's, because I've thought for some time that it would be an idea for one of you to go in there and flush him. I could never go, and C would never have sent Naldo."

Why?"—brusque, from Arnie.

"Because Naldo's too close to Caspar, and Tiraque would have firmly closed the door in my face. You'll understand when you've heard it all. Now, apart from Tiraque, who *did* you see, Arnold?"

"Only the guy called Manceau." Arnie rose and made a flapping gesture with his arms—just one movement, a flap, his shoulders drooping as his palms slapped against his legs. "Okay, Uncle Richard. I apologize. Yes, two guys tried to tail me after I left Manceau. They could have been the same pair. Excuse me, please. I got wound up because of Tiraque." He paused, reaching out for the photograph again. "You see, I was pretty sure it was Jo-Jo—even though she calls herself Jacquie now. You put me onto Tiraque. I figured you must have known about Jo-Jo."

"Did you?" Dick did not bat an eyelid, but anger rushed into his voice, like blood rushes to the face in a blush. "D'you think I wouldn't have been over there in a flash, with as many hoods as I could round up, if I'd known Jo-Jo was actually alive and well, and living in Paris with a cast-iron shit like Tiraque?"

"You didn't know?" Arnold appeared surprised.

"Of course I didn't bloody know, you fool! C's doing fandangos all over the place trying to find out what happened to Jo-Jo and Caro, isn't he? For God's sake, Arnie. Caro's my daughter. Jo-Jo's like a daughter to Sara and me. D'you think I haven't been doing my own looking?"

"Sorry, I—" Arnie began, and the telephone rang.

Dick's hand shot out like a striking snake, but it was some local woman for Sara. They all—probably the caller as well—heard Dick shout from the hall, "Sara, Mrs. Thingummy on the horn. You know, the woman from the Church Council. For God's sake get rid of her in double time, I've got calls coming in from Paris. Just get her off the bloody line!"

He came back into the General's Study, listened while Sara picked up an extension, then replaced the receiver.

"Right, Arnold," he said. "I gave you Marcel Tiraque's name for several reasons. First, I hoped you'd call on him and get some kind of reaction. Just anything, because I really thought we should have the whole *Night Stock* thing in the open. Caspar wanted it buried, and I don't think C was overly worried about hearing from *Night Stock* ever again. Wouldn't be surprised if he had a hand in the story of *Night Stock* going missing. Now, let's go over it again. You talked to Manceau, right?"

Arnold told him of the conversation by the Seine, near the Pont Saint-Michel.

"He actually said that?" Dick leaned over the desk. "He said Caro and Jo-Jo were fellow travelers but *not* members of the Comintern?"

"As far as he knew."

Dick took a very deep breath and exhaled loudly. "Oh, he'd know. Manceau would have known if they were Party members. He told you that, and then you spotted a tail on you?"

"A very obvious tail."

"Uh-huh. But you thought you'd shaken them?"

"Almost certain. They got me when I was quietly ejected from Tiraque's apartment."

"Tiraque didn't use force?"

Arnold appeared to be thinking. "Odd that. No. No, he didn't actually use force, but I felt as though he had. Didn't lay a finger on me, but I felt as if he'd taken me by the scruff of the neck and bounced me out."

"Yes." Dick almost smiled. "Yes, Tiraque has that effect on some people."

"What *about* this bugger Tiraque, Dick?" Naldo cut in. "I don't want to leave you all in the lurch, but Barbara's supposed to be going to see her family with me. So we can break the glad tidings."

"I rather think you'll have to forget that, Nald old son." Dick sounded quite cheerful. "As things've turned out, I suspect C will want all hands on deck."

"Oh, shit!" Naldo muttered.

"Hell hath no fury, I know." Dick was still cheerful. "Arnie, how would you read matters if Manceau put a pair of hoods onto you? Instructed them to see that you went missing?"

"He'd either lied to me about Caro and Jo-Jo or he wasn't happy about the news getting any further."

"Or someone else instructed him that all queries concerning either Caroline or Jo-Jo were to be treated as threats. *Someone else*. I stress that because Manceau's a nobody. Oh, he'd have known about the girls' political stance in '39. I'm sure of that. But Manceau isn't your born leader."

"Thought he was a courageous member of the Maquis? Decorated and honored by everyone?"

"Courage and leadership are two different things, Arn. Yes, Manceau was a useful *maquisard*, but not a leader, not so as you'd notice. Look." He got out of his chair and perched himself on the end of the desk, as though he wanted to be closer to Arnie. "Look, maybe you were right in the first place. Tiraque *did* know Manceau. Take that as gospel. I was aware of it, so was C and Caspar. There's a possibility that friend Tiraque retained a few old comrades to keep their ears open. It's a possibility—a definite possibility now you've seen Jo-Jo with him." He hesitated.

"Incidentally, you are one hundred percent sure it *was* Jo-Jo?"

"Two hundred." Arnie tapped the photograph. "Madame Jacquie Tiraque, née Josephine Grenot."

"Née Josephine Railton." Dick smiled again, though his eyes had in them a deep fire of worry. "You see, Arn—" The telephone rang again.

This time it *was* Paris. Dick muttered fluent French into the mouthpiece. Asking questions, almost fawning. "You telephone me quickly if there're any problems," he ended. Then a familiar "Good luck."

Hardly had he replaced the receiver when the instrument sprang into life again. Once more Paris, the other number. This time Dick was obviously giving terse instructions, adding a piece here and there, speaking quite softly, but with great authority. Whoever was on the distant end took the orders without question.

Naldo thought, People forget what a deep bloke old Dick is. He's so damned good that even the family forget how involved he is with the trade.

The conversation ended and Dick resumed command in the room. "Jo-Jo's going to be lifted, on my instructions," he said calmly.

"Can you do that, Dick?" Naldo felt uneasy. "I mean, have you got the authority?"

Dick nodded. "Yes. Yes I have. I spoke to their top man in the *piscine*. He's as good as anyone in France if you want illegal permission."

"*Piscine?*" Arnie queried.

"Can't ever keep track of what they call their bloody setup. But the headquarters is near a municipal swimming baths on the Boul' Mortier, hence *piscine*. Quite an apt name for that shower as well. So, young Naldo, I have permission."

"No. I mean can you lift her legally as far as this country's concerned?"

"Oh, I think so. I'll get around to telling C at some point. We need to talk with young Jo-Jo, Naldo. Especially if she's got herself romantically involved with Tiraque."

"About Tiraque," Arnold started. "Tiraque and Caspar. You said there was a story. Family business."

"Yes." Dick Railton Farthing moved back behind his desk, settling himself in his chair again. "Yes, there are things you should know. I've been thinking about that. I've come to the conclusion that Caspar should tell you the story himself. It's accurate enough—from him, that is. Incidentally, I presume he's still in that bloody pink monstrosity out at Northolt, reading the *First Folio*."

"What the hell do you know about that? This was a contained circle of knowledge."

"Symphony?" Dick raised his eyebrows. "Yes, it's very well contained. C wasn't going to see it suddenly stop. He didn't want any repetition of the old *C-Hornet-Harold* business. As acting Liaison between SIS and CIA, I was brought in before any of you were chosen. In fact, almost before the Joint Intelligence Committee decided that at least one dodgy *réseau* should be investigated. All in all, I think they chose well when they fingered *Tarot*." He cocked one eyebrow. "Mind you, they only thought *they* had made the choice. We organized it, like a magician forcing a playing card on an unsuspecting punter. There were many reasons for *Symphony* from the start—they included finding Caroline, Jo-Jo, and Hans-Dieter Klaubert."

"So you're not going to tell us the family story about Tiraque and Caspar?" Naldo looked concerned, worried, like a child who is not going to get a promised treat.

"I'll fill in the background. Caspar'll tell you the rest—even if we have to use the rack or some other form of torture. Caspar's not going to like it when he hears Jo-Jo's wandered off with the precious *Night Stock*—bastard that he is."

TIRAQUE WAS HIS real name. "Marcel Tiraque, out of Mrs. Eleanor Tiraque, née Winkmann, by Claude Tiraque—restaurateur and hotelier of New Orleans," Dick began.

Marcel Tiraque's grandfather had emigrated to the United States as a young man in the mid-19th century. He married reasonably well, having established six small restaurants. "Marcel's father, Claude, made them into what they are today—which is part of a well-known chain and includes twelve hotels," Dick said. "Old Claude invested well, nurtured his vineyard, and made enormous gains. His son Marcel had no desire to be a tycoon. He put others in charge and lived off the considerable profits. He's almost sixty years of age now, and he moved to Switzerland when he was barely twenty. No fool, spoke several languages, knew his way around, but could not do much about his build and looks—which, you will have noticed, Arnie, have similarities with a punchy ex-pugilist."

"With muscles to match, even at his age," Arnold said.

"Quite. A cultured, wealthy hoodlum, that's how you can best describe our Marcel. Also one who yearns for the glamour of adventure, even when there's no glamour attached." He stopped for a moment, as though for a dramatic pause, then continued—

"Living in Switzerland, speaking several languages, always longing for adventure. A natural, right? The Service recruited him, as a sort of loner, in the mid-thirties. Didn't tie him down to the embassies but worked him, mainly through Caspar—once they'd got Cas back into the fold. They hit it off very well to begin with. Tiraque became *Night Stock,* an important courier for us, so that was right up his alley. He had business cover in Geneva and Zurich—a dummy company he set up for income tax purposes actually, though they did produce high-quality paper. He sold quite a lot of it to the Nazis, which gave him a small profit on the side, and expedited his movements to and fro—to France, Holland, Belgium, even Germany: though it was mainly France, and almost totally work for SOE and Caspar. You know from the Enquiry that he serviced *Tarot* in the early days, and even later. There was some evidence about preparing *Felix*—the Frenchman Jules Fenice—for the *Romarin* op, I recall."

"Yes." Arnie tested his own memory. "He took in a lot of stuff after D-Day, including the details of *Romarin.* Gave them the warning codes, the DZ, and the instructions to steal transport. After which he disappeared 'in the carnage and chaos of battle,' according to Caspar after the Board asked if he could produce this Scarlet Pimpernel *Night Stock.*"

"That's about it." Dick's eyes appeared to twinkle. "You don't know how apt the Scarlet Pimpernel name is, Arn. *Night Stock* took stuff in and brought stuff out—including people. The Germans, for some unaccountable reason, never once latched on to him."

"What about—" Naldo started, but Dick held up his hand.

"There's one other thing you should know about Tiraque. He was a ladies' man. No, that's really the wrong word. In Tiraque's book if it wore skirts you tupped it, follow me?"

They nodded.

"Satyr," Naldo said. "I was going to—"

Again he was cut short. This time by the telephone. Dick grabbed it and, in a second, they realized that it was Paris back to him in exceptionally quick time. They heard Dick curse in French, and rapidly issue new instructions. From the conversation and Dick's face they could see the news was not good.

"Flown," he said. "Bloody up and left. During the night, from what my people could make out. Tiraque and his wife. Apartment empty. Clothes and jewelry gone. Not a scrap of paper in the place either. They're following it up and I've told them Switzerland's as good a bet as any." He stood up and looked out onto the rose garden. A breeze had sprung up and the bushes were shaking. The sky seemed to drop closer to the house, and it looked as cold as a winter's day. "Blast!" Dick said to himself, and did not even turn around when the telephone rang again.

On the fourth ring, Naldo answered. It was C, calling an immediate meeting at Northolt. "Caspar's cracked it," he said with some glee. "Thinks he's found a clue in one of the last letters. Thinks it might point us to *Harold*."

"It have something to do with Saint Augustine, Chief?" Naldo asked, as though disinterested.

"How the hell d'you know that?"

"Flash of inspiration, this morning. Haven't been able to check it yet."

"Well, I'm damned. Get over as quickly as you can, and bring young Farthing."

Dick had turned from the window. "That the Chief?"

Naldo nodded.

"A word." Dick held out his hand and took the receiver. "Dick, Chief. You calling an O Group? Right, yes, I'd like to be in on it. Young Arnie's run one of the girls to earth and we've lost her again." He paused as C spoke at the far end. Then—"Yes, Chief. It's okay, they know . . . Yes, I told them . . . No, Jo-Jo—but please don't mention it to Caspar. We need to talk with him first. We'll be there, Chief. Yes."

Naldo went off in search of Barbara to break the news to her. They would not, after all, be driving to her parents' in Surrey. As things went she took it well. She called Naldo's job by six different four-letter words; his superiors had both their lineage and sexual predilections questioned; and Naldo himself was dismissed with a string of abuse which would have gladdened the heart of any sergeant major. She then burst into tears, and Naldo had to console her, which took the best part of an hour.

Sara said she could quite well telephone them, and stay on— the others were to travel to Northolt in Naldo's Humber. If her parents were real old Army, Sara argued, then they would understand. She even offered to speak with the Burvilles herself.

At last they were gathered in the hall saying their goodbyes. "With any luck I'll be back late tonight," Naldo told Barbara.

In the car, Dick said, "You'll be lucky if you're back by next month, the way things're going." Then, just as Naldo was about to start the engine, he saw Sara running down the steps toward them.

Naldo wound down the window.

"A telephone call for Arnold." Sara's cheeks glowed in the late-afternoon cold.

"American accent? Sort of dry voice?" Arnie asked.

Sara nodded. "He says it's most urgent. He's apparently here. In Haversage anyway."

"You can't put him off forever, Arn." Naldo had already opened the door.

Arnie made a disgruntled noise, a cross between a harsh cough and a low cry of pain.

In the hall, the telephone was off its rests, waiting for him.

At the far end of the line, Fry's voice was reduced to a croak. "At the bottom of Red Hill, on the right, there is a public recreation ground. It's next to the Church-of-England boys' school."

"I know it, but I'm on my way to London."

"And I'm on my way to Washington, with you close behind me, I suspect. I'll wait by the old cricket pavilion just inside the gates. How long?"

"Ten minutes, and then only ten minutes with you. I'm under discipline to the Brits."

"Not if Fishman withdraws you."

"Has he?"

"Not yet. But I'll see it happens very quickly. Hurry. The air's cold and damp. Doesn't do me any good to stand outside for long."

The Humber, containing Dick and Naldo, was parked on the far side of the road, outside the gates that led into this "public recreation ground"—a rotting pavilion, seats for the elderly, and long grass, rising toward a wire fence. There were also ancient swings for children, made of stout wood and thick-linked chains. In the dusk their framework looked like a gallows. A notice said that adults caught using the swings would be prosecuted. Uncharacteristically, Fry was not beside the pavilion. He sat, breaking the law, on one of the swings, his shoes scuffing the asphalt.

"Well?" Arnold approached him.

"Well, indeed." Fry's throat was genuinely bad.

"I haven't got long."

"Tell me what's happening."

"I don't know what's happening. There's been some kind of breakthrough. I've just been trying to get some rest."

"You went missing." His tone was accusatory. "I was searching for you."

"You wanted some political in-depth stuff on the girls. I went to Paris. Doing my job."

"Paris?" Fry queried. "Then you'll have a report for Washington."

"There's no report," Arnie lied. Then, thinking better of it, he said it looked as though the girls had been fellow travelers, but not members of the Communist Party or the Comintern. He added, "I think they might have run one to earth."

"In Europe?" Fry sounded sharp and concerned.

"I believe so. In Europe."

Fry rocked himself back and the rusty old chains creaked on the swing as the wind grew slightly stronger. It was the first really cold wind of the year. At last Fry said he had news.

"From Washington?"

A nod in the gathering dusk.

"Well?"

"It would seem that the hit squad's been at work again."

"Who?"

"Screwtape."

"Jesus." He had to think for a moment to recall which was *Screwdriver* and which *Screwtape*. It was Nat Dollhiem—Klaubert's *Triangle*. "The same way? A cyanide pistol?"

"No, a straight revolver. Dollhiem was shot to death in a hotel room where, under normal circumstances, he would never have been seen dead—you know, *that* kind of hotel."

"When?"

"Two days ago. That makes four, interconnected. Buelow, our two guys who were dealing with Buelow, and now Dollhiem. Marty Forman wants to pull *Screwdriver* in. He also wants you back."

"But Fishman says not yet?"

"Fishman says not yet," Fry agreed. "I go tomorrow. Keep in touch with the Embassy, because I want you back home as well."

"I'll do my best."

In the car, he passed on the news.

"Nasty," Dick said. "It does begin to look interconnected."

"We could've given your chum a lift," grinned Naldo.

"Put a sock in it!" Arnie all but snarled.

"Witty chap your relative, Dick," Naldo laughed.

• • •

CHERUB STOOD GUARD over the small front door of the Northolt house. He hunkered down on his haunches, looking, in the shadows, like an overgrown dog.

"The Chief's been waiting for nearly an hour," he chided.

"We're here now." Dick nodded at him, and Cherub peered at his face in the darkness. "Oh, Mr. Railton-Farthing, I didn't recognize you. Nice to see you again, sir." Only Cherub would think of hyphenating the name.

Herbie almost blocked out the light in the hall. "Thought you'd all gone off with my Piccadilly friends, you was so long, eh! Thought you'd stopped for a quick one!"

"Stow it, Herb, it's been a rough trip." Naldo gave him a playful punch on the shoulder.

C and Caspar waited patiently in the pink room, which seemed even pinker than they remembered it.

"Cas has had a wonderful breakthrough," C began. "Really wonderful."

"I think you'd better hear what we have to say first." Dick, a stranger to the *Symphony* team until now, took the lead. "Arnie has a couple of things to tell you."

Arnold gave them the Dollhiem news first. Then—looking straight at Caspar—he told of his trip to Paris and the sighting of Jo-Jo with Tiraque.

"They know Tiraque is *Night Stock*, Cas," Dick said gently. "I feel it's time everybody should be put in the picture about him."

"I'll kill the bastard," Caspar said, so quietly and unemotionally that everyone in the room believed him. "Right, Dick. With the Chief's permission I'll brief them on *Night Stock,* then I'll go out and find him."

"I've given my people in Paris this number." Dick matched Caspar's tone in coldness. "I've suggested Switzerland, but not ruled out France altogether. They'll call Redhill first, then the private number, then here. We'll get a sighting soon enough."

There was an embarrassed pause. Then C spoke again. "Caspar's breakthrough. We might have pinpointed Klaubert if he's still alive."

"The Saint Augustine passage made sense?" Naldo had his eyes on his uncle's face.

"The Chief said you'd thought of it." Any happiness that Caspar might have felt before had evaporated with this latest news of Tiraque and Jo-Jo. "Yes, it makes sense. Take a look." He passed his sheet of paper to Naldo and they peered at the row of ten letters. The first three had translated into the letters OFM.

The remainder gave a name they all immediately recognized.

"What's OFM?" Arnie asked.

"Order of Friars Minor." Caspar managed a rather bleak smile. "I've checked, they are as thick on the ground as cops—in the city and the state." He pointed to the name. "It looks as though Klaubert intended to take the vows of poverty, chastity, and obedience: become a Franciscan friar. It appears the Franciscans make up the bulk of the Order of Friars Minor in that particular area."

"A Franciscan? A Monk? To make atonement?"

"If he's alive, with the way things are, he might not have long to go. Unless we get to him first," Arnie whispered.

"Getting Jo-Jo comes first." Caspar moved on the cramped settee. "Jo-Jo now. Then I'll settle *Night Stock*'s hash for good and all."

There was a silence, but for a tuneless humming that seemed to be coming from the tiny hall—Herbie performing his devotions to Gustav Mahler.

"I think you should tell them, Caspar." Dick towered above them all in the small room.

Caspar looked around, tight-lipped. Then he spoke—clipped and hard, as none of them had ever heard him before.

"Right, gentlemen. I'll tell you the story of *Night Stock* and how I wanted to kill him once before."

Nobody moved, but it was as though they had all gathered closer to him, to hear every word, and then put him to the question like the Inquisition of old.

35

▼

PHOEBE SAID CASPAR would have made a great politician. "I can
never tell when you're dissembling," she would tease him. "Dissembling" was just the kind of word Old Phoeb would use when
she really meant lying, Caspar thought. But the telling of tales
was part of his stock in trade, and he did it remarkably well, as
the *Tarot* Board of Enquiry had already discovered. Like all great
storytellers he had that ability to transport people to other times
and other places: hear unfamiliar voices and smell the air around
them.

He had not specifically lied to the Board, he told himself.
Only a slight bending of the truth, for he wanted to dodge the
issue as far as *Night Stock* was concerned.

C had been determined not to get mixed up with the Enquiry
—though, of course, he was, if only by the very nature of his
private operation *Symphony*. Before Caspar went anywhere near
the room where the Board met—on the second floor of the house
off St. James's—he had spoken to C about the *Night Stock* business. C agreed with him—"I don't think we should admit to your
last meeting," C said, not looking Caspar straight in the eye.

"Which means," Caspar replied tartly, "that we cannot admit
to one particular possibility in this whole business."

"True. Not to the Enquiry at least."

"They'll want to know how we got particular information in
and out—the details of *Romarin*, for instance."

"Oh, you *must* tell them about *Night Stock*, my dear fellow.
Of course you must. But let's hope he really *has* gone missing,
eh?"

C's words were tantamount to instructions, so Caspar had let it
rest there. Now, in the Northolt house, he told the full truth and,
as often is the case when all cards are laid on the table, the truth

altered many views of the *Symphony* team. For with the detail about *Night Stock* came a new perspective.

"I first met him in '38—just as I met so many new people toward the end of that year. He had already been spotted by our people in Berne, and one approach was made to test the ground. He was a vociferous Nazi-hater; it was no secret, but they told him to turn the volume down. It wasn't a good thing for any man to be blatant about things like that in Switzerland—not in '38 anyway. So I was sent off to see him."

Tiraque had two homes—one in Thun, the other on the shores of Lake Maggiore, outside Ascona. Caspar searched for him in the little fairytale town of Thun, with its perched castle that looked like something out of a Walt Disney drawing. When he finally located the house—"A mansion actually"—they told him that the master was away, in Ascona. So he took the train that rambled toward the Canton of Ticino, hard by the Italian frontier.

The house near Ascona lay right on the lakeside, square and pink with blue louvred shutters to keep the rooms cool on hot days. At the rear there was a manicured lawn which sloped down to the lake. "You could bathe right from the lawn, or watch the steamers plough in towards the jetty at Ascona itself," Caspar said.

"The guy from Berne—Brown was it?—said someone like you would be calling on me." Tiraque wore dark-red bathing trunks. He had been lying on the lawn, getting all the sun he could. An elderly housekeeper had answered the door to Caspar, and left him waiting in a cool room from which the sun was excluded. The pictures on the wall were real—a Whistler and an Eakins—and the furniture seemed old and well cared-for. The room smelled of polish and flowers. Outside—when the house-keeper took him to Tiraque—the scent was different. "In Ticino I swear you can smell the sun," Caspar said. In reality it was a mixture of cigarette smoke, sun lotion, and the cypresses, which grew everywhere along that shore.

Caspar shook hands with Tiraque, and felt a reassuringly firm grip. Tiraque's body was almost devoid of hair, though there was a muscularity about him that seemed to give the man another dimension. Was it power, or just a sense of great physical strength? His light-colored hair was cropped short, and the face was—as others noted later—that of a boxer, a pugilist: heavy jaw, bullethead, a slightly squashed nose, wide mouth, and amazing clear blue eyes.

"Come along and sit down. You want something to drink? Eat?"

Caspar had eaten in Locarno before taking the steamer, but he said a beer would be nice.

"Take your coat off, undo that tie. Relax, Mr.—"

"Just call me Caspar, that's enough."

"It certainly is. I'll get your beer—the boy has an afternoon off. Caspar? That's a name, all right." He laughed and Caspar realized that the power of his body, combined with the eyes and this exciting laugh, were the things that made the man attractive. It should not have been so—the stockiness and muscularity, together with his unattractive face, could have made Tiraque slightly repellent, yet somehow he was attractive. That is how Caspar saw him on the first afternoon.

For a long time they sat on the lawn—it was a warm autumn in Ticino that year—gossiping, looking at the view of the lake, which was like painted glass, with the awesome rising mountains on the far side. "The mountains across the lake are not huge, but they're an odd mixture of savagery and sensuality: long outcrops of rock, combined with lush green rises like huge breasts."

On the lake, the steamers trailed white water. As he remembered it, a string quartet played on one of them. Four old men bowing together, unaffected by the boat's movement, scraping out Strauss waltzes for the passengers, or maybe simply for their own pleasure. Above all, Caspar remembered the cypresses.

"For no reason, a poem came into my mind. It was something I'd read during the weeks before." Caspar did not look at any of the faces in the Northolt house. "I've only just recalled that, but it's true—God knows who wrote it or where I'd read it, but it went through my mind like a chant:

> *Along the avenue of cypresses,*
> *All in their scarlet cloaks and surplices*
> *Of linen, go the choristers,*
> *The priests in gold and black, the villagers."'*

"Lawrence. D. H.," C murmured.

In their present situation, Caspar thought it odd—"Religious ritual in a poem thought of on first meeting Tiraque, and the culmination with Klaubert's search for God, from that pit of horror which was his in Orléans. Yes?"

They sat together, Caspar Railton and Marcel Tiraque, two men getting to know one another, talking of nothing in particular

—life in Switzerland, England, and in America. The war in Spain, the money markets, and the growing clouds of war.

At last, Tiraque asked if Caspar had found a hotel.

"I'd better look for one—just a couple of nights if you can spare a few hours' chat with me."

"You'll stay here. Of course you'll stay here, Caspar. Please. I've gotten kind of lonesome this last week. Say you'll stay."

So he stayed, and they talked more—far into the first night; then on the lawn, in sunshine, the following day. Tiraque wanted action. "I guess they'll say I'm too old, but I can't wait for this war. We all know it's coming . . ."

"Yes, but give our young men a little more time," Caspar said, his memories crushed inside him—of the howling shells, the scream of horses, and the sobbing of other young men at Le Cateau in 1914.

"I'm sorry, but I'm a war man myself." Tiraque smiled. "I know, it's barbaric, horrible: turning countries into abattoirs. But this guy Hitler must be stopped now. Once and for all. Doing that means there'll be suffering, like the last time—the piled dead, the riddled corpses round Bapaume." He was quoting from a Siegfried Sassoon poem. "There'll be weeping women, and crippled . . . Oh, God, I'm sorry."

But Caspar shrugged it off, matching his Bapaume quote with another Sassoon poem:

> "Does it matter?—losing your legs?
> For people will always be kind,
> And you need not show that you mind,
> When others come in after hunting
> And gobble their muffins and eggs."

"Yes, they'll say you're too old. But, maybe, there are things you can do for us."

"Yeah?"

Caspar was pretty sure of his man, for they had checked—as far as anyone could check—on his background sympathies. "I should have spotted his weakness on that last night," Caspar said now, in the present.

On the final evening Tiraque wanted to go out—"To cele-brate!" He laughed that extraordinarily exhilarating laugh. They had arranged for him to come to London for training. "What tradecraft we had in those days; ciphers; check on his cover and languages. We thought he would only be required in Germany."

Caspar laughed aloud, mocking himself. "My God, if it had been *only* Germany; if the Maginot Line had really been able to hold Hitler. What uninspired strategists we were then."

They went along the coast to a restaurant with a small dance floor, covered by an awning entwined with flowers. They smelled wonderful. "Like some expensive scent. Lord knows what they were at that time of the year. It's possible that I smelled the women's scent, and not flowers at all." For there were women.

They ate lavishly, then the women came—half-a-dozen of them—crowding around Tiraque, calling him Marcel, flattering and touching him. "It was the touching that should have put me onto him." Caspar looked around in the pink room. "You know that business of people touching kings, in the old days, because they imagined it would cure them of scrofula or something? Old Samuel Johnson was touched by Queen Anne for it."

The women in this restaurant touched Tiraque like people touching a king to ward off, or cure, disease; and they did more than touch, they fondled. Later it was obvious that they knew the panting secret of his body.

Because Caspar was his companion—that was the *only* reason, Caspar said—two of them came and sat next to him, and started the same kind of thing. "They were blatant about offering me their bodies. I heard Tiraque whisper to one of them that I had a false arm and leg. That seemed to make them even more interested. I felt unclean. Well, you know, I'm not a prude but . . . Well, one hears about women who like doing it with dwarfs. I thought they felt like that about me—and Tiraque to some extent." In the end, Caspar found it so embarrassing that he made his excuses and left.

"There were two women in the house the next morning. I wasn't happy about it, but in London—while we trained him—he behaved himself. It was only much later that the trouble made itself wholly apparent. Tiraque undoubtedly had an incredible fascination for women. I saw it for myself later. If he set his mind to it, he could have taken anyone he wanted."

The thunderstorm finally broke over Europe, and, by the late summer of 1940 Caspar was running Tiraque as *Night Stock*. His first assignment was to activate *Tarot*. Later he serviced other networks, and behaved with great courage. He helped get people in, and he certainly brought a lot out. "There's no denying his courage. Tiraque is a born agent. But he's a flawed one. Dangerous."

Through the years, from 1940 to '44, Caspar and *Night Stock* met regularly. Only twice in Switzerland—"Because that was damned difficult"—but most of the time, like so many others, in Portugal.

By late 1943, Caspar was worried in case *Night Stock* compromised any of the networks. "We all know it now," he told them, in their Northolt magic circle. "One should be vigilant, look to one's agent's sexual predilections, and be guided by them as to how you use him—or her. We've all learned a great deal. We know there's a use for homosexuals, but they can be bloody dangerous—as we've all seen with Ramillies. He gave up his secret life of years because of the secret of his life. I don't know which is the more dangerous in wartime covert ops—a homosexual or a priapismic male. You see, with *Night Stock*, it wasn't just licentiousness. He not only wanted every woman he saw, he liked to talk about it; boast; proclaim if she was good, bad, or indifferent; tell strangers of a woman's tastes, sometimes even in her presence. He was quite disgusting, and he also had this unhealthy need to discuss the real, or imagined, sexual cavortings of others. He was an insatiable libertine, and at the same time a kind of voyeur.

"The whole business we're in is dangerous, and I blame myself for not picking up on Tiraque sooner than I did. By '44 we had learned lessons about sexual dangers. Wartime field agents are lonely. They snatch at sexual comfort, like a child grabs a favorite toy for security. Sometimes it cost lives—you all know what I mean: there was one incident when two agents were so engrossed in their lovemaking that they didn't hear the Gestapo arrive. One ended up dead, the other was decorated. They weren't the only ones."

Night Stock still did the job with exceptional gallantry, but Caspar became increasingly concerned. The final straw came when they met in Lisbon soon after D-Day.

Caspar had gone to brief Tiraque on the *Romarin* instructions for *Tarot*. "Never once had I let him know the girls called *Maxine* and *Dédé* were relations of mine." Caspar's face had set itself into a single angry pattern, as though he was trying to shut everyone else out of his spoken words. "To be fair, up until that night, *Tarot* was one of the few networks he had not boasted about."

They met in a small café, had a couple of drinks, and then went back to Tiraque's hotel room. "We observed all the rules— went separately; watched for surveillance—because the Abwehr had people in Lisbon. We took complicated precautions to avoid them, though it was a hundred percent safe in Tiraque's hotel. They weren't sophisticated enough to have the rooms bugged or anything like that, though they *did* have waiters and hotel staff on their payrolls. One had to use great discretion."

Tiraque slumped into a chair. There was a bottle of Scotch, glasses, and a soda siphon on the table. Caspar recalled the room as large, but plain, with a damned great bed, big enough for six couples, and a very bad print of something on the wall—he thought it was a Van Gogh. "There was also a crucifix, I remember. It was above the bed."

"So where does my milk run take me this time?" Tiraque had become arrogantly confident.

"Don't talk of them as milk runs, Marcel. You've been damned lucky..."

"Luck doesn't enter into it." He poured himself a very large Scotch, which went down quickly. He was drinking a lot by then. "It's not luck, Caspar. It's pure skill and professionalism."

"Make sure it is, because the one I've got for you now is *very* important."

"Oh, yes? Where do I go?"

"You pass on information to *Felix—Tarot*—Orléans."

"Ha! One of my favorite whorehouses. Good, I've a favor to ask about *Tarot*."

Caspar worked on keeping his anger down. He thought of Caroline and Jo-Jo, and was not at all happy about Tiraque's reference to whorehouses. "Favors will have to wait. Now get these facts into your head." He went through the details to be conveyed to *Felix*. ("And we know that *Felix* was briefed correctly, so he took it all in," Caspar said, in the present.)

Time passed, and they went through the information five or six times, until Caspar was wholly satisfied. Only then did the trouble really begin.

"*Tarot's* going to explode before long," Tiraque said, leaning back in his chair, a replenished drink in his right hand.

"Why?"

"Because their time *has* almost run out. I should know, I've had pillow talk with every eligible female in that *réseau*."

"Really?" Caspar's coldness signified nothing to Tiraque.

"Yes, really, Caspar." Tiraque seemed to mock him. "*Tarot*, at St. Benoît, *is* one of my favorite places. I've never told you, but whenever I'm in that area I pay them a visit."

Caspar's patience began to wear thin. "That's bloody unprofessional, as well as being insecure. Why haven't you told me before?"

"Because, Caspar, my dear man, you would have scolded me. I didn't want to be scolded, I wanted to have pleasure, and by heaven at least three of the girls around *Tarot* know how to give a man pleasure."

In retrospect Caspar admitted he should have closed things up there and then. But he did not. Instead he pressed Tiraque with more questions—"Which girls?"

The American put finger and thumb to his lips and blew a kiss into the air. "Oh, Caspar, you really must try them yourself. That is the favor I have to ask." He waited, but Caspar said nothing, so Tiraque continued. "While there's still time, I'd like to get two of them out."

"You'll do no such thing. They're there to get the job finished. It'll be over soon enough now."

"You're wrong." Tiraque raised his voice. "What if things *don't* work out? What if the push through France gets bogged down? You're going to have dead girls on your hands. I want to get Catherine and Anne out now. The Routon sisters."

It was Caspar's turn to shout. "You refer to them by their work names, Tiraque! *Maxine* and *Dédé*. Understand?"

"Oh, *Jawohl, mein Kommandant*. Caspar, you're getting damned pompous . . ."

"No, Tiraque—you're getting sloppy."

"Ask Catherine and Anne if I'm sloppy. . . ."

Caspar, in the present, swallowed and told them what Tiraque had then said about Caroline and Jo-Jo—every intimacy and sexual twist the mind could conceive. "I'm terribly sorry, Dick." He looked at Dick Farthing with ashamed eyes. "To make them understand, I have to tell everything."

Dick inclined his head, and, looking at Naldo and Arnie, gave a brief sad smile. "I know it all. Sara does not, and I'd be grateful if she never does—whatever the outcome."

In the hotel room, Tiraque had gone on, painting pictures of what both girls liked to do and have done to them. He made personal references that proved he was telling some of the truth, for he described a mole on the lower part of Caroline's stomach which only those who had known her in childhood would recognize. He had said, "It's heart-shaped. She says she has two hearts, one inside her and the other on the road to her—"

"Shut up!" Caspar yelled at him. "Stop it this moment."

But Tiraque was a little drunk, and he went on, "Then, of

course, there's the lovely little Sabatier girl, the schoolmistress —I'm sorry, Caspar, I must call her *Florence*, mustn't I? Well, she enjoys it in the most unusual way. Mistress is right for her, isn't it? I mean, *Tarot's* survived only because she's been sleeping with that SS bastard, Klaubert—just like *Maxine*, Caspar. Those two girls have saved *Tarot* being turned over and turned off because they've turned regular tricks for the SS—or didn't you know that?"

It was then, with a roar of scalded anguish, that Caspar launched himself at Tiraque, his fists—real and metal—flailing at the American's face.

"Of course I was no match for him." Caspar stared around, spreading his hands in a gesture of apology.

"No match at all." He sounded as defeated as he had been in the Lisbon hotel room. Taking a deep breath, he continued. "I must have hurt him, but not as much as he hurt me. He broke a rib or two, left a couple of teeth damaged. A few minor cuts and a split lip. What can a one-armed, one-legged idiot do against a very tough and fit fighter? The last thing I heard was him shouting at me. 'I'm going to get Catherine and Anne out. Soon I'll bring them out, Caspar, and nobody's going to stop me. Nobody.' He meant it at the time. I know he meant it."

There was silence in the Northolt room. Then—

"Don't you think we should have been given this information from the start?" Naldo, who had a right to be angry, was patient and very reasonable.

Dick opened his mouth, but it was C who spoke first. "We genuinely thought it was irrelevant. Now it appears very relevant. I was anxious to avoid the slur on Dick's family, as well as Caspar—even though it was a Service matter."

Dick leaned forward. He was also calm and seemingly unruffled. "We *had* virtually cleared Tiraque."

"So he didn't go missing in the chaos and carnage." Of all those in the room, Arnold looked the most angry. There were bright red patches high on his cheeks.

"For a while, yes, he did go missing." Caspar quietly lit a cigarette. "When I finally got back from Lisbon I reported the whole thing—directly to C. It was too late to recall *Night Stock,* and *Romarin* was practically under way. We started looking for him immediately after *Tarot* went dead."

C gave a shrug. "I sent out posse after posse. Even the military were alerted."

"Description circulated. Bring in unharmed. He was officially posted as being AWOL. That seemed the best way, though Caspar thought he might be dead." Dick Railton Farthing had apparently spent most of this time helping to coordinate OSS, SOE, and Resistance groups from London. "I spent a lot of the time with James," he added.

"And you obviously caught up with Tiraque in the end?" Naldo looked as though he was set for a long, probing interrogation.

"November, wasn't it, Cas?" Dick asked.

"He sent a telegram in November, yes." Caspar could even remember the exact wording: *"Sorry for delay. Held up behind German lines. Cut off for long periods. Have just returned. Await instructions. Night Stock.* Cool as the proverbial cucumber."

"The telegram came from—" Naldo began.

"Ascona. We sent him instructions." Caspar gave a grim little nod. "And they weren't 'Come home, all is forgiven.'"

"We requested his immediate presence in London." C was in no joking mood. "I ordered Caspar to remain clear of the whole business."

"Caspar, and myself," Dick added.

C grunted. Then—"I had Caspar give all relevant details to a team of good interrogators. Tiraque arrived in London within a week and he was taken straight down to Warminster. They had him there for a month. He was clean as far as the interrogators were concerned. I read their reports and spoke with them. *Night Stock* could account for almost every day since he had passed on the *Romarin* instructions to *Felix*. I had Dick and Caspar in, and we agreed that it would be safer if our American friend left the Service."

"So you fired him?"—Naldo, frowning.

C hesitated. "Not in so many words. You know how those things work, Naldo. We thanked him; said he was up for a decoration, and told him that if we wanted his valuable services again we'd be in touch. He knew what was meant."

"And we kept light surveillance on him." Dick stretched his long body, as though stiff from so much sitting around. "He sold the Thun property and after it was all over—the war, I mean—he went to Paris and purchased the place in the Rue de Rivoli."

"And you thought it would be a good idea for me to look him up—just for old times' sake?" Arnie asked, disgruntled.

"In a word, yes. There had been no hint that he knew anything about Caroline's and Jo-Jo's disappearance. No hint at all. I gave you the Paris address almost on a whim, and it's paid off. The very fact of his disappearance with Jo-Jo shows he's frightened. What I'd like to know is who he's frightened of. Caspar? Me? Any of the family? Or is he afraid C'll send some hoods over to drag him back for a further interrogation? Tiraque's no idiot. He must have weighed the chances of your recognizing Jo-Jo, Arnie. Up until now we've cleared him of any complicity in the events surrounding the girls' disappearance. Now he's linked in again. So why's he gone to earth? Is someone else after him?"

"You really think Caroline was Klaubert's mistress? That she shared him with *Florence?*" Naldo looked puzzled.

Dick said the probability was high. Then C took over, quickly, as though he wished to divert them from that subject.

"On the positive side," he began, "we now know that Jo-Jo Grenot got out alive. We cannot presume too much, but that suggests Caroline escaped as well. I agree that we should first concentrate on finding Tiraque and the girl." He looked toward Dick. "As Liaison with CIA, will you bargain for their assistance?"

Dick nodded and C continued to talk. "Now listen to me." He particularly looked at Arnie. "I apologize if I didn't put you fully into the picture, but many things can alter. In the beginning was *Tarot* and the 'Orléans Russians,' together with the two missing girls. We've all been obsessed by the Soviet threat—the moves they have made regarding what we like to think of as atomic secrets; and the question of Berlin. On the latter the wind blows very cold, incidentally. They'll try something drastic very soon. Our immediate intelligence is that they could attempt a blockade on Western Berlin." He paused, his little eyes sparkling as though relishing the thought of future troubles.

"I suppose that my own prying—into dead files and documents well hidden—sparked the possibility of further investigation. There's also a moral issue. Klaubert. Do we continue to look for him? Rehabilitate him . . . ?"

"If he's alive, why can't we hang the bastard?" Naldo became suddenly angry.

"Though we did not know it, he served us well." C looked at him blandly.

"And, in serving us, he kept his head by destroying hundreds —thousands—of innocent lives."

"Then I think we should try and find him. The whole thing remains a riddle, a mystery. And there are mysteries within the mysteries." Another pause. Naldo thought it was for effect. "Think," C said. "Think about the plots within the plots, and ask for the reasons. Everything was plain sailing when we started. Yet once you lifted Ramillies from the East, problems started to beget problems."

Arnie slipped in as C took a breath—"You mean as soon as we lifted Ramillies and you gave Buelow to my people in Washington?"

"Quite so. As I understand it, Buelow *and* his two interrogators were wiped out in one night. Which means?"

"A team effort. Not just one person acting on his, or her, own initiative," Arnold answered coldly.

C nodded like a Buddha. "Right. And it was a carefully coordinated effort. We presume that Buelow was removed because someone was afraid he knew too much—which meant taking out his interrogators as well. Then the trees began to move closer to home. First Munich, from which we had to move you. Then—though we did not alert you—people were sniffing around the Frankfurt area. The object?"

"To put an end to any further enquiries?"

"Or to Ramillies Railton. You see, there's been some activity near Warminster. Nothing we could pin down, but there have been strangers in the vicinity. So we moved Ramillies into London. He's a hard nut to crack. And now Nathaniel Dollhiem—one-time OSS officer and full-time Soviet infiltrator—is dead. One by one they go. Reasons? Grudges, or operational necessity? We won't know until we've had a chance to talk to Jo-Jo Grenot, Tiraque, and, if she's alive, Caroline Farthing."

"And Klaubert." Naldo sounded positive.

"Oh, yes, we have to talk with Klaubert."

"If he's alive," Arnie almost whispered.

C looked up sharply. "Oh, he's alive. I can tell you that. I put a good man onto him. Did you meet the ingenious young Shepherd during your move back home with Ramillies?"

Naldo answered for them all. "Curry Shepherd? Yes."

C said that Shepherd had followed Herbie's trail—"The one who called himself Klausen and claimed to have been a Norge Waffen SS officer. He got back to Norway, from whence he never came, of course. Then he disappeared. I suspect he somehow got papers and managed to bluff himself into your country, Arnold. Soon we shall have to take a look at the Franciscan houses here." His finger pointed toward the paper on which Caspar had written the Saint Augustine cipher. Under the letters
O-E-T-H-E-E-N-E-N-F-H-E was the decrypt—
O-F-M-N-E-W-Y-O-R-K-C-T

"One can only presume the CT means City. I'll brief people to peep at the Franciscans living out their holy lives among the skyscrapers. I suspect that you—Arnold—will be getting a recall to Washington soon. I also suspect that my little *Symphony* team will be heading towards Manhattan." He gave an uncharacteristic twinkle, using both his mouth and the piggy eyes. "We'll take Manhattan, the Bronx—and Staten Island, too," said the CSS.

PART THREE

▼

THE AMERICAN HOUSES

36

▼

THEY PULLED IN Tertius Newton at the end of the first week in October. He had been on the night shift at the Atomic Energy Commission's headquarters, and left at his usual time—seven-thirty in the morning. Everything was normal. Newton drove for half a mile to stop across the street from the drugstore, just as he always did, crossing the road to pick up his newspaper and buy cigarettes.

The moment he entered the shop, two cars pulled up, blocking in Newton's vehicle, front and back. There were four FBI agents in one car. The other held Marty Forman with another backup man from CA.

Two of the FBI agents went into the shop and browsed through magazines on a wire rack until Newton moved to leave. They followed him out, and on the sidewalk Newton found himself sandwiched between the pair already waiting and the couple behind him.

He showed startled surprise, but put up no resistance, merely asking if he could call his wife. They said he could do that later. Actually she knew already, for FBI men had arrived at Newton's apartment with a search warrant some thirty minutes earlier. Mrs. Newton was asked to go along with the agents, who were accompanied by a team of CIA people who knew what they were looking for.

Atomic secrets were landing in the Soviet Union like "sea gull shit on a beach"—Marty Forman was the coiner of this graphic description. So, with this in mind, the Agency team took the place apart, looking for filched papers, radio transmitters, one-time pads, and the usual paraphernalia of espionage. The fact that they found nothing in no way deterred them. They were spurred on by the fact that the British had already put away one traitor—Dr. Alan Nunn May, who had given atomic secrets to the Russians—and were investigating others, notably Klaus Fuchs, the German-born, naturalized English scientist who took part in work on the first atomic bomb in Los Alamos.

The FBI handed their prisoner over to Marty and his man, who drove Newton away to a clapboard house which stood in open country near Alexandria. Here, the CIA interrogators began their work. The house itself was ringed by officers from the security section of Counterintelligence. They left Newton in no doubt that he was there as much for his own safety as for the interrogation.

The decision to arrest Tert Newton was recommended by the CIA's head of Counterintelligence, who had secured the full backing of a small committee set up to analyze what was actually taking place in Washington.

James Xavier Fishman chaired the committee, which met regularly in his office. From there, through the one large window, it was just possible to see the Washington Monument spearing toward a lowering sky on the left, and a portion of the Senate House away to the far right. So it was Fishman, Marty Forman, Roger Fry, Arnold Farthing, and his uncle, Richard Railton Farthing, who made the final decision.

Some thought there had been too much prevarication already —particularly Fishman, who spent many sleepless nights concerned that the Agency had been penetrated by the Soviets. If they could have been infiltrated so easily into the OSS, with Dollhiem and Newton, how simple would it be to dig through the new walls which protected the Agency?

In London, as soon as they knew Arnie's recall to Washington was inevitable, C had decreed that it would be better if Dick went along with him. By this time Dick had been added to the charmed circle with access to the *First Folio,* together with all the *Tarot* Enquiry transcripts. It was also argued that, as Dick was their official Liaison officer with the CIA, he would be the best man to plead their case for assistance in the search for Tiraque and Jo-Jo in Europe. "I am also concerned for Tiraque's safety should Dick be around when we catch up with him," C confided in Naldo.

"What about Caspar? He'll hire thugs to kill him in the field." Naldo was seriously concerned about it.

C shook his head and tried to look wise. "I think not. Caspar feels responsible for Caroline and Jo-Jo. He'll want to see real justice done. Yes, in the heat of the moment, he can threaten, but he wouldn't act on his own. With the father it's a different matter."

Dick quickly secured agreement for what the Agency called the "skip search" in Europe, then he suddenly found himself being asked his opinion, by the head of CIA's Counterintelligence. Should they or should they not interrogate Tertius Newton? James Xavier Fishman wanted men around him who would come to a confident, unanimous decision, and it was to Dick Farthing that Fishman looked to explain how he saw the current situation and its dangers.

"Somewhere in this town you've got a hit squad, led by a professional agent with instructions to minimize danger to a specific operation." Dick's accent became more noticeably American whenever he returned to his native soil. "Whoever's giving the orders appears, in effect, to be dismantling an operation mounted either against the Agency or to gain access to atomic secrets." Dick had a clear, logical mind. He was putting himself in the shoes of the person at the heart of the killings.

"My personal theory is that the hit team arrived here too late. Hence Otto Buelow's death. Before he and his interrogators died, Buelow had already pointed the way to both your targets—Dollhiem and Newton.

"Let's say I'm correct: that the team got here only to find Buelow was already in town. They would know Buelow might be able to identify their two agents; somehow they realized he was being taken round on an identity parade that afternoon. So, when it was over, they killed him and clumsily tried to make the death of his inquisitors look like an accident. Whoever removed those three must have thought he had plugged a leak. Now, with Dollhiem's death, it would appear that the chief executioner has realized failure. It's a silencing operation." He gave Fishman a quizzical look. "You have no alternative. Grab Newton as quickly as possible. Drag him to safety and then go for him. Clean him out."

Fishman inclined his head gravely, like a bishop accepting the views of one of his clergy. "My sentiments exactly," he said. "But the Director takes a slightly different view. He wants to use Newton as a tethered goat."

"And snaffle the hit squad?" Arnie looked doubtful. "There are no points in that. These guys must feel very insecure about their agents."

"Very," Fishman agreed. "I've put that to the Director. If the killings are taking place in order to minimize damage, we can only assume Dollhiem and Newton know a great deal, much of which they would disclose under pressure. Can I take it that you all agree? We should lift Newton as soon as possible?"

The agreement was unanimous, as was their opinion regarding the hit squad—it could be as small as two people, working closely together, or as large as six.

The photographs taken by the surveillance unit outside Buelow's apartment building on the night of his death had been closely scrutinized. All those identified—including the girl and the man with military bearing, who had originally so interested Fishman—had been eliminated. Both the man and girl were honest upright citizens who lived in the building.

In short, there were no direct clues. One person had fired the cyanide pistol; one person had driven the truck which slammed into the car containing Herbert and King, Buelow's interrogators. The truck had been found, abandoned ten miles away, and there were traces of another car having picked up the driver. That could have been reasonably accomplished by two people.

As for the slaying of Nat Dollhiem, there was one clue only.

Even though surveillance on both Dollhiem and Newton had been stepped up, the teams working Dollhiem had been lulled into a familiarity which, in turn, bred its customary contempt. Nat Dollhiem had still gone through the same old antisurveillance routines which Arnold noted when he had first tailed the man. But by now these deviations had become part of Dollhiem's life —in themselves they formed a pattern. On the night that Dollhiem died, the surveillance crew had lost their target—waiting for him to turn up in his usual spot, trying to be too smart, knowing he always reappeared at this place before he went home. That evening Nat Dollhiem did not arrive. When the panic of truth hit them, the surveillance team had no idea where to go next. They tried the Dollhiem home, calling from a phone booth. He never went home again.

Both the surveillance team and the officers monitoring Dollhiem's telephones had been roasted. One incoming call on that day should have alerted everyone.

At eleven minutes after three in the afternoon Dollhiem's office phone rang. He answered, and a woman's voice asked—

"That you, George?"

"I think you have a wrong number," Dollhiem replied.

"Oh. Oh, I'm sorry. I'm trying to reach a George Bleecher."

"Not here, I'm afraid."

"Oh, my goodness. I *have* to contact him. We have an appointment at six-thirty tonight. You sure he's not there?"

"I'm sorry, you have a wrong number, caller."

"Oh, heavens. Could you help me, sir? I'm trying to locate the Crawford Motel. I'm due to meet him there and I haven't the faintest idea where it is."

"I'm sorry, lady, I never heard of it." These were the last recorded words of Nathaniel Dollhiem, who was found, with the top of his head blown away by a .38 caliber slug, in the Ford Motel, near the National Airport. He had arrived at seven-thirty —soon after the watchers assigned to him realized they had lost touch. The manager of the motel agreed that it was possible Dollhiem had an assignation. "You can't spot them all," he told FBI men. "Any motel is open to abuse. You just can't check on everyone."

The cops knew that the Ford was a well-known trysting place for hookers and their johns. Just as everyone with inside knowledge of the Dollhiem surveillance knew the logged telephone call was a most obvious tip for a meeting. For six-thirty, read seven or seven-thirty; for Crawford read Ford. It stuck out, as Marty Forman said so bluntly, "Like a cock on a honeymoon."

They listened to the woman's voice on the tape, but nobody could come up with any speech pattern that would help to identify her. One analyst suggested that the woman was not American born, but that was about as much help as the two other .38 slugs they pried out of the motel room wall.

A week after Newton's arrest, the committee was due to meet again, but at the last minute there was a message from Jim Fishman apologizing, saying that he would be late. He nominated Roger Fry to take the chair until he could get there.

"So what've we got?" Fry opened as though on the attack.

"As yet, nothing." Marty Forman had spent a lot of time out at the safe house, assisting in the interrogation of Newton. He was very good at making people talk. "Newton looks at us with innocent eyes. He says he doesn't know what we're talking about. We take him through the story again and again. He sticks to the same ancient fable. The *Romarin* shit. St. Benoît. *Tarot*, and his farewell to *Tarot*. When he went. Where he went. How he got picked up by the German unit and put in a stockade. How he was released and fought with that irregular unit, and ended up with the Ninth Army at the Remagen Bridge. All the stuff he's already given the Brits. No changes. And the hell of it is—it's all on record."

"And what about the Brits?" Fry asked, looking at Dick. "Anything?"

"You thinking about anything in particular?" Dick Farthing asked.

"Well, you've got this guy under the third degree—"

"What *guy?*" Dick snapped back. "And we don't operate the third degree, as you put it."

"The Russian."

"What Russian? I know of no Russian."

"You know damned well who I mean."

Very quietly Dick Farthing let him know he was off-limits by even mentioning this subject.

"We're to share the product." Fry became belligerent.

"Like you shared the product by letting Otto Buelow get murdered? It strikes me that your Agency leaks like a damned sieve." Dick knew this was not true, but he was aware that it was a touchy subject. "Now, Marty"—Dick Farthing almost took control of the meeting—"you want to share your thoughts about Newton with us?" Dick had already been granted the favor that he had come to Washington to get, "Agency assistance in the search for Marcel Tiraque and Jo-Jo Grenot." He did not care how many feathers he ruffled now.

This attitude seemed to have worked, for when Fishman arrived an hour later he brought with him an invitation for Dick Farthing to sit in on one of the Newton sessions.

"Am I allowed to contribute?" Dick asked immediately.

Fishman hesitated. "You met him when he was in London, yes?"

"Briefly." He did not mention his first encounter with both Dollhiem and Newton at the so-called Camp X near Oshawa, during the war.

"Okay, then, why not?"

"Do I get a look at his file—and, Jim, I mean his real file, not a few pages of filleted paper?"

"Why not? You can read it here."

Dick Farthing had been in the business for a long time, and ever since the day Naldo had come to him at Redhill to ask about Dollhiem and Newton at Camp X, Oshawa, the two men had stayed in his mind. The memories had returned, and slowly he had begun to see them in a clearer perspective, like a photographer bringing a subject into focus.

Dick also knew the first rule for people ferreting after traitors in his world. He had passed it on to many young officers, though God knew if they had understood. "If you want to wear a moleskin jacket," he would say, "you must first find out when the animal was possibly led away from the paths of righteousness."

In other words, in examining a suspect traitor's life, first find a period of time when he was in the right place, or the wrong circumstances; when he was most vulnerable; when he was sitting—or even lying—next to the people who most wanted to gain his soul. Once you had pinpointed that time in a man's life, you would find all the other signs stuck out like Indian signals— notches in trees, twigs crossed on a pathway, a mark on a fence. But first find the time and place.

He had already been able to examine the late, unlamented Nathaniel Dollhiem's life in some detail, and had come to the conclusion that there was only one time in that man's life when he was truly vulnerable. Could he find the same short period in Newton's existence?

When the meeting was over, he stayed behind to talk with Jim Fishman. "I'm sorry I can't allow you to take the stuff back to your hotel room, Dick," the head of Counterintelligence apologized. "But you of all people know about classified files. I can give you an office, with a telephone and the dossier. I'll leave the safe open. When you've finished, just put the files inside and close it." That way Dick could not be privy to the safe's combination.

"When can you come along and see Newton?" Fishman asked.

"Give me a couple of days."

Dick went straight to work, going through the available minutiae of Tertius Newton's life. At eleven o'clock that night he put the file into the safe and walked back to his hotel. The security man who had guarded the office wished him goodnight, then —like Dollhiem before him—Dick went through a series of tricks designed to both spot and throw off any personal surveillance.

When he knew that he was clear, he stopped at a public telephone booth and placed a person-to-person collect call to England. "The party will be at one of these three numbers," he told the operator. A few minutes later he was speaking to C, using a familiar double-talk which would mean little to anyone who might be listening.

The following afternoon he did the same thing, and got replies to the questions he had put to C. Then, finally, he made a series of calls—to the city halls in San Jose and Los Angeles, and the Records Office of UCLA. They asked him to call back in an hour, which he did. The answers he received from California now put Tertius Newton in his sights. He told Fishman that he would be free to see Newton anytime on the next day.

"Pick you up at ten in the morning," Fishman said.

"Fine. I might just have some surprises for you."

C TOOK DICK Farthing's call from Washington in his elegant private apartment in Queen Anne's Gate. Immediately after Dick was off the line, C telephoned Caspar, cryptically asking him for a meeting at the Northolt safe house.

Though Caspar had his hands full coordinating the British side of the now intensive search for Marcel Tiraque and Jo-Jo Grenot, C considered that he was the only person who could deal with the matters discussed by Dick.

Their meeting took place at midnight, C providing Caspar with a series of photographs and making it clear that he should be absolutely one hundred percent certain that the answers he obtained were genuine.

Caspar drove straight to the house, standing in its own grounds just up the road from the small military camp at Knook, near the garrison town of Warminster. They were expecting Caspar. Ramillies had been returned there on the previous day and, while he was taking some refreshment, the team of men and women who were still cleaning out Ramillies went to work.

Ramillies Railton—aka Colonel Gennadi Aleksandrovich Rogov, NKVD—had changed since Caspar had last seen him. He appeared to be fitter and more at peace with himself. The interrogation team had worked hard, making Ramillies come to terms with his situation, so he now acknowledged that while there would never be a time when he was wholly safe from his former masters in the Russian Service, life could be lived with a certain amount of pleasure and comfort. Yet this happy state could be obtained only if he answered all questions put to him with clarity and honesty.

They had reached a point which they called "filling in the gaps," which was a relaxed and easy time. So Ramillies was more than startled to find himself being wakened during the early hours of the morning to face questions. This was both unusual and unnerving, for it smacked more of the way they did things in No. 2 Dzerzhinsky Square.

For a second, on being shaken from sleep, Ramillies thought he was actually there. He had known the place when it was Lubianka Square, and even imagined the cathedral with its single cupola—the Church of Our Lady of Grebniev. They had already been pulling down the cathedral when he had last been in Moscow. Now, as he tried to shake sleep from his head, he thought of the plans he had seen for the new square, designed by Architect Shchussev.

They told him not to bother about shaving, but to hurry up. "Your brother has to talk with you," one of them said. Again the dark thoughts of Moscow came into his head and he found himself experiencing genuine fear. Why should Caspar invoke fear in him, like some evil wizard from a child's fantasy?

Caspar was drinking coffee, in the comfortable room they used for what they liked to call their "informal talks."

"Ram!" Caspar rose, going to his brother and shaking his hand. He was full of apologies for waking him at this hour of the morning. "I fear it's orders from on high, old son." He smiled warmly, offering Ramillies coffee and a cigarette.

"They say you're making great progress." Caspar sounded enthusiastic. "And, by heaven, you look well, Ram!" It was a good fifteen minutes before he got to the point.

"Look, Rammer, we have a problem. I'm going to be honest with you so that you can speak freely. I'm not trying to be tricky, but one of your old mob has got himself knocked off in the States. I *have* to do some checking with you." And he launched into an apologia in which questions were embedded like raisins in a cake. Slowly he came to the crux of things—

"While you were running your man, *Lightning*, did you get a sudden crash instruction? I'm talking about July 1944—six weeks or so after the D-Day landings?"

Ramillies thought for a few moments, then said yes. "I was asked to pass on details of the proposed OSS landing near Orléans—the one called *Romarin*."

"Who asked you to do that?"

"Moscow—as always."

"How would they have known?"

Ramillies hesitated again. You could not tell if he was trying to avoid the question or really had a problem of memory. At last he said, "From inside the OSS. I knew there was at least one penetration agent planted there—one, maybe two."

"And you sent the message to Klaubert?"

"Through our contact within the *Tarot réseau*, yes." There was no hesitation. Ramillies had learned that giving a little meant you might hide a great deal.

"So someone in the *réseau* would know—and Klaubert would also know?"

"There was a time element—but, yes."

"You said there were, maybe, *two* penetration agents within the OSS. In fact, didn't Moscow alert you to two possible agents arriving to assist *Lightning* at the same time as *Romarin?*"

Ramillies gave a little smile. He was still sleepy and his brother had caught him out with one simple slip. "There were two, yes. One was long-term. There was another, but I knew nothing concrete about him."

"The message that was passed to you from Moscow..."

"Yes?"

"Did they tell you the true object of the operation?"

Ramillies nodded. "Yes. It was one of those foolhardy things. Suicide—they were trying to kidnap Klaubert. Presumably to discourage further SS brutality. He wasn't the first Nazi officer your people, or the Americans, tried to lift. They even had a go at Rommel."

"Yes, I know. Now, Ram, this is *very* important—was the object of the *Romarin* operation passed on to your agent within *Tarot?*"

"No." Sure and quick. "Moscow gave strict instructions about that. She could have known from London, of course."

Well, Caspar thought, that was a blessing. London had passed orders to *Tarot*, but not the object of *Romarin*. By then Klaubert would have been desperate to get out to England. If he had known the true objective of *Romarin*, he might have tried to let it succeed. With the knowledge that two Soviet agents were coming to help, he must have been really split three ways.

"These agents—they had code names?"

"I can't quite remember if it went as far as that."

"Come on, Ram, don't piss about. We know most of it."

Ramillies went around in circles for a while, dodging issues, so Caspar changed the angle of attack. "Okay, let's go back even further." He reached into his briefcase and withdrew a number of photographs which he lined up on the table in front of Ramillies. "Let's go back to the time you spent at Bykovo—the spy school."

"Yes?" Ramillies looked blankly at the photographs.

"We know that one of the men in those pictures was at Bykovo." Caspar was a competent liar. "If you recognize him as having been there in your time, just push the photo towards me. The man concerned is dead now, so it is of little consequence."

"Of so little consequence that you have to get me out of bed to confirm it?" Ramillies gave a sly smile, then, as though playing a game, he pushed a photograph toward Caspar. "You win. *He* was there. Pavel Denisovich Rosten."

Caspar nodded as though he had known all the time. It was the right photograph. "Now, Ram, give me the rest—work names of the two agents who were to arrive with the OSS people."

Another long silence, then—

"One was called *Dumas*. The other . . . I can't quite . . ."

"Try, Ram. Try. Yes, it's important."

"*Dumas* and *Noble*." Quick, as though getting it off his chest in a hurry.

"Did you know the identities of these people?"

"No." Without hesitation. "No, only the work names."

"Were there signals?"

Ramillies nodded. "I seem to recall that they had to flash the Morse letter S. Where from I'm not sure. You know what it's like in the field, Cas, nobody tells you quite everything. I passed on the time and place of the drop, and that two of our people would be there to link up with *Lightning*. I gave their work names and said they would flash the letter S in Morse code. That's all."

"Yes." Caspar looked happy. "Yes, that is all, Ram. Thank you."

He stayed, chatting—family talk, for Ramillies had expressed a wish to see some of the family again once they would allow him more freedom of movement. Then Caspar left, driving to London. He wanted to get Ramillies' answers to the Chief, then get on with what he saw as the most important work—looking for Tiraque and Jo-Jo.

Much later, when it was all done, he said to his cousin James that—in spite of the criminal horrors Klaubert had committed—he felt some sorrow for the man. "Fancy being split three ways," he said. "Being a noted SS officer, feared by so many; staying loyal to us, though we gave him no assistance; and being in the moral pay of the Russians."

James had said the Russians must have thought him a worthwhile source, even though he gave them only chickenfeed. Then he laughed. "There's some irony in it, Cas. They went to a lot of trouble penetrating the OSS. Really it was rather bad luck for them to discover their two penetration agents were *both* involved in an attempt to kidnap a man they regarded as their source within the SS."

Caspar had laughed also. "Serve the buggers right," he said.

"Klaubert *was* good to them—even with his chickenfeed. He must have had lines in everywhere: friends in high places—generals of the Wehrmacht; other SS officers; people in the Abwehr; then the Berlin connection. If only we had taken some notice."

Yet, as he drove back to London after the interview with Ramillies, Caspar could think only of the two men who went in, cloaked with their own duplicity, by parachute on the *Romarin* operation. It took exceptional courage to descend from the sky, among enemies, desperately using small flashlights to flash out the constant dot-dot-dot of the letter S while bullets meant for others flew around you. Men who would do that were, in some measure, to be admired.

C passed the answers back to Dick in Washington, who by this time had obtained answers to other questions from California.

The true sweating of Tertius Newton could start.

THE HOUSE OUTSIDE Alexandria was very plain, with only the bare necessities as far as furnishings went. There was, of course, a cellar in which the recording machines turned constantly. Every room was wired for sound.

Newton looked fitter than when Dick had last seen him in England. He sat, with Marty, in a room which sported four comfortable chairs, a small table—bolted to the floor—and color-washed walls in lime green. Some psychiatrist had suggested the shade was more conducive to relaxation. There were no pictures on the walls.

"Well, look who we have here, Tert." Marty slowly got to his feet as Dick entered with one of the security guards. Fishman had driven him down, but preferred to stay outside, sitting and smoking in his car. "You remember Mr. Richard Farthing from England, surely?"

Newton frowned slightly, as if trying to place Dick's face.

"We only met for a very short time. I don't know if you remember me, Mr. Newton." Dick smiled and settled into one of the chairs. "I visited you while you were clearing up a few points after the Enquiry on *Tarot* and *Romarin*. Remember now?"

"Gee, I guess I saw so many people, I—"

"I don't want to take up too much of your time, Tertius, but we met somewhere else. Don't you remember that either?"

"Where? Where else were we supposed to have met?"

"Well, it wasn't Little Chicago, was it?"

"Little Chic— What you talking about?"

"The camp where you trained. Not Camp X—that was where we *did* meet for the first time. But you weren't really trained there, were you, Tertius? By the time you got to Oshawa, you'd already done a long course of training elsewhere."

"I'm sorry." Newton looked nonplussed. "I don't follow you, Mr.—er—I didn't get your name."

"And I didn't get your name, Pavel. Not until yesterday. You see, we have very good sources now. I know your true name, which you probably want to forget. They taught you to forget your real name at Bykovo, didn't they? They preferred you to think in terms of your legend—the cover they provided for you. Your legend was Tertius Newton—just as your wife's legend was Mrs. Olive Newton. You were born in San Jose. She was born just up the road in Tinsel Town itself. I could go to those places and look up your birth certificates, couldn't I? Tertius Freeman Newton and Olive Wilson Carey, isn't that right?"

Newton sat and looked at him with cold eyes.

"Sure it's right, Tert." Dick allowed himself a smile. "Your legend was great. Except they let you down on one thing. UCLA has absolutely no record of you. You, and Mrs. Newton, suddenly appeared, like characters from outer space in a science-fiction comic book. One minute you did not exist, the next there you were, the nice young married couple moving into a nice little house, in a nice residential area of San Jose. The all-American boy with his all-American wife. You came from nowhere—certainly not from UCLA—in 1940. There's no trace of you before then, though there is a trace, if someone bothers to take a careful look. I've taken a very careful look. Tertius Freeman Newton died when he was only eighteen months old. Olive Wilson Carey died when she was less than a year old. But you so loved your country that you volunteered for the Service immediately after Pearl Harbor. You put quite an accent on your proficiency in languages, though I guess it was pure luck that you got invited to join the OSS—just as it was a nice piece of luck when you met up with Nat Dollhiem, who had political leanings to the left. Did it take long for you to recruit him, Comrade Rosten?"

He turned to Marty Forman. "What you have there, Marty, is an 'illegal'—to use the NKVD term. He and his wife were quietly infiltrated, fully grown, into the United States, sometime in 1940 or early 1941, I guess. This guy's real name is Pavel Denisovich Rosten. He's never been near the campus of UCLA, but he is an alumnus of a very special school—the NKVD school at Bykovo."

"Shit," said Marty Forman without any emotion.

"Yes, he is," Dick snapped. He had gone through Newton's file a hundred times and could find no suitable time in the man's life when he could have been recruited. In the end he realized that Newton did not exist until 1940 or '41. Ramillies had confirmed, by identifying his photograph, that Newton had trained at the so-called spy school—Bykovo.

"You'll have to fill in the other details for yourself, Marty." Dick Farthing dropped a buff-colored folder onto the table. It was his personal check on Newton's background, and an outline of his own theories concerning the recruiting of Nat Dollhiem. "There's a lot of good stuff in there, Marty." He gestured to the file. "Have a nice year piecing it together." At the door he turned and looked back at Newton, who sat upright, his face gray. "Which one were you, Tertius? *Dumas* or *Noble?* My guess would be *Noble*."

Newton's eyes flared briefly with anger, but he did not even throw an oath in Dick's direction.

"No doubt you'll tell Marty. Oh, I almost forgot, Colonel Rogov, one of your old teachers at Bykovo sends his best wishes. He's with *us* now."

Dick Farthing went out of the house, anxious to get on with what he considered to be the real business—finding Tiraque and Jo-Jo; putting faces to the ghostly figures who were the Soviet hit squad in Washington; and—best of all—meeting Hans-Dieter Klaubert and choking the truth about Caroline from him.

37

▼

CASPAR WAS IN charge of the British effort to seek out Marcel Tiraque and Jo-Jo Grenot. After all, he had run Tiraque as *Night Stock* and was considered the best man for the job. In London there had been meetings between C, Caspar, and senior CIA officers based in Europe. Military Intelligence had also been circulated—docks, ports, and the growing number of commercial airfields were on alert. It seemed impossible that the couple would escape the huge net being trawled for them.

Tiraque's house near Ascona was put under discreet surveillance, and Caspar went through his personal notes, checking for places he knew *Night Stock* had used during the war—houses, lofts, barns, and cellars, and the people associated with them in towns, villages, and cities where for a time Tiraque had disappeared and gone deep.

They even covered the old ground of the *Tarot réseau*, with Naldo returning to Orléans accompanied by an officer of the French Service. He went to the safe house in the Rue Bannier which had been used by the visiting "pianist," Drake, and was also known to have served as a lovers' meeting place for Klaubert and his mistress *Florence*, and—if you believed the secret gospel according to *Night Stock*—Caroline Railton Farthing as well.

They found nothing. The safe house had been turned into three small apartments and was now occupied by a trio of families who had no contact with the Resistance. Jules Fenice had retired to Orléans, and at St. Benoît-sur-Loire the pig farm and the house, where *Tarot* had gone about its business in an amateur but well-meaning manner, was now derelict—the roof caved in, and a public notice, peeling on one unsteady wall, proclaiming that the property was due for demolition and rebuilding. It was to be some kind of community hall, and Naldo wondered what ghosts would rise up among the good parishioners of St. Benoît as they went about their meetings, or *Le Bingo* in aid of the tower restoration fund.

As for himself, he could sense the ghosts there as he stood silent and bareheaded, gazing as if to see his relatives or those who had died in the terrible events of 1944. For a moment he wondered if Caroline and Jo-Jo were in fact still alive, for he seemed to feel their presence close by. Was it Jo-Jo whom Arnie had seen in Paris? Or had Tiraque taken another who merely looked like Josephine Grenot? When they had put questions to him, Arnold had described her as a woman in her twenties, yet they all knew Jo-Jo, if alive, would now be over thirty. Could she have kept her youthfulness and looks living under the duress of deceit within *Tarot*?

Tiraque's Rue de Rivoli apartment was also under watch, yet, as the months changed from October to November, there was no sign of the missing pair.

Naldo returned to England and C granted him his promised leave so that he could be married, as planned, at Christmas. He spoke with Arnie on the telephone, and his American cousin said nothing would keep him from England to act as best man. Secretly he also wanted to spend a Christmas at Redhill Manor—the holiday season there was talked of as a ritual of fun and rest within both the Farthing and Railton families.

Meanwhile, all trails and traces appeared to have gone cold. It was as though *Tarot* had never been, and Caspar began to feel the onset of depression. The mysteries, he considered, would never be solved.

He was not to know that, in late October, C had received the CIA's blessing to go ahead with a search for Klaubert himself. To this end he instructed two of his most junior and inexperienced recruits. Curry Shepherd, who had assisted so well in helping to get Ramillies back to England, was to leave for New York in the first week of November. With him, still under instruction, would be Herbie Kruger, young indeed, but old enough for more field experience.

During the week of their departure, two things occurred in Washington that had an influence on both the families and the investigation.

IN LESS SERIOUS moments, when members of the Agency got together in groups or pairs, the talk usually turned to that kind of gossip which pervades any large organization. Who was sleeping with whom; whose wife or husband was having an affair; who, in this city where politics was the true growth industry, was being bribed; what was being planned in Washington behind the façades of those beautiful buildings, first envisioned by Pierre Charles L'Enfant.

So it was not unusual for Arnie Farthing to hear, second or third hand, of the continuing affair between his case officer, Roger Fry, and Miss Gloria Van Gent, who worked as personal assistant to one of the great but relatively nameless men at State.

The Fry/Van Gent saga was sometimes the cause of much hilarity, for Roger Fry—undoubted hero that he was—could not be in any way called dashing. He was certainly a dandy but, as some wag commented, "The only dashing thing about Roger is the way he dashes from meetings to airplanes, and from airplanes to Miss Van Gent." There was much talk about whether Roger had actually made it with Gloria—in fact he had. Even more speculation concerned the moment of transition, when Gloria would be named as Mrs. Roger Fry. Most people doubted that this would ever come to pass. "Roger hasn't the imagination or intelligence for Gloria," these folk maintained.

So it became known by the end of October that there was a serious rift in the lute which had for the past year or so played more or less in tune. Gloria's problem was said to be that of most ladies attracted to members of Roger's profession, he was always having to rush away from Washington, disappearing for weeks at a time; he was secretive; and, by no means least, he talked in a way which resembled clues to *The Washington Post* crossword puzzle, while Gloria was a bookworm. Roger just could not keep pace with her.

The love match was on in early October but off by the end of the month. Fry became more impossible than ever.

Arnie had never even set eyes on Gloria Van Gent, though he had heard extravagant descriptions of her from other members of the Agency. When he finally did meet her, at a small Halloween cocktail party in the home of an old family friend, his first thought was, How on earth did Fry manage to keep such a beautiful girl for as long as he did?

"Gloria, this is an old friend, Arnie Farthing. Arnie, Gloria Van Gent." That is how their host introduced them, excusing himself to deal with another late arrival as soon as the words were out of his mouth.

"Oooh!" Arnie heard his voice rise like that of a boy during the painful transition to manhood. "Oh!" he tried again, lowering the pitch.

"Do I take that as a compliment or are you working on your scales?" She had a voice which made Arnie think of honey being poured over piano strings that had first been wrapped in velvet. She wore her hair loose, so that it touched her shoulders. It was a kind of reddish blonde. Later he found that the hair tended to alter with the seasons. It was reddish blonde because the fall was well under way. Arnie sensed that his personal fall was also under way. Why, he silently queried, was he feeling so different all of a sudden? He had not wanted to come to the party. Now he would not have been anywhere else.

Gloria was more striking than beautiful, her face a shade too long, the nose a fraction too big, but the whole, when placed on top of a stunning figure, could cause even the most fastidious head to turn. Later he was also to discover that her gray-green eyes—"They're hazel really," she would say—together with the near-perfect mouth, made up for everything else.

"Ah, yes . . ." Arnie struggled. The idea of Roger Fry croaking his way through an evening of light banter—or heavy petting—with this most attractive creature appeared ludicrous to him.

"Yes . . ." He finally got control of his imagination. "I think we're connected. Not by marriage but rather by machination."

"Meaning precisely what?" The welcoming lips opened to show good teeth and a very warm smile.

"Meaning that I sometimes—for my sins—work for Roger Fry."

It was her turn to say, "Ah!" Then she added, a shade too quickly, "I think, Mr. Arnold Farthing, we had better go our separate ways and mingle at opposite ends of the room."

"We're not all like Roger, you know." Arnie realized that he said the line as though it had been rehearsed, but also as though he really meant it.

"I'm very glad to hear it." She smiled again, which—thought Arnie—was a step in the right direction. "If you were all like Roger, I would be exceptionally worried about the nation's security."

"I can only repeat it—we're not all like Roger."

For a couple of seconds there was a kind of stalemate. They both started to talk at the same moment, stopped, then started again. Arnie gave her a one-handed gesture meant to convey his apologies and that it was her turn in the conversation.

"Do you stand girls up at the last moment?" She came to the point immediately.

"Not if I can help it."

"Do you go away without telling your girlfriend you're going?"

"I have no girlfriend. If I had, then I would always try to let her know. I *am* going to England for Christmas."

"Really? By yourself? To plan skulduggery? Or what?"

"To be best man to a relative by marriage." He grinned. "Anyone can come, actually."

"Is that an invitation?"

"That would be presumptuous. Particularly as your former boyfriend is my superior."

Gloria finished her drink. "Tell you what." She had a nice way of smiling, the lower lip protruded slightly as her eyes lit up. "Could you be an angel and canter over to the bar and get me another stinger? I'll wait here for you and we can talk about presumptions." Once more he was later to learn that Gloria, though she never rode horses, always spoke in terms of the animals. She trotted here and there instead of walking, cantered when she was in a hurry, and galloped when she was incredibly late.

Within the week she had used another equine simile to Arnie Farthing. "Well." She smiled up at him from tousled sheets. "I didn't refuse that fence, did I?"

By the end of their first meeting, when they discovered they could speak each other's own kind of shorthand, they became friends. On the following evening, over dinner, Arnie discovered that, in spite of the honey voice and tantalizing figure, Gloria had hidden depths. Plainly she was the best-read woman he had ever encountered. Her greatest passions were Shakespeare, to which Arnie had been subjected in more recent days by Naldo, and opera, which Arnie had yet to experience. He could rub along with the books, and Uncle William of Stratford-upon-Avon, but the wonders of Verdi, Puccini, and even Wagner were closed to him.

No wonder Fry lost her, he thought after the third day, when they had talked almost constantly about movies—another of her obsessions. Fry's only conversation, as far as he knew, was politics and the Agency. Gloria was not only head and shoulders above Roger Fry, but also had an almost photographic memory, quoting from books, plays, and movies after one reading or viewing.

She was also a nice girl, in the best meaning of that word. Arnie heard her criticize Roger only once in those first few days. "Did you know that Roger hasn't read a single book of Graham Greene's?" she asked.

"Good grief!" Arnie had read only *Brighton Rock* and *This Gun for Hire*. He scribbled a note on his mind: *Read G. Greene*.

In that first week they met each night and dined in quiet restaurants in Georgetown, where her father lived. All of which made matters easier for Arnold.

The romance went straight through the sound barrier—too fast, some said. On the third night they kissed for the first time, and on the seventh, after returning to Arnie's little house, it was Gloria who said, "Mr. Farthing, would you care to lie down with me?"

"Only if you'll marry me."

And so it happened. Arnie walked around to Gloria's father on the next evening and went through the whole business of asking him for her hand in marriage. "It's wonderfully old-fashioned," Gloria told one of her closest friends. "Daddy was almost bowled over." She added that Roger Fry would not have dreamed of doing such a thing.

To be honest, on the night he proposed, Arnold also thought it was all a shade fast, as though he was on a runaway express. They both talked about it well into the early hours—Gloria did not get home until four—and when the morning came they talked again, for an hour on the telephone. Could someone be completely bowled over as quickly as this? Arnie had to admit that you could. By the time he went to Rear Admiral Michael Van Gent (Rtd) his mind was completely clear. Gloria's name, and the reputation she had gathered as Roger Fry's girlfriend, belied the person. Who, Arnie decided, could ask for anything more? He sent a cable to Naldo: GOT MYSELF ENGAGED STOP ARNIE.

To which Naldo replied, ALWAYS THOUGHT YOU WERE VACANT STOP TURN HANDLE COUNTERCLOCKWISE TO RELEASE LOCK STOP NALDO.

When the engagement was announced, Fry went straight to Jim Fishman and asked if he could be relieved of the duty of being Arnie's case officer.

"Funny," Fishman said in an abstracted way—his mind was on other, more serious, things, like Tert Newton—"Arnie's been asking for that all year."

On the day after the engagement was announced, a different kind of drama took place.

MARTY FORMAN WAS spending the bulk of his time at the safe house outside Alexandria. There were two other Agency interrogators with him, but Fishman—who was a good judge—could see that Marty was determined to crack Newton.

Yet, since Dick Farthing's visit, Tert Newton had refused to talk. "I've told you the truth. My own story, and I'm sticking to it. You can't hold me here indefinitely."

"You wanna bet?" Marty grouched. He was concerned, for Newton's wife had been just as stubborn. As well as their respective stories of what occurred during the war, they both claimed lives which they could trace back to childhood. "But the records don't show you lived in Idaho until you were seven, Tert!" Marty would almost scream.

"Then the records are wrong; or the records have gotten mixed up," Newton would reply. "My life's an open book."

"But the book's missing from the library."

"Then someone still has it out, and you oughta fine them."

The routine did not vary. They rose at around seven, breakfasted at eight, and went into an interrogation session at nine. At midday they had lunch, after which Tert Newton was allowed an hour's exercise, walking around the lawn at the back of the house, watched over by two of the security men. Others, now joined by armed Secret Service officers, ringed the house, watching skyline and trees for any signs of movement, and usually walking out to around half a mile from the house twice daily to circle it, looking for any signs of other watchers. There were no blind spots except for odd clumps of trees, which were raked regularly with field glasses.

During the week that Arnold was meeting and falling in love with Gloria, Marty Forman, depressed at both his lack of success and Newton's stubborn attitude, went to see Fishman. He had come to the conclusion that many interrogators, the free world over, would arrive at in future years.

"To get the facts, we gotta give something," he told Fishman. "The reason this guy ain't talking is that, deep down, he's afraid that we're gonna go public, give him a show trial, then burn him."

"Damn right that's what we're going to do," Fishman responded. "Dick Farthing's back in England now, getting a signed statement from Klaubert's Russian case officer. We've got cast-iron evidence against Newton."

"Look." Marty sighed. "With a clever lawyer this guy is gonna get away with it. Can't we give him some kinda immunity? Offer it to him in writing, everything legal and above board, with the Attorney General's signature? Tell him he gets this if he spills the beans? Because he isn't gonna talk without a piece of paper like that."

Reluctantly, Fishman agreed to talk with the Director, who clearly saw the wisdom in Marty's proposal and went to the Attorney General.

Forty-eight hours later, Marty began the first session of the day by pushing an official-looking document across the table toward Newton. "That's it, Tert. You sing for us and we don't take you into court. We'll even keep you safe for the rest of your life. Give you a new name, new background—like your guys say, we'll give you a new legend. All we want is the whole story."

He did not think his chances were high, even though he had patiently explained to Newton that the evidence included identification by one of the men who trained him in Bykovo.

Newton read the document, then quietly put it down and said, "My name is Pavel Denisovich Rosten, I was born in the town of Bobrka in the Ukraine and educated in Moscow. Because of my proficiency in languages, I was chosen by the NKVD to attend their special school in Bykovo in 1935. On Beria's personal orders I studied there for five years—I met my wife there. We were introduced and it was explained to us that we would be given a marital legend and placed in the United States to work for the cause of International Communism."

With those words they began the first of several sessions in which Newton gave a brief outline of his life, orders, and the object of his mission.

"It's a sketch map," Marty Forman reported to Fishman. "We'll have to fill in the topography later. There'll be enough raw material for two whole sets of the Encyclopaedia Britannica, and eventually we'll get to the heart of how these guys've been operating their illegals."

Newton/Rosten explained that he and his wife were sent to the United States expecting to be used in sabotage or straightforward espionage.

After Pearl Harbor he received new orders. He was to join the Service and if possible infiltrate Military Intelligence. "I did better than that." Now, in his true persona, Newton was infuriatingly smug and proud of what he had achieved. "I got into the OSS. Sure, we were all allies, but we weren't fools. Once the war was over, things would return to the status quo. We knew that eventually we were going to have to fight for our faith and the Revolution against the so-called democracies."

He went on to talk about the way in which he recruited Dollhiem while they were at the military school of languages together. When they completed training and moved to England, there was a complex yet almost foolproof system of communication. They had a control who, in these first sessions, he would only call *Simon*. They had dead drops, straight postcard ciphers, and telephone codes.

"This *Simon*," Marty Forman asked. "Was he British or a genuine Russian?"

"Russian. *Simon* was Russian born."

"Yea, but his cover—"

"Was cover." Newton opened his hands in a gesture which seemed to indicate that everything was plain—or, at least, that was all he would say about his controller.

Marty pressed, trying to grab the pieces of ectoplasm that had been the tradecraft used by Newton, Dollhiem, and *Simon*. His questions fell on deaf ears.

One morning Newton suddenly started to talk about *Romarin*. "It was Dollhiem who first had the details. Because he was fancied as a German speaker, they'd chosen him to impersonate an SS officer. He knew, weeks before the others—he told me, of course—that it was a do-or-die operation. Through Dollhiem we knew all the details: object, target, the how and wherefore. We fed it all to *Simon*, who in turn fed it to Moscow.

"Then the panic came—the night before we were all assembled at Gibraltar Farm.

"*Simon* got in touch. We couldn't believe it. He told us that the target of *Romarin* was really one of our people. He had been in place for a long time."

"So what were your orders?" Marty couldn't get through it quickly enough. He wanted to zoom in on the minutiae, and, like a leech, suck the man dry.

"We were to put the operation at risk. To let *Simon* know the exact time, date, and the DZ—that was tricky, but we managed it by telephone. They told Dollhiem in the morning, long before anyone else. *Simon* said we were to use our flashlights on the descent—flashing Morse code S's as we went down. Whatever

happened, we were at all costs to make contact with this guy
Klaubert. There was an arranged exchange of speech to prove our
bona fides. He must have been a reliable agent, because we were
to assist him in any possible way. Even if he told us to get lost,
that's what we were to do." Newton gave a dry laugh. "That's
what he did with me but Dollhiem stayed. I guess he tried to
help. He didn't need help, that Klaubert. A fucking cold-eyed
maniac bastard, that's what he was."

It was lunchtime, and Marty was as pleased—he said—as a
bull in a field of heifers.

After lunch, Newton insisted on taking his usual exercise. It
was a chilly day with a cold mist hanging just above the grass, so
the security men stayed in the lee of the house, watching the lone
figure walk in slow circles around the damp lawn.

They did not even hear the crack and thump of the rifle. One
minute Tertius Newton was pacing the lawn, the next he threw up
his hands toward his head, which seemed to have turned into a
ball of crimson cotton candy. The red cloud was still floating
down slowly through the air when Newton's body hit the ground.

Two of the Secret Service men on the outer perimeter claimed
to have pinpointed the exact spot, in the trees, from where the
one shot had come. They were about twenty yards out. The rifle
had been left at the place from which it had been fired—an
M1903A4, fitted with a scope. There were no fingerprints and
little in the way of clues as to how the sniper had escaped. The
only certain thing was that the job had been very well done.

"Well executed," Marty Forman said. "Professional."

In London, Caspar heard the news and immediately went to
C. "We'd better find Klaubert soon," he all but snapped. "Whoever's doing the killing knows his targets. Buelow, Dollhiem,
Newton. There's really only one choice for the next target, if he
hasn't been taken out already."

"Unless Jo-Jo and Caroline are still alive. They could come
before Klaubert." Quietly, C went on to tell him that Shepherd
and Kruger had arrived in New York.

"I think you'd best get the rest of the team ready." They were
in his apartment at Queen Anne's Gate, and C looked away and
out of the window, so that Caspar could not see the frown or the
deep worry in his eyes. "Make sure Ramillies is kept safe," he
said. "Get someone to check out the Warminster security again,
we've had one scare there already and there's still a lot of distance to go with him. Who knows, he might also be on this
strange death list."

38

▼

HERBIE KRUGER WAS not just going along for the ride—there was an important part for him to play in New York with Curry Shepherd.

"Star billing, Herb," Naldo said at the briefing. Apart from two grainy old photographs, Herbie was the only member of the team to have caught even a fleeting glimpse of the real Hans-Dieter Klaubert. A *very* fleeting glimpse, in one of the camps where the SS man was masquerading as Klausen. By the time Herbie had got back to anyone, Klausen had gone, and, though he followed the route, Herbie had missed him again. There had been talk of bringing *Felix* in, but this was ruled out as insecure.

Herbie's English was much improved, only lapsing into its odd parody during times of great stress or excitement.

"Curry, this is to be the greatest airplane ride I was ever taking." He gave his foolish wide grin to the somewhat languid Shepherd as they waited in the final departure lounge—a tent— at London Airport. "The greatest airplane ride ever," he repeated.

"Sure, Herb." Curry disguised his own excitement. Disguise was Shepherd's forte. Not the false beards, hairpieces, and funny walks so beloved of early spy fiction—and fact, according to the old school of the Great Game, and Baden-Powell.

Curry's disguise lay in his underplayed, bland, and slightly dissolute Englishman, who appeared to believe all the right things for the wrong reasons. With his lank, straw-colored hair and diffident, even dim, expression, he unknowingly taught Kruger a great deal about what the old hands called "natural cover."

Behind the façade of indifference, Shepherd was excited— and not only because of the operation. He was about to have an adolescent ambition fulfilled. New York! Even the sound of its name made his mouth water.

"You think we see G-men?" Herbie looked like a very excited overgrown child.

"I should think it highly likely." Curry yawned; he was dressed in what had become his uniform—cavalry-twill slacks, a double-breasted navy-blue blazer, white shirt, and old-Etonian tie. You could not detect the .38 pistol he carried under the blazer. On the other hand, any trained observer would have spotted Herbie's S&W .38/32, with the 2-inch barrel, for he was continually touching his hip, patting it as though to reassure himself it was there.

Permission had been granted on all sides for the two officers to go armed into the United States.

For the most part Curry remained silent—dreaming, perhaps, of bumping into June Allyson in Saks—during the very long flight, from London to Prestwick, on the northwest coast of Scotland; then the leap to Gander, Newfoundland.

Gander was fogbound, necessitating a diversion to Goose Bay, Labrador, where they sat, tired and uncomfortable in a log hut, drinking strong coffee and buying sealskin-covered paperweights as mementos. Five hours late they made it into Gander, and from there to New York's La Guardia airport.

In spite of the restless fatigue, Herbie did not sleep. He watched and examined everything about him, from his fellow passengers to the stewardesses' legs, which he found to be an increasing source of enjoyment.

His mouth dropped open when he saw the skyline of Manhattan for the first time, from around two thousand feet—the Empire State building clawing for the sun, the whole huddle of brick, concrete, and steel buildings like great man-made stalagmites: a huge medieval castle, with attendant defenses, all crammed onto an island, surrounded by the wide moat of the Hudson, Harlem, and East rivers—the long drawbridges down, to show there was peace. Knights could come and go as they pleased.

They came in low over the busy, flat, reclaimed land around Jamaica Bay where antlike vehicles moved below them, preparing what would soon be New York's International Airport. Like most air traffic from Europe, their four-engined DC-4 touched down at La Guardia after a flight—including refueling and the diversion stops—of twenty-seven hours, fifty minutes.

Arnie Farthing had flown in from Washington, and was there to meet them, with a couple of invisible Agency men in the background and another highly visible pair of FBI officers—

"There're your G-men, Herbie"—to check them through at top speed. Normal immigration, passport, and customs procedures were waived. Tired and bewildered, both Curry and Herbie gazed with wonder from the windows of the long black car that whisked them into the heart of Manhattan.

After so many years of drab, grim, wartime landscapes, neither man could believe the traffic, crowded sidewalks, and well-stocked shops. From their car they looked out upon what appeared to be a mouthwatering Aladdin's cave. Lights twinkled in trees and already, though they were only in November, an illuminated sign said that "New York is a Winter Wonderland." Here was affluence and bustle, backed by the music of motor horns echoing in the gulches between the tightly packed tall buildings, and the occasional counterpoint of a police siren.

Arnie saw them into the New Weston Hotel on Madison, at 50th—now long gone, but a luxurious paradise then, for Shepherd and Kruger.

"Get some food from room service, then sleep it off," Arnie advised them. "There'll be a lot for you to do tomorrow." He spoke flatly, and brought Curry and Herbie to earth with a bump. The long haul and dazzling arrival had almost driven the real purpose of their visit from their minds.

They ate, droopy-eyed, in Curry's room—chicken soup and steaks the size of dinner plates. Their shrunken, war-worn stomachs could not take such large portions. The waiter asked belligerently if there was something wrong with the food.

As he finally dozed, and dropped into sleep, Herbie thought that he had never seen bedside lamps as big as those in his room. Curry's last memory, as oblivion hit him, was, "Good night, baby—milkman's on his way."

Arnie met them in Curry's room where they were adjusting to breakfast—the fresh orange juice, bacon, eggs, thick black coffee that made your hands shake, waffles, and syrup.

"I hear it's congratulations, Arn." Herbie made his closed-mouth smile, splitting his face in a crescent, like a child's drawing. "Nuptials?" This last spoken like a password. He had only recently learned it—from Naldo.

Arnie nodded his thanks and began to talk. "You'd better have good warning. Some of the people I work for seem to think your arrival's unnecessary," he told them bluntly. "The guy who's my boss now, Marty Forman, is of the opinion that we should have handled the whole thing from Washington. His argument is that, as the killings took place here, we should see it through. If Klaubert is really in the United States, it's the CIA's business to root him out. But the deal's been struck, so everyone'll stick to the rules. Just be prepared to find Marty, and some of the FBI men, a little—well, brusque, heavy-handed."

They particularly did not approve of the agreed immediate extradition if Klaubert was brought in.

They talked about the problem for a few minutes, then Arnie said it was time for Curry to go into his routine. "You have the number?" he asked.

Curry nodded and went to the telephone. He dialed, and far away heard the long single *burrrs,* so different from the British *brrp-brrp-brrp-brrp.* When a voice answered, Curry asked if he could speak with the Father Guardian. He wondered if it was Hans-Dieter Klaubert who was at this moment alerting the Father Guardian to the telephone call.

IT WAS ODD, like leaving one planet and going straight to another. One minute they were getting out of a yellow cab, right down near Wall Street, where millions—billions—of dollars changed hands each day. The street noises of last night now seemed to be magnified, and that brash, roaring static which tingles the nerves in New York City was pushed up by several hundred volts. Then, within a dozen strides, the noise receded and they were in the midst of peace.

They had walked a few paces up a narrow side street, looked at the sign, engraved on simple wood—PRIORY OF ST. FRANCIS OF ASSISI—pushed open the metal gate set in the wall, and stepped into tranquillity.

The courtyard was bordered by stone walls on three sides, one was covered in wisteria, its color gone with the season; two pear trees, also now asleep after summer, stood near the wall to their right, and there were other bushes behind—to their left and right. In front of them was a short cloister, within the shadow of which they could see a Norman arch enclosing a heavy studded door.

Curry advanced toward the cloister and its door, followed by Herbie, who, as his cover, carried two expensive cameras. Arnold had brought them from Washington.

There was an iron ring bellpull to the right of the door. Far away, from inside, they heard an urgent clanking when Curry heaved at it. Then, silently, the door opened. A short, smiling man, in the brown Franciscan habit, bade them enter. Curry did not even have to give his name. "The Father Guardian is expecting you," the friar said, moving his hand as though they were donkeys who needed encouragement and guidance. The hallway was cold and small, but the one passage which led off it widened and rose giving a sense of spaciousness.

They stopped by another door, and the monk tapped lightly. From inside came a flat "Enter." The door was opened and their little monk quietly said, "The two gentlemen from England, Father Guardian."

"Thank you, Brother Martin. You are excused."

The monk gave a small bow of his head and retreated, closing the door behind him and leaving them alone with a tall, thin, severe-looking man. He also wore the Franciscan habit. His hair was shaved, and, between a pair of humorless eyes he sported a large aquiline nose. Later Herbie said the Father Guardian actually frightened him. "He was not a man of this world," he told Naldo. "This was a man who had seen other things. Other worlds. I think he had touched God."

"Gentlemen, please sit down. Welcome to our humble house." In spite of his appearance, the Father Guardian's voice was soft, almost gentle. Vocally he reminded Curry of one of the inquisitors at Warminster. Intuitively he knew this was a carrot-and-stick man.

"It's very good of you to find time to see us, Father—"

"Brother," the friar corrected him. "Yes, the Brothers call me their Father Guardian, but only on the first meeting of the day or when showing in guests. It is a rule of this house, for we are all Brothers—even those of us who are priests and can rightly be called Father. My name is Brother Peter."

The chairs were hard—little upright wooden things. They were meant to be uncomfortable. The walls were whitewashed, the only decoration being a large crucifix. Apart from the two chairs, only the Father Guardian's desk and chair furnished the place. Curry later pronounced it "Dead Spartan!"

"Now, on the telephone, I talked to—"

"Me," Curry said, a huskiness in his throat, which had become very dry. "My name is Shepherd."

"Ah, yes . . . Mr. Shepherd. And you are a journalist."

Curry nodded. "Yes. We work for a British magazine called *Picture Post*. I don't know if you've ever seen it—"

"But yes, of course. It is a sort of smaller version of our *Life* magazine. I fear that I have had to ban several issues—as with *Life*—from the Brothers' Common Room."

"Oh, dear—then you won't take kindly—"

The Father Guardian held up one hand, palm outward. "Please." He gave the wraith of a smile. "It is part of my duty to sometimes hold back certain periodicals—let me say, mainly for the peace of mind and body of the younger brethren—usually those serving their novitiate."

"I understand." Curry tried to smile.

Herbie shifted uncomfortably. There was silence. Then—

"Tell me what it is you ask." Brother Peter appeared to be looking into Curry's soul.

"We are doing—I mean, *I* am doing a feature for *Picture Post*." Why did he feel so damned uncomfortable lying to this man in the brown habit, Curry wondered. He knew nobody had sought permission from the famous magazine for him to pass himself off as one of their journalists. "This is my colleague, Mr. Kruger, by the way, who will be doing the photographs."

"Charmed, I'm sure," said Herbie, to Curry's dismay. Where in hell—in heaven? Oh, Lord!—had Herbie picked *that* one up?

Brother Peter looked hard and humorlessly at Herbie. "*You* are not English, Mr. Kruger." It was almost an accusation.

"No," Herbie bounced back. "I come from Austria. Before the war begins, my family get out of Austria."

Curry smiled. "We are doing a feature on the impact of the religious life on people who have gone through the war. Those who have, if I can put it this way, seen into the depths of despair and returned to embrace the religious life." He paused, wondering if he was going over the top. Then, seeing Brother Peter waiting for him to continue: "We have done several monasteries—and convents also—in France, Belgium, England, Germany even. Now I wanted to try the same thing here. We have to go to other orders—there are some Carthusians in Maine, and the Benedictines are also receiving us. What we're really doing for the moment is finding out, first if you have any returned veterans, or even foreign immigrants who have fled from the darker parts of Europe, and applied to join your order. Second, if the answer is yes, then we would seek your permission to photograph them, and, perhaps, speak with them—in your presence of course," he added a shade too quickly.

"I see." The Father Guardian looked very serious indeed.

"If you—" Curry began, but Brother Peter raised a hand once more. Even though the Father Guardian had taken the vows of *strict* poverty, chastity, and obedience, it was clear that he found great happiness in ruling, and overruling, those set below him.

"We have one such man," Brother Peter said. "Strangely, he

also comes from your country, Mr. Kruger. Austria. Unhappily, he did not get out as soon as you did. He suffered much at the hands of the Nazis. He is also a man weighed down with a deep sense of guilt. I cannot tell why, but I suspect it has something to do with the struggle for survival in the death camps."

"He went through the camps? *O Gott im Himmel!*" A piece of fancy acting from Herbie.

Brother Peter continued. "His personal permission will have to be sought before I can allow you to photograph and talk with our poor Brother. He has been with us for less than a year, so is still a novice."

"Can we see him?" Curry put it flatly.

"Even if he agreed, I fear not. He will not be returning to this priory—which is now his true home—for nearly a month."

Curry asked why this novice Brother was not in the priory at the moment. He tried to sound as casual as possible.

"He is here. In New York City." Brother Peter spoke as though forced to use great patience. "You see, my friends, our order bids us to go out among the poor, the sick, the lonely, and the despairing. We go to tend them, offer what assistance we can, pray with them, preach to them, and act as their friends. This is a hard, and sometimes thankless, demanding task. But we do it with joy, in Our Lord Jesus Christ."

"Yes?" Curry was trying to push him along.

"In New York alone we have several Refuges, where people can receive help—food, medicines, prayer, comfort. We rotate our Brothers as a good farmer of old rotated his crops. Each of our Refuge Houses is in the care of four Brothers. They do a month in one of the Refuges, then a month back here, in their true house. At the moment, Brother Clement—for that is his name in God—is serving for a month in our Refuge on the Bowery, which is possibly the most demanding of our Houses. The Bowery, my good friends, is a place of real despair. It will help him to see his own life from a different perspective."

"And he'll be there for a month, Brother?"

"He started but two days ago. So, yes, a month."

"You said his name in God is Brother Clement?"

"That is correct. We have no male saints whose name begins with the letter K."

"I'm sorry, I don't follow—" Curry began.

"Ah, no. Silly of me. I should not have mentioned it." Again the almost smile on the Father Guardian's lips. "Many of the Brothers, when they take their name in God, like it to start with the same initial as their surname in the world. Brother Clement's name began with a K. It's probably quite a common name in your country, Mr. Kruger. Klausen. Brother Clement's name in the world was Klausen."

"No, that is not so a common name in my country." Herbie's voice appeared to have lost a great deal of power.

Curry prayed for the big German boy, prayed that he would not show any sign; while in his own mind, one thing was being repeated, again and again, like a gramophone record that is damaged so that the needle sticks in a groove: *Got you! Got you! Got you, Klaubert, you lovely bastard! Got you!*

Herbie remained calm. All *he* could think of was the way he had just missed catching up with Hans-Dieter Klaubert after he had changed his name to Klausen in the DP camps. He smiled up at Brother Peter: a warm, open smile, as though he would like to kiss the severe Franciscan.

Klaubert was here, in New York City. Klaubert was now.

Oddly, for the first time, Brother Peter seemed to unbend. He also opened his mouth in a wide smile, and his eyes lit up as though to show the true joy which he kept hidden from the world.

39

▼

UNDER HIS BREATH Curry Shepherd sang, "I don't know what street—compares with Mott Street—in July." He still carried his revolver, but the smart slacks and blazer had gone. Now, like Herbie, who shambled ahead of him, Shepherd wore a scruffy jacket over what looked like a filthy shirt. His denim trousers—cast-off army fatigues—were ripped and frayed. Gone were the handmade shoes—his family had patronized Lobb's of St. James's for over a hundred years—and his feet were now shod in scuffed boots. The boots had no laces, and the sole of the left one had come away from the upper, so that it flapped like the opening and closing mouth of some strange beast.

Herbie, he thought, was more suited to this kind of disguise, but Herbie never seemed to care about clothes. Put him in something from Savile Row and the large German lad would look untidy within the hour, creased, rumpled, tie askew. In sartorial matters, Curry had given up Herbie as a lost cause. In fact, Herbie, dressed as a bum with a long, worn, shapeless coat over his rags and a strange, stained, black hat pulled down almost to his ears, just looked like Herbie.

This was the second time that the pair had walked up Mott Street, on the edge of Chinatown, their backs to the East River and the Brooklyn Bridge. They turned east now, into the Bowery.

The first time—two days ago—had been during the afternoon, a matter of hours after their conversation with the Franciscan Father Guardian.

"We have to make a sighting," Curry had said firmly.

They had set up a temporary headquarters in Rockefeller Center, unknowingly using the same office that "Little Bill" Stephenson—*Intrepid*—had inhabited when first initiating British Security Co-ordination, the secret cooperation between British Intelligence and the FBI, blessed by President Roosevelt and

357

aimed, first, at catching Nazi spies in the United States before America entered the war.

It was here, in Rockefeller Center, that a hot-line telephone had now been wired in for instant communication with London —straight into the Northolt safe house, where the remnants of the *Symphony* team again kept a round-the-clock watch just as they had done during *Brimstone*. In Washington they had another facility, carefully guarded and ready to house Klaubert during the short, but inevitable, time between his arrest and journey back to England. Everybody was aware that it could take several days to move the former SS man.

On their first visit to the Bowery, Herbie and Curry were accompanied by Arnie. One of the CIA cars had taken them—on the day of their breakthrough with Brother Peter—down to a point near the Brooklyn Bridge. From there, the trio had made their way on foot into that area of New York where Chinatown merges with Little Italy.

Arnie had suggested they approach the Bowery from the river instead of the more obvious route, taking them down through Little Italy. It was quickly clear that Arnie had made a careful check on the Franciscan Refuge, for it lay hard by what claimed to be the oldest pharmacy in America—Olliffee's at No. 6, the Bowery. Squeezed between two obvious flophouses was a green door, blistered by sun, scratched and cracked by more than normal wear and tear. Above the door hung a large board that had once been white. In faded black letters were the words REFUGE OF ST. FRANCIS. In smaller letters was a text in English, *Come unto Me, all ye that labor and are heavy laden, and I will give you rest*. When Curry Shepherd saw it he reflected that there were very few who labored in the Bowery, but a large number who rested—on the sidewalks or in doorways, mad, sad, bad, incompetent, alcoholic, drugged, or almost dead.

On the first occasion they walked this truly mean street for the best part of an hour, and hardly five minutes in that time passed without their being accosted, sworn at, or in danger of being manhandled.

A muttering woman, whose clothes seemed to be tied together with pieces of string, hung at their heels, even though Curry had dropped a few coins into her hand, misshapen and crusted with sores. "Fucking men ... my ruination, men ... men-men-men-men ..." she chanted through broken teeth.

A tall, gaunt figure, looking like a scarecrow, came close to them, thrusting his face near to Herbie so that the German could see the great red blotches around his lips and smell the decay and cheap liquor on his breath as he threatened them for money.

None of the three would forget the younger woman—her face like that of a doll, rouged and plastered with makeup, her clothes, once good quality, now stained with God knew what. She offered them her body: "Honey? Honey? Ya wanna good time? We can go fuck in the alley over there. I'll take the t'ree of ya for five bucks."

It was the only time they were nearly assaulted, for Herbie— who had experienced things like this in the ruins of postwar Germany—harshly told her to "Fuck off!" As he spoke, three men moved from the shadows—her protectors and self-appointed pimps. One had a bottle, and they had no doubt he would use it. Herbie's hand went to his hip and the Smith & Wesson nestling in its holster.

"No, Herb!" Arnie shouted, throwing some quarters into the street. The woman and her guardians leaped after the coins, biting, scratching, tearing at each other to get to the money first.

Cars went past—some idling as people looked out, morbidly or with a song in their hearts, knowing that but for the grace of God, or man, they also might belong to this terrible, ghostlike army. Almost paradoxically, a few Chinese restaurants appeared to be doing a reasonable trade in spite of the degradation.

Curry thought it was the nearest thing he had seen to those descriptions of the poverty-stricken areas of Victorian London. Arnie thought about Gloria, for he knew the Bowery had once been a small country road within the original Dutch community of this part of Manhattan. "Bouwerie" it had been called then, and he wondered if any of Gloria's Van Gent forefathers—who were originally from Holland—had passed this way. Only Herbie showed neither fear nor disgust. But he had seen the inside of DP camps and other places he would rather hold in his own mind than talk about.

Yet there were people who worked to reduce the despair. About four o'clock on that afternoon, on their fourth or fifth pass near the Refuge, Herbie suddenly whispered, "It's him. He's here."

Arnie and Curry looked up and saw the two friars, in their brown habits and sandals, leaving the Refuge. One was thin and red-faced; the other tall, straight, and with a scar visible down the right side of his face. His light hair had been shaved, but a soft down was beginning to form over his scalp. Under the monastic habit you could tell he walked erect, like a soldier, with his eyes moving warily as though he was crossing terrain which could house an enemy sniper or machine-gun nest.

They were the eyes of one who is always watching for danger, and they scanned Arnie, Herbie, and Curry, who all looked away quickly. Later Herbie said that Klaubert had seen them. Something had registered, fractionally, on the SS man's face.

"Fear?" Curry asked. "Fear that we might have rumbled him?"

Herbie shook his great head. For once any comic—or buffoonlike—traces vanished from him. The future spymaster emerged, the probationer who was father to the shrewd handler of secrets—"I detected hope. He saw us as a danger, but that, I believe, is what he wants. Didn't he leave a clue to where he would go? Isn't it why we're here, because he left a clue? I tell you that man feels he is lost. He wishes to pay some kind of penalty for his sins. Maybe he wishes even for death. In his eyes I saw hope."

In the office high above Rockefeller Plaza, Curry picked up the telephone and dialed London. It was Caspar who manned the instrument at the other end.

"He *is* in my father's house," Curry said.

"And there are many mansions?" Caspar asked three thousand miles away.

In New York, Curry answered, in agreement, "Many mansions," and replaced the receiver.

By the next night, Caspar, Dick Farthing, and Naldo Railton arrived in New York.

Now, here, on the following afternoon, with the plan laid and the briefing over, Curry sang under his breath and entered the Bowery, Herbie ahead of him. Within the next half an hour, Hans-Dieter Klaubert, aka Brother Clement OFM, would be lifted from the streets and, perhaps, some of the mysteries would be revealed.

It had become cold, with an icy wind blowing off the East River funneling up the streets. Curry felt miserable, silently cursing Herbie for choosing the torn, dirty, and long overcoat. He moved unsteadily across the street, waiting near the center for traffic to pass, swaying gently, head down, but eyes moving to and fro.

Finally he reached the far side and stumbled into the wall, rolling his body so that his back rested against the stone. He was stationed right next to the green door with the sign above it telling all, drunk, sober, insane, or desperate, that it was the Refuge of St. Francis.

The beat cops had been questioned subtly about the good brothers' comings and goings. They now knew that two of the friars left the Refuge at around ten in the morning, returning at three-thirty—sometimes with the odd vagrant or a person in dire need. The other pair left on their errands of mercy at about four o'clock.

It was three-twenty, so Brother Clement would either be returning or leaving during the next forty minutes.

Through his lowered lids Curry saw Herbie was in place, across the street and to his left. The cars were there also. Two were parked a few yards up the Bowery on Curry's side—the Refuge side—and to his left. The nearest contained three FBI officers, the other car held Marty Forman and Naldo Railton. A third car was almost directly across the street from him. Arnie, another CIA man, Dick Railton Farthing, and Caspar Railton sat quietly inside.

They were all armed—"A precaution only," Dick had said—and knew that only the FBI men had any authority to take the Franciscan into custody. "We're all really only along for the ride unless things get difficult or rough," Caspar told them in Rockefeller Center. Curry thought Caspar looked twitchy. He groaned and put his head back for a moment. He could see Caspar, sitting next to the driver in the car across the street.

SINCE HE HAD left the Northolt house—after making the three obligatory telephone calls—Caspar felt uneasy. He had ridden the subway back into London, and went through antisurveillance routines twice—getting off at stations, turning toward the tunnels that led to the exits, then scurrying back onto the train.

Instead of getting a cab to Queen Anne's Gate, he walked, stepping into doorways and doing several back-doubles.

Nothing. Only the odd feeling that he was not alone.

Once, passing down Northumberland Avenue, he turned abruptly and was convinced that a shadow had flitted into darkness behind him. He walked back to where he had seen it. Again nothing.

At C's apartment he stationed himself near one of the windows looking down into the street. Again, he thought there was a darker patch among the blackness. One of the Special Branch baby-sitters went down to investigate. Nothing to report.

They had made an agreement to meet at C's convenient quarters once a message came through. Each had packed a small

bag and left it at Queen Anne's Gate. There were seats booked
and ready, spanning a whole week, so that when the message
came—if it came—all three could leave on the earliest possible
flight.

During the drive out to the airport, Caspar still felt uneasy.
Finally he shrugged it off as the tension which comes toward the
end of a long field operation. And, for Caspar, this had all started
back in 1938. When they got Klaubert into the sweatbox, maybe
he would relax, for the truth—*whatever* it was—could only act
as a balm.

Yet, on arrival at La Guardia, on the journey into the city, and
even at the office high over New York, the alertness returned,
like a stomach ulcer burning and gnawing for a time, then reced-
ing, only to start again, unexpectedly.

He must have shown the stress, for Dick asked if he was
unwell.

In honesty, Caspar said, "No. Touch of the horrors. Probably
worried about what we'll find at the end of the road."

"Understandable." Dick smiled at him, wondering if they
would have been wiser to leave Caspar in England.

Now, as he awaited the final outcome, Caspar felt his nervous
antennae come into action again, and this time all his long training and experience told him that something was very wrong indeed. He couldn't put his finger on it, but it was there, out in this
street, which could have been lifted straight from Dante's *In-
ferno*.

"Here they come." Dick's voice was as calm and ordinary as
those of the fighter pilots in the Battle of Britain, giving their
"Tally-ho chaps, bandits at three o'clock, above us." They really
did speak like that, for some of the time anyway. There were
recordings to prove it: the ones with the screams of fear, near-
hysterical shouts of warning, and terrible agonizing cries had
been destroyed.

Two friars were coming down the Bowery, on the Refuge
side. They had a couple of vagrants and a crying woman with
them. From the corner of his eye Curry watched them, and saw
that Klaubert—Brother Clement—was not one of them. Slowly
Curry lifted his hand and scratched enthusiastically at his armpit.

"Not him." Arnie was in the back of the car with Dick. His
brother CIA officer sat in the driver's seat, next to Caspar.

Dick said to watch the door. "He'll be one of those coming
out."

Curry thought the same thing. Everyone now focused attention on the green door.

Traffic came by, in both directions. Some cars pulled in to discharge passengers, trucks stopped, and delivery men eased themselves out. A large boxlike van stopped directly behind the car containing Arnie, Dick, and Caspar, so they had no view of the black sedan which parked about three paces behind the van.

Herbie growled to himself, staggered from the wall, and moved farther down the street. The sedan had all but blocked his view.

From across the road Curry gave the sedan a surreptitious look. There was a man at the wheel, and he thought he discerned some movement in the back, but when he slyly looked again, nobody was there.

At that moment the green door opened and two friars came out onto the cold street, the wind whipping at their habits. One was tall, striding from the doorway like a holy hero about to do battle against Satan.

"Go! Go-go-go!" Marty almost screamed, looking incredulously at the car in front and cursing the time the FBI men took to get from it.

In fact it was only a second or two, but in those moments Marty and Naldo were out, standing in readiness, while Curry still performed his drunk act and began to walk unsteadily toward the friars—"Holy Fathers!" he slurred. "Will you not help a poor man who can't get work?" He even bumped against Brother Clement as he staggered, separating him for a moment from his companion.

The three FBI men moved in, and, as they did so, Herbie unstuck himself from the wall and began to walk forward into the street, his eyes on the tableau outside the Refuge.

Curry hung on to Brother Clement's habit, and one of the FBI men took the other Franciscan a few paces away, while the remaining pair began to speak—"Brother Clement?" one of them asked.

The tall man just nodded, then his face broke into a smile as though he had been waiting for this moment for years.

"We are officers of the Federal Bureau of Investigation. I must ask you to come with us and answer some questions, Brother."

Caspar, Arnie, and Dick were out of their car now, eyes fixed on the man they had sought for so long.

"Gladly, brothers. Oh, gladly." Klaubert smiled, then nodded. "You know of course that my real name is Hans-Dieter Klaubert?

That I was in charge of the *Schutzstaffel* in Orléans?"

"Yes." The agent gave a slow nod.

Herbie was halfway across the street now. Somewhere behind him he heard a car door open, then, out of the corner of his right eye, he caught sight of a figure moving past, on his outside. The figure came fully into his vision—a stocky, well-built figure, moving in a boxer's crouch.

It could only have been a tenth of a second before he realized what was happening. Herbie heard himself scream, "No!" The shout seemed to echo as it came simultaneously from Naldo and Curry.

Herbie launched himself at the crouching man, his huge hand going for the Smith & Wesson he had carefully strapped inside the long overcoat.

He hit, in a flying tackle, hearing the breath come out of the crouching figure. But even as he hit he knew it was too late. The stocky man had straightened at the last moment, his arms coming up in front of him. As Herbie struck, bringing him to the ground, he fired two shots.

It was all a mixture of sounds and noise—the crack as Herbie's shoulder connected with the gunman's legs, just behind the knees; the shots at the same moment; the thwack of both bullets finding their target; the breath exploding from the body now under Herbie; and shouts from all around.

Naldo saw it all, and for a moment could hardly believe it. He knew the intruder only from description—Marcel Tiraque: *Night Stock*—just as he knew Klaubert, now pitched backward off his feet and thrown to the ground, the heels of his sandals scraping on the surface of the street.

Naldo moved to Herbie's aid, though the German lad needed no help, apart from having the gun kicked away from Tiraque's hand. Then everyone turned looking toward the car from which Tiraque had come. There was movement from the rear, and one of the FBI agents took up the double-handed grip, his pistol an extension of both arms. Marty Forman did the same. Then the others, a ring of handguns pointing toward the sedan, the fingers taking up pressure on the triggers.

"Noooooo!" Naldo shrieked above the confusion and noise, running, putting himself between everyone and the sedan. "Hold your fire! Don't shoot!"

He saw Arnie moving along the sidewalk on the far side of the sedan, and Caspar coming into the middle of the road. There

were screams, the sound of feet running, and cars honking; a sea
of people; and voices all around.

Naldo had not even drawn his gun. Now his hand reached for
the rear door of the black sedan, wrenching it open. He found
himself looking down the barrel of a large Colt automatic. Behind the Colt was a small, dark-haired, very pretty young
woman. She looked like a darker version of Sara, and behind her
there was another girl, with an elfin face and long blonde hair.

In the wink of time between opening the door and seeing the
young women and the gun, everything fell into place within
Naldo's head. It was as though by some magic a jigsaw puzzle
thrown from a box had made itself into a picture on the table of
his mind.

In his head he saw the cyanide gun outside Otto Buelow's
door; the truck shattering the CIA interrogators' car; the bullet
splintering Nat Dollhiem's skull; the sniper blowing away the top
of Tert Newton's head. Most of all he was now nearly certain that
he knew about Caroline and Jo-Jo; knew how they had gone, and
who with; knew how they had been deceived; knew about the
now-dead Klaubert; knew about the intrigues and deviations of
Lightning/Harold; Thunder; and *Night Stock,* whom Herbie had
in an armlock with the stubby barrel of his S&W stuck into the
man's ear. *Night Stock*—Tiraque—was laughing hysterically:
"Got the bastard. Got the bastard traitor."

Naldo looked at the girl with the Colt automatic and saw the
tears running down her cheeks.

"It's okay, Caro. It's over. Give me the gun." Gently he took it
from her, glancing over her shoulder and nodding. "It's over now,
Jo-Jo."

Arnie had opened the far rear door and was helping Jo-Jo onto
the sidewalk, just as Naldo assisted Caroline.

He heard Caspar's voice, almost breaking emotionally behind
him—

"It's all right, Caro, Jo-Jo. It's all right. It's over for you. He's
dead. You've done what you thought best. The rest of us will
have to live with our mistakes. Forgive me if you can, please."

Naldo thought he heard one of the girls whisper, "Oh, Cas.
Cas. Thank God!" And he knew that there was little relief in her
words. For Jo-Jo and Caroline it was all far from over. In some
ways, for them, the hell was about to begin.

40

▼

It was not until the chaos following Klaubert's death began to recede that the full implication of what had occurred hit them. For almost half an hour the British team surrounded the cars. Tiraque had been cuffed and placed in one of them with an FBI man. The girls were separated and put in different cars, while various family members went to talk with them. The young women appeared to be frightened, and—in Caroline's case—almost hysterical.

Naturally, as her father, it was Dick who spent most of the time with Caroline, and it was to Dick that she whispered the name of the hotel where they had been staying. "I loved him, Daddy," she kept saying through tears. None of them knew whom she was talking about. At the time Dick was convinced she spoke of Tiraque.

The hotel information was passed to Arnie, who nodded and slipped away to speak with his CIA colleague. There were telephone calls, and the second CIA man disappeared to join a team already in New York, dealing with other matters.

In the end it was left to Marty Forman to explain the real problems. Until he spoke with Dick they were all under the oddly euphoric impression that it was now merely a case of getting Tiraque and the girls away, then taking them back to England for a full, lengthy, and demanding interrogation. It quickly became obvious that this could not happen.

"The guy should by rights face a Murder One rap," Marty said. "And the women should be held as accessories. I'm not a fool, so I can work out the possible connection with the Washington killings." He spoke of Buelow, Dollhiem, Tertius Newton, and the two interrogators.

Caspar looked outraged. "This was a combined Agency/SIS

operation. We have to take them back to the UK. *We had an agreement, damn it.*"

Marty slowly shook his head, saying that they had an agreement regarding Hans-Dieter Klaubert—"Who's going to the City Morgue. There can't be any agreement or understanding about this other guy and the women."

Arguments continued between the FBI and the British team. An ambulance took Klaubert's body away, and members of the NYPD moved the crowds on, their plainclothes officers talking earnestly with the FBI agents. While all this took place, Marty Forman disappeared.

When he returned, Marty beckoned Dick out of the car where he was still comforting his daughter.

"The situation's kinda fluid," he said. "They gotta appear before a judge *in camera*. No press, no nothing. But the guy Tiraque'll be on a Murder One charge, the women as accessories. Now, make sure you're hearing me right. I spoke to my boss, Fishman. He says it's a case for very long debriefing, and he's speaking with a judge now. The Director himself is having words with the Attorney General. In any case we'll have all three of them safe in Washington by late tonight."

So it turned out. Tiraque, who sat silent, shaking his head at questions from Caspar, was advised to reserve any plea at the initial court arraignment, scheduled to take place almost immediately.

Loath as they were to let either Tiraque or the women out of their sight, it was necessary for the British team, together with the Agency people, to give them up to the FBI.

Sadly, in Dick's case—and with much frustration for the others—three unmarked cars moved swiftly away, carrying Tiraque, Caroline, and Jo-Jo.

From that point things moved very quickly. Marty was a fireball of organization, getting the teams into cars, detailing the drivers, and moving them out. Hard, tough, and rough though he was, Marty Forman had a deep sense of fairness and truth. He knew how the Brits felt—particularly in respect of the fact that the women were relatives of most of them.

The only amusing incident in an otherwise worrying series of events was the arrest of both Curry Shepherd and Herbie Kruger, by overzealous cops, on charges of vagrancy and carrying concealed weapons. It was a sideshow, and the pair were eventually saved from spending a night in the drunk tank—which also housed vagrants—by the none-too-speedy intervention of the senior FBI agent of the section assigned to Klaubert's apprehension. The business brought a few smiles, but failed to lift the anxieties which pervaded the British contingent.

Early that evening they all stood in a small courtroom. The three defendants were still carefully separated, and each was now represented by an Agency-appointed lawyer. The charges were read out, but the names of the accused were omitted. The victim was also named only as Brother Clement OFM. When these preliminaries had finished, the judge ran his eyes over the small assembly and began to speak.

"I am advised by the Attorney General," he began, "that this matter contains certain aspects which concern national security and our security agencies. I am, therefore, not going to proceed with the arraignment at this time. The defendants will remain in the custody of the Federal Bureau of Investigation, who, I am assured, will see that they are delivered into the keeping of other agencies who need to make a full investigation regarding the killing of Brother Clement—a novice of the Order of Friars Minor.

"I have instructions from the Attorney General that the defendants will face charges at some future date"—he hesitated before adding—"if such charges are deemed necessary and valid following further investigation. The defendants are released into the hands of FBI agents now present in this court." He rose. The court rose. Tiraque and the young women were quietly led out of a side door, where Agency hoods waited to take them, by safe and guarded routes, to Washington.

"Okay," Marty told the British team. "We're arranging a special flight to get you all to Washington. There's a lot of work ahead, and I guess you folks'll bear the brunt of that."

THEY ALL MET on the following morning in James Xavier Fishman's office. Curry and Herbie were not present—by request. Instead, a couple of Agency men took them on a tour of Washington, with instructions to keep them happy and give them anything within reason until the preliminary interrogations were over. The Agency wanted no member of the British team leaving for England until at least the foundations of truth were exposed.

Fishman explained how things stood. Tiraque and the women had been kept separated from the moment they were taken in the Bowery. "I felt you'd want that." He spoke mainly to Dick as the most senior officer present. "Obviously there are possible matters of conspiracy, maybe treachery—and charges under your own beloved Official Secrets Act. We're naturally concerned about anything related to the killings of Buelow, Dollhiem, and Newton. We're also anxious about the possible leakage of secrets from the Atomic Energy Commission. Things Newton might well have passed on before his sudden death."

Fishman said that in the circumstances he felt the British officers should, as he put it, "Have the first shot." If these initial interrogations bore no fruit, then the results would be passed on to Agency people.

He left the clear impression that his own interrogation teams would not be gentle—he did not mean in any physical way—nor would there be any possibility of even discussing release of the women. They were accepted, he said, as "Gallant Resistance officers during the European campaign, *unless it was proved otherwise.*"

Dick did not wish to be involved. Caroline was his own daughter, and Jo-Jo had been brought up mainly by her foster mother, Marie Grenot, Sara, and himself. It was not right that he take any active part.

So it was agreed that Caspar, having run Tiraque as *Night Stock*, should begin to debrief his former agent. Naldo, together with Arnie Farthing, as the Agency's representative, would talk with the girls, who were still kept strictly apart. Caroline was in a house quite near Arnie's place in Georgetown. Jo-Jo had been lodged in the apartment in which they had once kept Otto Buelow. Both were heavily guarded by Agency people—men and women officers, with a ring of watchers nearby.

Marcel Tiraque had been taken to the house outside Alexandria. The house where Newton had died. Tiraque was held under an overkill of security.

Before they went their separate ways, Arnie not only disclosed what had been found in Tiraque's hotel room in New York but handed over the material. Caspar looked through it, not even disguising his bewilderment. This was a job that could be done best by others, he said, and shut himself away with Dick Farthing for almost two hours, going through the material, taking only one or two token pieces with him to the Alexandria house while Dick began to make long, detailed, and secure telephone calls to London.

In the first days it was clear that Tiraque had no intention of talking. Caspar's questions appeared to fall on deaf ears. "You really care about what happened?" Tiraque asked him. "I did you a favor. I did all of us a favor. I got rid of the Devil of Orléans for you—evened the score a little. I also saved your own relatives, Caspar, like I told you I would a long time ago. You think it wasn't done out of friendship? All we did was even the score. The fact that the war was technically over makes no difference. If you'd caught up with Klaubert, you'd have put him to death judicially—and those Red treacherous bastards Dollhiem and Newton would have been put behind bars. Christ, you'd have thrown the key away on them!"

"What about Otto Buelow?" There was no hint of Caspar's knowledge concerning Klaubert's almost ephemeral connection with the British Secret Intelligence Service.

"What about Buelow?" Tiraque countered. "He was Klaubert's deputy, wasn't he? He had blood on his hands."

"He was also related to my family by marriage—which means he was Caroline's relative. Which one of the girls got rid of him, Marcel?"

"I got rid of him." He banged his chest. "Me. I did them all."

"You?" Caspar raised his eyes incredulously. "You did Buelow, Marcel? You killed him with an ingenious piece of Russian equipment?"

"It was *my* ingenious piece of equipment," thumping his chest again. "*I* did it all."

"So you managed to get yourself into two places at once? You killed Buelow, then spirited yourself away, in a matter of minutes, stole a truck, caught up with Buelow's interrogators in the pouring rain, and smashed them into charred pulp on the freeway." He took a deep breath, smiling at Tiraque. "You find a telephone booth to change in, Marcel?"

Tiraque grunted questioningly.

"I mean, if you *are* the Caped Crusader—Superman—let's get it on the record."

"I did it all." Tiraque spoke quietly, snapping his mouth shut. "I saved the girls; kept them hidden; looked after them; swore vengeance with them and allowed them to see the results. That's all." Again the mouth closed, lips pursed.

"We need more detail, Marcel. You and me, we've known each other for a long time. Surely you can pass on the details to me. Why keep the girls hidden for so long? Why go to all that trouble?"

Marcel simply shook his head. "That's all I'm going to say." He then refused to answer any more questions, so Caspar had to

wait for the results of Naldo's and Arnie's work on Caroline and
Jo-Jo—together with the answers concerning material taken from
Tiraque's New York hotel room—before he could really lay the
news on his old agent.

NALDO WAS, NOT unnaturally, concerned with the time scale.
They were already into the last week of November, and he had a
date at the altar with Barbara on December 23. Arnie told him not
to worry. "If they cooperate, we have no problems. We only need
the baseline details."

They had been given permission to reveal the main *First Folio*
evidence—that Klaubert was an unserviced British asset who
was also playing a game with the Soviets—if they felt the need.
In the end they kept it to themselves, for, happily, Caroline appeared to be open and honest with them.

By the time of their first interview the initial shock had worn
off. Now Caroline was just pleased to see friendly faces, though
she pleaded a dozen times to see her father.

"Not until we've got this mess sorted out, Caro," Naldo told
her. "We need to hear your story. From the beginning. Let's hear
it, love. First, is there truth in the accusation that you were Klaubert's mistress?"

Caroline began to cry. It was eerie, for she cried silently, as
though with a grief which concerned only ghostly memories.
Then the tears ceased, she blew her nose, took a deep breath, and
began to talk. What she had to tell them put the whole matter into
a clear, sharp focus.

She knew nothing about *Florence*'s association with Klaubert
as mistress and secret emergency contact for the NKVD in general and Ramillies in particular.

"*Felix* advised us—Jo-Jo and me—to see and be seen," she
began. From the very moment they arrived in St. Benoît-sur-
Loire, as Catherine and Anne Routon, they were urged to mix
with the villagers and even make friends in Orléans. This was in
the first days of the Nazi Occupation, before the SS and Gestapo
began to show their teeth.

"Jo-Jo would make trips into Orléans, and I used to go each
Wednesday or Thursday. Just to look around, maybe seek out
contacts. Certainly to keep cover. I used to go into a little patisserie for what passed as tea—though how they managed I don't

know. Maybe the Germans befriended them—gave them extra rations."

She had been sitting in the patisserie one afternoon when Klaubert came in. "You could sense the atmosphere. People were hostile. We all knew this man had been appointed head of the SS. Nobody wanted to be seen with him. I suppose there were maybe six or seven women in the place that afternoon. When he came in, they all got up and left, with a lot of show. I felt I should stay. Who knew how it would turn out? But I was certainly not going to call attention to myself by leaving in an ostentatious manner."

Klaubert had come over to the table and asked—in excellent French—if he might join her. She had no option but to say yes.

"It was very strange. He was cultured. He'd read a great deal; liked art and music. We talked about Wagner—it so happens that I like Wag⌐ Naldo noticed that as she spoke about Klaubert her cheeks began to flush with color and her eyes looked feverish.

"We got on well together. I thought it might help the *réseau* —help *Tarot,* so I spoke with *Felix.* He said by all means I should foster this relationship, but he told me to keep it hidden. Neither of us was to discuss it with other members of the *réseau.*"

She became Klaubert's lover one month after they first met, and the relationship continued right up to the end. She knew of Hannalore Bauer—"He sent her away," she said. "At least that's what he told me. I don't know what to believe, though there was one small incident."

She told of how one summer evening she had allowed herself to be seen publicly with Klaubert. "He took me in his car to a deserted spot out of Orléans—quite close to Benoît, actually. A wood." There she seemed to stop, and choke. "It was the place where they shot and buried the priest; the doctor, and poor Annabelle—*Florence.*"

As though overcome by some horrific memory, she went white, her hands shaking, as she clenched and unclenched her fists trying to control herself.

"Klaubie . . ." She began. "Klaubie . . ."

"Klaubie?" Arnie asked.

She swallowed, took a breath, and forced herself to continue. "It was what I called him. I called him Klaubie."

Klaubert had kissed her in the wood, near a clearing. "His eyes glistened, as though he would cry. Then he said, 'My first love lies here.' He kept repeating it—'My first love . . . My first love lies here.'"

Naldo asked how she knew this was the place where they had taken the priest, the doctor, and the girl. He thought she was going to become hysterical. She balled her small fists and began to pound the table. "Because they made us watch it all. Jo-Jo and I were made to watch some of what happened to Annabelle, in the cellars. Then we were taken with them to the wood. We thought we were also going to be shot. They kept us each in a different cell, and the night before—when we had seen some of the terrible things they did to Annabelle—Klaubie sent me a note. He asked me to destroy it . . ." She gave a small, bitter laugh, "I did destroy it. He wrote this note in English. I think he had guessed I was English by then. He must have also known that I was finished with him. That I could not believe in him any-more."

"What was the note?" Arnie asked. The whole session had gone on a long time now, for there had been many pauses. Many moments when Caroline found it too difficult to speak of certain things.

"He said it was from a letter written by Henry the Eighth to Anne Boleyn—and you know what happened to her. The letter said he loved her, and wanted her—wanted to kiss her breasts. 'Whose pretty duckies I trust shortly to kiss,'" she quoted, then fell silent.

Both Naldo and Arnie tried to prompt her, but as she talked her mind went to and fro, moving backward and forward between her first days as Klaubert's lover to the last horrific hours of *Tarot*.

"I think he killed the other woman and had her buried in the wood—Hannalore, I mean. It was as though he was telling me this had happened. It was just before he began to take action in Orléans."

"You mean before he started to arrest people—deport them?"

She gave a little nod. "Jews. Honest French people. Men who had been in the French Army and managed to get home. Men, women, children. Then he started on the other *réseaux*. A terrible number of people died or just suddenly disappeared."

"And you went on meeting him?"

"Oh, yes. When something really awful had happened—peo-ple shot or taken away—he would be near despair. He would cry on my shoulder and ask if God would forgive him. Klaubie was

like a child at those times. It seemed such a long while ago, until
Marcel killed him the other day. He saw me in the car, caught my
eye just before Marcel fired. He . . . he smiled at me, and I remembered how he was, how distraught at the things he had to
do."

"But he did them just the same," Naldo said, trying to sound
hard, using the cutting edge of his voice.

"He did them, then wept on my breast. A paradox of a man.
Ruthless. Evil. Yet full of guilt. He let the guilt flow out of him
and tried to bury himself and his guilt in me. That was one of the
reasons why Marcel's plan seemed such a good idea."

Another long silence. Both Naldo and Arnie wanted to ask
what she meant by "Marcel's plan," but waited. Then they tried
to drag her mind back to the last days. "They made you watch
everything? After the arrests?"

"Everything. The execution in the garden. The rape. The
shooting in the wood. Then they brought us back. Took us into
Klaubie's office. He looked at me as though he'd never seen me
before and said we would not die. That he'd had a telephone
order about us. We would be taken to Berlin. They wanted to
speak with us there, but he had been assured of our safety. He put
out his hand but neither of us would take it. Then he smiled and
two of his officers came in."

"Otto Buelow?"

"No. Two of the young ones. They gave us cigarettes and said
some men were waiting to take us to Berlin. They drove us to the
station. They joked in the car. I remember we laughed, even
though we still thought they were taking us to some camp. We
couldn't believe our eyes when we saw Marcel." She gave a
smile which for once lit up her eyes. "You see, Marcel always
said he would get us out. He had ways. Documents. Papers.
Passports. He was there, with Dollhiem. They gave papers to
Klaubie's officers. Signed for us, then took us off by train—at
least Marcel did. He said he did not trust Dollhiem. He left Dollhiem in Orléans."

Tiraque had got them out, using his own strange, carefully
husbanded network and the passports and documents he always
seemed to be able to get his hands on. Caspar had once said the
man was a genius at deception—that he must have some forger
working for him. "For him alone. I could never have got such
authentic documents." Tiraque worked a particular magic in getting people in and out.

"He took us to Switzerland." Caroline said it as though it was a peacetime holiday. "We changed our appearance, and I said I wanted to come back to England. Jo-Jo said it also."

"He wouldn't let you?"

Caroline appeared to be thinking, her brow creased. "It wasn't that he would not let us go. He gave us motivation for something else—"

"Caro—" Naldo stopped her, then cursed himself silently. He could well have halted the flow of her thoughts. "Caro, two questions. First, were you ever Marcel's lover?"

"Of course." She looked at her cousin as though he was an idiot. "We all slept with him. Annabelle, Jo-Jo, myself. He was so wonderful. When he came to visit—with orders, or just passing through—at Benoît, it was like fresh air. We felt enclosed and trapped. He gave us pleasure. Made us laugh and have hope for the world. Surely you know how it was for people in the field, Naldo? People who had been sent by men like Uncle Caspar."

"You hated Caspar for what he asked you to do?"

"Is that your second question?"

"No, an extra."

"Sometimes. Sometimes I hated him. Then, when I saw him again, I realized that it was his job. That we had been asked and went. We were doing our duty."

Naldo said nothing. He did not even nod. "The other question. Did Marcel Tiraque call Klaubert and say he had orders from Berlin?"

"Yes. That's what he told us."

"And Klaubert just obeyed—like that? He didn't ask to see the orders?"

"No. No—I've thought a lot about it. Marcel says that it was a chance in a million. He knew where we were and he bluffed on the telephone. He simply said we were to be sent to the railway station and he would hand over the instructions there. I think Klaubie was pleased. He didn't want to make the decision about me. I knew him, Naldo. He would put off some of the worst decisions for days. Then, as I've said, when it was done, he would cry, take me, pray, call down damnation on himself . . . I . . . I didn't realize . . . realize . . ." She began to cry again. "I didn't realize how much I loved this strange, blind, ruthless, horrible man until I saw Marcel kill him in New York." She could not go on, so they called it a day and played back the recordings to Caspar that night.

"It makes sense," Caspar said. "Now you have to home in on how Tiraque persuaded them not to let anyone know they were safe. Get her to sing about what they all did together. They were the strangest *ménage à trois,* but Tiraque's been clever. Incredibly clever." Then, to Naldo's bewilderment, Caspar added, "And so has Ramillies."

41

▼

THE NEXT MORNING, Naldo and Arnie homed straight in on the events which followed the escape of Tiraque and the girls into Switzerland. Caroline had eaten well, they were told by the baby-sitters, and she looked rested.

"Caro," Naldo began, "yesterday you said that when Tiraque —when Marcel—got you to Switzerland, you both wanted to go home, but..." He looked at his notes, as if checking, though he knew exactly what he was going to ask. "You said Marcel gave you motivation for something else. What did you mean?"

"Please understand, Naldo. It took time to get out—right out of France, I mean. We hid for weeks on end. Sometimes we were very near the fighting. It was difficult. We got to Switzerland in about March—that would be 1945."

They had stayed at the Ascona house. Tiraque introduced them to women who helped them restyle their hair and make subtle alterations to their looks. "I was a blonde for some time. A blonde with spectacles. Jo-Jo became a redhead. We played games..." Her voice trailed off, and Naldo wondered what kind of games they played in that house hard by Lake Maggiore. He could guess.

"Then the war ended and you wanted to play games back home?" Naldo smiled as he spoke.

"Something like that. At first Marcel said yes. Why don't we telephone your people to let them know you're safe? We couldn't do that before. He said you never knew who was listening, and we were in Switzerland illegally. Then, just as we were going to make the calls, he asked us to wait."

Tiraque had thrown a dinner party especially for them. No other guests, but he arranged an elaborate dinner, with special table decorations, good wines, wonderful food, and extravagant party favors. When they reached the coffee, he handed cigarettes around and put forward his proposition.

"He said the war was over and, yes, probably our people were looking for us. But we still had a job to do. We'd all got used to living secret lives. Wouldn't it be better to complete the job first, and then go home, triumphant? We must have looked like two ninnies, because he laughed and we asked, 'What job? What've we got to finish?'"

Tiraque had bluntly said, "Vengeance."

They were puzzled, then he began to draw the picture for them. He told them that he knew—knew for certain—that Klaubert was still alive and in hiding. So was Buelow—his deputy, his second-in-command.

"We said that surely the Allies would round up people like Klaubert and Buelow, and he laughed again, calling us fools. He told us we were naive. The Allies would get the very big fish. The people who ran the death camps; people like Himmler and Goering. But Klaubert and those like him would get away and make new lives for themselves."

At first they were uncertain. But Tiraque was not to be put off. "Think of the adventure. The fun of the chase. What'll happen if you just go home now? Your families will welcome you back. Then you'll be expected to marry and settle down." He gave a great guffaw. "Can you see yourselves as obedient little housewives? After all *you've* been through? Take some time—a year. Have one more adventure. One more secret year to your lives. Just the three of us. We'll reap a harvest, I promise. A harvest of revenge."

Both Naldo and Arnie could almost hear the persuasion in Tiraque's voice. They would be so easily hooked.

"He was right, of course," Caroline continued. "Though it took more than a year, it was all great fun. Staying out of sight. Hiding. Buying the place in Paris. Searching a very dirty, disheveled Europe. But each day we hoped for revenge. I wanted to bring home Klaubert's head to Redhill Manor. I dreamed of walking into the dining room with his head on a silver charger, like the head of John the Baptist, and presenting it to Mummy and Daddy, saying, 'There you are. That's the bastard who sent thousands to their deaths, and who violated me.' I wanted just one of them—preferably Klaubert . . ."

"Who did not violate you. You loved him," Naldo said almost under his breath.

"Yes." She altered. Suddenly. Dramatically. Her eyes feverish again and the sweet voice harsh. "Yes. I wanted to see my Nazi lover dead. It was what *he* wanted, I'm sure."

"So you went out, looked, and could not find him?"

"Right." She was her old self again. The Caroline from the day before, and from the years before. "I don't regret it, though. Not one bit. And if they want to hang me for killing Buelow, or Jo-Jo for getting rid of the treacherous Dollhiem, then I'll hang happy."

"You? You killed Otto Buelow?"

"Yes." Matter-of-fact. Precise.

Naldo urged her to go on. "We searched Europe. Went almost everywhere. Paris was our base, but we were away for weeks, months, at a time. Sometimes Marcel would go alone."

"Where?"

"Berlin. London. Only last year he employed a free-lance surveillance team. They watched you, and others, in London. Then they lost you and Marcel was very angry." She swallowed, her eyes darting between Naldo and Arnie. "Marcel even went into the East, into Russian territory. He was dedicated. As each day, week, month went by, we all became dedicated." She threw back her head and gave a laugh—it was not hysteria, but genuine amusement. "We all went to London. Several times—only last week..." She laughed again. "I actually followed Caspar. Lord, it was funny. I was told—by Marcel, of course—to watch that terrible little house you all used in Northolt."

"You knew about the Northolt house?"

"Oh, yes. For the past few months, when we knew the only way to find Klaubert was for you to lead us to him." She looked at Naldo and giggled. "We came over here on the same flight as you. You, Daddy, and Caspar. Only a hundred people on that plane, and you didn't even notice us. Mind you, we were very low-key. Kept out of sight. I was padded and rather fat; Marcel had grown a beard—he shaved it off as soon as we arrived; Jo-Jo was pregnant. Marcel always says that the art of not being recognized lies in just being there, in a crowd, but in a condition nobody expects. He's right, you know."

"Can we go back a little, Caro?" Naldo was starting to follow everything now. It was what he had seen and felt when he opened the car door and saw the girls crouched behind the Colt automatic. "You spent months searching for Klaubert. When did everything really start to break for you?"

"When Marcel discovered the Americans—your people, Arnie—were using Otto Buelow."

"Yes?"

"He came back to Paris and told us."

"Came back from where?"

She shook her head violently, arms rising, hands, with fingers splayed, shaking. "I don't know. He was away for a couple of weeks. Then he came back and told us the Americans were sheltering Klaubert's deputy: Buelow. He ranted on about it. Said it was typical, that it was going on everywhere—England and America. They were actually using Buelow to help them in security matters. Allowing that damned Nazi killer to advise them—"

"I didn't know Otto Buelow killed anyone."

"Well, he gave orders, didn't he? He was Klaubert's lackey. Klaubie didn't like him. He told me, after Buelow arrived—he said that Buelow licked his boots, fawned and toadied."

"Really?" Naldo nodded as though to himself. "So you don't know where Marcel got this information about Buelow being in the States? You don't know where he had been, to find this out?"

"Does it matter? No . . . Yes . . . Yes, I do know. It was one of those trips to Berlin. I think one of the times he went over into the East even. He had sources everywhere." Suddenly she stopped, her mouth opening. "You're not going to do anything to Marcel, are you? I mean, he really has done everyone a service."

Naldo said he did not know what would happen. "Depends on the Americans." He inclined his head toward Arnie, who said he did not think any harm would come to Marcel. In his head and heart he considered Tiraque should be flayed, boiled in oil, hung, drawn and quartered. Nothing should be made easy for him—especially death.

Naldo urged her on. "So Marcel came back from one of his jaunts to the Eastern Zone and told you Buelow was working for the Americans?"

"In Washington, yes. He asked which one of us would like to deal with him."

"And you offered?"

"Of course. He'd been there, in the Rue de Bourgogne, during the atrocities—the *Tarot* killings. Of course I offered."

"And Marcel provided the weapon?"

"Yes. He had it in his case . . ." Her speech slowed down as though something had occurred to her. "When he came back. He explained the whole thing to me in Paris. Showed me how to fire it. Exactly how to get the vaporized cyanide right into his face. How to take the antidote pill just before using it. Oh, Marcel taught us so much. He taught us to drive, sail—"

"Kill," Naldo added. "And did you all go on this jaunt to Washington?"

"No, not that time. No, we didn't. Just Marcel and myself. I remember, we used the same name as we did after Arnie visited the Rue de Rivoli. We were Monsieur and Madame Jourdain. Marcel thought it amusing because Jourdain is a character in Molière's play *Le Bourgeois Gentilhomme*."

"What *did* you do after Arnie dropped in unannounced at the Rue de Rivoli apartment?"

She gave him a knowing smile, which he found disturbing. "We moved to a hotel of course. The Jourdains and the husband's unmarried sister. It was so easy, though I didn't think it necessary."

"Why?"

"Well, he had never seen Jo-Jo. Why should he think anything of it? You couldn't *find* Klaubert, so why should you be alerted by Jo-Jo? I didn't think Arnold could have recognized her."

"Marcel was right though." Arnold gave an unrealistic laugh, knowing that he was trying too hard. Attempting to appear relaxed when he was taut as a bowstring.

"Oh, yes. He insisted. We even had the furniture removed and placed in storage. He was wonderful at hiding in the open—where everyone looked for him."

"So the Jourdains went to Washington?"

"Yes, and it poured with rain. Poor Marcel, he got soaking wet that night. He hired a car and it broke down."

"Was that while you were—"

"Taking the first revenge? Yes." She looked solemn. "It was not as pleasant as I expected. Only later I realized I'd simply got rid of vermin." She frowned. "It was horrible for Jo-Jo. She was sick and had nightmares for days after Dollhiem. She had the more difficult one—a gun."

"Why was Dollhiem necessary?"

"Marcel found out from one of his contacts that Dollhiem was a Russian agent. He felt we might be compromised, and he knew the Pudding—that's what we called Dollhiem—had managed to get settled back in the United States. He was obviously spying for the Russians. He also knew far too much about us."

Naldo lit a cigarette. "Caro, this information. He didn't get it on one of those trips to Berlin, did he?"

She looked surprised. "Yes. Yes, of course he did. Marcel had contacts within the Russian Sector. That's where he got it from."

"Uh-huh. And Klaubert?"

"I told you. Marcel knew you were searching for Klaubert—no, that's not true. He said that if we kept an eye on you—on Caspar, and you, Naldo—you would probably lead us to Klaubert. I don't know what his reasoning was. He was right, though. We watched you a lot in London—"

"When you weren't taking trips to kill people in Washington. What about Newton?"

"Newton?" She looked amazed. "The American who we brought in after that ghastly night—the parachute business? What was it called? *Romarin?*"

"The same."

"Well, what about him?"

"You had nothing to do with his death?"

"He's dead? No. I had no idea."

Did Naldo see a small cloud of doubt form at that moment in Caroline's eyes? He was never quite certain.

There was something else of more immediate relevance which suddenly tied itself into Naldo's head. He heard C's voice—it seemed years ago—saying that his secret operation *Symphony* might have a bearing on two matters of great importance in the here and now—the question of preserving the secrets of the atom bomb and delving into Soviet forward planning.

Suddenly he wondered about Newton and the role he could have played as a sacrificial victim. He had been insinuated into a position of trust within the Atomic Energy Commission. As a chief security expert, he could be an agent nonpareil. Why then had he been removed by his own people? By now Naldo was completely convinced that Tiraque had manipulated Caroline and Jo-Jo for the Soviets—that Tiraque was certainly working both sides of the street throughout the entire war, and possibly even before that. Whatever the immediate answer, there could be but one conclusion.

Naldo put it to Caspar later: "If the Soviet Service, the NKVD, were prepared, or even forced, to take out Newton, it meant they already had someone else. Another traitor possibly even better-placed to glean secrets from within." It nagged at all minds for years to come, despite the trapping of scientists like Fuchs and Pontecorvo. It hung around all those entrusted as guardians of things secret—even after the sensational revelations of the 1950s, the '60s and '70s, when names like Burgess, Maclean, Philby, and Blunt became household words synonymous with betrayal.

Meanwhile, Caroline chattered on for some time, talking of

the places where they had hidden, the names adopted and, most of all, the revenge they had extracted. Klaubert at the end. Buelow and Dollhiem in the middle. Of Newton she knew nothing at all. The whole time—the experience—had been a gigantic game for her. The deaths were incidental. Deaths that were required, like passing Go in a game of Monopoly.

They played the recordings back to Caspar. Neither of them wanted Dick to hear. After that they spent three days with Jo-Jo, who told a similar story and seemed to take the same view as Caroline.

Caspar, and the recordings again.

"Yes." Caspar was obviously moved and sad. "I'll hit Tiraque with that, and the other stuff, tomorrow."

Oddly, both Naldo and Arnie did not think to inquire about "the other stuff." Only later did Caspar tell them.

In the New York hotel—to which Caroline had led them, by whispering its name to Dick—they had opened up a heavy briefcase. Inside were passport blanks: British, French, American, plus stamps and photographs. There were also documents of identity, cards, bank drafts, passes.

Samples had gone straight back to London; others were given to the Agency for examination. In the time Naldo and Arnie had been questioning Caroline, London had discovered the source. The passport blanks were all from a batch identified as having a Soviet origin.

Caspar moved in on Tiraque the next morning. In a calm and almost judicial manner he told Tiraque all he knew, and a great deal he suspected—but he told *that* as fact. "You worked with *Thunder* as surely as you worked with me," he said toward the end. "No wonder you were able to carry out jobs so convincingly. Did you assist in the servicing of *Lightning?* Did they discover, right after it was over, that *Lightning*—Klaubert—was working a three-way switch? Did you realize, Tiraque, that Buelow had been married to a Railton, or did they just order the job because poor old Otto was helping us? Why Dollhiem and Newton? Just orders because we were closing in on them and Moscow thought they would break? Or was it something more devious? Did you get rid of Newton to blind us? To make us think you'd lost your one highly placed man who was close to the most heady secrets of all—the A Bomb, and whatever else we concoct from the scientists' recipes?"

Tiraque merely smiled. Then he shrugged. "You appear to have all the questions and most of the answers. Yes, Dollhiem discovered the truth about Klaubert right at the end—on the day Klaubert left Orléans. Colonel Rogov ordered a complete liquidation. Everyone. He said that a single bad apple could contaminate others. That's how it was. Surely you understand? It was business."

"You bastard," Caspar concluded, his voice now betraying a little of the anger he felt. "To seduce those two girls—I don't mean sexually seduce—and make the whole thing into a terrible game. And you let *them* do some of the dirty work. Caroline for Otto, and Jo-Jo for Dollhiem. No wonder your people are such great deception artists, Tiraque. You offer the masses gold and heaven on this earth. Then you give them copper, corruption, control by the State, restriction, and death. You'll hang for this one, Tiraque. We'll get you. Even on circumstantial evidence. Or I might even manage to persuade my brother to testify. You worked under him long enough, I'm sure. Did you know we had him—*Thunder?* Colonel Gennadi Aleksandrovich Rogov? My brother, Ramillies?"

Again, Tiraque merely gave his enigmatic smile. He would never give them the opportunity to hang, or burn him in the electric chair.

Somehow, in an ultimate act of deviousness, he had managed to hide a cyanide capsule on his body, or in it—a hollow tooth was the favorite theory.

The baby-sitters found him in his bed the next morning. He had been dead for several hours.

42

▼

THERE WERE STILL problems. How to deal with Caroline and Jo-Jo was an urgent matter. One of the Agency psychiatrists—fully briefed on the business—after hearing the recordings and talking to them was convinced that near the end of it all, maybe at Klaubert's very death, Caroline knew everything.

Now she merely suppressed the truth. Why else would she have given the address of the New York hotel to her father? he argued. Rest, care, and watchfulness were required. Both women might know, deep down, how they had been used—seduced by an expert Soviet dissembler who had managed to remain hidden from the British Secret Intelligence Service for so long and had doubled through the entire war.

In the end all the arguments failed. During the following summer, Caroline and Jo-Jo faced a military court, made up from the American and British Judge Advocate General's departments and peppered with legal people drawn mainly from the wartime secret organizations.

The prosecution asked for the death penalty for both girls. They were charged with treason, murder, and—in Caroline's case—giving aid to the enemy.

Only by the brilliant pleading of an astute ex-MI5 officer retained by Dick Railton Farthing did they get off with terms of imprisonment: twenty years for Jo-Jo; twenty-five for Caroline. They served fifteen and seventeen years, respectively, in a special stockade close to a military base near Bangor, Maine.

The business did not even make the newspapers, and when they finally returned to Redhill Manor it was to a changed world. Life had altered and both women were utterly broken.

In the present—winter 1947—the British contingent returned to England for the Christmas wedding of Naldo and Barbara.

But before that day, Caspar traveled to Warminster. Ramillies was nervous and jumpy, he thought. Edgy, with his eyes constantly moving as though seeing threats in every passing shadow. The doctors put it down to the stress of his continuing, and demanding, interrogation. Caspar accepted their diagnosis, yet still felt unease.

"Why didn't you give us Tiraque?" Caspar's tone spoke of fatigue rather than anger.

Ramillies looked at him with blank eyes. Then, after a moment's pause, he turned away. He had cooperated, he said, to save his own neck. "The traitor and the betrayed are not always the same people." His voice also sounded tired. "We've all said it before, Cas. It depends where you're standing—like witnesses of an accident or even a bank robbery." He repeated that they had spoken of it at other times. "When I was taken into the Russian Service I was a traitor to you; the country of my birth was betrayed. I've cooperated with you, and so become a traitor to the Party and the State. I have betrayed my faith. Understand, Cas, that I've only given you what I thought could be safely lost. You asked for no other names, so I did not betray Tiraque, who had worked for me and others in the NKVD since the mid-1930s. Tiraque was a magician—a great manipulator. I had plans for him."

He was quiet for a while, then he gave a sigh. "You have Tiraque, then?"

Caspar nodded. "Yes—and the girls." He was not going to give away Tiraque's last act. "The girls are shaken, and I think emotionally and mentally bruised."

Ramillies gave a bitter little laugh. "*I*, of all people, understand that."

Before he left Warminster, Caspar told his errant brother of Naldo's forthcoming marriage. "Christmas weddings seem to be a tradition in our family."

"I wish..." Ramillies opened his mouth, like a fish, as though it was difficult for him to complete the sentence. "I wish ... that I could be allowed one more visit to Redhill. Just one Christmas. A few days to look at the family again. To see the house, gaze up at the Berkshire Downs."

Caspar merely nodded and left.

THE RAILTONS WERE an arrogant family. Always, when a male married, they tried to talk the bride's parents into getting permission for the ceremony to take place in Haversage. Most Railtons had been married from Redhill, driving down into the town and filling the church of SS Peter & Paul. In Haversage they were treated like royalty—after all, they owned almost the whole town.

On this occasion, however, it was not to be. The Burvilles were also high-minded and arrogant. Barbara, Colonel Burville decreed, would be married at their own church in the little Surrey village of Rowledge, near Farnham.

So it was, with every Railton present, together with numerous Farthings from the United States. Everyone thought it fitting that Naldo should choose Arnie as his best man, and they looked with inquisitive interest on Arnie's own future bride, Gloria Van Gent, whose clothes were the envy of many women present. "She's certainly a gilded glory," Sara laughed. "Our Gloria'll make some of us ladies pull our stockings up."

The new Mr. and Mrs. Railton arrived at Redhill Manor on Christmas Eve, having spent the first night of their marriage at a small hotel not far away.

Throughout the holiday, the couple remained quite unembarrassed at spending their honeymoon in the presence of a great phalanx of Railtons and Farthings. It was a cheerful holiday, kept in the traditional Redhill manner, even with the cloud of anxiety which hung over them regarding what would eventually happen to Jo-Jo and Caroline.

On the morning of Boxing Day, when the trees and bushes around the Manor were heavy and white with frost, Caspar was summoned to the telephone. The call was urgent, and from Warminster.

He made his apologies and left, after a hurried discussion with Dick, and his cousin James.

Along the main roads, as he drew near to the SIS house, Caspar came across police roadblocks. Closing the door after the horse had gone, he thought.

The Duty Officer told him in a simple manner, looking serious, for he knew his job and pension were now on the line. Yes, there had been a relaxing of vigilance over the holiday. It was natural, and Ramillies seemed perfectly at ease. "We knew him too well," the DO said. "Knew he wouldn't try anything silly. He felt safe here—one of the family, you might say."

"Not tense?" Caspar asked sharply.

"He's had moments of tension," the DO acknowledged. The interrogators' reports were there for all to see. "Last night, though, he was the life and soul of the party. In fact, I think we

almost forgot what his true situation was." In those few words the
DO had told the truth, and knew that in telling it he might have
damned his own future. Caspar said it was quite natural. If Ramillies had been allowed to take part in the festivities, then it was
easy for the staff to be blinded.

The details were straightforward. They all thought Ramillies
was probably a little drunk. Two of the baby-sitters who guarded
him personally—like permanent warders in a death cell—had
seen him to his room. "He was happy enough." One of them
looked embarrassed. "He wanted to kiss Jim good night." He
chuckled in spite of the gravity of the situation. "Jim got huffy
about it in the end, and Rogov apologized." At Warminster they
had always called him by his Russian name. "It ended without
anything untoward," the guard said, betraying his police background by his choice of words.

At five o'clock in the morning one of the guards patrolling the
perimeter of the grounds noticed a gap in the hedge, and saw the
wire had been cut. "They had neutralized the alarm. It's easy
enough with a battery and a couple of crocodile clips," the Duty
Officer said. "We *have* drawn attention to it before now. That
section has always been insecure."

The guard had alerted the main house. Ramillies was not in
his room, but there were signs of a struggle—a table overturned
and a lamp, still burning, lying on the floor.

Down the road, at the small military camp of Knook, the
young soldier on guard duty that night had seen a car slow down
and take the Warminster road. It had happened at around three-
thirty in the morning. No, he couldn't give them the make of
car—"It was big. Four doors. I didn't think to take the number
plate. There was all this carry on in the back, though. I thought it
was a lark. Blokes pretending to wrestle—skylarking in the
back."

On the following day a car was found—an old Wolseley that
had been missing from outside its owner's house in Warminster.
The police went over it for fingerprints. There were none. They
did find a small patch of freshly dried blood on the back seat, and
other drops on the door. The area around the car yielded more
blood spots, preserved in the frost, together with the tracks of a
second car.

Ramillies was never heard of again. The networks in the Eastern Bloc, and in Russia itself, had no reports. No body was ever
found. Caspar said it was as though Ramillies had never lived.
They were all in no doubt that Moscow had a very long arm.

Only one thing remained, and it was discussed in depth by everyone who had been involved. It concerned C's most secret operation *Symphony*.

How, they asked, had Tiraque or others known of *Symphony*? They had certainly been well briefed about the main protagonists. How in God's good name had they identified the objects of the exercise and even pinpointed that pink house in Northolt, which was such a secret house? Some of it must have been through Tiraque's "free-lance surveillance team," mentioned by Caroline. But that did not account for everything.

Years were to pass before there was the slightest hint, which came, together with the scandals that flushed Russian moles from both MI5 and the SIS. Even now they can only guess at who provided the Soviets with intelligence on *Symphony*. And the guessing still goes on—even into that land known by all Intelligence officers as "the wilderness of mirrors." It shows on no map, but it is barren and arid. Once in it, a man will jump at his own shadow, start at his own reflection, and become disorientated to the point of obsession. *Symphony* has never been mentioned in the plethora of books and articles about the penetration of the British Security and Intelligence Services, but it is there, marked, flagged "Classified," and sometimes dragged out by Naldo—under a fictional operational name—for lectures at Warminster.

As HAD BEEN predicted, the Soviets made their move against Berlin during the following year—before the trial of Caroline and Jo-Jo. In April and May the temperature between the Soviets, in their Eastern bastion of Berlin, and the Allied Commanders, sank to an all-time low. By June—just when Barbara Railton was confirming to Naldo that she was pregnant—the Soviets stopped all freight moving into the Western zones of Berlin. Then they cut the electricity supplies.

Russia was squeezing West Berlin in a stranglehold. The great siege began. It was overcome only by a massive, costly, and courageous airlift of supplies and necessities into West Berlin. That, and a new, harder intelligence offensive. They were now well into what became known as the Cold War.

Arnie Farthing knew of it first hand, as he was posted back into Berlin, bringing his new wife with him; as did Naldo, and Curry Shepherd, also working there.

Herbie Kruger was the closest of all—by June 1948 he was

already in East Berlin once more. This time they had sent him under deep cover—for he was now fully fledged. But that, as with the many secret shifts within the two families of Railton and Farthing, is a continuing wheel of deeds and words. As Caspar himself might say, quoting Shakespeare:

> And so, from hour to hour, we ripe and ripe,
> And then, from hour to hour, we rot and rot:
> And thereby hangs a tale.